IN THE MOON'S SHADOW

BOOK 1 OF THE FOUR SISTERS SERIES

ANAYA MACLEOD

❀ Created with Vellum

TO DREAM

No-one truly knows what they are capable of until they take a chance and believe in themselves. It is then they discover what it means to follow a dream and uncover the secrets that give their life meaning.

Anaya MacLeod

CHAPTER 1

* EARTH

*L*urthel kicked at her unconscious body. "What'd he say?"

Giordio strode across to Lurthel and slammed him in the stomach. He wanted to punch him in the jaw, but Lurthel was too tall. "You don't touch her without my permission. You got it?"

Lurthel rubbed his stomach "Yeah, yeah. So you gonna tell me what he said?"

The icy winds whistled around the two of them, forcing Giordio to pull his black woolen cloak even tighter around his stocky frame. He glanced at Lurthel, whose gaze was fixated on the brunette. Lurthel was two heads taller than him and built like a minotaur, his only coverings a light shirt, army pants and boots. How in Athena's name this man wasn't freezing in this Tasmanian winter was beyond him.

Giordio snorted loudly and spat on the rough stony ground next to the slim brunette. "The man said we're to make sure we keep her alive. He doesn't care if we hurt her, but she must be alive when he comes back."

Lurthel squatted and flicked the hair away from her face. "She's pretty."

Giordio whacked him across the head. "What did I say about not touching her?" He stepped around Lurthel, picked up the unconscious woman and, with a grunt, threw her over his shoulder. He knew he should give the brunette to Lurthel to carry. Lurthel was the strong one. But Giordio was the boss, so he had the woman first.

Lurthel stood, rubbing his head. "Once you have finished, are you gonna let me have some time with her?"

Giordo shifted the woman's weight on his shoulder in preparation for the hike home.

"Please, boss," Lurthel pleaded.

"You only touch her when I say you can. And none of your sick stuff. You clear on that?"

Lurthel rubbed his hands. "I promise I'll behave, unless, of course, she—"

Giordio turned to Lurthel and stabbed a finger into his chest. "You kill her, you'll pay the price. I won't cover for you."

Lurthel stumbled backwards and raised his hands in submission. "OK, OK. We going to the cave?" he asked.

"No. We'll take her to our cabin, keep her there for now."

"But how will we keep her quiet? What if someone hears her?"

Giordio squinted at the decaying forest ahead of them, rubbing his nose as if to wipe away the pungent smell of death. "Who'd hear her, you fool?" He rebalanced the woman's weight. "Only people like us live in places like this. Would we pay attention to screams here?"

"Nah."

They traipsed over the brittle bridge to their cabin. Giordio dug in his pocket to find the keys. "How bad must you be to be expelled from your own planet?"

"Worse than us," Lurthel replied.

Giordio unlocked the cabin door and pushed it open.

"Giordio?"

"Yeah?"

"Do you ever miss Eratus?" Lurthel asked.

"Nah, we were always in trouble. At least here no-one bothers us." Giordio patted the woman. "And now we get her."

Lurthel reached over to touch her, hesitated, then let his hand fall. "We could sell her clothes for a lot of money. They look real fancy-like. Who is she?"

Giordio strode into the cabin. "She's the leader of that group of mages on Eratus." He clicked his fingers as he tried to remember the name. "The Four...something."

"You mean the Four Sisters?" Lurthel asked.

"Yeah, that's it."

Lurthel took several steps back. "She can't do something to us with her magic, can she?"

"Nah, they took her magic when they removed her memory. If you're scared, when it's your turn you could keep her hands tied."

"I'm not scared." Lurthel rubbed his head. "I wonder how they took her memory away. That must've hurt."

"Yeah, I've heard stories about how bad it is. Many say the screams echo in the chambers long after the person has gone."

Giordio walked across the cabin, opened the door to the cellar and carried the woman's body down the brick stairs. He placed her against the wall, then checked the metal grids that barred the windows. They were secure. He left, locking the door behind him.

"You carried her down the stairs, Giordio. Going soft on her already."

Giordio twisted on his left foot as he expertly flicked his

right heel out to give a short sharp kick to Lurthel's groin. "Watch the mouth, boy."

Lurthel fell to the ground, moaning.

"There's no way I want her father after me. Not if this is what he does to his daughter. And, boy, if you know what's good for you, you'll be careful too."

SASCHA HUNKERED down in the corner of the dank, dark room. Pale moonlight shone in through the windows. The chill of the rough stone wall bit into her back, the torn shirt she was wearing giving her no protection. Her swollen eyes were starting to heal, but her vision was still blurry. She watched the wooden door at the top of the brick stairs, dreading what would happen next. The first time she had seen it she had hoped she could escape, but now she knew better.

A door crashed open in the room above her. The men had returned. Tears stung her bruised eyes, her stomach ached. Sascha wrapped her arms around her waist in a futile effort to ease the pain.

She shivered uncontrollably as she tried to push her body even further into the corner. The door to her prison slammed open. She quickly looked away and stared at the ground, as if the stones in the floor would somehow offer her the help she needed.

Footsteps stumbled down the stairs, stopped for a second, then continued across the cold stone, moving closer to her. One set of footsteps. Only one of them was here. She closed her eyes as rough hands grabbed at her shirt.

Don't show them any weakness. Be tough. Tears only make them hurt you more.

"Hi, honey, I'm home," the one called Giordio whispered

in her ear. He laughed, the pitch of it sending icy chills down Sascha's spine.

The sour fruity smell of alcohol was on his breath. He tied her wrists with a rough rope that cut into her skin and flipped her around so that she faced the wall. He looped the rope around Sascha's wrists over a hook on the wall and yanked at the torn shirt on her back. Sascha shivered as her back was exposed to the frigid air. A loud swish echoed through the room and then a stinging blow on her back, first on one side, then the other. Despite the need to stay strong, Sascha screamed. Lashes of intense pain burned deep into her skin until she passed out into the welcome relief of blackness.

FILTERED sunlight warmed Sascha's face. She tried to open her eyes, but the fresh beating had swollen them shut. The pain in her back throbbed as she pushed herself up so that she could sit. She reached around to gingerly assess the damage to her back. It was bandaged. Someone had treated her after the whipping.

I need to get out of here. But how? Where would I go?

Sascha tried to remember who she was, who her family was. Something. But her mind was blank.

The door to her prison crashed open.

"You're awake," Giordio said.

"Every girl needs her beauty sleep," another voice snorted.

More than one of them this time. She started to tremble. Pain crashed into her thigh as someone kicked her.

The mark on her hand tingled, then it throbbed. Heat flooded through her.

Don't let them do this to you, not again. Stop them!

Distorted screams filled the room, but this time they

weren't hers. The screams stopped, replaced by an eerie silence. She was exhausted. Despite the pain, the cold and the hunger, Sascha lay on the floor and promptly fell asleep, only partially aware of the stench of warm copper.

When Sascha woke, someone was wiping her face with a warm cloth. She shivered. A soft voice spoke. "Sascha, you're safe now."

The first thing she noticed was the smell of copper, mixed with the smell of rotten egg. Her stomach churned and her mouth tasted of sewage. Sascha covered her nose and mouth with her hand as she tried to stop herself from gagging.

"Easy," the voice said. "My name is Marco."

Sascha realized the swelling around her eyes had eased and she could see again. A man was squatting next to her. The light of the moon shone on his face. He had shoulder-length dark hair, bright blue eyes and a bandana across his face.

Marco pointed to the bandana. "Sorry about this. It stinks in here." He put his arms around Sascha to help her sit up. "We'll get you away from this foul odor."

"We?" Another set of footsteps came up beside her. She froze. This had to be a trick. She told her body to twist out of the arms that held her, but her muscles refused to move. "You don't need to be afraid of him either. His name is Connell. We are here to take you home."

"Home?" Sascha croaked.

"We know you won't remember anything," Connell said. "We are here to help you."

Sascha looked up at the man who stood over her, a burning torch in his hand. He had short dark hair and a slim build. He turned around and let the torch light up the room. Bile raced up Sascha's throat as she looked at the scene. Parts of bodies, blood and gore everywhere. The body nearest to her was whole but badly burned, its face contorted in the pain of death.

"Did you..." she gasped.

Connell glanced over at Marco. "We didn't do this. We assumed you did it to protect yourself."

"I can't remember." Sascha put her head in her hands. "I can't remember anything. If I did this..."

"Sascha, it isn't your fault," Marco said. "They kidnapped you. You did what you had to."

"But look at what I did to them!"

Marco stared at the body nearest to him, the color draining from his face. "These men tortured you. You defended yourself."

"May the Gods forgive me." Sascha buried her face in her hands and cried.

CHAPTER 2

"*C*onnell!" Drakon bellowed.

"What now?" Connell sighed. He turned to face the large oak door to his loft, his back to the roaring fire, the light reflecting off the polished shale floors. He smoothed his long white robe and waited.

Heavy steps stomped up the stone staircase, each step drawing nearer. Connell's stomach twisted. He wasn't ready for another argument.

Don't let him get to you.

The door slammed against the stone wall as Drakon entered. He stalked up to Connell, untied a huge mesh bag he carried, retrieved a lump of blood, scale and bone, and hurled it at Connell's feet.

Connell leaped sideways, dagger drawn. "Drakon, what in Athena's name—"

"Your friends are spying on me. Again! If you don't do something about those Sisters, I will." Drakon retrieved a cloth from the pocket of his long black hide jacket and wiped his bloody hands. He examined them by the light of one of the flickering torches mounted on the wall of Connell's studio. "And I don't think you need to worry about the dagger. The creature is already dead."

Heat rose in Connell's cheeks as he slid the dagger back into his belt. "You should know better, Drakon. Those creatures are dangerous, even when they're dead. You're lucky you survived."

Drakon raised his eyebrows. "You're worried about me? How touching."

The smell of spicy pine mixed with copper drew Connell back to the mess on the floor. A dragonling from Brun its once golden scales now a dark, rusty red, its neck and body twisted at awkward angles.

The poor creature.

"Why would they spy on you?" Connell asked.

"I don't know. You're father's spymaster. Go spy, go find out." Drakon's hand dropped to the bollock dagger tucked into his belt as he stretched himself to his full height - a head taller than Connell. "They're up to something. And if you don't want a repeat of what happened last time someone spied on me, then you'd better stop them. I'm warning you, Connell. Don't turn your back on them, even at the ceremony tonight."

"I know how to look after myself. I'll be fine."

"You're no use to me dead," Drakon said.

"Use. Interesting word. As for your threat—"

"Connell, I need your help." A woman stood at the entrance to Connell's studio. "I—oh, sorry." She turned to walk away.

"Come in, Laela."

Laela released her skirt from the tight fists of a young girl standing at her side and took a couple of steps into the room. The girl stayed in the doorway, her eyes focused on Drakon.

Laela bowed low, her jade gown tailored to show off her trim figure. Her polished ebony hair was styled to hide the mark on her face, the only indicator of her rank and race. "I didn't realize you were here, Prince Drakon."

"Obviously." Drakon stalked toward her, his hand still resting on the dagger. "I am pleased to see you still hide your servant marking, Laela."

Connell's body tensed as he readied himself to defend Laela.

"As High Priestess of the Four Sisters, I am a servant to my people," Laela replied. "I have found only those who are ignorant or cruel mock it."

"Oh, I know all about your people, or more specifically, you, Laela. Perhaps if your role is to serve, I need to—"

"Drakon!" Connell took a deep breath as he pushed past Drakon and moved toward Laela. "Leave her alone. And doesn't our law state that as princes, we are servants of the people of Eratus?"

Drakon cocked his head. "Ouch. Excellent comeback, little brother." He looked down at Laela. "But you don't do your position or our family any favors by believing that is true. Unlike Laela, we are true rulers, not servants."

"Do you want to sit, Laela?" Connell pointed to the tan lounge placed close to the large, curtained doorway leading to the balcony.

Laela twisted around toward the girl standing in the doorway. "Stay there, little one." She then took a couple of steps away from Drakon and faced Connell. "I'd prefer to stand."

"What's wrong?" Connell asked.

"One of my charges witnessed..." Laela's glance flicked over to Drakon. "Someone murdered her bonded pet."

Drakon walked toward the fireplace. "You mean this?" He smiled as he looked down at the remains of the proud creature. "It didn't need to die. A shame, really."

"Roluth, Roluth." The young girl left the doorway, pushed past Laela and raced toward the dead dragonling.

"Did you need to point the creature out to her, Drakon?" Connell grabbed the child moments before she saw the full extent of the mutilation to her pet. He used all his strength to hold her squirming body and stop her from breaking loose. "I'm sorry, little one, but its spirit has gone to join Athena now. Athena will look after Roluth for you."

"Roluth," she whimpered.

Laela turned to face Drakon. "How could you?"

"You shouldn't have sent the animal to spy on me, should you?" Drakon turned on his heel. "I've been fair and given you a warning. Next time it will be you, not a pet, that pays the price." Drakon slammed the door behind him.

The room fell silent except for the crackle of the fire and the muted sobs of the young girl. Connell nodded at the dragonling. "Do you want me to organize someone to..."

"No, thank you, Connell. We'll take care of the dragonling."

"Are you spying on him, Laela?"

"No. Why would we? We've bigger things to worry about." Laela leaned over and took the little girl from Connell. "I'll be back in a minute. We need to talk about tonight's ceremony."

Connell took a cloak from the back of the chair at his writing desk, walked to the dragonling and covered it. He strolled onto the balcony and looked down at the dark ocean. Tall solar lights decorated the shoreline, making it easy to see the white froth of the waves as they crashed against the shore. He breathed in the faint peppermint scent of the ocean. Drakon had always been cruel, but lately his dark lust soured everything he touched.

Leaning against the rim of the balcony, he glanced up at the night sky where the white cracks in the Shield which protected their planet were clearly visible. He listened to the whispers as the Shield tried to manage the pain each time the cracks expanded a little more. Tonight, however, the whispers were different. Connell frowned and pressed his fingers to his temple. Something was there, another group of voices.

"Not long now," he said to the sky. "Athena, I pray I do not let you or our people down."

Connell jumped as he sensed a presence beside him. "Must you always sneak up on everyone, Laela?"

"Sorry, Connell."

"How is the young girl?"

"She will heal. I heard what you said. You've trained a lot. You'll do us proud at the healing ceremony."

He stared at the burn scars on his hands from the many times he had tried - and failed - to use his magic. "I'm not Sascha."

"Do you miss her?"

Connell lifted his head and watched as the ocean crashed against the shore. "Why should I miss her? It's been years now. She made her choice."

"Time doesn't seem to heal as well as we would like," Laela said.

"I was hurt, but I'm over it. She said she hated Drakon, yet she chose to confide in him rather than me, her own brother! But that's her problem. Things might..."

"Might have been different if she had spoken to you?"

"Yes. Father always accepts Drakon's guidance when he's in a crisis and I don't understand why. Especially considering..."

"Considering what, Connell?"

Connell shook his head. "Nothing."

"Drakon is her brother, Connell," Laela said.

"Her adopted brother, not her true brother," Connell growled.

They stood looking over the balcony at the sparkling lights below. Connell stretched the muscles in his neck and shoulders. The soft breeze and peppermint scent of the ocean began to work their magic and he felt his muscles loosening, the tension easing.

Laela put her hand on Connell's arm. "You must release any anger you may have toward Sascha before the ceremony."

"I know, I know," he said as he moved his arm from under Laela's hand. After a few moments, he added, "Do you hear the voices?"

"Yes," she said. "What would it be like to sense yourself dying like this?" She glanced sideways at Connell before she continued. "The pain will ease after the healing tonight."

"Not the Shield, the other voices. Do you hear the other voices?"

Laela hesitated, twisting her head a little. She closed her eyes for a moment before turning back to him. "In our visions, we sense a darkness in the castle. There's a desperation to connect with the Shield, but no, no voices. Why? Do you?"

"Yes, I do." Connell rested his face in his hands. "We mustn't fail tonight, Laela."

"Stop worrying. This healing ceremony happens every fifty years." Laela looked up at the night sky. "And we have never failed."

Connell slouched forward and rested against the wall. "Something doesn't feel right. You mentioned visions. Has Athena given you any visions about tonight's ceremony?"

"Well..."

"What?" Connell challenged her. "I was right."

"We don't believe the ceremony is in danger. We're more worried about what happens afterwards. Over the past few months, one specific vision hasn't made any sense...until now."

"What vision?"

Laela cleared her throat. "We think someone sent Sascha the map of the ancients."

"No! You haven't mentioned this to anyone else?"

Laela glowered at Connell. "No, I'm not that stupid."

Connell rubbed his hands through his hair. "But why now? She wouldn't understand what it means."

"We don't know. But we believe that is what the vision is saying. And if we are right, we will need to find out if she has the map. Perhaps Marco can meet with her? He was, how do I say it, friends with Sascha."

"Marco is being initiated as a leader of the Fire of the Phoenix. We can't contact him."

"We need to do something, Connell, and urgently."

Connell shook his head. "I don't understand what is so urgent."

"I sent someone to Earth to see if they could find the map, but he stopped reporting in a week ago."

Connell stared at Laela. "What? I thought you said the vision has only become clear now. How come you...Laela, what is really going on?"

"In the name of Athena," Laela snapped. "Connell, if I could tell you, I would."

Connell pushed himself away from the wall. "I am a prince of Eratus. If you can't tell me..."

"The adopted prince," Laela muttered.

Connell turned and glared at Laela, before striding back into his loft. "Don't push me too far, Laela. After the ceremony, when Marco can join us, we will work out what to do."

"Sascha is your sister. I assumed you would care more than that."

"And I assumed you would have come to me when you knew that the matter was important enough to send someone to Earth. The ceremony is only a few hours away. I can do nothing before then."

"It may be too late after the ceremony," Laela snapped. "If you can't help us, Connell, may Athena give us all her extra protection in the coming days. We are going to need all the help she can spare."

CONNELL FOLLOWED the Four Sisters along the winding mountain track that led to the top of Zinnath's Peak. Each woman was dressed in fine white furs with golden hand-adorned silk mesh overlays and each carried the sacred ceremonial artifact they would use in the healing. A group of armed guardians, members of the Fire of the Phoenix, walked next to them. The red, gold and silver of the guardians' armor glistened in the flickering lights of the torches they carried to light the pathway.

At the top of the peak, Connell stopped, pulled his cloak tighter around him and surveyed the ceremonial area. A flat green creeper covered the surface outside the ceremonial circle. The area inside the circle was covered in golden tiles, engraved with images of ancient gods. He took a deep breath of the fresh air as Laela led the other Sisters to the edge of the cliff.

Buffeted by the icy winds, they gazed down at the dark river and the surrounding black forest, the soft lilt of their voices drifting toward Connell. He looked up at the sky as the stars disappeared and bright arcs of green fire and ice collided with the surrounding darkness. It was time to start the healing ceremony.

The guardians walked around the edge of the ceremonial

area and lit the ornate candles which had been placed there earlier in the afternoon. Despite the icy winds, the flames burned strong and true, and it wasn't long before the area smelled of beeswax and eucalyptus.

The Sisters turned away from the cliff edge and glided into position within the area lit by the candles. They tilted their heads back, arms outstretched, and prepared themselves for the ceremony. Each guardian took their place behind the Sister they were there to protect.

This was Connell's cue to take his position and commence his own preparations. He picked up his golden staff and moved to the center of the circle, now protected by the Sisters and their guardians. Once in place, he balanced the staff in his open palms and bowed his head.

"Athena, preserve us."

Standing up tall, he raised the staff to the skies - a signal to the Sisters. They retrieved the small vials of dragon's blood from the pockets in their silk mesh overlays and drank down the rich fruity liquid which Connell knew would help them perfect their concentration throughout the ceremony.

He centered on the power of the staff. He sensed the golden magic wind itself around him. The dragon-eye stone at the top of the staff began to warm. Connell retrieved his own vial of dragon's blood from the pocket in his robe and drank it.

The pain sliced at him, taking his breath away and forcing him to his knees. Sweat poured off him as he gripped the golden carved staff, propping himself up.

"What the..."

There must have been something in that dragon blood!

He forced his eyes open to check on the Sisters. They had commenced summoning their powers.

They're fine. The pain...

The guardians signaled Connell, asking if there was trouble. They moved in to protect the Sisters.

Connell signaled back. "I'm fine. Stay where you are."

The pain raced through his body, threatening to overtake him. Unbidden, the evening's memory flashed before him. Laela filled his vision as she tried to negotiate with him in his room. "We think someone sent Sascha the map...need to find out if she has the map...too late after the ceremony." And then Drakon's voice. "They're up to something. Don't turn your back on them, even in the ceremony."

Was Drakon right? The pain dragged Connell back to the ceremony.

He looked up at the sky. Is this what the end of the world would be like filled with slashes of light the colors of fire, ice and evergreen leaves, and howling winds whipping at all in its path?

All the years of training and I'm not going to start the ceremony, let alone finish it.

"No." He shook his head. "We must succeed." Connell used the staff to help himself stand straight and started to ready himself for the ceremony. He slowed his breathing, bringing the pain into the center, making it smaller. He could do this.

Connell turned his staff so its crystal faced true north. "Athena, I pray you cleanse this staff. Give it the power to heal and me the wisdom to guide its healing."

Soft, soothing music began to fill the air, a healing sound. Connell could feel his pain begin to ease. Where was the music coming from? He took a deep breath, allowed the music to calm him. A bright white light filled the area.

"Activate your artifacts now," he called out to the Sisters.

As the Sisters lifted their artifacts upwards, colored lights spilled into the sky, forming luminous arches of green, gold, orange and blue. In the same way a conductor conducts his orchestra, Connell moved his staff, merging the lights from the artifacts with the light from the staff and weaving them together.

"Blend together, let it be, the healing of the Shield for all to see."

The beat of the music increased, matched by the speed of the icy winds. The chant flowed faster and faster. As the lights continued to merge, they created a white line of glowing light.

"More power, Sisters. We need more power, more speed."

The beat of the music soaked into Connell's blood. The pace increased, but not enough. Energy drained from his body as he tried to compensate for the slower speed. He had to keep going. He would not stop until the ceremony was complete.

The light finally moved upwards, high into the sky. A few minutes later, the healing process began. The light started to knit in with the weave of the Shield. But too slowly.

"Help me, Athena."

Another power joined the ceremony a power Connell didn't recognize. At first, it tentatively explored what was happening within the circle, but in seconds the full force of the energy an angry and consuming power flooded in.

"We have help," Laela called out.

"No," Connell said. "We don't know its source."

"I do," Laela answered. "And we need help."

Laela was right. But he had to slow the energy down.

The Sisters started to draw some of the energy into their artifacts.

"No!" Connell yelled. "It's too powerful for the artifacts!"

"We can do this," Laela's voice boomed out. "Focus on what you need to do. The artifacts will hold."

Connell moved fast, knowing the power was greater than the Sisters realized. It wouldn't be long before the artifacts would reach their limits. Then they would be useless. They wouldn't be able to protect the Sisters.

The heat of the staff built as it consumed the new source of energy. Connell weaved the new power into the healing light. He slowed it down enough so the Shield wouldn't be damaged by the full brunt of its force. Perspiration was pouring off him. The air around him grew hot. A hint of fire and smoke mixed in with the fragrance of the beeswax and eucalyptus. Connell's focus, however, was on the Shield.

Everyone's attention was on the light as it regenerated the weave almost instantly. It then raced along the sky as it searched for and repaired all the damaged threads. Relief flooded through Connell. "We're going to make it."

Connell waited for the Shield to merge with the night sky. Meanwhile, the heat in the ceremonial staff continued to build.

Connell's stomach lurched as he stared at the staff. "Athena's ghost!"

The night fell deathly quiet. The winds held their breath. The owner of the new power pulled back, trying to shut it down. Now Connell noticed the change in the air, the growing heat.

It was the sound that made him turn, a soft crackle coming from one of the artifacts. Smoldering fire licked at the bottom of each of them. He glanced at the guardians and the Sisters. They were transfixed by what was happening. No-one moved. The Sisters looked at each other and then turned to Connell. It was as if they were saying goodbye.

Connell tried to yell, to tell them to move, to do something, but all his energy was gone. He fell to the ground, voiceless.

KABOOM.

The sky around them exploded, engulfing everything in its path. Plumes of fire bursting from the artifacts. He heard guttural screams from the Sisters and calls of help as the guardians tried desperately to save them. Connell could only watch as the growing ring of fire consumed everyone and then encircled him, moving to devour the only thing still alive, him. The winds joined the oppressive heat, hurrying the inferno on its path.

Connell knew he should be moving, doing something to save himself, but his body refused to work. The sounds of destruction seemed to go on forever. The overpowering stench of burning meat, charcoal and sulfur filled the air. Connell turned to look up at the sky. There was something wrong with the Shield. It should have been invisible, but he could still see it. And the color, there was something wrong with the color. No longer able to manage back the exhaustion and struggling to comprehend the horrific deaths of the Sisters and their guardians, Connell welcomed unconsciousness. His last thoughts were that the ceremony had failed. And now, with the Four Sisters annihilated, there was no-one to fix it.

CHAPTER 3

* EARTH

*T*he torchlight glinted on the blood splattered over the old man's hooded robe.

"Please, Sascha, spare her."

The young woman stood silently, tears rolling down her face, one arm resting on her stomach.

The old man moved to stand in between Sascha and the young woman.

The room smelled of death and was filled with the gargled groans of the dying. Sascha smiled, lifted the battle axe and trailed her finger along the sharp thin blade. She shook her head, amused by the old man's futile attempts to shield the woman with his body.

"There is no hope, only death," Sascha said.

Delighting in the metallic taste of the warm blood that spurted over her, she brought the axe down again and again. The mark on her hand burned, its flame scoring deep into her skin. Sascha ignored the pain.

The door to the room ruptured. Shards of wood drifted toward the pools of blood. It was the cries of horror from the doorway that woke her.

Sascha shoved the doona aside. The breeze from the air conditioner cooled her skin as she struggled to get her bearings in the dark. The air in her room was filled with the stench of copper and her hands were still sticky with blood. Stumbling out of bed, Sascha fumbled for the light switch. Turning the lights on, she swallowed hard and made herself look at her hands. They were clean. No blood. The coffee-colored mark on her hand tingled, but there was no damage, no burns. Salty tears stung her tired eyes. She looked over at the door, still intact.

Nausea built quickly and Sascha raced to the toilet. She remained hunched over the bowl for what seemed like an age. Finally, she hunkered against the tiled bathroom wall and pressed her cheek against the frigid surface as she waited for the stomach cramps to ease.

Please let it only be a nightmare.

Sascha stared at the tiles on the floor as images of the old man begging for the freedom of the young woman flashed through her mind. Shivering from sheer exhaustion, she wrapped her arms tightly around her knees, buried her wet face in her hands and wept.

The squawking of lorikeets filtered into the bathroom. It was nearing dawn. Time to move. Sascha leaned on the towel rack, pulled herself to her feet and stared blankly at her reflection. Her olive skin was pale, and her green eyes dark and bloodshot from a lack of sleep. The dark roots in her hair reminded her of what she wanted to forget, what had happened in the cabin. Perhaps that old man and that young woman were in the cabin, and she had killed them. She turned the tap on full, washed her face and staggered back to her bedroom and to bed.

The fear of falling back asleep stirred her. Sascha stretched her legs, swung them over the edge of the bed and took a mouthful of cool water from the glass sitting by her bedside.

She walked over to her oak tallboy and selected a teal-colored tracksuit. The copper stench of blood in her room had dissipated, replaced by the warm odor of ginger and ylang-ylang from the electric oil dispenser. Sascha pulled her long blond hair into a ponytail as a tear rolled down her cheek. She was so alone.

Stop being so pathetic. You need some sleep, that's all. You wouldn't do that. It's not possible.

Putting on her sneakers, Sascha picked up her iPhone and made her way to the kitchen, where she grabbed a chilled bottle of water from the fridge. She crossed through the family room, past the girls' bedrooms and down the narrow, twisty stairs to the wine cellar.

Flicking on the lights, she glanced around. The cellar was well-ventilated, but Sascha could still detect the buttery smell of wine aged in oak. She looked over at her wine fridge. Avoiding the temptation to pour herself several glasses of wine and give herself some time for dreamless sleep, Sascha strolled over to the treadmill, increased the height, switched up the speed and began her warm-up jog.

The old man's face flashed back at her. His plea to save the young woman echoed around the wine cellar.

Sascha increased the speed and raced even faster, trying to escape the images. After an hour, she turned off the treadmill, walked over to the steps to the cellar and sat on the bottom step while she caught her breath. The nightmares had been so real this time.

You need to face it, Sascha. Find out what happened.

"No!" Sascha stood and walked over to the treadmill to pick up her water bottle.

A quick movement in the corner of the room caught her eye. Sascha moved closer to see what was there and noticed a small bundle of papers sitting on the corner of one of the empty wine racks.

"I can't remember seeing this here before."

As she moved toward it, the temperature in the room plummeted. Sascha rubbed away the goosebumps, shook her head, sighed at herself and leaned down for a closer look.

It was a battered piece of parchment, yellowed with age. A note with the typed words, "It is time", was stuck to the front. The note wasn't aged but crisp and fresh with a water-mark of four female silhouettes embossed in the corner. Frowning, Sascha opened the parchment. It was a map with a smaller map attached to it with a dragon clip. The map was familiar, but where was Eratus, the place it referred to? And what were the portals that were marked on it? Sascha looked back at the note. A chill raced down her spine. "It is time."

Time for what?

Sascha stood and stared at the flow of water as she waited for the shower to warm. Lee and Ella had left for work. She was grateful the girls had offered to take Kira to school. It meant she had some time to herself. This weekend they would be celebrating being together for five years. The girls were gifts and had come into her life at the perfect time. They gave her a sense of purpose, a reason to live, a reason to not give in when things got tough.

The water had warmed, so Sascha stepped in and closed the shower door. She was about to lather herself up when a loud scrabbling of claws sounded at her bathroom window, followed by a bang and then silence. She flashed a glance at the window. The blinds were down. Another bang, this time inside the house.

Sascha stepped out of the shower, wrapped herself in her orange shower robe and, after arming herself with one of her high heel shoes, looked around the room. The sliding door to her bedroom was slightly open. "I'm sure I closed that."

Sascha gripped the shoe tighter, her heart pounding.

"Hello. Who's there?" The hair on the back of her neck bristled. "I've called the police," she lied. "They're on their way." No response.

Sascha forced herself to walk calmly through the house. She checked the front door. It was locked. She headed toward the back door. It was the silence in the house that allowed her to hear the soft click of a door closing.

The back door, someone was at the back door.

Sascha raised her shoe again, ready to stab the sharp pointy heel into the first thing that moved, and tiptoed toward the back door. The door was closed. She checked the handle and found it locked.

On her way back to her bedroom, Sascha glanced at the front windows. Maybe she should see if there was someone or something outside. She stepped down into the sunken lounge, walked to the curtain and took a deep breath. She reached for the curtain, half afraid of what would be there.

The shrill ring of the phone made her jump. Blood pounded in her ears. She stepped back, raced to the kitchen and reached for the phone.

"Hello."

"Hi, boss." It was Marcie. She had been with Sascha for a few years now, starting with her as an intern before she became a vet.

"Marcie. Hi, what's wrong?"

"Jenny hasn't turned up this morning. That's two days in a

row. And she still hasn't called in. I'm really worried now. This is so unlike her."

"Yes, we need to check on her," Sascha said, frowning. Marcie was right. In the two years that Jenny had worked as Sascha's bookkeeper, she hadn't once failed to explain an absence.

"We tried to call her, but no answer. Do you mind if I drive to her place, check if she's home? Her boyfriend's overseas, so she's by herself."

"Good idea. Take the company car and ask someone from the office to go with you. How are my patients?"

"They seem to have improved, even the rottie."

"Thanks, excellent. I'll be in soon."

Sascha hung up the phone, walked past the lounge and glanced at the curtain. There was no point in looking. Whoever might have been there would be gone by now. She checked both doors again. She knew she was being silly, but the morning had left her unsettled. When she was sure everything was secure, she headed back to finish her shower.

After the shower, she lay down on her bed to rest for a few minutes before heading off to work. Two hours later she woke from a dreamless sleep. She jumped out of bed and glanced at the clock. 11 a.m. Grateful for the sleep, but worried about the late hour, she rang the office. "Hi, Marcie. Sorry, I'm running late. I'll be on my way in a minute."

"No worries, boss. We've had a pretty quiet morning. By the way, we called in at Jenny's home. She didn't answer the door and the house looked empty. Do you mind if I talk to Ken?"

Sascha winced. She should have asked about Jenny. "Yes, that's a good idea. Give him a call. I'll be in soon."

As she drove into work, her mind drifted back to the day she had employed Marcie. A fantastic find - bubbly, caring and showing promise of being an outstanding vet. She had an incredible way with animals. Sometimes it was almost as if she could talk to them.

SASCHA PARKED in front of her veterinary clinic. The sun glinted off the stained-glass creatures Sascha had designed for the large glass entry. She wasn't sure where the idea for the fantastical creatures had come from, but she loved how they suited the lush garden area that surrounded her clinic. Designing them had distracted her from the need to obliterate herself with alcohol. She had struggled after Connell and Marco rescued her.

Sascha walked into the clinic, said hello to her receptionist, greeted the clients who sat waiting with their pets and then went to visit her patients. On her way to the kennel she stopped to talk to a couple of her nurses who were giving a reluctant patient a blood test. "Morning. How is the little patient doing?"

"Really well," one of the nurses replied. "This little one doesn't like needles. That's all."

Sascha laughed. "No-one likes needles."

Marcie greeted her as soon as she entered the kennels. "Hi, boss. I saw you arrive, so I phoned the coffee shop and asked them to drop over a skinny latte with an extra shot and a warm vegemite scroll."

"Thanks, Marcie."

The door swung open as Mike strode in. "And here it is," he said.

"That was quick, Mike," Marcie said.

"You know me, Marcie, always trying to impress with my efficiency." Winking at her, he strolled over to Sascha.

"Here's your coffee and your warm scroll." The aroma of the scroll and coffee reminded her she was hungry. "Enjoy.

Oh, I added a dash of vanilla." Mike smiled at Sascha, winked again at Marcie and then left.

Marcie turned to Sascha and grinned.

"He is a lovely guy." Sascha nudged Marcie in the ribs. "And he is a part owner of the coffee shop. A forty percent holding. He must be worth a bit of money." Sascha stopped herself from thinking of the person who owned the remaining sixty percent holding.

"Would you stop matchmaking?"

Sascha laughed.

For the next half hour, Sascha and Marcie checked the patients in the kennels. Some of them could go home, while a couple needed one more day under observation.

"Thanks for your help, Marcie. I'll go and call the clients and give them an update," Sascha said, turning in the direction of her office.

"Cool. By the way, that accountant dude, Roger something or other, asked me to phone him when you arrived. Urgent, he said. Sorry, but it slipped my mind."

"Tell him I'm here. And he can meet me in my office."

"Sure will, boss. Oh, and do you mind if I leave at two-thirty tomorrow afternoon? I'm going away for the weekend."

"Wow. You're actually listening to me and taking time off."

Marcie blushed. "I always listen to you, boss."

"The clinic is closed this weekend anyway." Sascha glanced around the kennels. "And all our patients will be discharged by then. I'll organize for one of the nurses to be on call this weekend. Are you going somewhere nice?"

"Yep, to the beach."

"Lucky you. That sounds like the perfect escape."

"I'll call Roger."

"And, Marcie," Sascha said as she strode toward her office,

"you're slipping back into your bad habits. Would you do me a favor and stop calling me boss?"

"Yes, b—I mean, Sascha. I can't help myself. You suit boss."

AFTER SASCHA HAD CALLED her clients, she swiveled in her chair and took a minute to gaze out the large window that looked out on the grounds surrounding her clinic. She loved the way the pines and eucalypts contrasted with the well-manicured gardens. Magpies and butcherbirds called out to each other as they swooped in and out of the tree line. Crows cawed in the distance. Sascha stretched her arms above her head and yawned as someone knocked on the doorframe. She turned to see Roger stepping into the office. "Sorry to disturb you, Sascha. Do you have a moment?"

"I can't give you long, Roger," she lied. Sascha didn't feel up to a long-winded discussion with Roger.

"It shouldn't take long."

"Take a seat." Sascha pointed to a chair near her desk as she glanced at the scar above Roger's eye. The scar made him look as if he was permanently angry. "What's wrong?"

"Did you get a call about Jenny?"

"Only from Marcie."

"No," Roger said. "I mean from Jenny's lawyers. I received a call from them to say she won't be back. She's in trouble for stealing."

"Jenny? You must be kidding!" Sascha stared at Roger. "It's not possible."

"I didn't believe it at first either, but I—"

"Why did the lawyers call you?" she said. "Did you know about this?"

"No way! I would've told you. I guess Jenny gave them my number."

Sascha's throat tightened. Her stomach clenched.

I thought we were friends. Why didn't she call me? Unless...

"Something isn't right, Roger. She would never steal. Are you sure about this?"

"Well..." His glance wandered around the room as his fingers toyed with the handle of his briefcase.

"What is it?" Sascha snapped.

"I reconciled the bank accounts. Money is missing."

"Missing? How could money go missing?"

"I'm trying to work it out."

"How much?"

"Five thousand dollars."

"Shit. Five thousand?" Sascha sat back in her chair as she scrutinized Roger. "Are you saying you think Jenny took it?"

"I don't know for sure, but I am looking into it. I just thought I should check with you first."

"How could she have stolen the money? No-one can make withdrawals without my sig..." Sascha stood and moved to the corner of her desk, where she sat and stared at Roger. "There are only two people who can take money out of my account - you and me."

"What, me? I would hardly steal money and then come and tell you."

"I have known Jenny for a couple of years, you for a couple of months. I may owe you an apology, but you must see how strange this all seems."

Roger snapped out of his seat and stood, glaring at Sascha, his fingers gripped tightly onto the handle of his briefcase which he held close to his chest. "I'm not going to stay here and be insulted by you. I don't need this. Get someone else to check if you don't believe me."

Roger strode toward the door and then turned to face Sascha. "And for your information, I rang the bank to try and find out where the money had gone. They're the ones who said Jenny took the money." The door slammed behind him.

Sascha left the office and walked out to find Marcie. "Marcie, have you got a moment?"

"Sure," Marcie replied.

Sascha led the way into one of the examining rooms and closed the door.

"What is it, Sascha?"

"Did you call Ken?"

"Yes. He's coming here at 1 p.m."

"Good. Can you send him to me first? I need to talk to him."

"Sure."

"And, Marcie, did Jenny ever talk to you about any troubles she was having?"

"No, she was happy. She told me on Tuesday, and swore me to secrecy, that she's engaged. She promised to introduce us soon. They wanted to wait until they had told his family before they said anything."

"Thanks, Marcie."

"Do you think Jenny is OK?"

"I hope so. I will let you know when I find out more." Sascha left the examining room and strode back to her office. Ten minutes later, she had reviewed her bank account and was picking up the phone to call the bank. A quick knock sounded at the door and Ken walked in. He was still in his uniform - a police superintendent.

"Hi ya, honey." He walked over and pulled Sascha up into a hug. Ken always reminded her of a big bear. He was tall and muscular with a beard that was as dark and thick as the curly thatch of hair on his head. Streaks of gray in both gave him a grizzled appearance. "You need my help?"

"Hi, Ken, wonderful to see you. You do look gorgeous in your uniform. Pat better be careful or I might steal you."

Laughing, Ken sat down in one of the two large lounge chairs in the meeting area of her office.

"Coffee?" Sascha asked.

"No, thanks. You look terrible, honey. What's going on?"

"Nothing, I'm fine."

"If you say you're fine, then there is definitely something wrong."

"Ken, please."

Ken studied her. "Let's change the subject...for now. What did you want to discuss?"

"Roger told me Jenny's in trouble for stealing." Sascha gave Ken a quick update on the events of the morning. "For some reason, I think Roger is lying to me, but I don't know why. I find it too hard to believe Jenny stole anything."

"Honestly, Sasch, the number of times I hear people say it's not possible their friends or employees committed a crime, specifically white-collar crimes. But don't worry. I'll investigate and find out what's going on. I'll meet with the bank first. So what else is wrong?"

"Nothing. I told you."

"So how long have we been friends?"

"A while."

"A while? More like five years. I know when you're worried. I'm not leaving until you tell me what it is." Ken sat forward, formed his hands into a steeple and looked directly at Sascha.

She sighed. "I'm having nightmares about an old man and I'm not sleeping. All I need is something to knock me out for a few hours. I'll be fine."

"How long have you been having the nightmares for?"

"A couple of months now," she replied. "But in the last week, the nightmares have worsened, become more graphic."

"Do you recognize this old man?"

"He's familiar, but I can't place him. There's something..."

"I could help you find him."

"How?" Her stomach churned at the thought of finding the old man, or rather, what was left of him.

"I could organize for one of our sketch artists to visit you, take a sketch of the face?"

Sascha shook her head. "No, thanks, Ken. I'm fine. I'll talk to the doc and get some drugs."

"If the nightmares are getting worse—"

"Ken, don't make it into a big deal. And I have no idea how to describe the face or give enough detail for the sketch." Her stomach clenched.

"Sasch, it is a big deal. You must do something. Even your doctor will tell you the drugs are only a temporary answer. You need to find out the cause. Perhaps a sketch is the first step."

"Why are you stressing about this so much, Ken? Let's forget it."

"No. I can see what it's doing to you. Please, Sascha, let me help. This is what I do, find missing people."

Sascha sat on her hands to stop them from shaking. "I will agree to the sketch on one condition."

"Name it."

"The sketch artist gives me the only copy of the sketch. And you won't do anything until we've discussed it."

"Deal," Ken said. "Shall we spit on it?"

"What?"

"Spit on our hands and shake."

"Gross, Ken."

He laughed. "You smiled. You should do that more often."

"No, I didn't smile. It was more of a grimace."

Ken chuckled. They both got up and walked to the door.

"How's Pat?" Sascha asked. "And how is my gorgeous Rusty? I haven't seen you guys around for the past week."

"They're both doing well. We've been visiting Pat's friends in Sydney and we took Rusty with us."

"I bet Rusty didn't like the flight. You know I'm always happy to doggy-sit. I love that animal. Why don't you and Pat come over for dinner next week? And bring Rusty. I'll make something special for her too."

"I'll look forward to it. Let you know what I find. Bye for now, kiddo," he said as he waved goodbye.

CHAPTER 4

ERATUS

A distant voice split apart the comforting darkness.

"Connell, you are going to be fine. We are here now."

His breath quickened.

Where am I?

"The healer gave you a healing draught," the voice said. "The pain will ease soon."

Connell didn't want to leave the darkness, but the voice pulled at him. As he came closer, the full force of the pain hit - white and burning agony. His lungs and his eyes were on fire. Every breath was torture. All he could smell was charcoal and sulfur. The pain...

"My head," Connell groaned. He tried to move to make it easier to breathe, but his body wouldn't obey, wouldn't respond.

"Connell, don't move."

Move? I can't move!

He flinched as the voice boomed out, "Healer, he is waking. He's still in pain. Sweet souls and angels. How long before the blasted medication starts working?"

Another voice spoke. "Don't worry, Connell, we've treated your injuries. Your eyes are bandaged, so you won't see anything. You'll find it hard to breathe. The fire damaged your lungs, but they will heal. I promise you that your pain will soon ease."

The Sisters' screams of agony and the guardians' calls of help echoed in his mind, and all he had done was lie there like a log, waiting for death. Connell grunted in agony as someone repositioned something beneath his shoulders. A fresh whiff of spices and musk drifted over him. Owain. Owain held him.

"Father?"

"Yes, son, it's me. Thank Athena..." Connell sensed the movement as Owain took a deep breath, quiet for a moment. "Thank Athena you're alive."

Connell waited for the relief to come. But instead of subsiding, the pain worsened. As he was about to cry out for help, the pain started to dissipate. It was replaced by a cool sensation and then numbness. He sagged against Owain, weak and exhausted.

"Where are we?"

"We're preparing to take you back to the castle. The healer said to leave you here until the treatment worked."

All Connell wanted to do was sleep. As he lay there, he became aware that Owain was arguing with Drakon. He kept his eyes closed and listened in silence.

"You'll see," Drakon said through gritted teeth. "The people of Earth, the ones you still wish to protect against your peoples' wishes, they're the ones who did this."

"Drakon, as I said, this is neither the time nor the place to discuss this."

"Sokentash!" Drakon snapped.

Owain shook his head. "In Athena's name, do you have to use that foul language?"

Drakon ground his teeth, then growled, "We need to protect Eratus. Athena has been fooled by the humans."

"Athena is a god. She cares about everyone, not just humans."

"I know what the humans are planning. I can stop this from ever—"

"Drakon, I'm not discussing this with you now."

"It never is the time or place for you, Owain. Unless, of course, it's your dear Connell. Look at you, a High King sitting in the dirt like a commoner."

"I would do the same for you, Drakon."

"I would be ashamed if you sat in the dirt holding me. You're the High King. You should have more pride."

For a moment there was only silence.

"Father, this disaster is another example of the damage Earth inflicts on us."

Owain sighed.

"The sabotage here," Drakon continued, "the wars, earth-quakes and storms on Earth. Humans are at the center of what is going wrong. We need to stop them, protect Eratus and Earth."

"Earth? Are you suggesting—Drakon, we'll discuss this later."

"You're too soft, Father. You're using Athena as an excuse."

"Challenge me if you like, Drakon. If you can find people to support you."

"Oh, there are plenty of people who will support me, dear Father. Plenty."

Metal boots turned on gravel as Drakon strode off, his guard detail close behind him.

～

CONNELL'S HEAD SPUN. He felt weak. Every breath sliced through him as if the air was acid. He tried to force his eyes open, but they refused to move. Everything was black. Panic clawed at him.

Think, Connell. Think!

Connell forced himself to relax back into the soft sheets and feather pillows. He focused on the gentle swishing of the silk as the breeze blew in through the curtains and the clear sounds of the crashing waves of the sea. The sweet sea air filled the room.

There had been the explosion, the fire. He was alive. How had he survived? The soft lick of a rough, wet tongue on the top of his hand told him George lay on the bed next to him. He raised his hand and the bed moved as George pulled her leather wings closer to her body and snuggled nearer to him, positioning her heavy fur head neatly under his hand. "Hello, beautiful."

George nudged him gently with her nose. "I am healing, girl. You don't need to worry." A heavy thud sounded on the door. "Come in."

"Who's finally awake then?" Owain's voice reverberated around the room.

"I'm young, I need my sleep."

"But three days?"

Connell's mouth dropped open. "Three days!"

"And your creature hasn't left your side."

Connell patted the mane of hair beneath his hand. "She's my favorite lady."

"The healer is here," Owain said. "I'll come back when he's finished your treatment. You up to talking?"

"Yes, of course, Father."

Connell heard the soft footsteps as the healer moved toward him. The pressure eased as the healer unwrapped his bandages.

"Things would be a lot easier for me if you could tell your creature to stop staring at me so closely," the healer said. "And swishing that deadly tail of hers."

Connell laughed. "She knows you're helping. You're safe."

"How are you feeling?"

"Better than before, but—" Air brushed against each of his wounds, reigniting the white-hot pain.

"I'll be as quick as I can." The healer applied a cool, moist spray over Connell's body. Most of the pain disappeared, replaced by the pressure from the bandages as the healer reapplied them. "Just hang in there, Connell."

It seemed like an eternity before the healer spoke again. "Now, I'm going to remove the bandaging off your eyes. Keep your eyes closed until I tell you to open them."

Connell dreaded having the eye bandages removed. What if he couldn't see? "I am in your hands, healer." The pressure eased as the bandages loosened.

"Now, open your eyes slowly. Things will be a bit blurry for a while, but it won't be long before your vision returns."

He opened his eyes. Panic set in. He was surrounded by blackness. "Healer, tell me it's fine that I still can't see anything."

"Close your eyes again," the healer said. After a minute, he said, "Now open them."

"It's still—oh, wait a minute." Relief flooded through him. "As you said, everything is a bit fuzzy, but they're wonderful. Thank you, healer, thank you."

"Here's a concoction for you to drink. It will help with the pain and the healing."

"What's it made of?"

"Just drink it, Connell." The healer paused. "When we first arrived at the site, we couldn't find you. We eventually found you in a cave at the edge of the disaster area. Someone had treated you to help you breathe and put a healing salve on your eyes before bandaging you. Those treatments saved you and your sight."

"Who treated me?"

"We're not sure. No-one was around when we arrived. We hoped you knew."

"I don't."

"Mm, strange," the healer said.

There was a loud thump on the door as Owain strode into the room with Marco, putting a stop to all conversation.

"Father. Hello, Marco."

"You look a lot better." Owain studied Connell. "A big improvement."

Marco walked to the bed and sat on the edge of it, his hand automatically reaching out to pat George. "I should have been there."

"I'm glad you weren't. At least you're still alive. You're my friend, not my bodyguard."

Marco stood and stretched his legs. "George sensed you were in trouble. She went crazy. It's hard enough keeping people calm at the best of times with a manticore strutting around the place as if she owns it, but the panic she caused...we had to send guards to bring you back."

"She's not a pure manticore," Connell argued.

"She's close enough," Owain replied. "She may not be pure, but she is just as terrifying to the people."

"Anyone else alive? The Sisters..."

"The ceremonial site was a mess." Owain massaged his forehead. "Packs of deathtails gorged themselves on the remains, so it was hard to find out if anyone had survived. The only reason you're still alive is because someone moved you to the crystal cave. Those creatures are terrified of crystals."

"Father, I need..." Connell looked pointedly over at the

healer, who was busy working at the table on the next batch of treatment.

Owain nodded. "Healer, would you mind giving us a moment?"

"Yes, Your Majesty." He bowed and backed out of the room.

Connell turned to George. "The door, George." George flexed her wings and jumped gracefully off the bed. She moved to the door, her sharp claws clipping on the stone floor, and sniffed along the gap below the door, then lay down. Connell relaxed. George would growl a warning if anyone was listening in.

"Father, the ceremony was sabotaged. We had practiced so many times, but this time when I drank my vial of dragon's blood...I think it was poisoned. Somebody wanted the ceremony to fail."

"Poisoned, but why? Who would want to kill you and stop the ceremony?" Owain sauntered toward the balcony and gazed out toward the ocean. "Why would anyone want to sabotage a ceremony to heal the Shield that keeps this planet safe? We would die without it."

"It doesn't make sense." Connell watched his father's heavy movements, slow and deliberate, as he leaned against the door frame. "You're tired, Father." The breeze blew Owain's long gray hair about his face. Though Owain was half a head taller than Connell and broader across the chest, there were many similarities between the two of them, surprisingly more than between Owain and Drakon.

"I'm getting old," Owain said. "Too many battles."

"We need to find out who is responsible for the disaster." Marco walked to the oak desk in the corner of Connell's room and perched on the edge. "Our people are saying humans sabotaged the ceremony. They're starting to rally against the ones living here. We need to protect them."

When no-one spoke, Marco continued. "And we need to think about how we're going to fix the Shield."

George's breathing echoed in the silence as they contemplated Marco's words.

"Where do we start?" Owain stared out at the ocean.

"Sister Laela came to visit me several hours before the ceremony," Connell said.

"Why?" Owain turned to face Connell.

"She said one of their visions had shown Sascha being given the map that shows where the ancient weapons are buried. She wanted me to find out if that was true."

"But the map is locked away," Owain said. "How could someone have found it? And why didn't Laela tell us if it was missing?"

"I don't know."

"Are you sure she said Sascha?"

"Yes," Connell answered. "We need to find the map. Maybe it is time to bring Sascha here. Perhaps that's our starting point."

"I don't want that ungrateful wretch back on Eratus," Owain snapped.

"That is unfair," Marco said. "Sascha went through a lot."

"What!" Owain roared. "Sascha went through a lot, but what about us? She gave up on all those who loved her - Soleil, her family—" Owain took a deep breath. "I was ready to protect her, despite what she did, but she threw everything away and hurt everyone who loved her, just so that she could feel better."

"It might not matter what we think, Father," Connell said. "We have to get the map back, and we have to protect Sascha and the girls. You know, the one thing I'm curious about is why the Sisters, with their power of precognition, didn't know about the healing disaster."

"What if they did know?" Owain said.

"You might be right, Owain." Marco stretched his legs and stood. "I've been searching the records in the headquarters of the Four Sisters and I found a bundle of notes on how to awaken the powers of someone who has been through the transition process."

"So you think they wanted to awaken Sascha's powers, but why?" Owain rubbed his arms.

"I'm not sure, but if you combine that with the missing map..." Marco said. "We will need Sascha to help us heal the Shield. You certainly won't survive another ceremony, Connell."

"It's been too long for Sascha," Connell said. "Even if we can get her memory back, will she remember her training? And who will take the place of the Sisters? You need more than Sascha."

"She's our only lead," Marco replied. "Do you think the girls could replace the Sisters? They were being hunted by their own people because of how powerful they were. Maybe they're powerful enough to help with the ceremony."

"We can't afford another disaster," Owain said. "Sorry, Connell."

Connell looked down at his hands. "You're right, Father. There must be a chance that Sascha can get her memory back if the Sisters made notes about awakening her powers."

"You saw what she did to those men that kidnapped her," Marco said. "She still has some of her old abilities."

"I hadn't seen her be so destructive before then, but after what they did to her..."

"How did you explain your presence there?" Owain asked.

Marco snorted. "Connell said he was a police detective. He said he received a tip on a group of men who were kidnapping unsuspecting young women and torturing them. I was his sidekick."

"And she believed you?"

Marco glanced over at Connell. "We think so, yes."

"Sweet souls and angels." Owain scrubbed his face with his hands. "We do need to find out what's going on. I guess the only way we can do that is if we bring them back here. Marco, can you contact Sascha?"

"If only Connell could travel," Marco answered. "I'm not exactly in her good books and she related well to Connell. I wish we had someone she could trust."

George thumped her tail on the floor, turned her head to the balcony and roared at the golden creature that had just landed on the balcony rim.

"Soleil!" Connell said. "Sascha and Soleil had a connection stronger than any bond we have seen between a pet and its master. If there's anyone who can help, it's him."

"Don't let Soleil hear you call him a pet." Marco turned to smile at the fiery golden raptor with onyx-colored eyes, its legs covered in scales of yellow-gold with rose-colored talons.

"Marco, would you bring me Soleil's necklace?" Connell asked. "It's in the top drawer of the desk you were using as a stool. I'll need to let Soleil know what we need him to do. And we will have to organize to get this necklace to Sascha. She won't understand Soleil until her power is restored, so she'll need it."

Marco retrieved the necklace and held it out for Connell to take.

"Would you mind putting it around my neck, Marco? My hands..." Connell waved his bandaged hands uselessly in the air. When Marco had placed the necklace around Connell's throat, Connell called out to Soleil. "Soleil, I have good news. I need you to travel to Earth with Marco. We need you to protect Sascha."

Soleil took off in a gust of wind. He twirled, twisted and dived up and around, emitting a sweet harmonious song that brought a smile to Connell's face and increased if it was possible the speed at which George wagged her tail.

"Soleil, calm down. I need to talk to you. You'll need to give her some time." The sounds stopped as Soleil flew down and landed on the balcony rim, tilted her head to the side and continued to listen. "She lost her memory, so she won't recognize you. You have to be gentle."

Suddenly, Soleil shimmered, then disappeared.

George jumped up and looked at the door, a low roar rumbling in her chest. Owain opened the door. "Come in," he said to the healer. He turned to Connell. "I will visit you tomorrow morning after you've had some more rest. Come on, Marco, let's get organized."

"And, Marco," Connell said as they were leaving, "would you check in on Jenny when you return to Earth? She should be safe with Sascha, but we haven't heard from her this week. With everything that is happening, I'm worried about her."

"Yep, sure thing."

CHAPTER 5

ERATUS

*D*rakon sat quietly on his father's throne, bored. His guards stood on either side of the throne area, alert, ready to protect their Prince. His soldiers drank, ate and grabbed at the serving wenches.

"Prince Drakon." His aide-de-camp bowed before him.

Drakon frowned at the source of this interruption. "Yes?"

"We've received word from Lieutenant General Chiane. He's advised that since the healing ceremony disaster, the people of Eratus are uniting. They are saying Athena has deserted them and they are ready to make a stand against the humans. Every day recruits flock to join him. The Awakening has increased a hundredfold to well over thirty thousand." The man's eyes lit up. "There have been many victories."

Drakon crossed his arms. "Pass on my approval. And arrange for me to make the journey to the mountains to visit him before dawn tomorrow, but make no mention of the visit to him."

"One more thing, if it please you, Prince Drakon. The

young lady over there," he said, pointing to a table at the back of the hall, "is Mage Isabella."

"*The* Mage Isabella?"

"Yes, My Prince."

Drakon looked at the woman with interest.

"She is the most powerful mage in her land of Breyth. There are rumors she is more powerful than Sascha was when she lived on Eratus," the aide said earnestly.

"I doubt that, but what about her?"

"She asked me to pass on her compliments on the decorations for tonight's banquet. She said she has seen no finer."

The young lady raised her glass to toast to Drakon. He nodded in acknowledgement.

Attractive enough. Could be fun, but my Reya is still the prettiest.

Drakon gazed around the hall. Red and black decorations glistened in the light of the wall torches. The solid stone walls of the hall were painted with scenes of battles from the Eratian history the ones his army had won. His prized possessions, specially trained fire dragons perched on the roof beams, observing his men and ready to attack on his command should he decide any of them needed to be taught a lesson for poor behavior. Musicians played raucous ballads to keep the men amused and the tables were full of roast meats, baked sweets and plenty of wine.

She seems deliciously naïve. The women are here to entertain the men, not to enjoy themselves, so perhaps I—

The golden carved doors to the hall were thrown open. The sounds of talking and eating stopped as Reya entered the hall, followed by her bodyguards. She glided in, tall and elegant. The blue shimmer of her fine silk gown skimmed her lean, delicately carved body and full breasts, and highlighted her perfect porcelain skin.

The men stood and saluted her. All except Novo,

Drakon's newly appointed Lieutenant General. He alone continued swilling down wine and eating the roasted meats, laughing loudly as he did so. One of his men nudged him, warning him to be quiet, but Novo was drunk. "She's not the prince. We don't answer to her," he said.

Drakon raised his cup and took another sip of wine. "She's your general, you fool," he muttered.

"But, sir..." a young man stuttered as he tried to pull the drunk Novo to his feet.

"Sit down and listen to me," Novo said. "You don't need to answer to some woman."

Reya turned. She had heard him.

Drakon smiled to himself.

This is going to be fun. You are about to find out why this woman is in control, you silly fool.

As etiquette demanded, Reya bowed low before Drakon. "Prince Drakon." She then moved over to Novo. She laughed, a soft tinkling sound, incongruous with the building tension in the room. "Lieutenant General Novo." She smiled at him, tilting her head to the side. "Have you found Jenny yet?"

Novo picked up a portion of roast lamb and took a large mouthful. Grease dripped down his beard. "I answer to Prince Drakon and, as yet, I haven't briefed him. I don't believe I need to answer to you."

A gasp echoed around the hall. Reya signaled to her bodyguards, who dragged the drunken man to his feet and turned him to face her. She leaned closer to him and pressed her palm briefly to his chest. "I'm sorry, Lieutenant, what did you say?"

The boom of a heartbeat echoed around the hall. Novo tried to speak, but nothing came out. His hand flew to his chest and his head jerked backwards as his drunken mind tried to work out what was going on. He began to moan. The heartbeat became louder and louder, faster and faster.

Drakon laughed as the color drained from the faces of his men as they stared at Novo's thrashing body. Many of the women covered their ears to block out the sound of the heartbeat. A grinning Mage Isabella appeared to be the only person enjoying the show.

Interesting and promising.

The fire dragons were still but for their eyes, which followed the action with a furious intensity that betrayed their desire to attack. He signaled them and they rested back on their haunches.

Reya's bodyguards dropped Novo to the ground. He writhed in agony at her feet. He would die if she continued. Not many men had the stomach to carry out the plans Drakon had in mind. This one did. "Reya, the man has learnt his lesson and we may still need him." Her charcoal eyes met Drakon's. She glanced down at Novo and took a step away from him.

The echo of the heartbeat started to slow, then stopped. Quiet filled the hall. Novo lay still on the floor. "Lieutenant General Novo," Reya said. "I expect you to deliver a report to my room before the night is out." She called out to the hall, "Continue, everyone. This is a party after all."

Drakon felt the desire start to build as Reya glided toward him. There was nothing more attractive than a powerful woman. He flicked his finger at his aide. The aide topped up his wine and produced a fresh cup for Reya as she lowered herself into the seat beside Drakon. They watched the festivities in silence until they had drained their glasses.

"Let's go to my chamber." Drakon pushed himself out of the throne and walked toward the hall's large entry doors. His guards led the way out, Reya's followed them. He enjoyed owning Reya, especially at times like this when everyone else was terrified of her and the power she wielded. He knew better than to let his guard down with her, but it satisfied him to keep her around. For the moment.

When they arrived at his chambers, he turned to the guards. "We don't want to be disturbed under any circumstances."

"Yes, Prince." The guard nearest the door brought his clenched fist to his chest in salute, turned on his heel and closed the door behind them.

REYA SASHAYED TOWARD DRAKON, her flowing raven-colored hair gleaming in the light, her full red lips curved and full of promise. Drakon moved to the drawer and retrieved the chains. He walked toward her, ran his finger gently down her neck and then quickly ripped the dress from her, leaving her naked but for a fine silver cord around her waist. He looped the chain around Reya's wrists and threw it up over the roof beams where he pulled it tightly, stretching her up so her feet just touched the floor. He ignored the small cry of pain as the chains bit into her wrists and stepped behind her. Drakon took her from behind, enjoying the pleasure of controlling her, forcing her to satisfy him. Sated, he released the chains, dropped into the lounge chair and watched as she dropped to the floor. Reya picked up the remnants of her ruined dress and walked toward the showers.

"Stop."

She stopped, clenched her fists and turned around to face Drakon.

If she thinks she can control me by flaunting her body in front of me, she can think again.

"What happened at the ceremony?" Drakon drawled.

"What do you mean?"

"Connell told Owain the healing ceremony was sabotaged. He thought his vial of dragon's blood had been poisoned. Poison is a woman's weapon. Again, I ask, what happened?"

"I didn't poison Connell. How would I have had time? I was too busy helping the fire mage who was setting everything alight instead of modifying the Shield. And she still needed to set up the connection to the second Earth portal."

"Another disaster. Is it true the second portal doesn't work at all?"

Reya cleared her throat. "Yes, it's true."

"What you are talking about, Reya, was during the ceremony. The vial was probably poisoned before the ceremony. You could have done that."

"I didn't, and I swear I don't know who did."

The tendons in Reya's jaw flickered. The pulse in her long elegant neck beat visibly faster. She had seen how he punished those who displeased him, so she would be afraid. But her anger. Drakon loved her anger.

"The vials are prepared in secret by the Sisters," Reya said. "No-one else is given access to them, not even me. The only ones who could poison the vial are the ones who were a part of the ceremony."

"What? Are you saying one of the Sisters or guardians poisoned Connell? I don't believe you. It makes no sense."

"Well, it wasn't me."

He leaned forward, his hand reaching for her throat. Drakon saw the panic as she realized what he was going to do.

"I swear, My Prince, I would never double-cross you. I'm not a fool."

He walked over to his desk and picked up the photo she had put there only a matter of months before. He studied it. How much everything had changed in the last few days. She seemed different. He wasn't sure if she was lying to him or not. "If you ever let that thought cross your mind, Reya, you know I'll make you pay."

"I swear I'm the one person you don't need to worry about. I'll never betray you. I owe you everything."

Drakon allowed the threat of silence to descend upon the room. He walked over to his bar and poured a glass of red wine for himself and Reya. "Why didn't your mage make the connection to the second portal, as I asked?"

"She lost control of her power and couldn't pull it back fast enough before the ceremony ended. Once the ceremony was over, it was too late. She killed the Sisters, which is what you wanted, well, at least..."

Drakon waited for her to continue, but when she didn't, he said, "At least what?"

"She hadn't seen the Sister tending to Connell when she put the protection barrier around him. The barrier protected one of the Sisters as well."

"It what?"

"She thought she was doing the right thing."

"She failed to make the connection to the second Earth portal and failed to kill the Sisters. Send me the mage. I'll deal with her."

"I've given orders for her to be punished," Reya said. "She can learn a lot from us and she is powerful. She'll be useful for you and me."

"You either send her to me or you stand in her place. Your choice."

The color drained from Reya's face. She couldn't hide the shudder.

"And you'll need a replacement for the mage she'll have lost her usefulness once I'm finished with her." Drakon took a swig of wine. "As for the surviving Sister, you will use whatever resources you need to find her! Before the ceremony, I overheard the Sisters asking Connell to bring Sascha back. The Sister must not speak to Sascha."

"Should we kill Sascha?" Reya asked.

"We may need her. Connell's too wounded to perform the next healing ceremony himself. But don't worry, when I get my hands on her..."

Reya was waiting for Drakon to finish, but he decided to leave his threat unspoken.

"More importantly, we need the second portal. I'll talk to Connell. Now, have your shower. I'll get us some fresh wine."

LATER, Drakon sat in bed, studying Reya as she slept. He reached over and ran his hand down her naked back. What would happen if he tired of her and sent her to the dungeons? The whip would destroy her smooth, soft skin in no time at all. The thought aroused him. But he had work to do and for that, he needed to wake her. He ran his hand down her back again, hard this time. She woke up, extended her arms and stretched like a cat. She glanced at the window. "It's still dark."

"I couldn't sleep," Drakon answered.

"What's wrong?"

"After everything that has happened, I want to be certain the search for the ancient weapon is going as I asked."

"We found out the codes you need are marked on the original map but hidden by a magical spell. It's easy to reveal once you know the spell. We sent Roger to Earth a couple of months ago to steal it back from Sascha."

"From Sascha?"

"Yes. Kalurth got her claws on the map and decided it should be sent to Sascha."

"Kalurth? Sokentash! That damned dragon."

"She and Zinnath thought they were being clever."

"Damned beasts. I think the Four Sisters had the right idea in trying to get rid of them."

Reya peeked at him from beneath heavy eyelids before continuing. "We wanted to be prepared, so we sent Roger there early. His job was to watch the house for when the map arrived and steal it back. He was also supposed to keep an eye on Jenny."

"Let's hope he has done a better job of finding the map, considering he lost Jenny."

"Yes," Reya replied. "He will pay for that mistake."

Drakon sensed the subtle movement of the mattress as she sat up in bed. She tried to pull the sheet to cover herself, but he held it down. It didn't take long for her to realize he wouldn't allow her to cover up.

"When is Roger due back?"

"I am expecting him in the next day or two," Reya said.

"The army is at your disposal. I don't want any excuses for this not working."

"I will personally make sure it all works out, My Prince."

"Well, you'll be held responsible, so I would make sure of it if I was you. Have you gathered the test subjects for when we find the weapon?"

"We've gathered over two hundred and fifty subjects and they've all been tagged," Reya said. "They're locked away in the dragon's cave below The Awakening's headquarters, but I'm having a few issues with some of our leaders."

"Why? What are they doing?"

"Most subjects are being tagged so if they run away the tags will explode, killing them instantly. Some of the men are tagging the subjects to maim, not kill, and then releasing them for sport. They explode the tags of those they don't capture and then leave them to die or be eaten by the wildlife in the hunting park."

"My men do love their sports. But that is not my problem. You manage it. That's your job."

"I'll need to punish some of the men, make an example of them if I'm going to stop it. Do you give your permission?"

"Do what you need to do." Drakon put his hand to her face. She pulled away, as if she thought he was going to hit her. The fear aroused him even more. Admittedly, he had thought about it. He traced his hand down her body. As her muscles relaxed, he grabbed her arms and pulled her toward him. Her head arched back and he took her deeper into the covers, finding release in the pleasure of her touch and the smell of her perfume.

CHAPTER 6

* EARTH

"We raided Roger's office and his home." Ken's voice boomed from Sascha's car speakers. "He's missing, along with the bookkeeper. It's all rather convenient. Is it possible they're both in on it?"

The street lights flicked on. Her house was only a short distance away. She let out a deep breath and smiled.

Nearly home.

"I don't believe Jenny has done anything wrong and Marcie told me she's engaged to someone. She would hardly play up with Roger and I...shit!"

The figure, shrouded in mist, appeared from nowhere. Sascha slammed on the brakes. Her car spun off to the side of the road and came to a rest inches from the edge of the creek near her home.

Her heart pounded as she searched for the figure. She could see nothing, but the crack of a twig and the crunch of gravel underfoot told her she wasn't alone. The usual night sounds - frogs croaking, crickets chirping - were absent. Sascha checked her car doors. Locked. She jumped as the loud screech of an owl shattered the silence.

She barely heard the knock on the passenger side window.

Don't look. Don't look.

The knock sounded, louder this time. She did the only thing she could do, she looked.

Glowing beady red eyes stared back.

Sascha tried to scream, but a high-pitched squawk was the only sound she could manage.

"Talk to me, Sascha. What's wrong? I'm on my way. Where are you?"

Ken! She needed to say something.

Sascha glanced at the phone and then back at the window. The eyes had disappeared. She twisted in the seat as she looked around her. Again, nothing. She gasped and clutched at her chest as the boisterous laughter of a family of kookaburras acted as a signal to the other creatures, who resumed their noisy chatter.

I need a drink.

"Sascha, talk to me."

"Ken—"

"Thank Athena...ah, God, you're safe. Where are you?"

"Somebody is here," she whispered. "They ran out on the road right in front of me. I didn't see them until the last second. I swerved off in time. I didn't hit anything. But it's here."

"Where are you, Sascha? Don't get out of the car. I'm coming."

"I'm a block from home, Ken. I can drive there." She fumbled for the keys, her hands shaking. She turned the key in the ignition. The engine refused to turn over, so she turned the key off and then on again. This time, the engine roared into life. Sascha smiled shakily and slapped the steering wheel gratefully. She slammed her car into reverse and then raced for home.

"Stay on the phone until you're home. I'll organize for the local patrol to look around."

"That'd be good. But I'm fine. A bit shaken up, that's all."

She twisted the steering wheel and pulled into the driveway. "I'm home," she said. "All good."

"I'll drop by after work. I did call your house earlier and left a message with Kira."

"Don't tell the girls about this, Ken. They don't need to worry."

"Why? You need to start trusting people."

"Please, Ken."

"If you say so. But you need to trust them more, Sasch. They're good kids. Hey, before you go, some good news. Someone's just handed me a note. Roger's neighbor called the local station when Roger returned home. A couple of officers are on their way to pick him up. I'll let you know what he says. Time for a stiff drink and a rest."

The mark on her hand tingled and the garage door opened. Sascha stared at the mark. Would she remember how to use it if she needed to protect herself again?

No, not if protection means what I did to those men. Even if it was life and death.

"I'm lucky. Ken is my protector. I don't need anything else."

Sascha parked the car and then leaned into the back seat to pick up dessert, half a blueberry cheesecake. She glanced out the back window as the garage door started to descend. Nothing there. Once the doors thudded down, she sat for a moment, holding the cheesecake box, until her breathing slowed. She clambered out of the car. Time to face the girls. She entered the house.

The girls' laughter lifted Sascha's spirits. Kira stood at the kitchen bench, pouring glasses of wine for her sisters. Lee and Ella sat on bar stools, still chuckling at whatever they'd been joking about.

Sascha took this rare moment to breathe in the sight of the three girls. Even in their casual gear they looked gorgeous. The three of them were slim and fit. Kira's fiery strawberry-blond hair was loose and fell halfway down her back. Her lightly tanned skin highlighted her fine features. Lee's raven hair contrasted with her pale skin, and Ella's darkly tanned skin and long white-blond curls had men following her in droves.

Kira saw Sascha first. "Hi, Sasch."

"Hi, girls. You beat me." She walked into the large kitchen. "Here's dessert." She placed the box on the kitchen cupboard and opened the lid.

The girls squealed with delight. Sascha smiled. She had chosen well.

Kira opened the cupboard door, took out another glass, poured some wine and handed it to Sascha. "Ken said you'll need this. He called earlier and checked we would be home. He's dropping by at 7 p.m."

"Thanks." Sascha leaned over and looked at Kira's glass, then glanced up at her.

Kira placed her hands on her hips and scowled. "Yes, yes, I know. It's only mineral water. It's not fair that I'm the only one that can't drink."

Lee stepped off her stool, walked over to Kira and hugged her. "That's 'cause you're the baby of the family, Kira. But the next couple of years will go fast."

Kira humphed as she turned to Sascha. "So was it tough today?"

"I'll tell you all over pizza. I'll order."

"Too late." Lee glanced at Sascha, then chuckled. "All ordered. Your favorite. The girl on the phone said it would be here in twenty minutes."

"Thanks. What do I owe you?"

"Nothing." Lee took another sip of her wine. "Special deal tonight all pizzas are free."

"I must remember to ask you to order pizza in future if you get them for free." Sascha chuckled. "Thanks, Lee. I'll change and meet you all in the lounge."

A few minutes later, she joined the girls, sitting beside Kira on the three-seater lounge. She glanced at the curtained window.

Today was a huge day.

Kira leaned over and topped up Sascha's wine. Sascha took another mouthful and the muscles in her stomach started to relax.

Lee moved forward in her seat. "Okay, Sascha, spill. What happened today?"

"Roger, the accountant I hired a couple of months ago, came in to tell me Jenny was in trouble for stealing."

The girls gasped.

"That's not possible," Lee said.

"That is exactly what I said too," Sascha answered. Fifteen minutes later, the girls sat quietly, digesting everything she had told them.

"I don't like Roger," Ella said. "He's a total jerk."

Sascha flexed her neck as she felt the muscles tense up. "Marcie doesn't like him either."

"On a different note," Kira said as she placed some crisps and a fresh bottle of wine on the coffee table, "we've all noticed you're not sleeping. Consider this an intervention. What's going on?"

Sascha's stomach lurched.

Oh, no. I forgot to tell Ken not to mention the sketch artist. I will have to tell the girls. Damn it.

She took another mouthful of her wine while she planned what to say. "I've been having some strange dreams lately."

"What sort of dreams?" Kira asked.

"I keep seeing an old man. And a young woman. At first I couldn't work out the details of the faces, but last night the old man's face became clear. There was something about him." Sascha put a hand to her mouth. She needed to slow down. She was speaking too fast, saying too much. She took another mouthful of wine, hoping the action would slow her down. "Ken gave me a hard time today, said I looked terrible. He wanted to organize a sketch artist to see if he can sketch the face of the man from these...dreams."

The girls glanced at each other.

I shouldn't have told them.

"What is it about the old man you find scary?" Kira studied her glass of mineral water.

"I didn't say he was scary, Kira."

"You didn't need to," she replied.

Sascha fiddled with the glass in her hand. "He's, um, he's brutally murdered."

Silence.

"Say something, girls."

Again, silence. Sascha cleared her throat. "What's going on?"

Kira answered first. "We've all had the same dream, but each of us see ourselves killing the old man and the woman."

"Oh!" The glass slipped from Sascha's hand, spilling the wine on the carpet. "What? How's that possible?"

Lee raced to the kitchen and came back with a cloth to mop up the wine.

"We thought it was a memory from our past. We didn't want to tell you. We were ashamed." Kira brushed away a tear.

The conversation broke off as a knock sounded at the door.

"Pizza must be here," Ella said as she pushed herself out of the chair and walked to the door. "Oh, hello, Ken. Sorry, I thought you were the pizza man."

"Nope, not the pizza man, but that might be."

"Yep, you're right," Ella said. "Thanks, Ken. Go in. Sascha's waiting for you."

"Hi, Ken," Sascha said.

"I won't take long," Ken replied. "Your dinner's here and Pat is waiting impatiently for me at home." Studying the women one by one, he asked, "Is everything alright? You're all unusually quiet."

Sascha straightened up in her chair. "We're fine. We've been discussing today's events."

Ken moved to sit on the edge of the coffee table.

"Don't sit there," Lee said as she walked toward the kitchen table to find a chair for Ken. "Wait, I'll get you a seat."

"Lee, you are way too superstitious for such a young 'un," Ken said.

"It's bad luck. An omen." Lee positioned the chair next to Sascha.

Ken laughed as he stood. "An omen of what?"

"Death," Lee answered. "Or poverty."

Ken pulled at his collar and flexed his neck. "Now that's weird." He sat down on the chair and turned to face Sascha. "Sasch, we found Roger."

"And?"

"There's no easy way to say this. He's dead."

"What? He's dead? How?"

"It appears that he hung himself, but hanging is inconsistent with the bruising on his face and hands. We're still investigating. He left a note. It said, 'Forgive me'. We also found another note attached to some cash. Someone wrote a number on it."

"Some cash?"

"Yes, five thousand."

"So he died over my money? If he needed it, why didn't he talk to me? Money is replaceable."

"It could be a coincidence. Do you recognize the number on the note?" Ken said, showing Sascha a piece of paper.

The blood drained from Sascha's face. This couldn't be a coincidence. She read the typed words on the note "It is time" and a handwritten number. Stamped in the corner were the silhouettes of four females, identical to the silhouettes on the note she had found attached to the map earlier that morning.

"Sascha, you are white," Ken said. "What is it?"

"It's a shock to hear what happened to Roger," she lied. Sascha wondered if she should mention the map, but sensed that she should keep it to herself.

"No-one deserves to die like that," Kira said. Sascha jumped at the sound of her voice. She'd forgotten that Kira was sitting beside her.

"We'll get to the bottom of this. Don't worry, Sascha." Ken leaned over and patted her hand. "Jenny's story is strange too. We still haven't found her and she's not in trouble like Roger said. We checked. There are no records of a matter involving Jenny."

"God, I hope she's not dead too," Sascha said. The cushions moved beneath her as Kira slid closer and put an arm around her shoulders.

"I hope not, Sascha," Ken answered. "Now, about the other matter..."

"What other matter? Oh, right. You can talk about it. The girls know about the sketch artist."

"Okay, well, one of our artists would be happy to help. And he's totally trustworthy. Do you mind if I give him your number?"

She sighed. "Only on the conditions we agreed to, Ken. I keep full control of this."

"For sure. I hope it helps, Sascha. You do need to do something." Ken stood, leaned over and hugged her. "Don't worry, we'll sort out what's happening. See you tomorrow. Bye, girls."

"Bye, Ken." Sascha drank the rest of her wine in one swig.

~

LAST NIGHT'S conversation came back to Sascha as she drove to work.

"Why don't we wait until the sketch is done?" Ella had said. "The picture will tell us if we're all having the same dream."

"And what if it's not the same dream?" Sascha's stomach knotted at the thought.

She parked at the clinic, walked to Marco's coffee shop and picked up an extra strong coffee and a vegemite scroll. Her heart ached every time she visited Marco's coffee shop. She missed him.

Sascha went to her office and sat at her desk. Her mind was numb. With Roger dead and Jenny still missing, work was the last thing she wanted to think about. But there was so much to do before the weekend. She needed to focus.

The map. No-one was around, so it was the perfect time to look at it. She grabbed her bag and checked the pocket. It was gone.

"Shit."

She emptied the bag's contents on her desk. It wasn't there.

What have I done with it? I'm sure I put it in the pocket of my bag. I must have left it somewhere in my room.

She decided to search for it when she got home that night. The girls always went out on Friday nights.

Work soon claimed all her attention. Marcie left at 2.30

p.m. and Sascha had been working at her computer solidly since then.

"Hello, Sasch."

Sascha glanced toward the doorway. Kira stood there, smiling at her. "Hello, Kira. What a lovely surprise. What're you doing here?"

"It's time to leave for Caloundra for the weekend. For your birthday."

"Oh, right. Sorry, I forgot."

"We've a special party organized for you. You'll enjoy it. And we all need something *normal* to do at the moment. Lee and Ella dropped me off. They'll meet us there."

The girls had been planning this weekend for the last month. How could she have forgotten? "Give me a minute. I'll tidy up. Then we'll go home. I'll need to pack some clothes."

"We've already packed you a bag. We figured if we were tired, you would have to be as well. We wanted to do something nice. We hoped you wouldn't mind."

Panic flooded through Sascha. They had been in her room. Could they have found the map? Kira would have said something if they had found it, wouldn't she?

Kira fidgeted, bit her lip, as she stared at Sascha.

Be nice, Sascha. She needs to hear you're fine with what they did.

"True, I'm exhausted. It's good you girls were kind enough to organize my bag for me."

Kira walked over to examine the feature wall filled with ancient folding fans. "Sascha, what is it with you and fans? They're beautiful, but they look...dangerous."

"I don't know. I just love collecting them."

Kira pointed. "These two look more like weapons than fans. Are they made of some kind of metal?"

"Yes, they are. Don't touch them—"

"Ouch," Kira said, pulling her hand back. "They're sharp."

"I know. I cut myself when I put them on the wall. They were sent to me last week. There were no contact details, so I'm not sure who sent them. They may be dangerous to handle, but they're exceptionally well-crafted."

"Yes, they're gorgeous." Turning back to Sascha, Kira asked, "Are you ready to go?"

"Yes, I am. But give me a minute to close up here."

Kira gave Sascha a cheesy grin. "Can I drive?"

"Did you bring your L plates?"

"I sure did." Kira walked to the window and studied the red BMW parked in the carpark. "Heads turn when a red BMW convertible drives by. And it's a great way to pick up cute guys too."

Sascha laughed. "Yes, you can drive my car, but no speeding and no picking up cute guys."

"Party pooper," Kira replied.

Sascha tossed her keys to Kira. "I'll meet you at the car in a minute."

Sascha washed her face and freshened up. She decided to use work as an excuse to leave the weekend earlier than the girls, giving her time to search the house for the map.

The map isn't going anywhere in the meantime.

She grabbed her bag and walked toward the door. As she did so, the hairs on the back of her neck prickled. Goosebumps dotted her skin. She breathed deeply and forced herself to stop panicking. Nothing was here. She was being silly. Sascha walked slowly around the office to make sure. She looked out her office window. Nothing.

The tooting of the horn told Sascha that Kira was getting impatient. She berated herself for being ridiculous and locked up. As she hurried to the car, she psyched herself up for the weekend. She hated being the center of attention.

Behave yourself. The girls have gone to a lot of effort for this. Don't mess it up for them.

~

THE APARTMENT at the resort was spacious and airy, with floor-to-ceiling sliding glass doors that gave the best views of the ocean. Sascha stepped onto the balcony and breathed in the tangy, salty ocean air. She felt the knots in her shoulders begin to unravel. Colored kites dominated the view as wind-surfers made the most of the breeze. A couple walked on the beach, wrapped in each other's arms. Memories of being here with Marco flooded back. They would swim in the cold ocean until they were exhausted. Then they would clamber up to the beach and collapse on the warm sands as they waited for the sun to dry them off. Once they were toasty and warm, they would help each other up and walk arm in arm along the beach laughing at silly jokes. Marco's laughter still echoed around her.

Sascha had felt so utterly alone when he left for Scotland. Every little thing reminded her of him and even after all this time, the pain still lingered.

The door to the apartment opened as the girls returned, laden with bags. Sascha pulled herself back from her abstraction and forced herself to smile.

"This is lovely, girls. Thank you. Just what the doctor ordered," she said.

"Let's go exploring," Kira said.

"Girls, I might have a night in tonight. You three go out and enjoy yourselves."

"Why don't we all go out for dinner?" Ella said.

"Not me, but you girls go. I'll get something delivered." When the girls, in a whirl of make-up and teased, straightened and curled hair, eventually left, Sascha flopped into the nearest bucket chair. She picked up her phone and ordered dinner.

Roger had lived out this way. It was hard to believe he was dead. And Jenny. Where was she?

I don't believe what Roger said. She wouldn't steal from us.

Sascha sat and forced herself to block everything out. She opened a bottle of Angel Cove the girls had organized for her, took a sip and sank back into her chair. A knock on the door signaled the arrival of her dinner.

As the delivery boy was busy getting her dinner out of the bag, she looked over at the rooms on the opposite side of the resort. Lights were on and people were sitting on their balconies, enjoying the warm spring night. Her attention was drawn to the resort's grounds by the sound of children laughing as they splashed in the pool. A tall muscular man ambled past the pool, heading toward the exit, his dark shoulder-length hair blowing about in the breeze. He glanced over at the laughing children. The light from the balconies highlighted the contours of his face. Sascha's heart stopped. Marco! It was Marco.

"Here we go, ma'am. Chilli prawn and chorizo linguini."

"Oh, of course, thank you." She turned back to the delivery boy and handed over some money. When he had left, she looked down at the pool again. Marco had disappeared.

CHAPTER 7

* EARTH

*S*oleil swooped out of the portal and landed neatly on the concrete rooftop of Marco's apartment complex in the middle of Brisbane City. The golden glow of the setting sun warmed Marco's back a stark contrast to the freezing cool winds in the portal. Marco yawned, unstrapped himself from the harness on Soleil's shoulders and climbed down to the roof. He rubbed his legs to ease the cramps from the trip.

"Thanks, Soleil. I—"

Soleil clicked his beak, strutted to the edge of the building and then flew off.

"Hey, wait," Marco bellowed. "Where are you going? We need to..."

Marco shook his head as Soleil disappeared.

Damn creature. He was so much like its master.

He reached into his jacket pocket and retrieved his phone. Twenty-two missed calls. "What in Athena's name?"

Marco unlocked his phone. The calls were all from one person, Eham. He sighed. "That's just what I need." He dialed the number.

"Thank the shadows. About time. I've been calling and calling for—" Marco held the phone away from his ear as Eham vented his grievances. He considered hanging up, but instead, once the voice at the other end of the phone fell silent, he put the phone back to his ear.

"Now, what is it, Eham?"

"I need you here in Caloundra. You'll need to organize yourself somewhere to stay."

"Why? What's happened?"

"I can't talk on the phone. I'll tell you when you get here. You need to hurry."

"I'll be there as soon as I can. Where will you be?"

"Out the front of the Ocean View Resort, Bulcock Street, 8.30 p.m."

Marco walked to the stairwell door and made his way down to his apartment. He changed out of his leather travel gear and into jeans and a navy-blue shirt, before packing an overnight bag and leaving for Caloundra. An hour and a half later, Marco had checked into a resort not far from where Eham was staying. He looked at his watch. He had enough time for dinner before his meeting.

As Marco walked toward the restaurant, he glanced at the raucous children playing in the pool. His skin prickled. He was being watched. He smiled at the children as his eyes scanned the apartments surrounding the pool.

He saw nothing unusual, just people eating and drinking on their balconies and a delivery boy standing outside one of the apartments.

MARCO ENJOYED his dinner of steak and chips, washed down with a glass of beer. He was ready to face Eham. As he stood, a bright orange light flashed past him. The creature crash-landed in the middle of a group of pine trees, upsetting the sleeping lorikeets and leaving a trail of broken branches and scattered leaves in its path. Soleil was here.

Are you following me or is Sascha here?

His gut twisted, a familiar reaction. He wasn't looking forward to seeing Sascha again, but he knew the day would come when he would have to face his demons.

Marco drove his blue MG out of the carpark and focused on what he had to do next. The Ocean View Resort. At the top of the exit to the carpark, he plugged the address into his GPS.

Minutes later, he pulled over to the side of the road in front of the resort. Marco hadn't been waiting long when Eham clambered into the passenger seat.

"These cars are bloody difficult to climb into, Marco. Why don't you own a normal car? I wouldn't have thought *you* needed to stroke your ego by owning one of these."

Marco glanced over at Eham's neatly trimmed gray hair and beard, his perfectly tailored pants and shirt. "That's funny coming from you. You're jealous."

"Humph, I don't need to prove anything. Obviously *you* do."

"Let's not start arguing already," Marco said. "What did you need me to do?"

"I have a lead on Jenny from Roger. He said he wanted to help, but he wasn't saying anything until he could talk to you."

"Whoa, Eham. Let's take a step back. What do you mean? You know Jenny's working with Sascha. And who's Roger?"

"How the hell did you get to be the leader of the Fire of the Phoenix if you can't even keep up with what's going on in your own town?"

"I only arrived back today," Marco said. "I haven't had much chance to catch up on anything."

Eham gave an exaggerated sigh. "A couple of days ago, I

went to visit Jenny at work and that stupid receptionist of Sascha's said she wasn't in the office. She wouldn't tell me when they expected her back. She brushed me off like some commoner."

"She wouldn't have known who you were. It's not surprising she didn't say anything."

Eham dismissed Marco's comment with a flick of his well-manicured hand. "Anyway, I kept the place under surveillance but Jenny didn't return. Later that evening I went to her unit, but no-one was home."

Eham looked out the window of the car and was quiet for a few seconds, before turning back to Marco. "Yesterday morning, I returned to Sascha's clinic, but still no Jenny. Then this bloke Roger sees me standing outside and comes over. Long story short Roger tells me he's worried about Jenny too. He said she had been accused of stealing. My Jenny stealing!" Eham shook his head. "Roger agreed to let me know if he heard anything, so I told him where I was staying. He called me not long after, sounding real scared. Said he had some info about Jenny, but he didn't want to say anything until he spoke to you. Said he wanted protection."

"To me?" Marco asked. "Did he say my name?"

"Yes, he specifically said you."

"Who is this Roger? And how would he know me?"

"You can ask him that," Eham answered. "I need to find where my Jenny is. She's the only family I have left. I can't lose her."

"What sort of protection did he want?" Marco asked.

"He wouldn't say anything until he spoke to you."

"Let's go." Marco turned his GPS back on. "What's the address?"

～

THEY TURNED onto Roger's street. As they neared the address, they saw that Roger's house was lit up like a Christmas tree and that police officers were everywhere. Out of necessity, they parked a few houses away.

Marco glanced at Eham. "This doesn't look good."

"What the..." Eham stuttered.

"Let's see what we can find out." Marco got out of the car and walked toward the house.

A neighbor was out in his yard, leaning against a tall beech tree and watching the police go about their business.

"Hi," Marco called out. "We're here to visit a friend who lives in this house. What's happened?"

"Where were you when the poor bugger needed a friend," the man said.

"What do you mean?" Marco asked.

"Your friend is dead. Whispers say he hanged himself."

"Hanged?" Marco swiveled toward Eham.

Eham shook his head. "There's no way he would have killed himself. He knew I was helping him. Something else is going on here."

"Let's go." Marco started to walk back to the car. "Did Roger say anything else, anything that could help us?"

"He said something about Jenny wanting them to both book a flight overseas."

"So why didn't they do that?"

"Roger said that, as far as he was concerned, they couldn't run far enough away to ever be safe. It's probably why he wanted to talk to you, but we'll never know, will we?"

Eham's cell phone buzzed. "Thank the shadows. It's Jenny. She's safe."

"What does she say?" Marco asked.

"She said she'll meet us where the sun doesn't set, tomorrow at 8 p.m."

"Where the sun doesn't set? What does that mean?"

Eham smiled as his fingers worked the keys of his phone.

"Eham, what does she mean?" Marco asked again.

"She loves spy movies. It's a code she came up with." Eham scrubbed his face with his hands. "She's alive. You need to come with me. You need to give her whatever protection she needs. She can't end up like Roger."

"Of course I'll help protect her," Marco answered.

Eham wrung his hands. "I should have stayed at Roger's house instead of gallivanting all around the place. And if you had answered your phone when I called you, then Roger would be alive and Jenny would be safe."

Marco bit back his response. Eham might have been right, but there was nothing Marco could do about it now.

"I need a drink," Eham said.

"We can go to the RSL." Marco started up the car and waited for Eham to climb in. "It's not far away."

They were nearly at the club before Eham spoke again. "I've been told Drakon will be arriving on Earth this weekend. He's after Sascha. Someone has told him you're trying to bring her back and he wants to get to her first."

"I wonder how he found out so fast," Marco said.

"Probably from the servants. They're terrified of him. Not much is secret from Drakon."

MEMORIES OF MARCO haunted Sascha's dreams, but at least the nightmare was leaving her alone. After a relaxed breakfast of fruit salad, Eggs Benedict and a couple of cups of strong coffee, Sascha and the girls strolled along the boardwalk as they headed toward Kings Beach. When they arrived, Sascha sat on one of the silver benches facing the ocean while the girls, after sitting for only a matter of minutes, raced down the beach, eager to face the chilly waters. Sascha loved springtime, but today the winds were cool and the water too cold for her. The girls squealed as they splashed in the sea, the waves crashing around their feet.

The first time Sascha had brought the girls to this beach was two days after Connell found them at Marco's coffee shop. They had been abandoned. Connell asked Sascha to look after them while he searched for their family, but he never had found them. The sounds of the girls' laughter carried on the breeze. The desperate urge she felt to care for these girls surprised her. Somehow, despite her best efforts, she had grown to love them, though she understood that one day she would lose them.

The day she had agreed to care for the girls had also been the day that she received the call from Marco. She had thought he was in Scotland for a couple of months on business, but then he had called to say he was getting married. Married! How could she have missed the signs, not notice there was someone else? Sascha realized she was grinding her teeth, and her jaw was aching with the tension. She had to forget him. If he was too gutless to tell her face to face, he wasn't worth her time.

Determined to push the pain aside, Sascha studied the pelicans as they glided in graceful circles, their heads held back in their shoulders, their bills resting on their folded necks. A brightly colored bird appeared above the pelicans. A glittering orange flash of light. The bird changed direction and hovered high above her. It was larger than the pelicans, and its color reflected the molten golden colors of the sun.

It's beautiful.

A mournful whistle, long and low, filled the air. Sascha had a strong sense of déjà vu. She had seen this creature before, heard its call. But where?

The intensity of the call increased, the pitch awakening a

deep sense of loneliness, of longing. She was confused. Why would the bird's call evoke such a reaction in her?

Minutes later the girls arrived, grabbing for their towels. Without turning away from the bird, Sascha pointed at the sky. "Look, girls, the orange streak near the pelicans. Isn't it beautiful?"

"What?" the girls asked.

Sascha pointed up in the air. "Above where the pelicans are gliding."

The girls talked amongst themselves as they tried to locate whatever it was she was pointing at. "There are only pelicans," Kira said. She giggled. "Sasch, how much wine did you have last night?"

"What?" Sascha turned away for a moment to face Kira.

"You're hallucinating. Too much alcohol." The girls all laughed.

Sascha looked back at the sky, but the bird was gone. A sense of incredible sadness flooded through her.

It was late afternoon when they ambled back to the apartment. The girls decided to head to the gym to work off the calories from their lunch. Sascha grabbed her iPad and some cashews, poured a glass of wine and sat on the balcony.

A soft crooning sound came from across the road, somewhere near the pine trees. The bird was back. Sascha walked to the edge of the balcony and searched the trees. She found it sitting on top of a light pole on the opposite side of the street. The creature stared at her. It was exquisite, a large golden creature with a long elegant tail the colors of fire and rich emerald green.

"Hello, you beautiful thing," Sascha whispered.

The bird flew toward her and landed on the balcony, taking up most of the space.

"You're so much bigger than I realized," Sascha said as she moved toward it. The balcony filled with the aroma of pine and cinnamon, the warmth of its body reminding Sascha of a warm summer day. She reached her hand over to touch it. The tone of the call changed to a high-pitched whistle. The sudden blast of pain in her head was crippling. She gripped her head in her hands and staggered back to the table, dropping into the nearest chair. The whistle stopped, and the pain eased immediately. There was a loud whoosh of wings, and warm air whipped around her. Sascha looked over in time to see it fly away.

"No, come back," Sascha called out. Seconds later the creature had disappeared. She searched in the vain hope of finding it flying overhead. Nothing.

"Bugger."

Something moved at her feet. A single golden feather. She picked it up. It was still warm to the touch. "Wait until I show the girls."

Sascha's phone beeped. A text.

Hey Sasch, we will meet you at the Tides Restaurant at 6 pm for your birthday dinner. We've showered and changed at the gym. You might have missed it, but we left a little birthday gift for you on the kitchen cupboard - behind the toaster. We hope you like it. We're told it will bring you good luck. We will give you your real gift at dinner tonight. See you soon. Love, Kira.

Sascha was dreading the birthday party, as she did anything which forced her to be the center of attention. She walked into the kitchen and found a golden envelope propped up on the kitchen bench beside a slim carved wooden box. Sascha opened the envelope and read the card. She wiped away a tear with the back of her hand before picking up the box and opening it. For a second she forgot to breathe. Sitting on a bed of soft black silk was a slim gold chain. Attached to the chain was a pendant in the shape of the bird that had been on her balcony only moments before. The body was gold and the tail a mixture of reds, greens and burnished gold. Its eyes were ochre-colored jewels. Inside the lid of the box, carved in gold, was inscribed, "2769 AGS Bonding Ceremony S and S. *Only those with a true heart, can achieve the power over life and death.*"

As soon as Sascha put the necklace on, it warmed against her skin. She closed her eyes and heard the sounds of crashing waves and tasted peppermint on the sea breeze.

Peppermint? That's strange.

She let out a deep breath. It was like coming home.

MARCO AND EHAM arrived at the Swedish restaurant two hours before they were due to meet Jenny. Eham had been restless, so Marco agreed to getting there early.

"I'll buy us a couple of drinks," Marco said as he headed to the bar. "You find our table." Marco placed his order and then glanced over at Eham. He was sitting at a table near the window, watching everyone who passed by. Eham had lost weight since the last time Marco had seen him on Eratus.

Eham had tried to kill himself when he lost his family in a fire. When that hadn't worked, he stopped eating. The only member of his family who hadn't been killed was his grand-daughter, Jenny, who was living at the craft school for magic. She had heard what he was doing to himself and started to visit him every night after classes. She cooked him dinner and prepared his breakfast and lunch for the next day. If something happened to Jenny, it would destroy Eham. Marco took their drinks from the bar and made his way over to their table.

"Here you go, Eham," Marco said as he handed over a glass of beer.

By eight-thirty Jenny still hadn't showed.

"I'm really worried," Eham said. "The only reason she wouldn't show is if something or someone stopped her."

"Let's give it a little longer," Marco said.

"What do we do now? I don't know where to go, how to find her." Eham had been checking his phone every few minutes for the last hour, his fists tightening and loosening each time. He couldn't keep still.

"We will find her," Marco reassured him.

"She could be lying somewhere badly injured or dead..."

"She's too clever for that," Marco said. "Something spooked her and so she stayed away."

Eham's phone buzzed. "It's a text from Jenny."

"What does she say?"

"Destroy phone, bugged. You must protect Sascha. BIT GOS. J"

She can't mean this phone is bugged." Eham stared at the phone in his hand. "No-one would get the chance to bug this. It's with me all the time."

"Text her back and ask." Marco took a sip of his beer. "What does BIT GOS mean?"

"BIT is be in touch, but I have no idea what GOS means."

"You haven't used GOS as a code for something?"

"You ask me all these bloody questions. How the hell am I supposed to know? All I do know is that she must be in danger and I can't help her." Eham sighed and then texted.

"I wonder why she's worried about Sascha," Marco asked.

Eham opened his mouth to say something, but stopped when his phone buzzed again. Eham read the message, then threw the phone on the ground and crunched it underfoot. "It's my phone. And GOS means she's going overseas."

Marco stared at the crushed phone. "That was a dramatic response."

"She said it was bugged. What else should I do?"

Marco skulled the rest of his beer. "It would have been

good if we could have asked her where she was planning to go."

"You text her, Marco. Say you're doing it for me."

"She won't recognize my number."

"Please, Marco."

Marco exhaled, entered the number, typed a brief message and pressed send. They waited for a response. Half an hour later, they knew Jenny wasn't going to reply.

"We can work this out," Marco said. "Is there a place she talked about?"

"I have no idea. No idea. She doesn't know enough about Earth. She was going to come back to Eratus after this...assignment. She had been accepted into the Four Sisters, their Coven. I..." Eham buried his face in his hands.

Marco waited silently while Eham composed himself. The realization hit him. "The Sisters, of course. I may have an idea where she is going."

"Where?" Eham croaked.

"The Sisters have, for want of a better description, a safe house in Scotland," Marco said. "Jenny would know where the house is. If she has been accepted into the Four Sisters, then she's talking to them and she's trusted. They would have told her about the safe house in case she needed protection. Perhaps she's gone there. It would explain the trip overseas."

"That makes perfect sense," Eham responded. "Let's go there then."

"We don't know where it is," Marco said. "It's in a secret location that only those who are part of the inner circle of the Four Sisters know."

"Don't you have a brother who's over there? In the police or something?"

"Yes. Alex."

"You trust him?" Eham asked.

"Of course I trust him. He's my brother. He'll help us find

the safe house. I'll call him when we get to your place. We will sort it out, Eham. Don't worry."

Eham didn't say another word until they were back in the car. "We need to make sure Sascha is safe. And the girls. If Jenny is worried about their safety, maybe she's worried that whoever is chasing her will go after them."

"I'm pretty sure Sascha is here in Caloundra," Marco said.

"Yes, the girls brought her here for her birthday."

That's right, it would be her birthday.

"How did you find that out, Eham?"

"I have my contacts."

"If Sascha sticks to her old habits," Marco said, "she'll go to that coffee shop on the esplanade for a coffee before the girls get up. We could get there early to meet her."

"And if she doesn't turn up?" Eham asked.

"Then we go to her house," Marco said. "Connell told me he sent the necklace to you, the one we have to give to Sascha. Do you have it with you?"

"She should have the necklace, or, should I say, the girls have it," Eham replied. "The girls were at the Brisbane markets. I organized it so that they bought it as a present for Sascha's birthday."

"What do you mean, *organized?*"

"I set up an arrangement with one of the store owners. The fates must have been on our side, because as soon as they saw it, they bought it."

"Soleil flew past me earlier tonight, so I know he's here too," Marco said.

Eham spat in disgust. "I really do hate that bird."

"Why?" Marco asked.

"The creature is always watching me, waiting for an excuse to attack me."

"Soleil wouldn't do that," Marco said. "Not unless you attacked Sascha."

"And it gets on way too well with Connell's half-breed. Manticores should be caged."

"Whatever," Marco said, "Let's just hope that the girls give her the necklace this weekend.

Marco parked the car and they caught the lift to Eham's apartment. As Eham opened the door to his place, Marco saw that the curtains were pulled back. The lights of Caloundra glinted in the darkness beyond the windows, their reflection sparkling in the mirrors.

Once Eham had turned on the lights, Marco put his phone on the coffee table in the dining room, put it on speaker and dialed Alex's number. It wasn't long before a croaky voice answered the phone.

"Alex speaking."

"Hi, Alex, it's Marco."

"Hello, stranger. It's been a long time."

"You sound terrible, Alex," Marco said.

"I'm tired. It's been a long day."

"I'm here with Eham."

"Oh, hello, Eham. How're you? How's Jenny?"

"I have no idea how she's—"

"That's why we're calling you," Marco interrupted. "Jenny's missing. We believe she's heading overseas, but we're not sure where. I had an idea that she might have gone to the Four Sisters' safe house. We need your help to see if she's there."

"We've tried to find that house before," Alex replied. "I'm not sure what I can do, but if Jenny's missing, I'll do what I can. Any clues?"

"Nothing yet," Marco replied. "It's all guesswork. I'll see what I can find in the library of the Fire of the Phoenix. There might be something there we can use."

"You've got to do whatever you can," Eham said. "It's Jenny we're talking about."

"We will, Eham," Alex replied. "Don't worry, she's important to me too."

"Thanks, Alex," Marco said. "Speak to you soon." Marco hung up the phone, slid it into his pocket and prepared to leave. "After we catch up with Sascha tomorrow, I was thinking that we could go back to Roger's place. See if we can find anything that might reveal who killed Roger and who's after Jenny. I have a feeling that everything is somehow connected to Eratus."

"Let's hope you're right," Eham said.

Marco stood and ambled toward the door. "I'm off then. I'll see you at the coffee shop tomorrow."

"What time?"

"Seven," Marco replied.

"See you then."

As Marco turned at the lift to say goodbye, a black weasel-like creature popped its head around the corner of the hallway and raced toward Eham. Marco was about to yell a warning when he saw the creature twist around Eham's legs in much the same way a cat twists around the legs of its owner. As Eham started to close the door, the creature turned to look at Marco, its red beady eyes reflecting the light in the hallway. It opened its mouth in a knowing grin, showing sharp white teeth. Eham clicked his fingers and the creature disappeared.

Marco was still looking at the closed door, trying to work out what it was, when the lift door opened.

Could it have been a dread wisp? Only dark mages own dread wisps. Could Eham be a dark mage?

CHAPTER 8

* EARTH

*S*ascha woke early the next morning. The party had been a lot more enjoyable than she'd expected. Marcie had been there, along with a few others from her team. And the present from the girls was something she had wanted for a long time, a dolphin cruise to the Tangalooma wrecks. They'd all had a few wines (maybe a few too many), beautiful food and a fun evening.

The girls were still asleep. Deciding to make the most of the peace, Sascha dressed in a short summer dress, fluffed up her hair and wrote a note to the girls, before making her way to the coffee shop. The day was warm, but the gentle breeze freshened the air.

It was when the waitress had taken her order and walked away that Sascha noticed him. Marco. He sat at a corner table on the other side of the little brick ledge that separated the sheltered section of the coffee shop from the open-air section. A tall lanky man sat at the table with Marco, his shoulder-length gray hair blowing about in the wind. His back was to Sascha.

Her heart ached. She pushed down the emotions that

raced to the surface, the pain, the anger. She would never again allow herself to fall in love the way she had fallen in love with Marco. Sascha searched for her purse as she debated whether she should disappear.

"I love your dress," the waitress said when she returned with Sascha's coffee. "And I love the color. I love jade."

"Thank you," Sascha replied as softly as she could, hoping Marco wouldn't hear her. No luck. Marco had heard.

He lifted his head and turned toward her. Sascha stopped breathing as his eyes held hers. She tried to nod, but her head wouldn't move. The man with Marco turned around. Her blood turned to ice. Her nightmare had come to life. She didn't need the sketch artist. This was the old man, the one she had killed.

They both stood and made their way toward her. She couldn't breathe, couldn't move. She watched them move closer.

"Sascha, hello," Marco said, bending down and pecking her on the cheek. She still hadn't found her voice. "Can we sit down?"

Sascha must have nodded, because they pulled out chairs and joined her at the table.

"Marco," Sascha muttered.

That's all you can say? His name?

"And this is Eham," he said, gesturing to the other man.

Sascha couldn't take her eyes off the tall dignified old man. He started shifting under her stare, first glancing at Marco and then back at Sascha.

"Sorry," Sascha said. "I know I'm staring, but you're very familiar. Do I know you?"

"Not that I'm aware of, but you know my granddaughter."

"Your granddaughter?" She frowned.

"Jenny," Eham replied.

Sascha finally understood why the old man's face was

familiar. He and Jenny were so much alike. Her blood chilled. If the old man in her nightmare was Eham...

"Explain why you didn't protect her," he said.

"Hang on, Eham," Marco said. "It's not Sascha's fault and you know that."

Sascha stared at them both. "You know she's missing?"

"Of course I know she's bloody missing," Eham snapped. "She's my granddaughter. Roger said that he had found a clue, that he knew where Jenny was. We were supposed to meet him last night, but when we arrived at his place we found out he was dead."

"Roger? Do you mean—"

"I don't know what he does for you," Eham replied. "But I do know he works for you, and he was the only one prepared to listen to me when I was looking for Jenny."

"What's the connection between Roger and Jenny?" Sascha asked. "He's the one who told me the bank blamed Jenny for stealing my money, so they can't be too close. He would have tried to cover it up if he—"

"How much are we talking about?" Marco asked.

"Five thousand dollars," Sascha replied.

"Roger told me you all thought Jenny took it," Eham said.

"I never believed she stole the money."

Eham smirked. "Are you saying you think she's innocent?"

"Yes, I do," Sascha replied.

"Well, that's something I suppose."

Kira's laugh sounded from the stairs, growing closer every second. The girls must have read Sascha's note and were on their way to meet her. She glanced at Eham. She needed to grab the girls and warn them about him.

Too late.

"Hey, Sascha," Kira said. "We didn't want you to drink

alone on your birthday weekend so we thought we'd come and join you, but it looks like you already have..."

Kira and the other two girls gaped at Eham.

My God. This is the man we've all been dreaming about, not just me.

"Excuse me," Sascha said as she pushed herself back from the table. "I need to talk to the girls for a second."

Sascha gestured for the girls to follow her. When they were far enough away, she said, "Listen—"

"That's him," Kira whispered. "That's the old man."

"Yes, I know. He's Jenny's grandfather."

"What? Jen never mentioned anything about a grandfather."

"Well, that's what he said."

"So if we were dreaming about Jen's grandfather, was it Jen..." Lee's voice quivered as she broke off.

"We wouldn't kill Jen," Kira said.

"I'm sure you're right, Kira," Sascha replied. "But until we know what's going on, let's not say anything."

The girls looked at each other before nodding their agreement.

They returned to the coffee shop, where the girls dragged over some more chairs while Marco pulled over a second table. When everyone was seated, Sascha glanced at Marco. He had started ripping one of the coasters into bits, a sure sign he was uneasy. What would be making him nervous?

As Sascha sat down, Eham leaned over, his icy cold hands briefly touching her throat as he pointed to the necklace she was wearing.

He grinned. "Soleil's necklace."

"It's a birthday present from the girls. Who is Soleil?"

"We've a lot to talk about," Eham said. "Maybe we should go somewhere more...private."

"No. I would prefer to stay here," Sascha said.

Eham shrugged. "Well, let's begin. We know that none of you can remember your pasts, and that is what makes you vulnerable now. At least Jenny remembers her past, remembers who she is."

"Sascha remembers hers too," Kira intervened. "It's the three of us who don't remember."

"Don't correct me, you stupid girl," Eham replied. "Sascha can't remember hers either." His eyes focused on Sascha. "Surely you've told them."

"Eham, stop being so rude," Marco growled. "If you don't, I'll tell Alex to stop looking for Jenny."

"What—you can't!"

"Your call, Eham," Marco said.

"Sascha?" Kira asked. "Is that true? You don't remember your past either?"

Sascha couldn't speak. An intense pain gripped her, like something was squeezing her, squeezing her lungs. She was sure everyone in the coffee shop was looking at her, sucking the air out of her, pulling the ground from beneath her.

Eham laughed, an uneasy sound. "So you never mentioned anything to the girls. I've put you in a sticky situation then, haven't I?"

"Shut up, you evil little man," Kira said, jumping to Sascha's defense. "She has a right to keep her past a secret. Everyone has secrets."

"I'm so sorry, girls," Sascha said. "I didn't want it to come out like this."

"The reason none of you remembers your past," Eham interrupted, unperturbed by the increasing tension, "is because your memories were expunged."

"What does that mean?" Sascha said. "How can a memory be expunged?"

"It's a medical process," Marco answered.

"Well, I've never heard of anything like that before," Sascha said.

"The process was different for you, Sascha." Marco answered, "But perhaps we—"

"Have you known about this all this time, Marco, and yet you never told me?"

Eham tutted. "So many secrets."

"Why was my memory expunged?" Sascha asked.

"Because you wanted to forget the pain of what happened to you," Marco said.

"It was a punishment," Eham corrected.

Marco twisted in his seat to glare at Eham, and turned back to Sascha. "You chose to have your memory taken away. We found it hard to accept your choice at the time, but it was your choice. We had to respect your decision."

"How bad was what happened to me?"

"Bad," Marco answered.

"Worse than what happened when...".

I can't talk about what happened to me at the cabin in front of the girls.

"Did I kill someone?" Sascha said quietly.

Marco looked over at Eham and back at Sascha. "What made you ask that?"

"I was trying to think of the worst thing someone could do, and that's all I could come up with."

"No, you didn't. Although you wanted to kill the person you believed was behind everything that happened to you."

"And who was it I wanted to kill?"

Marco winced, picked up his coaster and continued breaking it. Sascha clearly wasn't going to like his response. "Your adopted father."

"My what?"

"For this to all make sense, we need to start at the beginning," Marco said. "What if Eham and I come to your place tomorrow? We'll bring something to eat and drink. We'll tell you everything then."

"Why not today?" Sascha asked.

Marco bundled the shredded coaster into a neat pile. "We need to do some digging around at Roger's place."

"Why?" Kira asked.

"We're trying to find answers to questions we have," Marco said. "Eham, you happy to go to Sascha's tomorrow?"

Eham grunted, sat back in the chair and folded his arms. "Do I have a choice?"

"But what happened to us?" Lee asked. "Did we ask to have our memories taken away because we had something bad happen to us too?"

"No," Marco said. "Your memories were taken away for your protection. When your parents were told how well Sascha was doing in her new life, your parents wanted you to have the same chance. Look, it's a long story. We can talk more about it tomorrow. Just know that your parents loved you so much they would do anything to protect you."

"Our parents are...alive?" Lee asked.

"Yes," Marco answered.

Lee and Ella both gulped, while a shy smile spread slowly across Kira's face. "So where are they?" Lee asked. "We have to find them."

Marco gulped. "This is the difficult part. How do I say this?"

"Oh, for God's sake," Sascha responded. "Tell the girls what they need to know."

"None of you are from Earth. You're from a place called Eratus, another star system connected to Earth's solar system."

Sascha jumped up, sending her chair flying backward. "Have you really sunk so low? You're a cruel man, Marco.

You know how much the girls want to find out about their pasts and then you feed them this garbage."

"It's true, Sascha," Marco said quickly. "And we can prove it."

"How?"

"That necklace you have around your neck. That is to help you talk to the pet you were bonded to on Eratus. Hold it and call Soleil."

"Soleil? Is that the bird I've been seeing around here?"

"If you've been seeing a bird that looks like the pendant, then, yes. You were bonded to Soleil when you were young. As you got older and your bond strengthened, you no longer needed the necklace. But it has been a long time and—"

"If it is the same creature, we can't call Soleil here," Saschsa said. "It's too large. What will the people in the coffee shop say?"

Marco peeked around the coffee shop. "There's only one couple left, and it looks like they're going. Now would be the perfect time to do it."

"Call Soleil," Kira said.

Sascha straightened her chair and sat down. She put her hand around the necklace. It warmed to her touch.

"You don't have to say it aloud, Sascha," Marco said. "Think it."

There was a flurry of heat and wings as the creature she had seen yesterday landed on the brick wall not far from their table. The girls gasped.

"Talk to him," Marco said.

Sascha glanced at Marco. "Soleil? Is your name Soleil?"

The bird strutted along the brick wall, moving closer to Sascha. "Yes, it is. You can hear me now?" A sense of warmth, of belonging, flooded over Sascha as the creature's onyx eyes studied her with an intelligence that was breathtaking.

"Is it talking to you?" Kira asked.

"Yes, I can hear it."

"I'm not an *it*. I'm a *he*," Soleil said, raising himself to his full height and puffing out his chest.

"Sorry, Soleil." Sascha turned to Kira. "Soleil is a he."

The girls chuckled.

"Ask him where he's from, where we're from," Kira said.

"Soleil, are you from Earth?" Sascha asked.

"No, you and I are from a long way away. Not Earth. But you will find out for yourself soon."

"So was Marco telling us the truth?" Kira said.

Sascha avoided looking over at Marco. "It's early days yet. We need to find out more information before we know for sure."

Soleil pushed his chest out, held his head high. "I don't lie!"

"I'm not saying you're lying. This is all just a bit tough to accept," Sascha answered.

Kira stood and moved closer to the brick wall, her hand outstretched, ready to caress the beautiful creature. "Can I have a go with the necklace?"

"Kira wants to speak to you."

"Is that the girl with hair the same color as me?" Soleil asked.

"I hadn't noticed the similarity, but yes."

"OK, take the necklace off and give it to her."

"Here, Kira, have a go."

Kira put the necklace on and moved closer to Soleil. "My God, I can hear it...I mean him. Such a beautiful sound," she said, staring at Lee and Ella. "It's incredible. Here, Lee, you have a go." Kira stopped mid-movement. "Sorry, Lee. Soleil has said that Sascha and I are the only ones who can use the necklace." Kira turned back to Soleil. "But why?"

"What did Soleil say?" Sascha asked.

"He said Marco will explain it all to us. Here's the necklace, Sascha. Soleil asked me to give it back to you."

Sascha put the necklace on and looked over at Soleil. He seemed to be smiling.

"I've got to go now, Sascha. But I'll always be around if you need me." He took off in a burst of feathers and warm air.

After Soleil left, followed closely by Marco and Eham, Sascha and the girls sat in silence, trying to digest everything that had just happened. The waitress suddenly appeared behind them.

"Can I get you anything else or would you like the bill?"

"The bill," Sascha answered.

CHAPTER 9

ERATUS

"Connell, how are you?"

Connell's stomach clenched. He pushed himself up, moving the plush cushions so that they supported him in a sitting position. George had woken up the moment Drakon entered Connell's chamber, a soft growl rumbling low in her chest.

"Bloody creature," Drakon said. "Way too temperamental. Don't know why you don't get rid of it. I could do it for you."

George snarled, showing her large sharp teeth, and inched toward Drakon.

"Down," Connell commanded, despite having enjoyed the sight of Drakon backing off when George had moved toward him. She was the only creature Drakon couldn't threaten with his magic, and she had enough venom in her claws to kill an army.

"I hear you've been up in the mountains, Drakon."

"Yes, I have. Catching up with some of my men. Good to see how my armies are growing in numbers, especially since you did such a terrible job at the healing ceremony."

Connell winced when Drakon's words hit home.

"I had a word with your healer. I was worried he wasn't looking after you properly."

Connell picked up the jug next to his couch and poured himself a glass of water. "What do you mean?"

"How do you know he's not working for the Sisters? He might be doing what they didn't manage to do, kill you."

"Drakon, if this healer leaves us..."

Drakon walked over to the balcony door, pushed back the curtains and stared out at the ocean. "Since when is it my responsibility to worry about servants leaving?"

"Since the last time you used *persuasion* and we lost all our servants. We couldn't get anyone to work for us for months."

"I was young."

"You murdered a young girl. Youth is no excuse."

Drakon turned to Connell and grinned knowingly. "Prove it. There's no point in saying anything. Father didn't believe you the last time you tried to convince him."

"Our pasts have a way of catching up with us, Drakon."

Drakon smiled. "You can't talk. Because of your failure, everyone's now worried about the Shield breaking down. People are rioting all over Eratus. They're blaming the humans and many are being, let's say, punished. All because you were unable to do the one task you have been trained to do. So who has committed the greater crime?"

Connell felt the guilt slice at him. "What do you mean, *the humans are being punished*? What have you done, Drakon?"

"It's not me, Connell. It's the people. Even I can't control what the masses think, can I?"

"And who would've put the idea into their heads, Drakon?"

"If people choose to believe rumors, that's their problem, not mine. Or, should I say, it's humankind's problem." He sniggered.

"What did you come here for, Drakon?" Connell asked, keen to get Drakon out of his chambers.

"I overheard you telling Owain you are bringing Sascha here. Is that true?"

Overheard? How could he have overheard? George was at the door. She would have alerted me.

Connell's eyes flicked over to the picture that hid the secret entrance to his chambers. Quickly realizing his mistake, he looked back at Drakon, but it was too late. Drakon had seen.

"Oh, Connell, another example why you can never be High King. You are totally incapable of hiding what you're thinking. You still think you can keep things from me? I know everything that happens in the castle. I know you're off to find Sascha."

George's growl deepened. Connell reached over and patted her.

"You're going to have a hard time convincing Sascha to come back here," Drakon said. "Do you want me to help?"

"No, thanks. I've got it in hand."

"If she does get her memory back, you know I'll be the only one she will trust. I'm the only one who she believes didn't betray her."

"I didn't betray her."

Drakon smirked and tilted his head to the side as he studied Connell. "We know that, but she doesn't. Remember what she said just before we transferred her to Earth? She said our dear father was responsible for her fiancée's *murder*...and her mother's. And she figured you must have known about it."

"You hate her. You've always hated her. And she knew it."

"What a terrible thing to say," Drakon said.

There was a knock on the door.

"Enter," Connell commanded.

The healer bowed as he entered Connell's chambers, careful to avoid looking at Drakon.

"Ah," Drakon said, turning back to Connell, "it's time for your next treatment. You must look after yourself. You'll need your strength for what is to come."

Connell stared at Drakon's retreating back. Drakon was starting a war, and he was in bed, unable to stop him.

DRAKON TURNED TO HIS GUARD. "Bring Reya to my chambers now." It had been a good couple of days. Once the second portal was activated, Chiane's army would be ready to go through it to retrieve the weapon from Earth. Chiane was certainly proving his worth.

Drakon strolled out onto the balcony, walked over to the table laid out with drinks and savory treats and grabbed himself some ale and something to eat. He looked down on the training grounds where his men were fighting each other in preparation for the trials at tomorrow's feast. Though some of these men wouldn't survive the trials, the best ones would. Drakon only wanted the best.

It wasn't long before Reya knocked on the door and glided into Drakon's chambers. She was wearing the tight-fitting leather tunic his warriors wore when training.

It's hardly surprising men look at her with desire, despite their fear of her. What man wouldn't want to possess that beauty?

"I met with Connell an hour ago," Drakon said. "I found out he has a secret entrance to his chambers. I need you to find out how we can access that."

"A secret entrance? How did—"

"I have my ways. And I'm right in deciding to go to Earth to meet Sascha. Connell has already begun preparations to get her back here. I'll meet with Ken and Pat. They will tell me where she is. It's time for them to start taking their roles seriously. And I need the charm bracelet. Without her own magic working properly, Sascha won't be able to resist the magic in it."

"How do you know her magic isn't working? She could have been using it all along."

"She may have some residual magic, but her memory of magic was taken away as part of the transfer."

"The charm bracelet could kill her. You will need to use it with care." Reya flinched as she realized what she had said.

"What did you say, Reya? Surely you weren't telling me what to do?"

"I only wanted to protect you, My Prince."

Drakon smiled as he saw the fear in her eyes. "Before you go, I need you in my bed."

"I'm a mess and I smell," she said. "And you did want me to find that secret entrance to Connell's chamber. Why don't I shower first, get my advisor to start the search and then come back to you?"

"Now," he said as he walked to his bed, stripping his clothes off as he went. Drakon smiled to himself as he glanced back and saw a flash of hate in her eyes. The hate quickly dampened down when she saw him looking at her and was replaced with fear. She knew he was about to make her pay for that indiscretion.

WHEN REYA HAD LEFT, Drakon summoned Fenix. He had been bonded with her when he came into his powers at the age of thirteen, and, until recently, the creature had served him well. Of late, however, he had found himself constantly punishing her for spending time with Soleil.

Soleil! That damn bird!

When Sascha was transferred, her essence died. Soleil should have gone to the fifth dimension and died like all other pyrans did when they lost their masters. But he refused. Fenix told Drakon that Soleil believed Sascha would return and that he wanted to be ready for that day.

The click of talons on the window ledge announced Fenix's arrival. Her onyx-colored eyes watched Drakon, waiting for instruction. "It's time to visit Earth, Fenix."

She warbled, flew down to the balcony outside his window and waited for him. Her silken ebony and scarlet feathers glistened in the light of the moons. Drakon clambered onto her back. He knew he only had a small window of opportunity to get through the first portal to Earth while the guardians, the grotesque creatures that guarded it, slept. He tapped his hand and the embedded transportation chip flashed. Still working.

CHAPTER 10

* EARTH

*W*hen Drakon landed on Earth, he sent Fenix to the Awakening headquarters to await his call. One of Drakon's minions had organized an Earth vehicle for him, and when Drakon exited the building the small man stood next to a red Ferrari, cowering before his gaze.

Drakon enjoyed the sound of the whisper-quiet engine as it came to life. He leaned back into the soft leather seats and draped one hand around the leather-wrapped steering wheel as he used the other to shift into gear. He smiled. There was nothing like an Earth machine, though the time it took to drive from one place to another would be frustrating if it was a way of life. Drakon put the roof down and turned the music up, savoring the pound of the beat coming through the speakers.

It had been a while since he had been on Earth. The last time had been when he disposed of the hit men who had kidnapped and tortured Sascha. Thinking she was dead, he had tormented her kidnappers for several hours, trying to determine who had given the instructions to kidnap her. But, even at the end, they had still denied knowing anything. It was only after he had returned to Eratus to collect the burial wrappings that he was going to use to bring Sascha's body back that he found out she was alive. Marco and Connell had turned up and *rescued* her.

One day I will tell Sascha what I did to those men, what I did to save her.

Half an hour later, he arrived at Pat and Ken's place.

Ken answered the door. "What the—" His mouth dropped open as he stepped back, gripping the door handle.

"Ken, is that any way to greet your prince?"

"Sorry, Prince Drakon," he said, quickly bending low before Drakon. "I was shocked to see you. It's been a long time."

"A pleasant shock, I trust." Drakon's words were met with silence.

Interesting.

Drakon moved past Ken and into the house. Pat jumped out of her lounge chair and bowed before him. "Welcome to our humble house, My Prince."

Drakon was pleased to see Pat still recognized Eratian law for commoners and didn't raise her eyes until he touched her shoulder.

"Stand," Drakon said. "I thought I would come and say hello."

Ken hadn't moved from the doorway, but his eyes followed Drakon, trying to work out why he was here.

Drakon looked around. Everything was clean and tidy, but the amenities were basic. He noticed a yellow note sitting on the coffee table with some words scribbled on it - Sascha's name and a second name he didn't recognize. Underneath the second name were the words, "sketch artist, happy to do job, confidential". The word "confidential" was underlined a couple of times.

Was Sascha looking for a sketch artist? Why?

Drakon glanced over at Pat and Ken. Ken was watching his every move.

"I won't be long. I just wanted to check up on Sascha. You've both been watching her, haven't you?"

"Yes, sir—I mean, My Prince," Pat spluttered.

Drakon laughed. "Pat, relax. I haven't come to do anything to you. Unless, of course, there's something I don't know about?"

Ken walked over to Pat and put his hand on her shoulder. "We have nothing to tell you, Prince Drakon. No-one from Eratus has contacted her. Her memory hasn't returned either."

"Does she still live next door?"

Ken frowned and glanced over at Pat before turning away. "Sascha has never—"

Pat answered instead. "Yes, she does, My Prince. We've been able to keep a close eye on her from here."

"Excellent," Drakon said, pleased that this was turning out to be much easier than he had expected.

What had Ken been going to say that Pat had to shut him down? I'm going to have to keep an eye on him. Ken might have become too attached to Sascha. It would make him a liability.

"Is she home now?"

"No, Prince Drakon. The girls organized a birthday party for her at a resort in Caloundra," Pat answered. "They'll be back on Monday. Ken hasn't been well, so we didn't make it, which turns out to be a fortunate thing. We would have missed you."

"Does she still live by herself?"

"No, she lives with three girls Kira, Lee and Ella," Pat said.

"So that's where the girls ended up." Drakon rubbed his hands together. Pat was proving to be useful. Ken, however, wasn't saying much at all. Drakon smiled at Pat. "Anything unusual happen at her place lately? Has she had any strange visitors?"

"Nothing. Sascha did call Ken in to help her with something at her workplace..." she said, turning to Ken.

"That was more of a staffing issue. Stealing," Ken answered. "Nothing Prince Drakon would be interested in."

"Isn't that where Jenny works?" Drakon said, scrutinizing Ken. "Reya tells me she has disappeared?"

Ken frowned. "Yes, My Prince. She took some money and disappeared. We're looking for her. But she was the bookkeeper. Why would you be interested in her?"

Pat slammed Ken in the ribs with her elbow. "Sorry, Prince Drakon. Ken forgot who he was talking to. We've been on Earth too long."

Ken flicked his eyes downward in submission. "I apologize, My Prince. I didn't think you would be interested in Sascha's staffing issues, so I didn't mention it."

"In future, I would appreciate it if you didn't decide what I do or don't need to know. Is that understood?"

"Yes, My Prince," Ken answered.

"Sit," Drakon said. "Let's all sit and have a civilized conversation." He sat on the corner of a large tan lounge. Pat sat next to him. Drakon leaned toward Pat and brushed her hand. He knew how much women responded to the sympathetic touch. "Maybe it's time to bring you back to Eratus. It must be tough living in these primitive conditions."

Drakon stood and walked around the small lounge room while he worked out what he was going to do next. "Ken, I want you to ring Sascha and tell her you want to meet her at —where is a good meeting place?"

"The local RSL is where she always seems to end up," Pat responded.

"Excellent. Ken, tell her you want to meet her at the RSL."

"But what excuse will I use? She'll be suspicious."

"I'm sure you'll know what to say. Unless, of course, you don't want to do what I'm asking you to do?"

"It's not that I—"

"Tell her it's urgent. Tell her it's about Jenny."

"Yes, My Prince." Pat elbowed Ken. "Straight away."

Drakon walked to the front door. As he put his hand on the doorknob, he turned to Pat. "Do make sure Ken makes the phone call to Sascha." Drakon smiled.

"Yes, My Prince. I'll make sure. He'll make the call."

"And I want you both to focus on finding Jenny. Reya tells me Roger was supposed to keep an eye on her. You remember Roger? That young boy you and Ken cared for on Eratus?"

"Roger?" Pat frowned. "Yes, that's right. I remember him. That was a long time ago. He'd be a grown man by now."

"You would still recognize him. He hasn't changed that much, except for the large scar above his left eye from where he lost in a sword fight." Drakon stepped onto the verandah, then looked back over his shoulder at Pat. "Which resort is Sascha staying at?"

Pat raced back into the house. She returned with a piece of paper. "Here, take this. We don't need it. This is where she's staying."

"Excellent."

Pat stood in the doorway and watched as he walked down the pathway and opened the gate. Drakon waved absently as he stepped into his car. A few moments later, he heard raised voices. He didn't trust either of them, but he was particularly concerned about Ken.

Drakon fingered the charm bracelet in his pocket, grateful for Reya's efficiency. Ken might never organize that meeting, despite Pat's promise. He glanced at the paper Pat had handed him and decided to drive to the resort.

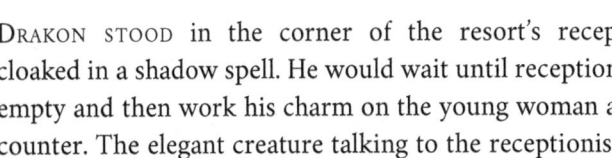

DRAKON STOOD in the corner of the resort's reception, cloaked in a shadow spell. He would wait until reception was empty and then work his charm on the young woman at the counter. The elegant creature talking to the receptionist had a sexy figure, curves in all the right places. Drakon didn't mind waiting. As the woman moved her floppy hat, he caught a quick glimpse of her face. His nails bit into the palms of his hand as he glared at her.

Reya! What the hell was she doing here?

Drakon was about to move toward her when he heard the sliding doors swish open. Marco walked into the reception area and stood beside Reya. "Here, Sascha. Let me help you with your bags," he said.

"That's Sascha?" Drakon stepped back into the shadows.

"Thank you, Ms. Morgan. It was lovely to have you stay with us, and we're glad you enjoyed yourself. It's a shame you have to leave early, but sometimes life gets in the way, doesn't it?"

Turn around, you bloody female. Let me have a look at you.

As if she heard him, Sascha turned toward him.

In Athena's name! How could I have not seen it before? Reya and Sascha they're almost identical.

Drakon stood, stunned. What did it mean? Drakon saw Marco stop for a minute and glance in his direction. Marco had sensed his presence.

Drakon pulled up the collar of his jacket, adjusted his cap and stayed in the shadows. He had to make sure Marco wasn't going with her. Drakon hadn't counted on them becoming friends again. Ken and Pat hadn't said anything about Marco being here.

Drakon returned to his car and waited.

~

SASCHA WAS SURPRISED when she heard Marco offering to help with her bags. There was that familiar flutter of excitement when their hands touched as he took her bags from her. Though she told herself she didn't want to be near him, the passionate nights they had spent together were ones she would never forget. She was determined not to let anything happen, but it seemed her body wanted something different.

I wouldn't survive a second fallout with Marco. Hell, I'm not even over the first.

She followed him down to the carpark. Marco had apparently been talking to her, for he had turned to face her and was now waiting for her to say something. "Sorry, Marco, what did you say?"

"I was giving you my contact details, in case you need me. We were planning on coming to your place around 1 p.m. tomorrow. Will you be home then?"

"I'd prefer you didn't come around at all, but I don't have any choice in this now, do I?"

"We always have choices, Sascha."

"Talking about choices...how's your wife?"

There was silence for a couple of minutes as Marco loaded Sascha's bags into her car. "I'd rather not talk about it."

"Trouble in paradise, Marco?"

Marco squirmed beneath Sascha's gaze. "I said I'd rather not talk about it. I should never have—I have always loved you, Sascha."

Sascha snorted. "Loved me? Loved me so much married someone else? Don't lie to me, Marco. I don't need your sympathy."

Didn't he just tell me what I've wanted to hear him say? That he shouldn't have married her? That leaving me was a mistake?

Sascha stifled a sigh.

It doesn't help, whatever the truth is.

"Marco, I can't have this conversation with you. Once we have discussed whatever it is you and Eham need to tell us, then I would prefer we keep our distance."

Marco stood silently and watched as Sascha started her car. When she looked in the rearview mirror, she saw him still standing there, watching her drive away.

Tears welled in her eyes, making driving difficult. She needed a distraction. She put her soft top down, turned up her music and pushed back the whirlwind of emotions that threatened to tear her apart. She took a deep breath and focused on the tasks ahead. First, the meeting with Ken, and then the search for the map.

Sascha was looking forward to catching up with Ken. She felt safe with him something she didn't feel when she was around Marco. Ken's call had been unexpected. It was so unlike him to be mysterious. What was it about Jenny that he couldn't tell her over the phone? The girls had wanted to come along with her, but Ken had made it clear he needed to talk to Sascha alone.

Sascha heard what was starting to become a familiar call. She glanced up in the sky and saw heavy black clouds moving in. Against the dark backdrop, she saw a glint of gold. Soleil was following her. Her necklace warmed. She felt a connection, a sense of home, of belonging. She could do this. Marco would not destroy her, not this time.

A COUPLE of raindrops splattered on Sascha's windscreen as she arrived at the RSL. The rain was on its way. Rumbles of thunder echoed around her as she stepped out of her car and entered the club. Her favorite spot - a table with a view out over a large green oval that backed onto the ocean was empty. She ordered a bottle of wine and waited for Ken to arrive. Maybe he would stay and join her for a quiet dinner. A flash of lightning sounded, followed by a loud boom. The storm had moved in a lot faster than she had expected.

Her cell phone buzzed. A text from Ken. *"Sorry, Sascha, I can't make it. Would you mind dropping over to our house?"*

"Bugger." She sat down at the table with her bottle of wine and tapped a response. *"I'll be there as soon as I've had this glass."*

Ken's reply arrived a minute or so later. *"Not a good idea to drink and drive, especially after the trip from Caloundra. I have plenty of wine. Come soon. I'll make dinner."*

Sascha texted back, *"I'll be there soon, but have poured my wine, so can't waste it."*

She closed her eyes and leaned back in her chair as the rain crashed against the club's windows.

CHAPTER 11

* EARTH

*D*rakon hadn't needed to worry about missing Sascha leaving the resort carpark. She had the soft top of her red BMW down, her music blasting, her long blond hair blowing in the wind. She was certainly a lot more attractive than he remembered.

As Drakon watched Sascha get out of her car and walk toward the club, he decided to wait a few minutes before joining her. When he thought she would have had enough time to get a table and order a drink, he walked into the club, shaking off droplets from the heavy rain outside and rubbing his arms to massage warmth back into his body. He checked his reflection in the window entrance and saw that his camouflage spell had worked. His shoulder-length curly dark hair was now short and blond, his dark olive skin a pale tan and his blue eyes green. His disguise was in place.

Sascha sat by herself at a table in the corner of the club. How perfect. Drakon put his hand in the pocket of his full-length leather jacket and fingered the bracelet resting there, waiting.

Sascha glanced up at Drakon as he moved toward her.

Sitting up straight, she flicked her long blond hair back over her bare shoulders as she crossed her long legs and smoothed her yellow summer dress. Being this close to her again was like a fist to his stomach. Until now, he had forgotten just how much he had cared for her.

"Yes?" she said.

"I'm sorry to disturb you," Drakon replied, "but I have a message from Ken. He asked me to tell you he couldn't make it."

"Oh, you know Ken?"

"Yes, he's a work colleague."

"Thanks, but he has already texted to tell me he couldn't make it."

Drakon clenched his jaw and bit back what he wanted to say. Ken had tried to stop this meeting from happening.

"Was there something else?" she asked.

"I'm the sketch artist. I don't know if he mentioned me to you."

"Oh, I forgot to ring Ken. I found the person I was looking for this weekend."

"Normally people comment on results after I have started working for them," Drakon said, "not before. Do you mind if I take a seat?"

"Sure," she answered. "I'm sorry about this."

"Not a problem. Plans change."

"How did you know what I looked like?" Sascha asked.

"I've seen you a couple of times with Ken. You're an attractive woman, hard to forget."

"Thank you."

"You obviously didn't notice me. That could knock a man's pride, you know." Drakon put his hand on his heart and lowered his head to his chest. When he glanced up, she was smiling.

"I'm sure you would easily find someone to bolster your ego," she said.

Drakon laughed. "What happened when you found this person that you wanted me to sketch? Ken didn't tell me why you wanted a sketch artist."

"Nothing exciting, but I was pleased to find him." She sat back, crossed her legs away from Drakon and looked at her watch.

"Ken told me it was your birthday this weekend. I hope you had a lovely time."

"Yes," she said. "I was spoilt." She peeked at her watch again and then finished her glass of wine.

Damn it, she was leaving.

"I hate to be rude, but Ken invited me over for dinner when he couldn't make it to the club. I'd better go."

"No, no," Drakon said. "That's fine. You have a lot happening. Sorry to hold you up." He leaned over and touched her shoulder. A sharp bolt of electricity shot into his arm.

"Oh, I'm sorry," she said. "Static electricity. Always happens during electrical storms."

"The storm *is* getting fierce." As if in response to Drakon's statement, a large lightning bolt split the night sky open, followed by a loud crack of thunder that rattled the windows.

Sascha stood, picked up the bottle of wine and wrapped it in a serviette.

The bolt of electricity had told Drakon that Sascha still had her powers. And it was doing what it had always done, protecting her from him. Drakon would need to change his approach.

I'll have another chance, but next time I will organize everything myself. Ken will pay for this.

"Bye, Sascha," Drakon said as she walked off.

"Bye," she answered.

Ken showed his true allegiance tonight. He would need to have him followed.

Drakon made a call. A few moments later, everything was in place.

∾

THE CLUB HAD FELT strange today. The meeting with the sketch artist...Sascha didn't even know his name. She made a mental note to talk to Ken about it.

Sascha drove home, parked, took out her umbrella and walked over to Pat and Ken's. She knocked on their door. A loud crash echoed in the house a couple of seconds before Ken opened the door for her.

"What happened?"

"Nothing," he answered, his gaze bouncing up and down the street. He ushered Sascha into the house and shut the door behind her.

"Is something wrong?"

"Everything's fine. Being careful, that's all."

"What smashed?"

He waved his hand in the direction of the dining room. "Oh, I sent a glass flying. Knocked it off the table."

"Where's Pat?" she asked.

"She joined some friends for a girls' day out. They were going shopping, then out for dinner and a movie."

"She'll enjoy that," Sascha said.

The doggy door in the kitchen flew open. Rusty raced up to Sascha, her tail wagging so hard her whole body shook. As Sascha bent down to say hello, Rusty leaped on her, pinning her to the floor, her long tongue licking Sascha's face in welcome. Sascha laughed as she hugged her.

Ken grabbed Rusty by the collar to give Sascha a chance

to clamber up. "She's uncontrollable when you're around. That animal loves you more than it does us."

"And I love her too, don't I, gorgeous?"

"Ar-ruf."

Sascha leaned down and scratched Rusty under the chin. She couldn't help but smile at the huge grin on Rusty's face.

"I'm sorry I didn't meet you at the club, honey."

"It all worked out. Also, your sketch artist colleague caught up with me and passed on the message."

"My sketch..." His glance flicked over at the door as he cleared his throat.

"Ken, what's going on?"

"Nothing. I'll pour us a drink." Sascha pulled the open bottle of wine out of her bag. "Here's the wine I opened at the club. Let's finish this one off first."

Ken carried the wine to the kitchen. Sascha followed him. "You're edgy, Ken. Is it something about Jenny?"

"Sorry, it's been a long day. I'm tired."

"That's not all it is. Ken, talk to me."

"How was your birthday with the girls?"

"You're trying to distract me."

"No, seriously, how was it?"

"It was a fun weekend. Look what they bought for me." Sascha showed Ken her necklace. "And they organized a trip to see the dolphins at Tangalooma. I was so spoilt."

Ken moved closer to examine the necklace. "Where did the girls buy that from?"

"They found it at the markets. And you'll never guess—"

A voice sounded clearly in Sascha's head. "Don't let him know I'm here, Sascha. He cannot be trusted."

Soleil?

"What were you saying?" Ken interrupted.

"What did I start to say?"

"You said something about me never guessing, something to do with the necklace the girls gave you."

Sascha shook her head. "I can't remember. It must have been a lie." She laughed. "But more importantly, there's something wrong with you and you're trying to distract me."

"A lot happened today," Ken said, letting out a deep sigh.

"Like what?"

He turned toward the oven, but not before Sascha saw him wipe away a tear. "I'd better check the casserole. You want to pour us some wine?"

Ten minutes later they were sitting at the table eating the chicken casserole Ken had dished up and drinking their third glass of wine.

"What did you want to tell me about Jenny?" Sascha asked.

"I've been told she took a flight overseas. We're trying to learn exactly where she went. Do you have any ideas where she could have gone?"

"No, no idea. The girls might have. Let me check with them if you—"

"I'd prefer you didn't talk to the girls yet, Sascha."

"Why?"

"Jenny is in grave danger. I don't want the girls involved in the case, it also puts them at risk."

"What sort of danger?"

"We don't know yet, but we believe it has something to do with Roger's death."

"So do you have any leads?"

"No, not yet, but I'll let you know when we do. And now I have something else I want to tell you." Ken stood and cleared the table. "I visited the doctor today."

"What's wrong?"

"Not good news, I'm afraid."

"What does that mean?"

"The worst news, unfortunately. I only have a month or two left. It's a rare disease with one of those funny long medical names."

Sascha's eyes stung as she pushed her chair away from the table and stood. She walked over to Ken and hugged him. "We will find a specialist, organize whatever help you need."

"It's complicated, but it's too late." Ken walked back into the kitchen and Sascha followed him. She leaned against the kitchen bench and watched as Ken started to fill the sink with hot soapy water. "Does Pat know?"

"No. Don't say anything to her."

"Of course not."

"Knowing you're dying changes your perception, gives you the courage to do what you need to do. I have some errands I need to run, then you and I need to talk."

"We could talk now."

"No. You must trust me. Give me a couple of days and then I'll tell you everything."

"But—"

"I need you to trust me. Can you do that?"

Soleil was being overprotective. Why couldn't she trust Ken? She'd known him for years. He'd become like a father to her.

"Yes, I can do that."

She picked up a tea towel to dry the dishes as Ken washed them. He leaned over and took the towel from her. "I'll do this, Sascha. Gives me something to do when you've left."

"You cooked. I want to clean up for you."

"Honey, please."

She threw her hands up. "I don't like it, but if you're sure."

"I'm sure. Thanks, Sasch."

Sascha gathered up her bag and umbrella and pulled out her house keys. "Thanks for dinner, Ken."

At the door, she turned back. "Hey, Ken, what was the name of the sketch artist?"

Ken blushed. "I should remember, but his name won't come to me. Leave it with me. By the way, do you mind if I drop Rusty off to you tomorrow morning? Pat and I have to fly to Sydney."

"Not a problem. See you tomorrow." Sascha searched for Soleil as she walked back to her house, but he had gone. She did, however, notice a black Rolls Royce parked a couple of blocks down the street. It was the glow of the cigarettes that caught her attention. For some reason, two people were watching her street.

Sascha called Ken about the car as soon as she stepped in the door. "I'll find out about it, Sascha," he promised. After a moment of silence, he continued, "And please keep what we talked about to yourself. I don't want you or the girls in danger."

Unable to sleep after that, Sascha cleaned the house as she searched everywhere for the map. It was gone.

What on earth did I do with it?

Still awake at 3 a.m. Sascha heard a muted hum as an engine started and then the soft drumming of tires on the road as it drove away. She looked out the window. The black car was gone.

She couldn't face work the next morning, so decided to catch up on paperwork at home.

"Before I do anything else I need a run." Sascha changed into her navy tracksuit, pulled her hair back into a ponytail, strapped on her iPhone and walked out onto the front lawn to stretch.

Ken was watering his garden, assisted by Rusty, who was

chasing the water shooting from the hose. Ken turned and waved. "Hi, Sascha. You off for a run?"

"Yes, feeling tired. I need some energy."

"Not surprised. You still happy to take Rusty?"

"Of course. What happened about the black—"

Pat stepped out onto the verandah. "Ken, are you ready? We're leaving in a few minutes."

"Yes, I'm ready. Look who's here."

"Oh, hello, Sascha," Pat said as she walked over to the fence. "I didn't notice you there. By the way, happy birthday. Did the girls buy you something nice?"

"Yes, they did." Sascha's fingers brushed the necklace. "This is one of the gifts the girls gave me." She walked over to join Pat. "Isn't it beautiful?"

Pat raised her hand to touch it, then hesitated. "Um, yes, it's beautiful. Ken, did Sascha show you her birthday present from the girls?"

"Yes, she did."

Sascha's skin prickled as they glanced at each other. "Is something wrong?"

"No, not at all," Pat said, a little too quickly.

"I'd better start my run before I change my mind," Sascha said.

"Thanks again for looking after Rusty for us," Pat called after her. "Let yourself in when you return from your run. We'll be gone by then."

"I'm looking forward to having her," Sascha called back.

After her run Sascha collected Rusty, then returned home and spent a good portion of the day finalizing her accounts. It was nearly lunchtime when she sat back in her chair, pleased to have finished the work. She stared down at Rusty, who was sleeping at her feet. She was wearing a new collar embroidered with rainbows and stars. A small silver locket in the shape of a bone was attached to the collar. Pat must have bought the collar and locket yesterday.

The ambient sound of a motorbike revving and then pulling away broke into her thoughts. "Mailman's noisy, isn't he, Rusty?" Sascha reached over and stroked Rusty's head "Come on, gorgeous, time to fetch the mail." Her tail wagging, Rusty jumped up and raced across the room, turning at the door to wait for Sascha to catch up.

Chuckling, Sascha opened the door. She walked over to the letterbox and retrieved the local newspaper. No letters, but underneath the paper was a rose-colored box tied with a red ribbon. A pale-yellow envelope was attached to the box.

A sudden blast of warmth blew past her. She turned to see Soleil disappearing behind a copse of trees in Pat and Ken's front yard. Sascha had felt his presence during her run this morning, but he hadn't talked to her since last night, despite her attempts to talk to him. She turned toward Rusty, who was happily waiting to take the mail inside. Rusty reached up, grabbed the newspaper from Sascha's hand and raced to the front door. Sascha looked at the envelope, noticing that there was no stamp. A muffled bark told Sascha that Rusty was getting impatient. "I'm coming. I'm coming."

She opened the door and let Rusty inside. Rusty raced to her mat, dropped the paper and sat waiting for her reward. Sascha leaned over, patted her and gave her a couple of chicken treats.

She carried the box and envelope to the kitchen table, deciding to open the box first. Inside the box was an ornately crafted wooden pen. The flash of recognition disappeared as quickly as it came. "Why would someone send me a pen?"

The pen was made up of four pieces of white scented wood with a different creature etched onto the surface of each piece. Different shades of gold brought the creatures to life - blue, white, yellow and ochre. On the cap of the pen was an ochre-colored stone carved into the shape of a dragon's head. The eyes of the dragon were dark empty holes. It looked as if something fitted into the holes. She checked the box. There was nothing else there.

Next, Sascha opened the envelope and took out a folded note. On it was the picture of four female silhouettes with the words, "It is time". There were some additional handwritten words written below the first words, "Your journey begins now".

A cold shiver raced through her as she stared at the note. It made no sense. First, the map, which had since disappeared, and now a pen. What did either of them have to do with a journey? And what was with the silhouettes?

Rusty barked and raced for the back door. Sascha walked to the door and opened it, so distracted that she forgot to consider how Rusty might react to the big golden bird that sat on top of the water fountain. Rusty let out a blood-curdling howl before racing toward Soleil.

"Rusty, no—"

Soleil screeched, then flew off as a knock sounded on Sascha's front door.

CHAPTER 12

ERATUS

"*N*o," Connell screamed. He clawed at the darkness. Loud piercing cries of agony surrounded him as victims were torn apart by the minions of the creature that was about to devour him.

He could smell the brimstone, taste the ash as it filled his mouth.

The darkness moved aside to allow the gaping maw to move closer to its prey. Connell tried to push away the fear that was coursing through him. A distant voice called to him. "This isn't real. Listen to my voice."

"What? Who are you?"

"It's Laela."

"You're not real. Laela's dead."

"I'm alive, Connell. I'm here to help. You need to focus on where you were when this started. What were you doing?"

"What is this? Where did this creature come from?"

"You don't have time to worry about that. This is an ancient force and it wants to destroy you. It will win if you don't stop panicking."

The slurping sounds of the maw grew closer.

"Focus, Connell. What were you doing?"

"I was sitting on the cliff top."

"That's good. Keep going," Laela said.

Connell ignored the saliva dripping on his shoulder, the smell of the maw's foul breath as it moved toward him. He started to bring back the image of where he really was.

He was sitting on a lush mat that padded against the rocky surface of the cliff top. The scent of incense wafted around him. George's delighted high-pitched call sounded from the beach below. Tears pricked Connell's eyes as love for George flowed through him. The wind blew softly on his face and the light of the morning suns shone through the darkness that had surrounded him.

Then he was being licked, licked by a large wet tongue. He opened his eyes. He was back on the cliff top, the evil gone, blown away in the wind. George was sitting in front of him, her head twisted on its side, ready to give another lick if needed. A smile broke over Connell's face as he pulled George's head closer to him and hugged her. "You saved me, George. You brought me back." George gave a short soft roar, thumped her tail and lay down.

"I might have had something to do with it too," said a voice to his left.

"Athena's ghost," Connell said. Laela sat cross-legged on a mat next to him.

"Admittedly, it was George who told me what was happening in time to reach you."

"What? How did she do that?" Connell clenched his trembling hands and forced himself to calm down. He was safe.

"George messaged me. She knew when the darkness came and called out to me. When I arrived, she was standing over you, going wild." Laela looked over at George. "I didn't know she knew I was alive or that she could message."

"She is an amazing creature," Connell said, patting

George. George seemed reluctant to sit next to Laela, instead preferring to sit on his right, closer to the cliff edge. "How did you survive the ceremony, Laela?"

"I was tending to you after the fire consumed..."

Connell put a hand on her shoulder.

Laela gulped. She wiped her hands on her robe and carried on. "I think it was a mage who brought the extra power into the ceremony, a young woman. The darkness used the mage's power to access the ceremony. It wasn't long before it became too powerful for her to control. That's when everything changed. She realized what was happening and tried to withdraw her power. She couldn't stop the fire, but could protect you. I had raced over to try to help you so when the mage protected you, she protected me too.

"I thought you said you knew where that additional power was coming from."

Laela hung her head and rubbed her eyes. "I was wrong, completely wrong."

"Who did you think it was?"

"I'll tell you when I know for sure. I don't want to be wrong again."

Connell sat for a moment, digesting what Laela had said. It didn't make sense. Laela was hiding something. "The mage must be talented. How come we have never sensed her magic until now?"

"I'm not sure. She could be an apostate who never enrolled in one of our magic schools."

"Do you know where she is?" Connell asked.

"I've overheard a couple of mages gossiping at the Academy of Magic. They say Drakon has had a mage taken to the lower level of his chambers for punishment. Everyone believes it's connected to the healing ceremony."

"We have to stop him. You know what he's capable of."

"We can't. He would find out that I survived. I want to

keep my survival a secret for as long as possible. Anyway, Drakon would deny it. But if the mage is as powerful as we think, even Drakon would have to consider his options before attacking her."

"Maybe, but I think I'll still get someone to look into it." Connell looked over at Laela, "How come you're not hurt?

"I have used simple glamor magic." Laela lowered her magic to reveal the large weeping blisters that dotted her swollen face and hands. The skin that wasn't blistered was bright red.

"Your hands. And your face," Connell cried out. "My healer will help you. The pain must be—"

"I have treated it. Most of the damage will heal in time. I'll be fine."

Connell watched as Laela renewed her glamor magic and the burns disappeared.

"When I was tending to you," Laela continued, "I heard it, the darkness. Have you listened to the Shield lately?"

"Yes, I've heard the whispers, but sometimes they're hard to decipher. I assumed it was because of damage from the ceremony."

"Some of the whispers use the language of the ancient," Laela said. "The Sisters have chants that are based on the languages used in ancient times, so I recognized it when I heard it."

"Why would the language have changed?"

"The darkness I told you about, the one we sensed before the ceremony, it communicates using the ancient language. It has found a way into the Shield, and it's slowly consuming it. But it is weak. It needs more power. So it attacks those it thinks are physically or mentally weak and consumes their power. You're a powerful mage and you're injured, so it attacked you. The more power it gets, the quicker it will destroy the life that makes up the Shield."

"And if the darkness consumes the Shield?"

"That can't happen," Laela answered.

Connell ran his hands through his hair. "Why would the darkness want to destroy the Shield? If the Shield dies, so does the planet. If the planet dies, so does everything that lives on it."

"I don't know yet, but we think Drakon might be the connection."

"Drakon? How?"

"We started to feel a change when Drakon turned thirteen," Laela said. "Do you remember when Drakon was young and he stumbled across the secret room where the map showing the location of the ancient weapons was hidden?"

"The map you think was sent to Sascha?"

"Yes," Laela answered. "When Sascha was here, she warned us that Drakon had sketched a copy of it. We didn't believe her. We thought he was too young to understand its significance, so it made no sense for him to have copied it."

"Then Sascha shouldn't be in danger," Connell said.

"But she is. The original map has the codes needed to access the ancient weapons. The codes can only be revealed using a specific magical spell. Drakon wouldn't have known that at the time, so he wouldn't have copied the codes. He would know about the codes now, so he knows he needs the original map. What Drakon doesn't know is that the weapon is somehow connected to this darkness. When Drakon started the search for the weapons, he inadvertently opened a connection, allowing the darkness onto Eratus."

Connell leaned over, dragged his cane closer to him and brought his knees close to his chest as he prepared to stand. Laela got to her feet. "I'll help you, Connell."

Connell waved her away. "You're injured too." George jumped up and stood beside Connell, giving him something to balance against as he struggled to his feet. "Good girl," Connell said as he patted George's head. "How do we heal the Shield this time?"

Laela sighed. "I don't know, but it is going to require a lot of power. Not only do we need to heal the Shield, but we also need to destroy the darkness that is killing it."

"Is Sascha capable of doing that?"

"Sascha was more powerful than anyone we had ever seen and so were the girls she is looking after." Laela pulled back her hair. "This mark - I had it tattooed on my face when I was appointed enchantress of the Four Sisters. Sascha was born with this mark. That means she was chosen, that she is special. It's the same with the girls. They were also born with their marks. We hope their purpose is to help at the next healing ceremony."

"But they've all had their memories taken away. Will they still have the power?"

"We hope so. "In the meantime, you need to bring Sascha and the girls here and keep them safe."

"Marco left for Earth a couple of days ago. He will meet with Sascha and the girls." Connell sighed. "I wish you had been honest with me before the ceremony."

"We thought it would distract you from what you had to do. We couldn't take that chance." Laela walked to the edge of the cliff and stared out at the ocean. "What happened to you today, Connell, was a warning. We have now had two warnings. Let's not need a third, because that may be too late."

DRAKON SLAMMED the door as he stormed into his room. "Guard, bring me Lieutenant General Novo."

"Yes, My Prince."

Several minutes later, the heavy clump of metal boots entered Drakon's chambers. "You wanted me, My Prince?"

Novo was wearing the armor of the Awakening. Their emblem, a red fist holding a raised sword, was engraved into his chest plate.

"Do you have a report on what has been happening with Ken and Pat?"

"Yes, My Prince." Novo coughed, then started to read from the transcript he was holding. "2000 hours. Sascha arrived at Ken and Pat's residence and stayed until 2215 hours. Pat was out." Drakon tuned out until he heard, "0630 hours. Sascha left for a run after a short conversation with Pat and Ken. Followed them to the airport, where they boarded QF326 to Sydney. 0645 hours agent in Sydney instructed to follow them. Report from agent due within the hour."

"I want you to keep a close eye on them. I will not accept failure. You understand me, Novo?"

"Yes, My Prince."

"I need to know everywhere they go and everyone they meet. Understood?"

"Yes."

"You may leave. Advise Reya that she is to report to me immediately, and do not mention our conversation."

"Yes, My Prince."

Drakon smiled to himself. Reya would be furious when Novo relayed his order. It amused him to keep her on her toes.

When Reya arrived, Drakon stepped behind her and ran his fingers across her bare shoulders. "You are tense, Reya. Something wrong?"

"No, My Prince. Any chance to serve you is a pleasure."

Drakon turned his back to her, unable to hide the pleasure he felt in her anger.

"Have you heard from Roger yet?"

Reya gulped. "I was going to tell you, but I haven't had the chance to see you."

Drakon turned to her. She fidgeted with her bracelet, unable to look at him. "Tell me what?"

"Roger is dead. The police are investigating the death."

"How did that happen? Who's investigating the death?"

"The name of the investigator?" She repeated, frowning at Drakon.

"Yes, the name. It's a simple question."

"It's Ken," she answered. "I assumed you knew, that he would've told you. Didn't you see him?"

"He didn't say anything." Drakon drew in a slow and steady breath, barely controlling the growing anger. "And what about the map Roger was supposed to steal? Did you find that?"

"It's missing," she whispered.

Drakon picked up the nearest chair and threw it across the room. It smashed into little pieces. "How could we have lost it? Again? Must I do everything myself? Maybe I should have given the task to Novo. He seems a lot more reliable." Drakon swung around. "Guard!" He watched as the color drained from Reya's face.

One of Drakon's guards stepped cautiously into the room. "Yes, My Prince?"

Drakon flicked his fingers and an invisible band wrapped around the throat of the guard. As the band tightened, he dropped to his knees, his fingers scrabbling at his throat. The man gurgled as the life was strangled out of him. Drakon continued to tighten the band, then let his finger flick forward. The guard's neck snapped and his lifeless body slumped to the cold stone floor.

Drakon strode toward Reya. "That man paid the price for your failure. Next time it will be you. You have until the second sun sets behind the seas to give me the news I need."

"Yes, My Prince," she stammered.

"Leave. Now."

Reya scampered toward the door.

"And, Reya." She tensed, but didn't turn.

"Organize someone to dispose of this body so that no-one finds it."

"Yes, My Prince," she answered.

Once Ken and Pat return from Sydney I need to deal with Ken. He lied to me. But first, I need to find out how loyal Pat is.

After a few glasses of prumble ale, Drakon sat and stared out over the castle training grounds, his thoughts turning to the day he had found the map.

He was only thirteen, and he dared not use his magic for fear of discovery. He pushed himself into the corner of the alcove near the stairs to the basement. Every sound was magnified. He could even hear the servants breathing in their quarters as they grabbed a few hours' sleep before their day commenced. As he waited for his father to arrive, the cold winter winds whistled through the open castle windows above his hiding spot, bringing the chill of the snow and the sweet salty tang of the ocean into the castle. He wrapped his bed jacket tighter and continued to wait.

Soft padded footsteps sounded behind him. His father was close. Pushing himself even harder against the icy wall, he waited for him to pass. Careful to stay well behind, he watched his father climb cautiously down the stairs, leaning on the ancient crumbling wall for balance.

How easy it would be to push him. Then he would become the youngest High King in the history of Eratus.

No, not yet, but it was an idea.

His father turned to the left at the bottom of the stairs and tapped three times on the wall facing him. The wall opened quickly and silently. His father stepped into the void and the wall closed behind him. Drakon heard whispered angry voices. Minutes later, the wall opened and his father emerged, a young woman in a cape following close behind him. His father tapped on the wall and the wall closed again.

When the sounds of their footsteps had disappeared, Drakon walked over to where his father had stood. He stretched up and tapped the wall as he had seen his father do. Nothing happened. He tried again, but the wall remained closed. The third time, he jumped as he tapped the wall. It opened. "Yes!" he said, fist-pumping the air.

Drakon walked into a large room lit by sculpted torches placed in wall sconces. The walls were filled with ancient maps and old scripts. A large glass box rested on an ornately carved table in the center of the room.

I hope there's more to this room than old papers.

Drakon began to chant quietly.

"There's a secret here I know, element of air, the secret show."

A glow appeared over the glass box. He walked over to it and looked inside. The only thing there was an ancient map stretched out on a board. He shook his head and cursed. "Is this all there is?" But he knew that if the magic had shown it to him, the map must mean something. He examined it more closely. Four circles were etched on the map, and a smaller map of a land he didn't recognize was attached to the bigger map with a dragon clip.

Drakon toyed with the idea of stealing the maps, but then had a better idea.

"Powers of Earth let it be, a sketching of these maps for me to see."

It wasn't long before he was holding sketched copies of the maps in his hands. Parts of it were familiar but—

"Drakon, what are you doing here? What is this place?"

"Connell," Drakon said without turning around, giving himself time to stuff the sketches into his pocket.

Connell sidled up to him and glanced down at the table Drakon was standing before. "This room is amazing, isn't it?"

"What're you doing, Connell? Are you following me?"

"Boys." They both turned to the doorway. Their father and the girl in the cape were watching them.

"Sprung." Drakon surreptitiously stuffed the sketches further into his pocket. He noticed the young woman watching him. He looked back at her, challenging her, trying to catch a glimpse of the face beneath the hood.

"Get out of here. Now!" their father said.

Drakon shook his head as he watched Connell scamper out of the room without a backward glance. "You're gutless, Connell," he muttered.

Drakon decided to take his own time in leaving the room. He glanced around pointedly, stared at his father and the woman, then casually walked out. Once out of the room, he stopped a few steps away from the door, where he cast a shadow spell to hide himself. The young woman and his father retreated into the room, but Drakon could still hear what they were saying.

The woman spoke first. "How did your sons find this place? They shouldn't know about it."

"Don't challenge your king," his father said.

"That map must be hidden," the woman said. "We cannot allow anyone to find it. What will happen now that Drakon and Connell have seen it?"

"They're young boys," his father replied. "They'll forget. Young boys are easily distracted. But perhaps you should consider moving it to your headquarters. The chronicles do charge the Four Sisters with the protection of the map."

Footsteps moved closer to him and then the wall closed as his father and the woman exited the room. Drakon pushed himself deeper into shadow as he fingered the sketch in his pocket. "This must be important."

The woman turned to whisper something to his father. He couldn't hear what she said, but the hood of her cape started to fall. She pulled it back quickly to hide her face, but not before he realized it was a young girl, not a woman.

Drakon woke. The face. He had always thought it was Reya pretending to be the enchantress for the Four Sisters, but it wasn't. It was Sascha. How come he hadn't noticed it before now? Could Sascha and Reya be sisters?

CHAPTER 13

* EARTH

*E*ham threw himself into the front seat of Marco's car.

"What time are we supposed to be at Sascha's?"

"One o'clock."

"That's not enough time," Eham grumbled.

"It's plenty of time. What's eating at you, Eham?"

"It's Connell...and you."

"Me? What did I do?"

Eham stabbed his finger at Marco. "You let Connell use Jenny."

Here we go.

"What do you mean?" Marco asked.

"It's Connell's fault that Jenny had her magic taken away from her, leaving her vulnerable to the idiots that live on this planet. If it wasn't for Connell, she would have easily fought off her enemies, and she wouldn't have had to run."

"What are you talking about, Eham? She didn't have her powers taken away."

"He took her powers away. He must have. She would have

destroyed her enemies if she had her powers, not run from them."

"Eham, you need to check your facts. Connell did no such thing. If Roger decided against running because he didn't think anywhere was safe, destroying the enemies chasing her wouldn't be the answer either."

"If she had her magic, she would have stayed here to fight with us," Eham said.

"We don't know why she left and we don't know if she would have stayed. Just wait until Alex gets back to us, until we know more."

Eham let out a deep breath. "This waiting is killing me. Let's call him."

"It's early morning in Scotland. I'm not phoning him now. Maybe later."

"He shouldn't be sleeping," Eham said. "He should be looking for Jenny."

"Alex needs—" Marco slammed on the brakes, narrowly missing a short squat woman who had just raced out of Sascha's house. She stared through the windscreen at Marco.

Marco jumped out of the car. "Are you hurt?"

"I... I'm sorry," she muttered.

Marco turned as Sascha raced to join them, a dog chasing after her, barking at the confusion.

"Sorry, Sascha, I..." The woman waved her hands uselessly in the air, then raced into the house next door.

"What was that about?" Marco asked. "What happened?"

"I have no idea," Sascha replied. "Let's go inside. C'mon, Rusty."

"I didn't know you had a dog," Marco said.

"This is Rusty." Sascha pointed to the house the woman had just run into. "She's their dog. They were supposed to have flown somewhere this morning. And then Pat arrived at my place, saw the pen and raced off, nearly getting killed in the process. I'm not sure what's going on."

"Pen? What pen?" Eham raced up the path and into the house.

Sascha yelled after him, "Excuse me, this is my house."

When Marco entered the house after parking his car, Eham was standing in the dining room, waving his hands agitatedly. "Where is it?"

"What's the big deal, Eham?" Sascha pointed at the table. "There it is, in the box." She walked past Eham, to the back door and let Rusty outside.

Marco glanced out the window. "I didn't realize Soleil was here. How do the two of them get on?"

"Really well since Rusty saved Soleil from a snake."

"A snake?"

"Yes. After the pen arrived Rusty wanted to go outside. I opened the door and Rusty raced out into the backyard, toward Soleil. I thought she was going to attack him. But she wasn't, she was after a snake that was about to bite Soleil. She saved him."

"Did she kill it?" Marco asked.

"No, the snake was sensible, it took off."

"That's amazing. But she was lucky it didn't attack her," Marco said as he stood looking at Soleil and Rusty sunning themselves in the back yard. He turned to Sascha. "I brought lunch with me. Where can I put it?"

"Sorry, I didn't realize you were carrying that around," Sascha said. "In the kitchen, on the bench. I'll show you."

Marco followed her into the kitchen and he put his car keys and the food on the bench, and the wine in the fridge. Then they walked back into the dining room. Eham was sitting at the table, staring at the pen.

"I don't know why this pen has caused this sort of angst," Sascha said. "It looks pretty, but it doesn't work."

"What? You tried to write with this?" Eham snapped.

"Of course I did," Sascha snapped back. "It's a pen!"

"I need tea," Eham said. "I'll wait while you make it for me. We have a lot to talk about."

"I'll show you where the kitchen is. You make your own tea."

"Making tea is women's work," Eham spat.

"I'll make it," Marco said. "You two talk."

"No, I'll make it," Sascha said, stomping off to the kitchen. "It's my kitchen."

"When did it turn up?" Eham called out to Sascha.

Marco heard doors and drawers being slammed shut.

"Today," Sascha answered.

"But how? Who would have sent it to you? The Sisters are all dead and no-one else knew where it was."

"What do you mean?" Sascha asked. "Who are the Sisters?

"How long before that cup of tea?"

Silence.

Marco leaned over to Eham and whispered, "Back off, Eham. We're not here to insult her. We need her help."

"That woman recognized this?" Eham picked up the pen and let it rest in his hand.

"I'm not sure but—" Sascha called back.

"What do you mean, *you're not sure?* She raced off, left her dog behind and nearly managed to be run over by Marco's careless driving in the process."

"If it is all so clear to you, why ask me? And another thing," Sascha said, storming into the dining room, armed with tea, beer, mineral water and wine, "this is my house and I will not be spoken to like some child."

"Then don't act like a child."

"Eham," Marco shouted, "that's enough. You owe Sascha an apology. You're being rude."

"Marco, I don't need you to fight my battles for me."

Sascha's face was flushed, and the muscles in her neck quivered.

"You didn't let me finish, Eham." Sascha took a step toward him. "I was going to say that I wasn't sure, but that when she touched the pen, it must have hurt her, because she dropped it like a hot rock and then raced out of here."

As Sascha sat down, there was a crash as the front door swung open, signaling that the girls had arrived home. "Sascha, we're home."

"We're at the dining table, girls," Sascha called out.

Ella and Lee walked up to the table and sat down. Kira walked to the kitchen, poured herself some mineral water and some wine for Lee and Ella and then joined them at the table.

"We're all here," Sascha said. "Let's begin."

Eham took a sip of his tea. "You were a powerful mage, Sascha, even as a young girl. We had never seen power like yours."

"Who's *we?*"

"I advise the Four Sisters. We work together on Eratus to protect the planet and heal the Shield that keeps it safe."

"Who are the Four Sisters?" Sascha asked.

"They're a group of powerful female mages," Marco responded.

"Your parents were murdered when you were young," Eham continued, "and you were adopted."

"You were adopted by Owain, Owain Grayfang," Marco added. "He's the High King of Eratus, leader of the Grayfang realm."

"Where is this planet and why have we never heard of it before?" Sascha asked.

"It's part of a star system connected to your solar system," Eham answered. "The Shield that protects the life on the planet also keeps the planet, and the star system, invisible to Earth."

"What do you mean, *protects the life on the planet?*" Kira asked.

"The system is so close to the sun that it would be destroyed without the Shield," Eham answered. "Life as we know it would die. The Shield maintains the temperature and the air so that life can survive. It is a living magic that must be healed from the damage it sustains over the years. It protects life in the same way as your atmosphere protects you, but I guess you can't heal Earth's atmosphere."

"It must all sound strange," Marco said. He could see Sascha was still struggling. Confusion was etched on her face.

"If I was so powerful," Sascha said, "and the adopted daughter of the…"

"High King," Marco said.

"Yes, the High King, how come I ended up here? And why did I try to kill him?"

"It took you a long time to recover from the murder of your parents, but you did," Eham said. "You were getting married."

"Married!" the girls said in unison.

Marco glanced at Eham.

"You were attacked at your wedding ceremony." Eham's eyes flicked over in Marco's direction.

Marco's pulse started to speed up. Eham had better stick to the story they had agreed to.

"You were able to defend yourself," Eham said. "But your fiancée was overwhelmed and killed."

"Killed?" Sascha's mouth dropped open as she stared at Eham, the girls gasped.

"Why would someone attack me at my wedding?" Sascha asked.

"We still don't know the reason for the attack," Marco answered. "You said you recognized the cloak the leader was wearing over her battle armor."

"*Her* battle armor?" Sascha asked.

"Yes, it was a woman, and she was leading a group of assassins called The Elite. You believed the High King was behind it all. You wanted revenge, so you attacked him."

"Why would the High King—was he behind it?"

"No," Marco answered.

Sascha frowned. "But what if I was right? What if he confessed to me and then I attacked him?"

"Owain didn't do it," Marco answered. "When you attacked him, you gave him the perfect opportunity to kill you. The penalty for assaulting the king is death."

"Wow!" Kira breathed.

"When your attack failed, you asked for the law to be applied. You wanted to die. Owain refused. When you realized Owain wasn't going to change his mind, you asked to be sent to Earth and for your memory to be expunged. Owain desperately wanted you to stay, promised to help you recover and find those responsible for the attack, but you were adamant. He eventually agreed."

Sascha's head was in her hands. Marco could see that she was trying to take everything in. Kira moved closer to Sascha and put her arm around her shoulders. "I don't understand. I would have..." Sascha said. "There must be more to this."

The chirps of the finches in the forest across the street echoed around the quiet room. Marco glanced outside. Rusty and Soleil lay next to each other, their heads tilted to the side, as if listening to sounds Marco couldn't hear.

"What about us, Marco?" Kira asked.

"Your mothers asked me to find a way to save you from a darkness we believed and still believe was searching for you. The Four Sisters sent your parents to me. They were told about the process Sascha had undergone. How she had been sent to Earth without any memory of her life on Eratus and was living a happy life."

"A happy life?" Sascha said angrily. "Have you forgotten what you and Connell had to save me from? Do you have any idea how hard it is to have no past? To not know what you're capable of? Or who you are? And these poor girls were sent to the same fate."

"You asked for death," Eham said in a soft voice. "I would say you got off lucky, girl."

"Why would our parents want our memories to be taken away?" Lee asked.

"They didn't want you to suffer," Marco said. "They thought forgetting them would make your life easier. It was a hard decision for them to make."

"Can this be reversed?" Lee asked. "Can we return to Eratus, to our parents?"

"We don't know if it is possible to bring your memories back," Eham answered. "But we want to try. As for returning to Eratus, we think there is a way. There are portals we use. Normally those who wish to use the portal have a chip embedded under their skin to enable them to travel safely. Your chips were removed when you were transferred to Earth. We did have a couple of examples where people had to use the portal without the chips. Marco is one example."

"In my job, I need to travel incognito." Marco shrugged his shoulders. "I couldn't take the chance of someone using the chip to track me."

"Anyway," Eham said, shaking his head, "Our scientists developed a keystone which Marco could use." Eham retrieved a keystone from his pocket. It looked like a gold coin, with the emblems of fire, earth, water and air engraved on both sides of it. "But we haven't tested it out on humans yet. Having lived on Earth for five years, your tolerance levels would be more like a human's."

"Tolerance levels?" Kira asked.

Marco shifted uneasily in his chair. "Travelling through the portal damages the body. People on Eratus can deal with the impacts of the travel. It kills most humans, though some have survived."

"Sascha, there is a portal in the city which we can access," Eham said, "but we thought that if we could convince you to return to Eratus, you would test the keystone before the girls use it."

Sascha pushed back her chair and stood. She opened her mouth to say something, but instead she turned and left the room.

"She has a lot to deal with, Eham," Kira said getting up from the table. "Give her time." The three girls followed Sascha out of the room.

"We don't have a lot of time before this cycle closes," Eham called after them. "She must make up her mind in the next few hours, otherwise we'll miss our opportunity." Eham tapped his fingers impatiently on the table as they sat and waited for the women to return.

Marco sat back and crossed his arms. "Do you have to do that, Eham? It's most annoying."

"Tell the bloody women to hurry up and not be so dramatic about it all."

"Eham, they need a moment alone," Marco said. "I think we can give them that. I'll get lunch ready," he said as he headed to the kitchen.

"Talking about time, Marco, I can't sit around and wait for Alex to give us updates on what's happening with the search for Jenny. I need to be there when he finds her."

"What are you asking?"

"When you leave for Eratus with Sascha, I need to join Alex and help him find Jenny."

"Alex is a loner. He doesn't like company."

"This is my Jenny. I'll stay out of his way, but I know more about her than he does. I just...I need to be there when he finds her."

"OK," Marco agreed reluctantly. "You can stay at my house on the cliffs. It's two houses up from Alex's. But if you—"

"I will let him do his job," Eham said. "Thanks, Marco."

Marco snorted. "Some thanks from you. You must be grateful."

"Let's not push it," Eham said, smothering a smile.

SASCHA WAS FINDING it difficult to breathe. Her mind was numb. She had tried to kill her adoptive father and then asked for death. And she accepted being sent here, without any memory of who she was or where she came from. She lost a family, a fiancée. What would the High King do to her when he found out that she had returned? Her stomach fisted into a tight ball, and her head started to ache.

"The High King loves you, Sascha," Soleil's voice called to her. "He might be angry, but he loves you."

"Sascha, one of us will use the transporter instead of you," Kira said. "We want to find our families, find where we are from. You must be terrified of going back."

Sascha's shoulders drooped forward. Part of her had always known that she would lose the girls one day. It looked like that day was about to arrive. But she had to be there when they met their families, just in case they needed her. Which meant that she had to face the transporter and the High King.

"Thanks, Kira, but it must be me. If it doesn't work..."

She returned to the dining room. "Marco, I'll do it. How long before we have to leave?"

"A couple of hours. Let's have some lunch first, then I'll drop Eham off at the airport. We've booked him on a flight to Scotland. He wants to work with Alex to find Jenny."

"Oh! I haven't even asked about Jenny."

"I noticed—" Eham started to speak, but Marco silenced him with a glare.

"I've prepared some lunch," Marco said. "Let's have something to eat first."

"A man who prepares a meal without being asked to do it," Lee said, "Be still my beating heart." The girls laughed.

AFTER LUNCH, Marco grabbed his keys off the kitchen bench. "I'll be back after I drop Eham off."

When Marco and Eham had left, Sascha called the office. "Hey, Marcie, I have to take some time off. I will be away for a week or two."

"That's fine, Sascha," Marcie said. "If there's anything I can do, let me know."

"Thanks. Just keep an eye on the clinic for me. If anything urgent comes up, leave a message for me here and one of the girls will call you back."

"Look after yourself, boss," Marcie replied. "We'll see you when you get back."

Sascha sat back in her chair and looked out the back window. She watched as Soleil swooped down, teasing Rusty. Rusty did her best to catch Soleil, but she was all legs and paws, and didn't have the grace and speed Soleil had.

Sascha's stomach tensed as she thought about what she had to do. Surely none of this was real, but the sight of a boxer dog playing happily with a creature she had never seen before told her it was.

The girls came and sat at the table with her. Kira carried in a tray of hot coffee and sweet biscuits.

They all sat in silence as they drank their coffee. As Kira put her empty coffee cup on the table she cleared her throat. "Sasch, can we come with you? Please?"

"Kira, this is a gamble. The keystone might not work. I would prefer to be the one who tests it out."

"How will we know if you...if you're hurt or need our help?"

"Kira!" Lee said. "Sasch would be worried enough. You're only making things worse."

"But we won't know, won't be able to help if she's in trouble. We'll be left...waiting," Kira said.

"I'll come back and tell you," Marco said as he walked in the front door. "And unfortunately, you girls can't go because each of you need a keystone and we only have one for Sascha. We need to move, Sascha, we have forty-five minutes left."

"Yes, let's go."

~

THEY PARKED under a tall brick building that overlooked the Brisbane River. Marco retrieved a card from his pocket and swiped it through the card reader.

"Lift 3." Marco pointed to the first lift.

After they got out of the lift on the top floor, they walked up a stairwell to the roof top. Sascha took one step onto the roof and froze, unwilling to release her tight grip on the door. She couldn't see anything to hold onto. A good gust of wind and she'd be over the edge.

"This isn't good, Marco," Sascha said as her stomach

lurched. "Do we have to do this up here?"

"This is your keystone, Sascha," Marco said, ignoring her protest. "It is essential you have this with you at all times. It will save your life. Do you understand?"

"I'm not a child, Marco. Of course I understand."

"I'll open the transporter."

"You can do this, Sascha." Soleil's voice echoed in her mind.

Marco walked to the edge of the roof top and looked down. Then he closed his eyes and moved his hands, mumbling something she couldn't hear. The idea of anyone standing on the edge of the building, with nothing to stop them from falling, terrified her.

"For God's sake, be careful, Marco. We're a long way up."

A soft whirring sound came from the edge of the building as a large circle of spinning air opened. Marco moved the vortex until it touched the edge of the building.

"Are you serious? I have to...I have to walk off the edge of the building into...into that!" Sascha turned to walk back down the stairs. "I can't do it."

The girls.

If she didn't do this, one of the girls would. And then they would find their families and she would never see them again. She turned back.

Marco walked over to her. "The girls need you to be strong."

"That looks bloody terrifying," Sascha whimpered. "You're asking me to walk off a tall building into space. What if it can't carry my weight? What if I fall to the ground?"

"Sascha. Of all the things to worry about." Marco chuckled.

"Glad you're amused," she snapped.

"It doesn't have a weight limit. The transporter is like a step. The portal is a door. You step up onto the step, walk through the door and end up in your old home. But first, you have to liberate the door you're holding hostage."

Sascha looked down at the white fists that were still gripping the edge of the door.

"We will walk into the transporter together. I just need to do one more thing and then it's time for us to leave." Marco turned back toward the portal.

"Sascha," Soleil screamed. "Behind you."

Sascha turned. A cloaked figure was charging toward her. Sascha saw herself collapsing in a heap on the rooftop, the keystone dropping. Her neck stung as the necklace was ripped from her neck. Darkness descended as Marco rushed forward, calling her name. The last thing she noticed was the familiar smell of watermelon and ginger.

GENTLY, Marco gathered Sascha in his arms, holding her close. The cloaked figure picked up the keystone Sascha had dropped and headed for the portal.

Soleil screamed toward the escaping figure, beak snapping and claws slashing. Marco heard the grunting and cursing as Soleil's claws ripped at the back of the figure, blood oozing through the tears in the coat.

Determined to make it into the portal, the figure staggered toward the transporter Marco had created and, within seconds, he was gone.

Marco examined Sascha's injuries. Blood was flowing freely from the wound on the back of her head. She needed medical attention, but without the keystone, she wouldn't make it through the portal. He could make another transporter, but it would be useless without the keystone. "Damn it. Now what?"

Soleil landed on the roof top, emitting a sad crooning

sound. Soleil walked to Marco, put his head under Marco's arm and nudged, trying to push in between him and Sascha.

"Stop it, Soleil. She's hurt. I need to work out what to do."

Soleil leaned toward Marco and tapped at the keystone in his hand.

Soleil could take her if I put it in the pocket of her top. He's carried her before. But she'd be alone. What if she panics when she sees the guardians? They might both die.

Marco stared at Soleil.

The portal was closing. He had to make up his mind now.

Soleil tapped on the keystone, harder this time.

"Alright, alright, you damn bird."

He put the keystone in Sascha's shirt pocket, mainly to shut the bird up. He stood and turned toward the portal. Time was fast running out. Soleil shoved Marco out of the way, wrapped Sascha in his claws, brought her close to his body and flew toward the portal. A whoosh of hot air and then he and Sascha were gone.

CHAPTER 14

ERATUS

George's booming roar shattered the peaceful, sunny afternoon.

Connell jumped in his dragon-bone chair, wincing as his bandaged arms banged against the sides of the chair. "George! In the name of Athena. Quiet."

George glanced back at him, a wide grin spread across her face, tongue lolling. Then she raced for the balcony, her talons clipping on the floor.

Connell levered himself up. He adjusted his loose pants and tunic, leaned on his cane and hobbled outside to join George. The second sun had nearly set, and with the two moons rising, the sky was filled with the colors of fire and green ice.

"Soleil. What are you doing here? Where are Sascha and Marco?"

A piteous cry echoed from deep within Soleil's chest, sending an icy chill up Connell's spine. He shivered. Soleil twisted his head to the side and stared at Connell, before letting his gaze drift downwards. Connell repositioned his cane as he followed Soleil's gaze.

"What have you got there?" Connell reached toward the bundle Soleil carried in his claws. His hand froze mid-movement as he stared. "Sascha!"

Blood covered the claws holding Sascha's head. "Healer," he yelled. "Quickly."

The door flew open as the healer raced toward Connell. "Connell, are you hurt?"

"No, not me."

Soleil's wings stirred the air, creating a warm breeze, as he lowered Sascha gently onto the balcony floor.

Connell pointed. "Healer, that's Sascha. There's a lot of blood."

"Sascha?" the healer asked. "Did she come through the transporter injured? That could have killed her."

"I don't think she was alone. I think Soleil brought her here."

"It still could have killed her," the healer muttered as he sat on his haunches. His long thin fingers explored Sascha's head, moving her hair and the collar on her top as he examined her neck. "She'll be fine." The healer moved his lanky body sideways, giving Connell a better view. "She's been hit on the head, but no other injuries apart from these strange bloody indents on her neck."

Connell leaned forward as much as he could without toppling over. "A necklace - could that cause that sort of injury? She might have been wearing Soleil's necklace."

"Yes, that would make sense," the healer replied. "The marks could be from the chain."

Connell glanced over at the balcony rim. Soleil was perched there, his eyes following every movement the healer made.

"I'll get one of my novices," the healer continued, "and we can take her to her old chambers." He put his hands on his knees and pushed himself up with a grunt. "Ciara," he called out.

A petite young woman with fiery red hair rushed to him. "Yes, master."

"Help me move Sascha to her chambers. We will use the transporter cone."

"Yes, master," she said as she raced off to get the wrap they would use to move her.

Connell stared after her. "Is she from Brun? And she practices healing magic?"

"Yes, the red hair is a giveaway. She's an excellent healer, but she has no real talent with fire magic. Luckily for Ciara, we stole her away from her people before they realized."

"I'm glad you could save her," Connell replied. "Let's hope she appreciates what you did, unlike some others..."

Connell caught the healer's quick glance at him. He sighed. Sascha and Kira had been born in Brun. His heart broke a little as he thought of how much they had all lost when Sascha had left Eratus for Earth. They could have been happy.

A whoosh of warm air whipped around Connell's legs. He twisted around. Soleil had gone. He turned back and watched Ciara and the healer gather Sascha and place her into the wrap.

The healer and Ciara guided the floating wrap toward the cone shaped transporter in the corner of Connell's chambers. "We will meet you in Sascha's rooms." They touched the cone and disappeared.

"Guard."

The guard dashed into the room. "Yes, My Prince?"

"Ask the High King to join me in Sascha's chamber."

"Right away."

"And when Sister Laela arrives, send her to join us."

The guard brought his clenched fist to his chest in salute, turned on his heel and left the room.

Connell tapped the ring on his finger twice, waited two seconds, and then tapped the ring three more times. Laela would arrive here soon.

Connell hobbled over to the transporter cone and looked at it. He hadn't been to the northern section of the castle, Sascha's chambers, since the day she had left. He took a deep breath, stepped forward and touched the metal cone.

THE FAMILIAR SMELL OF HONEY-WOOD, pine and cinnamon greeted him as he appeared in Sascha's room. Everything was the same as he remembered the large polished amber and honey-wood bed with white silk sheets and a coverlet painted with images of pyrans. The wall next to her bed was filled with delicately carved hand fans from every region across Eratus. Soleil's nest still sat in the corner of the room. Decorated with various dyed vines, the nest reminded Connell of a bonfire. Being back in the room was like stepping back in time.

He glanced over at the ornately carved door to her chambers and his thoughts flew back to the last day he'd been here. He'd wanted to stop Sascha from doing something she'd regret. Arriving at the door, he'd heard voices from within the room. He flung the door open and found Drakon and Owain discussing their regret at Sascha's choice to leave. He'd known Sascha was determined to get her revenge. But he'd thought she was after the Sisters and had wasted valuable time racing to find Laela. When the guard advised him that something had happened between Sascha and Owain, he realized he had been wrong. He'd wanted to tell her he'd taken Marco to Kalurth, the Dragon Queen, and she had saved him. He could have helped her, but she had chosen to leave without even talking to him. Leave! His heart had shattered that day.

Connell drew in low and steady breaths as he pushed down the anger that bubbled inside him.

Stop thinking about it, Connell. No matter what she did, Eratus needs her now. Breathe...

The soft chatter between Ciara and the healer intruded on his focus.

"Is this *the* Sascha, the leader of the Four Sisters?" Ciara asked the healer.

"Yes, my child," the healer replied.

"I've heard so much about her. Is she as scary as people say?"

"You surprise me, Ciara," the healer said. "I didn't think you listened to gossip."

"I don't. I've always wanted to meet her. She's from my home town in Brun, Black Hollows. And she was a healer. Like me! That is, until..."

"I know."

Ciara was quiet for a few seconds as she stared down at Sascha. "The servants say that after Sascha left, Soleil snuck into these chambers every evening when the second sun set and cried his little heart out for her?"

"As I said, Ciara, you should know better than to listen to gossip. Now, put this balm on her neck while I talk to Prince Connell."

"Yes, master," she replied.

The healer pushed himself up and walked over to Connell.

"How is she?" Connell asked.

"She'll be fine, but she may be unconscious for a while. If it pleases you, I will direct Ciara to act as Sascha's maid until she is healed."

"Agreed."

"Then you should rest. Ciara will come and tell you as soon as she is conscious."

Connell shook his head. "No, I'll wait with her. Ciara can carry on with her other duties until it is time for Sascha's next treatment. I'll call if Sascha has need of her before then."

The healer bowed, then walked over to where Ciara stood. He whispered something in her ear and they both left.

Connell hobbled over to the windows and pushed them wide open to let in the fresh ocean breeze.

The sudden whoosh of air nearly knocked him over. Soleil crashed into the room and, breathing heavily, positioned himself on the exposed beams overlooking Sascha's bed.

Cursed creature.

Connell shuffled over to the chair next to Sascha's bed. He slowly positioned himself in the soft cushions. Seconds later George raced into the room and threw herself onto the floor next to him with a loud thud, panting as she smiled up at him. "What have you two been doing, George?"

George thumped her tail, then lay her head on the cold slate floor. Connell leaned down and stroked her. He sat back in the chair and stared at Sascha.

The bedsheet was tucked around her shoulders, and bandages covered most of her head.

The tears surprised him. It seemed that, despite his anger, he still cared for her. Maybe now he would find out why she abandoned them all.

He leaned over and gently brushed a loose strand of hair from her face. "By Athena. I've missed you so much, Sascha."

A silvery voice spoke from the doorway. "I came as soon as I received your message."

"Sister Laela." Connell turned away from Laela to wipe the dampness from his face.

She moved to the bed and stared down at Sascha. Connell straightened his dark green tunic, picked some invisible dust off his long charcoal colored pants and waited. Finally, she spoke. "Do you think she will get her memory back?"

"I'm hoping she will. We need her to regain her full powers."

Laela turned to face him. "Careful what you wish for, Connell. You might find the person you thought Sascha was never existed. She kept a lot of secrets from all of us."

"I'm fully aware of that," Connell snapped. He pressed his lips together and stretched a hand toward Laela. "Sorry, Laela, seeing Sascha here has brought back a lot of memories."

"Do you remember Drakon's reaction to you both when you first arrived?" she asked.

"How could I forget? He disappeared for over a week. He was so angry with Owain for adopting us. No-one ever understood his decision to take us in."

"Did you ever ask Owain why?"

"He doesn't want to talk about it," Connell replied. "He evades the topic every time I broach it."

Laela raised her eyebrows. "He's never told you?"

Connell shook his head. "No."

"I'm surprised."

"Why did you ask that now?" Connell asked. "Do you know something?"

"No. Well, nothing I wish to repeat."

"What does that mean?"

"You know what gossip is like in this castle," Laela answered. "I don't know the truth. I hoped you did."

"To be frank," Connell answered, "I don't care. We were lucky to be adopted by such a generous man."

Laela turned back to face Sascha. "Sascha obviously didn't think so."

"Whatever she thought, she was wrong," Connell answered.

"I know but..."

Heavy footsteps announced Owain's arrival. "She's here!" he called out.

"Father, she's sleeping."

"I can see that, Connell." Owain turned to Laela and nodded his head in acknowledgment. "Laela."

"She won't be sleeping for long," Connell said, "if you keep talking so loudly and—"

A powerful flap of wings stopped the conversation, and the three of them looked up to see Soleil glaring at them.

"It appears the bird is telling us to be quiet," Owain said.

Laela bowed low to Owain. "I'd better go. I'll come back when she's conscious and see what I can do to help."

"No need to leave on my account," Owain said as he watched Laela leave. "She's always skittish around me," Owain whispered in a voice scarcely quieter than his usual roar.

"You must be scary, Father," Connell replied.

"Ha!" Owain looked around the room. "Where's Marco?"

"He didn't come back with Soleil and Sascha."

"Have you been able to work out what happened to her?"

"No way of knowing. Soleil would be able to tell us," Connell answered, "but someone ripped the necklace off Sascha when they attacked her. Her neck has several long deep abrasions."

Owain walked over to the bed. He stood silent for a moment, staring at Sascha in the same way Laela had. Then he moved the covers and examined her neck.

"What would they have wanted with the necklace?" Owain asked. "Anyway, didn't she have another one hidden here somewhere?"

"It could be anywhere. The healer said she'll be fine, so we should find out what happened soon enough."

Owain pulled up another chair and sat next to Connell.

"It's hard to see her back here," Connell said.

"I know."

"How could she have abandoned us all so easily? And to just leave Kira after everything we did to help her adopt her?" Connell glanced up at the bird perched on the beams above Sascha's bed. "And to leave Soleil when it could have meant his death."

Owain closed his eyes and let out a deep breath. "After seeing the damage she did to the family, I swore I would never let her come back, never let her get close to any of us ever again. She has too much of her father in her. But I must think of Eratus. When this is over..." Owain scrubbed his face. "Sweet souls and angels. I didn't expect this day to come."

The sound of George's snoring echoed around the room as Owain and Connell sat next to each other in silence. Presently, Owain slapped his hands on his thighs and stood. "I have some business to sort out. I'll be back soon." As he walked toward the door, he turned back to Connell. "If she wakes before I return, send the guard for me."

"Yes, Father."

Connell stared at the empty doorway after Owain had left. A chill blew into the room as a dark shadow appeared in the doorway. Connell shuddered as it halted for a moment, peered into the room, then moved away. He struggled out of the chair, limped to the doorway and looked up and down the corridor. Nothing. He rubbed his eyes.

I'm seeing things.

Connell went back to his chair and settled in, ready to wait until Sascha woke.

Sᴀsᴄʜᴀ'ꜱ ʜᴇᴀᴅ ᴘᴏᴜɴᴅᴇᴅ.

Where am I?

Waves crashed in the distance. A cool, peppermint-scented breeze wafted around her.

Somewhere near the ocean. Are we still in Caloundra?

Sascha raised her arm to massage her forehead, but stopped mid-movement as sharp jabs of pain hacked their way through her head. She needed some painkillers.

"Be still," a soft female voice instructed. "You received a nasty gash to the back of your head. I'll give you something that will help." Sascha felt a cool spray of moisture on her forehead and the pain started to ease immediately. She sighed, grateful for the relief.

It all came flooding back. Someone had attacked her. After all that build up, she hadn't even made it through the portal. Her hand reached for her necklace. It was gone.

With the pain in her head easing, Sascha slowly opened her eyes. She blinked as her eyes adjusted to the golden glow from the setting sun. A soft sweet chatter sounded above her head. She moved slightly to get a better view of where the noise was coming from. Soleil was perched on a wooden beam, studying her. He grinned, then floated down onto the bed, his large claws gripping the cover. He towered over her and his unique scent of pine and cinnamon wafted around him. Soleil leaned down, put his beak next to her hand and nudged it. In response, Sascha brushed her hand against his face. He was warm and silken soft. It was then she noticed the necklace in his beak.

"My necklace? You got it back, Soleil." She reached over and took it from him.

"You damn bird, you had the necklace," said a familiar voice. "You could have given it to me before."

Sascha jerked at the sound of the voice and then twisted to see who was there.

"Did you ask him for it?" a female asked, the sound of laughter echoing in her words.

A slim dark-haired man sat in a carved wooden chair. White cushions decorated with images of Soleil surrounded him. "That's beside the point."

"Connell. What are you doing here?" Sascha glanced around the room. "Where am I?"

A sudden movement next to Connell drew her attention. A large creature lay on the floor, its broad head resting on its paws. It had the face and body of a lion, but a lion with wings. Its wings were folded at its side, and its tail, which had a fat spike on its end, swished in the air. Its eyes focused on her.

"You're on Eratus. These are your private chambers," Connell said.

"How did I get here? Where's Marco?"

Soleil nudged the hand Sascha had resting on the bedcover, next to the necklace.

A slim fiery-haired girl with iridescent green eyes walked toward Sascha. "I think Soleil wants you to put the necklace on. Here, I'll put it on for you."

"Thank you," Sascha said.

"To answer your question," Connell continued, "we don't know. We don't know how you got here, and Marco didn't come with you." Connell glared at Soleil. "I would have been able to tell you more if that damn bird had let me use the necklace."

Soleil snapped his beak at Connell. "Marco gave you the keystone so you could travel," Soleil answered. "but it meant he had to stay behind."

"What did *it* say?" Connell asked.

"*He* says Marco stayed behind."

"About time you woke," a voice boomed. A lean, muscular older man with long gray hair and cold gray-blue eyes stood glaring at her, his arms crossed across his broad chest. Next to him stood a tall, lanky man with twinkling blue eyes, polished pink cheeks and a large, toothy smile.

"You're lucky to be alive," tall and lanky said to her. Gray hair stayed at the doorway and stared at her, while tall and lanky walked over to her bed. "I'm the Master Healer for the Grayfang Realm. Ciara, help her up so she can drink her medicine."

Ciara plumped a couple of pillows and pushed them behind Sascha's back. The healer leaned over, a wooden cup shaped like a conch shell held in his hand. "Drink this," he said as he handed her the cup. "It will help you heal."

The thick green drink smelled sweet. Her stomach turned. Sascha felt the acid rising in her throat and shook her head. She didn't want to drink this green stuff. How was she to know what was in it? Sascha lifted the cup to give it back to him.

"Drink it. You and your brother are pips in a dragonberry. He didn't want to drink his medicine either. If I made him drink it, I'd hardly let you off, now would I?"

The sound of her own breathing reverberated in her head. "My what?"

He pointed in the direction of Connell. "Your brother. Oh, I'm sorry. You wouldn't..." His face flushed bright red. "I'm sorry."

Connell's my brother? But that's not possible.

Sascha drank the medicine and handed the cup back.

"We'll leave, now," the healer said. "The medicine will send you to sleep, so you might not have long to talk before it works. Come, Ciara."

Silently, Ciara followed the healer out of the room.

"Was that true, Connell? Are you my brother?"

He studied his hands. "Well, I—"

"Are you a police detective?"

"No."

"So what were you doing on Earth?"

Connell cleared his throat. "Marco told me you were in danger. We had to rescue you."

"Marco?"

"Yes, he found where you were being held."

Bile rose in the back of Sascha's throat.

No! It can't be true. They both lied to me for all these years?

She swallowed, breathed in slowly until her stomach settled. "How did he find out what happened to me?"

Connell glanced at Owain, then back at her. "The contact we had organized to help you set up a new life on Earth was found dead. You'd disappeared. Marco searched for days. When he finally found the cabin, he sent for me and we rescued you."

"Why didn't you tell me who you were? Why lie?"

"I had to lie. How would I have explained it? You're the one who wanted to forget Eratus and me and everyone who ever cared..."

Gray hair coughed. "Connell."

"Sorry." Connell turned away from Sascha and reached down to pat the creature next to him.

"What does Marco do if he doesn't work with you?"

Connell gave the creature a final pat and turned back to face her. "He is the leader of the group I asked to help me keep an eye on you, the Fire of the Phoenix."

"So Marco lied too?" Her chest ached, and the pain in her head was returning. "Everything we did together was a lie. I assume the one he married in Scotland was his true love. God, I'm an idiot. How could I have been so stupid, so gullible?"

"Sascha, there's a lot more to this," gray hair spoke up. "There's a lot you don't know."

"And who are you?" Sascha snapped.

"You're in my castle. *I* am the High King of Eratus."

"The High King," Sascha stammered. "You're the one I..." Her heart fluttered against her ribs as a thought occurred to her. "Was this all an elaborate plot to get me back so you could punish me for trying to kill you?"

Owain turned to look at Connell.

"I haven't told her anything," Connell said. "Marco must have."

"If I wanted you dead," Owain said, "you wouldn't have been sent to Earth. You'd be dead."

"I'm not going to be punished?"

"No," Owain answered. "If I had my way, you wouldn't be here but—" He took a deep breath. "What happened in the past is a long story, one better left for when you've had some more rest. And you need your rest too, Connell."

Sascha glanced over at Connell, but the room had started to spin. She yawned several times. Darkness started to descend, and the last thing she remembered before she passed out was a shadow in the doorway. It looked at her and grinned, showing its sharp yellow teeth and flashing beady red eyes. Sascha smiled.

CONNELL SAT in Owain's chambers and stared out at the mountain range that backed along the eastern side of the castle. The season of the third moon would be upon them soon, but the end of the season of the two moons was still comfortable – chilly but not icy. During the season of the third moon, ice covered the mountains and the winds that blew down into the castle grounds cut through whatever you were wearing. It was only the ingrained magic in the castle walls that kept the castle and the surrounding gardens warm.

"She's grown into a beautiful woman." Connell snorted. "Time away from her family seems to have been good for her."

Owain leaned against the balcony railing, studying him. "Connell, I understand you're trying to work through this, I am too. She tore this family apart when she left, but we need her to help us save Eratus."

"I know. It wasn't only us who suffered, Soleil did as well. The healers said that Soleil has been going to her chambers every night."

"I know," Owain answered.

"You knew about Soleil?"

"Yes, the servants wanted me to help him. If Sascha gets her memory back, she might be able to explain why she made the choices she did. But we must be patient with her. She seems almost vulnerable now, totally unlike the Sascha we knew. Maybe she's changed."

"When I watched over her," Connell said, "I kept trying to work out what made it so hard for her to turn to me when she needed help. She trusted Drakon but not me."

"Hard for her, how?"

Connell put his head in his hands. "I don't know, but I must have done something."

He felt Owain's hand on his shoulder. "Connell, you can't start second-guessing everything. We will take it one day at a time."

Connell lifted himself out of the chair and grabbed his cane. "I'd better go and get some rest before dinner." When he reached the top of the stairs that led to the hall below Owain's chambers, he turned back to Owain. "Father, I'm sorry about the ceremony. If I hadn't messed up, we wouldn't be in this situation with Sascha. But I can't help feeling that if we hadn't let Sascha go in the first place, things might have turned out differently."

"Connell, do you really think that?"

"Yes, I do."

"She was taking green lyrium. If she'd stayed here, it probably would have killed her."

Connell looked at the tall, muscular figure of Owain as he stood in the center of his chambers, the wind blowing his gray hair about his face, his gray-blue eyes sparkling. He looked like a god. "I'll see you at dinner, Father."

CHAPTER 15

ERATUS

*S*ascha reached up and touched the bandages on her head. A small amount of tenderness, but that was all. She took in a deep breath of the sweet air as the morning sunshine warmed the room. The coffee-colored mark on her hand tingled, and her skin glowed. It was as if her body was reacting to something in the air. Her conversation with Connell rushed back, but Sascha pushed the thoughts away. She wasn't yet up to dealing with what he had said.

Sascha swung her legs off the bed, careful not to jar her head wound. She smoothed down the long white silk shirt she was wearing. She felt strangely self-conscious when she realized someone had changed her clothes.

It was probably the girl, Ciara, who changed me. I hope it was.

She looked under the shirt. She was naked. She needed to get some decent clothes.

A soft trilling noise echoed around the bed chamber. Sascha looked to the corner of the room where Soleil was sleeping in a large nest, his head buried beneath his wings.

A nest!

Sascha stared.

Well, this has got to be a first a bird sleeping in a bird's nest in my bedroom.

"You're awake," Soleil said.

"Hello, Soleil. I hope I didn't wake you."

"I wasn't asleep. I only closed my eyes for a minute."

Sascha smirked as she stood and walked to a large open window near her bed. The soft green ocean crashed against the white sands. She could taste peppermint on the breeze.

"This is beautiful," Sascha whispered.

"You loved being here." Soleil stood and ruffled his feathers. "When we stayed here, rather than the Four Sisters headquarters, you used to unwind by sitting outside on your garden balcony at the end of the day."

Sascha turned away from the window. "What garden balcony?"

Soleil trotted over to the teal-colored silk curtains, which were being gently buffeted by the breeze. "Here."

"Why would I stay at the Four Sisters headquarters?"

"You were their leader."

Sascha frowned. "I was?"

"I can take you there if you like."

"Not yet. I've enough to deal with at the moment. And I need to get back to Earth. I promised the girls I would bring them to Eratus as soon as I could. It's their home. Soleil, is this place... safe? Is it a bad idea to bring them here?"

"Sascha, they want to find their families. They know their families live here. They will come here one way or another."

"You're right." Sascha was about to walk out onto the balcony when a glint on the wall next to her bed caught her attention. On the wall was a display of beautifully crafted hand fans. Sascha shook her head. "This is surreal." She walked to the wall and examined the fans. "Did I collect these?"

"Yes. You gathered fans from each of the regions you visited in Eratus."

"I still do," Sascha whispered as she fingered a large charcoal and lemon-colored fan with images of various strange creatures engraved on it. They looked just like the creatures she had designed for the front of her veterinary clinic. "Wow. So this is where the idea for the creatures came from?"

"You used to practice with them for hours on end," Soleil said.

"Practice with them?"

"Yes, they're weapons. But you would always do your training in secret. Not even Connell knew."

"Weapons? I guess that makes sense. But didn't I trust Connell?"

"I'm not sure why you kept it a secret," Soleil said, "but I believe there would have been a reason."

Sascha turned and walked out onto the balcony. She leaned against the wall and looked out at the view. Large purple and green-feathered birds swooped down into the orange and yellow-leafed trees that edged the area. Tiny orange and black-feathered birds frolicked in the breeze. The air was filled with the beeps, coos and honks of the various bird species. The beautifully landscaped garden and lawn provided the perfect playground for some fluffy white toy poodle-sized animals, who were chasing each other in and around the trees and bushes.

Soleil jumped up onto the balcony railing.

"This is gorgeous, absolutely gorgeous," Sascha said. "And these gardens. They're so much like what I have back at home. The girls would love it here."

A flock of birds flew overhead and circled the garden. They seemed to be the same species as Soleil, but some had pure gold feathers and others orange.

"I can understand them," Sascha said to Soleil as she pointed to the circling birds. What are they?"

"They're pyrans, like me. You were able to understand our language when we were bonded, but you need the necklace now."

Sascha touched the pendant. "Will I be able to understand your language again without this?"

"Yes, when your magic is reawakened."

"How can Connell use this?"

"He is your brother. We share blood, so your kin your blood can also use the necklace."

"Share blood?"

"Yes, it's like a bonding ceremony."

A pyran with ebony and scarlet feathers sat on one of the balconies not far from them, watching the other pyrans diving into and twirling along the wind currents. A strong sense of loneliness overwhelmed Sascha.

She pointed the creature out to Soleil. "Who is that?"

There was silence as Soleil stared at the bird.

"Who is that, Soleil?" Sascha repeated.

"Fenix was bonded to Drakon. She's not to be trusted. She does Drakon's bidding and can be cruel." Soleil dropped his head. "We used to be friends, but..."

Sascha looked over at Fenix. Fenix stared at her intently for a few seconds, emitted a low protracted warble and then flew off.

"I think she's lonely, Soleil. Why aren't you still friends?"

"She has chosen to be unhappy and to serve a master she doesn't care for. She could fly into the fifth dimension, but she won't. Others who have been forced to work for cruel masters have done that."

"What happens when they fly to the fifth dimension?"

"They die."

Sascha stared at Soleil. "Death is the only way they can be released from their bonds? How can that be right?"

"That's the way it's always been. Once, you thought you had found another way, another option for us, but...you left."

Sascha grimaced. Had she found a way to help these beautiful creatures, but not told them. How could she have done that?

"We understood, Sascha. There were complications."

"I'm sorry, Soleil. I can't believe I was that cruel."

"We understood," Soleil said again.

"Soleil," Sascha whispered, "did you like me? Or was I like this Drakon?"

"You were my best friend," Soleil said after a few minutes. "I understood you leaving me, but it tore out my heart. The pain burned for a long time. But I always knew you'd come back, you had to. I just had to be patient."

"Why did you know I'd come back?"

"You told me you would."

Sascha looked up at the sky and took a deep breath as tears stung her eyes. Large dark clouds started to move across the planet's two suns.

"Eratus has two suns?" Sascha asked Soleil. "Summer must be a killer."

"That is why we have the Shield to protect us from the extreme climates."

Without the full glare of the suns, Sascha noticed fine white lines in the sky. She pointed. "What are those lines, Soleil?"

"They're the cracks in the Shield. They're why we need your help."

"All the way up there? How am I supposed to—I don't know if I can do this, if I have the power that is needed to fix this."

"You do," Soleil answered. "I have sensed it. And that's

why I knew I could carry you through the portal, even with your injury. Your magic protected you."

"Why is the Shield so important, Soleil?"

"Many years ago, our planet was dying, destroyed by the heat of the suns and the flying space rocks. The people prayed to our god, Athena, for help. Athena and the Masters of the Elements - the Dragon Lord, Zinnath, and his queen, Kalurth - heard our prayers and made the Shield. It protects us and maintains the climates we need to survive and grow our crops."

"And if the Shield isn't healed?"

Soleil stared up at the sky. "Eratus won't last long. We will all die."

Sascha pushed herself away from the wall and flexed her neck. She needed to do something. "Time for me to get dressed."

She turned to search for her clothes. "Soleil, look. Who made the bed? I didn't notice anyone in here."

"It reverted."

"It what?"

"It's the material. It reverts back to its original shape."

"Wow, we could make millions out of this idea back on Earth."

A soft whir sounded behind her and Sascha turned to see Ciara standing next to a metal cone in the corner of her room. Though she was holding a tray loaded with strange fruits and sweet bread rolls, she managed a small curtsey without spilling anything. "Princess Sascha."

"Ciara. Where did you come from?"

"Sorry, I didn't mean to scare you." She nodded toward the metal cone. "It's a long way from the kitchen, so I used the cone."

"Really?" Sascha walked over to the cone to have a closer look. "So the cone transports you when you touch it?"

"Yes, but you must get a clear picture of where you want to go before you touch the cone, otherwise it won't work."

"Amazing. Thanks for the food. I wouldn't mind having a shower and getting dressed."

"Here, I'll show you where everything is." Ciara walked over to a door Sascha hadn't noticed earlier and pressed a button mounted on the wall beside it. The door swung open, revealing a massive bathroom.

Intrigued, Sascha walked into the room.

"Good afternoon, Sascha. Do you want me to run a warm bath for you?"

Sascha jumped. "What the—"

"Sorry," Ciara said as she came up behind her. "I should have warned you." She pointed to the bathroom mirror. "That's Mirror."

Sascha gasped. Almond shaped amber eyes with large dark lashes stared out from the center of the mirror. "There are eyes in the mirror."

"Um, yes," Ciara said. "We let it know you were here, and it wants to help."

The eyes were watching Sascha's every move. "Will it watch me while I bathe?" Sascha asked, feeling distinctly uneasy.

"No, you have total privacy. But you can ask Mirror to play music, read a story, whatever you want."

"So what if I wanted to know more about Eratus?"

"It has access to our reference sections. When we programmed your details in, you were automatically given permission to access most of our historical records."

"Programmed my details?"

"Yes, it knows your height, weight and clothing prefer-ences, and orders in whatever you need."

"How did..."

"From the bed. There's a scanner in the bed. It gives

Mirror your vital details. You've...you've changed since you were last here, but it has updated everything for you."

"Changed?"

Ciara looked at her, blushed, then walked over to a wardrobe that stood near the bathroom door. "Here are your clothes."

Soleil chuckled. "She's saying you're fat."

"Fat? I'm not fat," Sascha said, automatically standing up straighter and sucking her stomach in.

"No, no, I never said that," Ciara said.

"It's alright," Sascha said as she pointed at Soleil. "It was that creature over there that said I was fat."

Sascha caught Ciara smothering a smile. Ciara froze, color draining from her face. "I'm sorry, Princess Sascha. Forgive me." She dropped to the floor and bowed, head touching the floor.

"Ciara, get up. Look, if we're going to get on, you're going to have to relax around me. I need friends, not people who fear me. Can you be a friend?"

"Yes, Princess Sascha."

"Good, that's settled. And you can start calling me Sascha, not Princess Sascha or any other name."

"Yes...Sascha."

Sascha walked over to the wardrobe. In the corner were the clothes she had been wearing when she arrived on Eratus. They had been cleaned and pressed. Next to them were beautiful silk kaftans, pants and tops, with matching boots and shoes sitting underneath. Sascha fingered the fine materials. "Whose are these?"

"They're yours. Mirror ordered in what you used to wear."

Sascha headed straight for a sheer jade top with white camisole, pants and boots, and headed back to the bathroom.

"I can't call you Mirror. Your eyes look like a girl's, so I'm calling you Crystal."

"Crystal. I like that name," the mirror replied.

"Good, Crystal it is. Crystal, would you please run me a bath? And are you able to lock this room so that people can't get in while I'm in here?" Sascha peeked over at Soleil and grinned. "Or birds?"

"Yes, certainly," Crystal replied as Soleil snapped his beak at her, strutted over to the balcony, then flew off.

"Ciara, are you able to get me some coffee?"

"Coffee?" she queried. "What's coffee?"

"Is there a hot drink that people here drink in the mornings to give them energy for the day?"

"Ah, yes, vimberry."

"Can you pour me a mug of vimberry then?"

"I'll pour you some and then leave you to have your bath."

"Thanks. And would you show me around the castle later?"

"Yes, Sascha." Ciara curtseyed. She walked to the bed and pointed to a button on the wall beside it. "Press this button to summon me. I will show you around the castle grounds after I've changed your bandages."

"Thank you again, Ciara."

"Crystal, lock the doors, and would you mind shutting the mirror or doing whatever it is you do to give me some privacy?"

"You always have privacy. Do you wish to read any of our ancient records, or would you prefer music or stories?"

"I want to find out more about Eratus," Sascha said as she stepped into the warm bubbling bath water and breathed in the soft scents of honey, pine and cinnamon. Her shoulders relaxed as she lowered herself into the bath.

This is heaven.

The room darkened. Scenes from around Eratus came to

life on the walls of the bathroom. A soft voice spoke to each of the changing scenes.

THIRTY MINUTES LATER, Sascha was bathed and dressed. She pressed the button to summon Ciara. She could still smell the soft, sweet scent of the water on her skin. As she waited for Ciara, there was a knock on her door.

"Come in."

The door opened, and her stomach lurched when she saw Connell standing in the open doorway. He reminded her that she was here for a reason. Sascha watched as he hobbled in, leaning heavily on a cane. "How are you recovering?"

He glanced up at her. "Best way to heal is to move."

Ciara appeared at the cone, dressed in a dark green tunic and long dark pants. "I'm here, Sascha. Ready to do your bandages?"

Connell frowned at Ciara. "Sascha?".

"Oh, sorry, Prince Connell, I didn't realize you were here."

"Obviously not since you didn't use her title."

Sascha walked out onto the balcony and gestured for Connell to follow her. "I've asked her to call me Sascha."

"You never did follow protocol," Connell grunted. "Do you mind if I sit for a minute while Ciara does your bandages? I need a moment of your time."

"That's fine."

"I came to ask if you would join Father and me at Ocean's Mouth."

"Ocean's Mouth?"

Connell rubbed the back of his neck. "I forgot, sorry. Ocean's Mouth is the High King's private meeting place."

"It sounds pretty," Sascha answered.

"It is."

Sascha knew it was important that she meet with Connell and the High King, but she didn't want to go with Connell. She felt uneasy and guilty around them. "Rather than keeping you waiting, Ciara can show me there after she's finished."

"I could wait for you," Connell said.

"No, I'm sure you have plenty to do. Ciara, do you mind taking me?"

"I would be happy to."

Connell stood and looked at Sascha for a few seconds before turning and hobbling back out the door. "I'll let Father know you'll join us shortly."

"Thank you, Connell." Sascha released her breath when she heard the door close. She wasn't looking forward to this.

CIARA LED her down a stone staircase to a grassed area. A cobbled pathway, edged by large white trees, led down the grassy slope to a large cave. Sascha enjoyed the swish of the jade top against the soft white pants. In the end, she had settled for white slip-on shoes rather than the exotic-looking boots. She thought they might be more practical for the beach.

A glowing barrier barred entrance to the cave. "What's that for?" Sascha asked.

"It protects the meeting place from unwanted visitors. It's another version of Mirror—I mean, Crystal. It's told who to let through. If your name isn't on its list, it attacks."

"It attacks? Would it kill you?"

"Not if you're sensible enough to get out of its way."

"Is your name on the list, Ciara?"

"No, but yours is. If I'm with you, I can't be harmed."

"Oh. Do I have to go first or something?"

"No, it's already sensed you're here. If it was going to attack, it would have done so by now." Ciara waved her hand in an arc and the barrier disappeared.

Sascha stood at the entrance and stared into the blackness. "I thought we were going to the beach, not into a cave. Are you sure we're going to the right place?"

Ciara laughed. "This is the entrance to Ocean's Mouth. Connell and the High King will be waiting for you at the meeting area at the other end of this cave."

"It's awful dark."

"Wait until you see what happens when we get in there." Ciara rubbed her hands together and giggled. "C'mon, let's go."

Sascha glanced back at the pathway that led to the castle. A shadow moved and hid in the copse of trees near the path. Sascha peered into the tree line to see what it was, but it didn't move again.

"Sascha, are you coming?"

"Sorry, I...yes, coming."

The barrier reappeared the moment they stepped into the cave, and tiny glowing creatures began to light up the space. A waterfall near the entrance to the cave was filled with glistening fish. Emerald-leafed vines, covered in purple, orange, yellow and blue flowers that looked like large snapdragons, grew along the walls of the cave. A breeze ruffled her hair, carrying with it a hint of rose, vanilla and cinnamon. Little lights lit up a grassed path that led further into the cave. The path was edged with tiny trees and small multi-colored birds darted in and out of the branches.

"It's beautiful, isn't it?" Ciara watched the fish splash at the base of the waterfall. "I love it here. When I'm allowed in. Magical creatures live in the cave. They're called crudouraks. They protect the cave. If you enter here without permission or harm a creature in here, they will kill you."

Sascha cleared her throat as she glanced around the cave. "Where are they now?"

"They live beneath the floor of the cave, but we've never seen them."

"How do you know they exist then?"

"When the High King was being attacked by his enemies from the kingdom of Breyth, he asked the crudouraks to help him. All that was left of the High King's enemies were the clothes they had been wearing."

Sascha shivered. "The High King and Connell will be waiting for us. Let's go, Ciara."

The walk to Ocean's Mouth took only a few minutes. For a moment, Sascha stood in the maw of the cave and looked out at the pale green ocean crashing against the shoreline. The bright blue horizon was slashed with gold, red and orange. Sascha stepped out of the cave.

Ciara pointed. "They're over there."

Connell and the High King were sitting in a circular pergola with a thatched roof. The beams of the pergola were covered with the same emerald vines that grew along the walls of the cave. They were both dressed in white flowing gowns that resembled the robes Catholic priests wore. She gulped and the knot in her stomach tightened. The massive creature Sascha had seen sitting next to Connell yesterday was sitting in between the High King and Connell. It turned its head to Connell, swished its tail and then jumped up and raced toward Soleil.

How did Soleil get here?

"Ciara," Sascha said, pointing at the massive animal, "does that creature have a name?"

"That's George, Connell's bonded pet."

"George? Why did Connell decide on that name? It doesn't seem to suit it."

"You chose the name for him, Sascha. Well, that's what village gossip says anyway."

"What type of creature is it?"

"It's a half-breed," Ciara said. "We know one parent was a manticore, but no-one seems to know what the other creature was. I'll leave you now, Sascha, but if you need me, send Soleil. He has a knack of finding people, even if they don't want to be found." Ciara turned and walked back toward the cave mouth.

Sascha arrived at the pergola to see a table laid with drinks of various colors, a selection of bread rolls and an assortment of meats and fruits. Her stomach rumbled. The vimberry she'd had earlier hadn't sated her appetite.

"Have something to eat, Sascha," Owain said as she sat down on the chair opposite Connell.

"No, thank you. I'm not hungry," she lied.

Owain walked over to the table, poured a glass of some purple liquid and handed it to her. "At least have a drink."

"Thank you." Sascha took the drink from Owain and watched as he walked back to the table and sat next to Connell.

"You would have lots of questions," he said.

Sascha took a deep breath. "Connell is obviously angry at me for leaving. I'm assuming you are as well. Can I call you Owain, or should I be calling you High King?"

Owain looked down at his drink. "You used to call me Father."

"I'm sorry," Sascha replied. "It must be hard for both of you. But you are strangers to me. Strangers who know more about me than I do, which is rather terrifying."

"Yes, we can understand that," he replied.

Sascha took a sip of the purple liquid. It tasted like wine. She felt the muscles in her stomach start to unwind. "What I don't get is why you're both angry at me for leaving. I thought I was forced to leave as punishment for attacking you, Owain."

"No, you weren't forced," Owain replied. "You chose to leave. We never understood your choice."

"I must have had a reason."

"Connell and I don't have the answers you want, Sascha. Maybe everything will make sense when you get your memory back."

Sascha stared at Owain. "I need to know what I did to you, Owain. Marco and Eham told me I tried to kill you, but why would I do that?"

"It was your wedding day. A group of men attacked you and the shots they aimed at you hit your fiancée."

"I was told he was killed."

Owain glanced at Connell. He coughed. "You thought the ones that killed your fiancée worked for us. You attacked me with a sword."

"Attacked you? If I believed you had killed my fiancée—

"I didn't," Owain said.

"I must have demanded an explanation. I wouldn't have just attacked you. I would have wanted to know why. It doesn't make sense. And why would I use a sword? Why not magic?"

"You were trained in battle skills, including magic and weaponry. You were a dangerous woman. I tried to find out what happened, tried to calm you, but you kept raving about my Elite guard and the color of the leader's cloak, a woman."

"The color of their cloaks?" Sascha asked.

"Yes. I wasn't sure what you meant at the time, but you wouldn't stop and talk."

"And who was the woman?" Sascha asked.

"I didn't have a woman controlling my armies so what you were saying made no sense," Owain said. "You were too angry, saying you had been betrayed. Connell told me later that you recognized the color of the coat the leader wore. You thought it was the same group that killed your mother."

Tears stung her eyes. "Killed my mother? Why would they kill my mother?"

"Mother was a famous Fan Warrior," Connell said.

"Fan Warrior? What is a Fan Warrior?

"They have specially crafted fans, made from the finest metals. They are deadly warriors, able to kill silently and quickly."

"That's why I collected them?"

"You loved Mother. You said the fans reminded you of her. You were terrified of forgetting what she was like."

"What was the point of killing her?"

"Various political factions believed the Fan Warriors were becoming too powerful," Connell continued. "I still wish I had been old enough to help you, but I was only four years old. You were seven. During the night of the Screaming Blades, our mother and all other Fan Warriors were killed. You witnessed the whole thing, but you never told me exactly what happened."

"What about our father?" Sascha croaked.

"He disappeared, leaving us behind. After the attack at your wedding, before you raced off," Connell glanced at Owain, "you told me you recognized your fiancée's killers. You said they were the same ones who killed our mother, that you could tell by the color of the leader's cloak. You were after revenge. I didn't realize that you meant Owain."

Sascha turned and stared at Owain. "I believed your people had killed my mother and my fiancée and all I have is your word that it wasn't. Now it all begins to make sense. I need to walk." Sascha stood and walked out of the pergola and toward the ocean. Chairs scraped on the ground as Owain and Connell pushed their chairs back and followed her.

"We won't talk about it anymore," Owain said. "It must be hard to hear all of this and not be able to remember."

Sascha's headache was threatening to return. She massaged her temple. "How did you stop me?"

"Drakon stopped you. I was hurt, but not badly. My biggest concern was to work out how I could break the laws set out in our Chronicles without losing the respect of my people."

Sascha heard the footsteps behind her stop. She turned to face Owain.

"You see," Owain continued, "the penalty for attacking the High King is death. I wasn't prepared to do that. I sent my private guards to see if they could find out who it was that attacked you so that I could stop the death penalty from applying."

"Did they find anything?" Sascha asked.

"They didn't have time. Drakon came back to me an hour later to say you were adamant that I was guilty. No matter what I said or the evidence I found, you swore you would kill me. Drakon and I discussed it. If we sent you to Earth through the transporter with your memory expunged, the intent of the law would be satisfied, and your life would be spared. May Athena forgive me, I gave the order and you were sent away."

"Why didn't you talk to me, help me to understand what happened?"

"In those days, you took green lyrium and it had changed you. Everyone, including me, was afraid of you, afraid of what you would do when you were in one of your tempers." Owain ran his fingers through his hair and sighed heavily.

"What's green lyrium?" Sascha asked.

"It's a drug. An addictive drug. Those hooked on green lyrium will do whatever they can to get some more. You were hooked, and I was the last person you would have listened to. We struggled with your decision. You left us all behind without even giving us a chance to explain, to tell you the truth. We didn't attack your mother or your fiancée. And we don't know who did."

Sascha sat down on the beach. Owain sat next to her. "We believed it was the lyrium that stopped you from listening to reason. It had to be. We were a family, and it made no sense for you to leave without giving us a second thought."

"Father," Connell said softly.

Owain's shoulders drooped and his head hung forward. He was silent for a minute, then lifted his head. "Sorry, Sascha. We want to know, to understand. But what we should be doing is working to gain your trust so that you will want to help us resurrect the Four Sisters and heal the Shield. You led the group until you left."

Sascha picked up a handful of sand and watched as it filtered through her fingers. "Soleil told me."

"We also believe the girls you have been looking after are powerful enough to join the Four Sisters," Owain said.

Sascha wiped her hands clean of sand as she stood. "I've no idea if I have the power you are looking for, let alone what powers the girls have."

"We have someone who wants to help," Owain said. "One Sister survived the disaster at the ceremony and—"

"And here I am." A light pleasant voice sounded behind her.

Sascha turned. The ground moved beneath her. Memories of a life flashed before her eyes and then disappeared as quickly as they had come. Sascha lost her balance and stumbled backwards, but Owain scrambled to his feet and steadied her by putting a hand on her back.

The Sister rushed toward her. "I didn't mean to alarm you."

"You didn't. It's—I had a sudden memory of..." Sascha closed her eyes and put a hand to her whirling head.

"Have something to drink and sit for a moment," Laela said.

"You remembered something?" Connell asked. "That's a good thing. Maybe you will get your memory back after all."

"On Earth I thought I needed to remember who I was but since I've been here I've realized I don't need to," Sascha answered. "And I don't want to. Why would I want to go back to being someone that everyone was terrified of? I'm not her, I'm me. I'm different."

"*I* wasn't scared of you at all, and I missed you." Soleil's voice echoed in her mind. "I miss who you were. And if you remembered everything, you could help us like you said you would."

Tears stung Sascha's eyes. She sighed, her heart heavy. "I know, Soleil. I'm sorry I let you down."

"We were close friends once," Laela said. "I want that friend back, and Connell and Owain would like their sister and daughter back."

"No, they wouldn't," Sascha sneered. "They only want me here because they're desperate. I wasn't brought back because they loved and missed me."

Connell and Owain stayed silent.

"See," Sascha said, pointing at them. "They can't deny it. And I wouldn't be here if the girls hadn't wanted to find out about their past. I'm doing this for the girls, not for strangers who don't want me here."

Owain glared at her. "Don't make us out to be the bad ones. You chose to leave. I begged you to stay, but you thought only of yourself. You caused more damage when you left than—"

"Father," Connell said, standing up and putting his hand on Owain's arm. Owain shook Connell's hand off and strode to the edge of the water. He stood for a moment, gazing out at the ocean.

"Sascha," Connell said. "Have you thought about the fact that getting your memory back could help us find Mother's killers?"

"I don't want to be that person from my past. If my memory comes back, I might become her again. I want to be me as I am now. Can't we leave the past in the past? I don't need my memory to find Mother's killers. We can do that anyway."

"I don't agree, Sascha," Connell said. "If it was possible to have found them, we would have."

Unless the killers were organized by Owain.

Sascha shook her head. "Connell, I think you can't see the truth of what is happening in your own family. You need to—"

"Sascha, let's go for a walk," Laela said. "It might be good for everyone to cool off." Laela stepped forward and put her hand on Sascha's shoulder. The mark on Sascha's hand flamed and the air crackled with electricity. Laela whipped her hand away, stood back and stared at Sascha, shaking her hand to ease the pain. "Well, that's one question answered, Sascha. Your powers are still there."

CHAPTER 16

A sudden jolt of pain shot up Drakon's arm as a burst of power whipped around him.

Where had that come from?

Drakon glanced over at Reya. She was still sound asleep. The last time that had happened was when Sascha lived on Eratus. Surely she hadn't arrived already? It couldn't have been that easy to convince her to come here. But the signs were there. Drakon climbed out of bed and walked over to Mirror.

"Yes, My Prince."

"Quiet, Mirror. Type script only. Light up the keyboard."

"Yes, My Prince," Mirror typed back.

"Show me the castle room by room," Drakon typed. Mirror flicked a view of each room.

"Those are all the rooms. Do you want me to go through them again?"

"Show me the lawns and the gardens." Drakon still couldn't see anything. "The Ocean Mouth."

"I'm sorry, but something is blocking me from seeing beyond the entrance to Ocean's Mouth."

That's where she must be then.

There was only one thing to do. Grateful he had changed his appearance before meeting Sascha at the club, Drakon dressed quickly and made his way to the Ocean's Mouth.

Drakon shadowed until he was at the maw of the cave. His intention was to shadow until he was close to the pergola and then suddenly appear at the table, taking them all by surprise. As Drakon looked out, he saw Sascha talking to a dark-haired female. The female turned slowly in his direction, as if she sensed his presence.

Laela!

Drakon watched as Laela moved Sascha away from the cave. He clenched his jaw as he bit back the anger that sizzled through him. Laela was the one who had survived and Sascha was speaking with her. He had a whole army and Reya and he still hadn't been able to stop Sascha from meeting with Laela. Drakon slammed his fist against the cave wall, ignoring the pain as his knuckles grazed against the stone. He had to think, work out what to do.

First, he had to know what was going on. Drakon closed his eyes, imagined the darkness surrounding him and sent himself further into shadow before moving close enough to Sascha to listen in.

SASCHA WATCHED Owain and Connell wander back to the pergola.

"You did have a strong reaction when you saw me," Laela said.

"It was strange," Sascha answered. "It's like you are part of a jigsaw puzzle, but I can't seem to work out where you fit."

"Did Connell and Owain tell you why we need you?"

"Yes, but I'm concerned that I don't have the power you think I have. I've already said I won't go back to being the person I was."

"Who do you think you were?

"A cruel and selfish person. Someone who put her own needs above those she loved."

"You were definitely confident and powerful, but I wouldn't necessarily say you were cruel. For the most part, you tried to be fair."

"Necessarily?" Sascha asked. "What do you mean?"

"Sometimes you had to make decisions that some might have considered cruel, but you didn't let that define you. As for your powers, I think it's safe to say that they're still there."

"Yes, but is what I have enough?"

"Did you have any powers on Earth?"

Sascha looked down at the mark on her hand. "I was able to do some strange things," she admitted.

"Like what?"

"Sometimes I could move objects or open doors just by thinking about them, but it was random."

"You're vulnerable in this state, Sascha. If Drakon found you like this, he would know exactly what to do to take advantage of you."

"Who is this Drakon? I've heard his name mentioned, but I'm not sure where he fits into all of this."

"Drakon is Owain's son."

"My brother?"

"You're his *adopted* sister. Changing the subject slightly, who do you think attacked you at the transporter?"

"You know about that?" Sascha asked.

"Yes, Connell told me. I came to see you, but you were unconscious. Did you see who it was?"

"I didn't, but I thought I recognized the smell of his aftershave." Sascha waved a hand. "I don't know. Maybe it was a coincidence."

"A coincidence? Is that what you really think?"

"It's what I hope."

"You think it's someone you know then?"

"Yes, though I'd prefer not to talk about it until I'm sure. He's a friend, but his behavior changed recently." Sascha fingered her pendant. "When I showed him this necklace, it seemed to mean something to him."

Laela nodded in the direction of the pergola. "Did you tell Owain and Connell?"

"No, I don't know how I feel about either of them yet. And this man is my friend. I trust him. He's been like a father to me."

Laela stuck her hands in the pockets of her long purple cloak and looked down at the sand. "Sascha, I wasn't sure I should bring this up now, but I know of a way we can test your powers. It's a test we give recruits at the Academy of Magic before they graduate. Would you be comfortable taking it?"

"Will it tell me how much power I have?"

"Yes and what type of power."

What happens if they find out I don't have the power they need? What then? Can I go back to my old life? But I would lose the girls.

"We can keep the results private," Laela said as if she sensed her reluctance. "But I think you will be surprised."

"Is there something I can read to find out more about this test?" Sascha asked.

"Yes, the paperwork we give to potential graduates to prepare for the test. I'll need to leave you for about half an hour to go and get it. Will you be fine with Owain and Connell?"

"Yes, I'll be fine." Sascha watched as Laela raced toward the castle. She turned back toward the pergola and shivered at the cold chill that swept past her. She caught a movement out of the corner of her eye. A shadow raced past the pergola up to the cliff wall and then clambered up the rock face at speed. It stopped at the top of the cliff and turned. Beady red eyes stared back at her before the shadow sprinted off.

CHAPTER 17

ERATUS

*D*rakon was striding through the cave toward the castle when he changed his mind and veered left toward the bridge. He needed privacy.

"Guard," he snapped at one of the soldiers patrolling the bridge, "send for Reya. Tell her to meet me in my war room."

"Yes, My Prince."

His knuckles hurt. Drakon flexed his fingers to ease the swelling. Laela was going to be a problem. But the results of the test she wanted Sascha to take could be useful. Sascha appeared to be unaware of how powerful she used to be.

And the creature that had flown past Sascha was a gibleree. Where had that come from? He could have sworn she recognized it.

"No." Drakon shook his head. He would have sensed if Sascha had befriended such a creature. It would have taken powerful dark magic to conjure it. Even he would think twice before trusting one of those deceitful and greedy creatures.

One of the two guards opened the door for him as he arrived at his war room.

"My Prince." The guards stood to attention, but remained at the doorway. They never entered this room. They were terrified of the fire dragons.

"No unusual activity, My Prince," one announced.

Drakon snorted.

Never have you been so wrong.

The muscles in Drakon's neck relaxed as he entered the room and his anger began to dissipate. This room was his escape from the castle and home for his fire dragons.

Drakon clapped his hands and the lights in the overhead beams started to glow. The room was warm and smelled of pine. Red eyes glistened in the corner. His pets were awake.

"Hello, my beauties."

They answered with a swish of their tails and a soft trill.

"Hungry? Mirror, get the map and some food for my dragons."

"Yes, My Prince."

A soft blue glow surrounded the carved marble table that stood in the center of the room. Shapes emerged from the table as the map a three-dimensional representation of the site of the ancient weapons on Eratus came to life. Drakon walked around the map as he studied the site which had so far been inaccessible. Once he sent his army to Earth through the second portal, he would craft a map of the second site. He hoped that the magic barriers protecting the ancient weapons on Earth would be weaker. Earth didn't have healing ceremonies which meant that the magical barriers that locked the weapons away wouldn't have been constantly renewed like they were on Eratus. The map disappeared as soft footsteps sounded behind him.

"Yes, My Prince?" Reya said.

Drakon stood and stared at the table, which now showed a map of the castle. "When were you going to tell me that Sascha is here?"

"That's not possible."

Drakon turned slowly toward her. "I'm beginning to worry about you, Reya. To wonder whether you are still capable of performing your role. Connell is on the beach with her. And with Laela!"

"La...Laela?" Reya stuttered.

"Yes," Drakon snapped. "I have you and the army at my disposal, yet none of you were capable of alerting me to Sascha's arrival or stopping the only surviving Sister from talking to her. How could that happen?"

"I don't—"

"What damage has Laela done already?" Drakon paced around the table. "The more time they spend with Sascha, the harder my job will be. I want Sascha followed every second of every day she is on Eratus. Is that clear?"

"Yes, My Prince."

"Now, move!"

Reya spun on her heel and sprinted out of the door.

Drakon called out to the guard. "Guard, send Novo to me. And I'll want my aide when Novo leaves."

"Right away."

A few minutes later, heavy metal boots ground to a stop at the doorway to his war room. "My Prince."

Drakon waited a moment before turning to face Novo. "Novo. Reya doesn't seem to be her usual self. I am entrusting you with an important task."

"Yes, My Prince." Drakon caught him smothering a smirk.

"And, Novo, if you fail, I will feed you to my pets." Drakon glanced over at the dragons. The ravenous creatures were feasting on a mischief of rats that were trying unsuccessfully to avoid them.

Novo gulped. "I won't fail you."

"Good. My plan is to capture Sascha and the girls she has been caring for. I need you to locate some suitable quarters. Somewhere Owain and Connell would never think to look."

"Right away."

"You have until the end of the season of the two moons to have everything finalized."

"Yes, My Prince." He saluted and turned to leave as Drakon's aide-de-camp arrived.

"That young girl from the festival the other night, Mage Isabella," Drakon said to his aide, "bring her to my upstairs chambers after the second moon rises. And tell her to make any necessary arrangements, because she will be staying with me tonight."

"Yes, My Prince." The aide hurried out of the room.

Drakon's pets were asleep. "Goodbye, my beauties." Their eyes opened suddenly. They hissed and backed away as a red band of light appeared in front of Drakon, its pulsating glow filling the room. Drakon's hand moved to the hilt of his sword as he took a step away from the light.

"There's no need for panic," a voice called out as two men shimmered and then appeared directly in front of Drakon."

Drakon nodded his head slightly, his eyes watching the two men carefully. His hand gripped the hilt of the sword tighter.

"Ares. Hades. You honor me," Drakon said.

Ares chuckled. He strode toward the dragons and stood watching them as they retreated further into the corner of the room. "You know," Ares said, "everyone bows before gods. Except for you. Why is that? All you do is nod your head."

"I apologize if I've insulted you, Ares."

"On the contrary, my dear chap, you have proven to my comrade that you are worth watching. You have an aura about you, but neither of us knows what that means." Ares looked to Drakon's sword. "And yet you still hold tightly onto that sword of yours. Do you really think that could protect you from us?"

"Why would I need protection from you, Ares?"

Ares laughed. "You have no fear. We heard you discussing the capture of Sascha and the girls. That is good. You can't access those weapons without Sascha's magic. But we're not here to discuss that."

"Why are you here?"

"There is a master who lives in the shadow of the Earth moon. We need you to find him and destroy him. He lives in the Peaceful Valley."

Hades snorted. "A stupid name for that place."

"What is so special about this master?" Drakon asked.

"He is the one who initiated you into your powers, but he has...changed. We believe Athena has been working with him. We need him destroyed and you need to do it. In fact, you're the only one who can."

"Because he is my father?"

Ares laughed. "You always were the smart one. Sometimes a bit too smart, but we can work with that."

"And when do you want me to kill him?"

"The sooner the better. But a word of warning, do not listen to him. If you do, he will destroy you. He is powerful. He has survived this long for a reason and now he appears to have Athena's protection."

Hades touched Ares' shoulder. "We have to go, Ares."

Ares nodded.

"And how do I get there?" Drakon asked.

"The same way you did when you activated your powers."

A loud clap of thunder forced Drakon to cover his ears. Then Ares and Hades were gone.

Why is it so important I don't talk to him? What is it about him that puts fear into the hearts of gods like Ares?

Drakon calmed his pets, then left his war room and headed for his chambers. It was time to put his plan into action and to even the odds following Laela's meeting with Sascha.

When he reached his chambers, he entered his bathroom. The bathroom door closed behind him and the room filled with visions of the histories of the ancients. Drakon stepped down into the warm bath.

"Sascha, destiny has given instruction. It's time for us to meet."

SASCHA STARED at the sheer face of black rock beyond the pergola. She recognized that tall shadow with its beady red eyes. Her skin tingled. It was a friend. She was sure of it.

Sascha searched the area for Soleil. He sat on the edge of the pergola, where he guarded George as she slept. Sascha walked over to join him. "Soleil, did you see the strange creature on top of the cliff?"

"What?"

Sascha pointed. "Over there. A few minutes ago."

"No, I didn't see anything." Soleil scanned the cliff top. "What creature?"

"It looked like a spindly ape, but it was made of mist. And it had these glowing red eyes and large red talons—"

"Sascha, we need to tell Owain and Connell. What you're describing is a gibleree." Soleil ruffled his feathers. "They're vile. And if it appeared here, someone in the castle must have summoned it."

"What, but I..." For a couple of seconds, Sascha forgot to breathe.

If giblerees were so evil, then how come I thought it was a friend?

Soleil stood and spread his wings. "Sascha, you must tell them. Now."

"In a minute, Soleil," Sascha snapped. "I need a minute before facing them again."

Soleil clicked his beak. "Females!"

Sascha walked to the edge of the ocean, took off her shoes and ambled along the water's edge. The wet sand massaged the soles of her feet. She flexed her neck to ease the building tension in her shoulders. Her mind drifted back to her conversation with Owain and Connell. And the shadow creature that she thought was a friend.

Who was I? What was I like?

The idea of becoming *that* person again, the one everyone seemed to be afraid of, seemed to hate, made her shiver. Sascha couldn't become *her* again.

You might not even be able to get your memory back.

The thought came from nowhere. Sascha stopped walking.

Of course. Why am I worrying about something that might never happen? They can want it as much as they like, but it doesn't mean it will happen.

A flicker of hope sparked.

She looked over at the pergola. Connell and Owain were still in a huddle, whispering animatedly.

Her stomach churned as she watched them. She couldn't put this off any longer. Her footsteps squeaked in the warm white sands as she dragged herself back to join them. She was struggling to know how to react to everything she had found out since she had arrived.

I could pretend none of this happened and find a way back to Earth. Or return to my chambers, crawl into bed and die quietly under the covers. But the girls, what would happen to them?

A blood curdling scream echoed around the beach. Sascha froze.

George and Soleil lifted their heads and listened for the source of the sound. The scream sounded again, and they both sprinted toward the cave.

"Crudouraks," Soleil called out. "Someone has woken the crudouraks."

Her blood ran cold. Maybe it was the gibleree. What sound does a gibleree make? Sascha hurried after George and Soleil.

Footsteps sounded behind her. She glanced back to see Owain sprinting toward the cave, followed by Connell, who was hobbling to catch up.

A body fell out of the maw of the cave and scrambled toward the cliff face. "Sascha," the body cried out. "Help me."

Sascha stopped mid-stride.

That voice!

The air filled with George's thunderous roar and Soleil's high-pitched screeches as they cornered the figure, trapping it against the cliff face. For a moment, bright purple eyes glinted in the maw of the cave.

"Sascha! Help!" the body called again.

She moved closer. The figure winced as it stood, brushed sand and dirt off the white shirt and khaki pants it was wearing, hesitated and then turned toward her. "Hello, Sascha."

"Ken?" Her mouth dropped open as her hand reached for her necklace, "How did you—"

"You know him?" Owain asked.

"Yes, it's Ken. A friend," Sascha answered.

Connell called out. "George, here!"

George took a single step backward, a deep rumble echoing in her chest.

"George! Now!" She backed away from Ken and moved to stand guard in front of Connell, her tail swishing dangerously in the air.

Soleil flew toward Sascha, deliberately gliding in low over

Ken's head and causing him to duck. Soleil chuckled and landed next to Sascha, where he stood guard, his full focus on Ken.

"I'm sorry, Sascha." Ken grimaced in pain as he tried to bow before Connell and Owain. "I apologize for the intrusion, My King. My Prince."

The air buzzed around her, and the hairs on her arms stood on edge. She looked to her side to see Connell standing there. A white ball of electricity glowed in his palm. Sascha shook her head. This was all so surreal.

Owain stood with his dagger drawn, glaring at Ken. "How did a *friend* of yours get in here?"

"How did you get in here, Ken?" Sascha asked. "The barrier should have stopped you."

"I snuck in as Drakon left. I've been here with him before and the mirror recognized me from then."

"He's lying," Owain snarled. "Drakon hasn't been here."

"He was, My King. I swear it on my life. He left a few minutes ago and—"

"You know Drakon?" Sascha asked. Her head started to spin. "And you know Connell and Owain?"

"Yes. Pat and I are from here. We used to work for Drakon."

"You and Pat used to work for Drakon? Doing what?"

Ken started to fidget. His gaze bounced around the beach.

"What are you hiding, Ken?" Sascha asked, not sure she wanted to know the answer.

"We were sent to Earth to watch you and report on what you were doing."

"You were sent to *watch* me?"

Ken flicked a glance at Connell and Owain. "I didn't know you in the beginning. We were doing as we were instructed to do. As we became friends, I slowly stopped reporting. I was hoping he had lost interest in you."

"No!" Sascha shook her head. "This can't be true. You were spies? You have been spying on me all this time and were just pretending to be my friend?" She stared at him, her mind numb. Sascha saw his mouth moving. He was saying something, but she couldn't hear him.

"First Connell, then Marco and now you, Ken?" Sascha backed away from him and stumbled toward the ocean. She dropped onto a little boulder near the crashing waves. Squeaking sand told her they had followed her. Soleil came up to her and rested his head on her hands as they sat uselessly in her lap. He felt warm, reassuring. Sascha's eyes stung. Love for Soleil flooded through her as she stroked his warm feathers. "I've no idea how I could have left you," Sascha croaked.

"You had to. You had no choice," Soleil replied.

Ken lowered himself onto the sand next to her. "I'm sorry, Sascha."

Sascha spun toward him. "I trusted you, Ken. You were my rock."

Tears glistened on Ken's dusty face. "I still am. I will do whatever I need to do to protect you."

"Ask him how his back is," Soleil whispered.

"His back?"

"I clawed him when I took your necklace back. I thought I had killed him. He must be sore."

"Was it you who attacked me?" Sascha asked. "Is that how you got here?"

"Yes."

"So much for him being your friend," Connell said.

Sascha glared at Connell. He sat on the sand next to Owain, his back to the ocean. He and Owain were watching the interaction between her and Ken. "This is my fight, Connell. Ken, you hurt me. What were you trying to do?"

"I didn't mean to hit you hard. You moved back too quickly."

"So now it's my fault?" Sascha put her head in her hands. "I'm going to wake up and find out this is only a nightmare."

"Sorry, I didn't mean it was your fault."

She sat back. "Why did you take my necklace?"

"I had to take it. Pat was watching."

"What do you mean? You're not making any sense."

"Drakon came to see us two days ago," Ken replied. "I realized then that he hadn't lost interest in you. When Drakon asked us for help Pat was only too willing to oblige." Ken stopped talking and looked down at his hands. "I thought we were free of him and that Pat would stay with me."

"But you two are married," Sascha said. "Why wouldn't she stay?"

"We're not married. We only pretended to be married to carry out our job, but I really do love her. What Drakon doesn't know, is that she is in love with him and not me. Anyway, when you showed her the necklace she knew someone had been in touch with you, someone from Eratus. That was the only way you could have had Soleil's necklace. When she saw the artifact on your table, she believed the Sisters were behind everything."

"Artifact? You mean the pen?"

"Yes," Ken answered. "The Sisters are the only ones who could have sent it to you, which meant they needed you back on Eratus. When Pat saw Marco and Eham, she knew they were there to give you a keystone. Pat was determined to steal the necklace and the keystone back. She planned to tell Drakon what she knew when he returned. I had to stop her."

"Why did she want to wait for Drakon?" Sascha asked. "She had the keystone, so she could have used the portal."

"The portal nearly killed her last time she used it. I tried to persuade her to let me sort it out, but she didn't believe I would betray you."

"But Pat could betray me?"

"Pat would betray anyone for Drakon," Ken said. "I had to agree to steal the necklace and keystone. She hid behind the air-conditioning unit on the rooftop and watched me. I had no choice. My instructions were to tell Drakon everything when I arrived."

"Did you...did you update Drakon?" Sascha stammered.

"No. I am only interested in saving you."

"Saving me from what?"

"Drakon."

Owain jumped up, glowering at Ken. "What a ridiculous thing to say. It was Drakon who saved Sascha. He showed me how I could obey the intent of the law and not kill Sascha. He loves his sister."

"With respect, My King, there is a lot you don't know about your son," Ken said. "And he doesn't want to *kill* Sascha. He wants to resurrect the Four Sisters, but under his control, not yours." Ken struggled to his feet. "And he wants you to lead them, Sascha."

"As I said, ridiculous." Owain slapped the sand from his pants. "I hope you have something more substantial to offer Sascha than lies and gossip. We will continue this conversation over dinner tonight."

"I must leave soon." Ken rubbed the back of his neck before shoving his hands in his pockets. "Before Drakon knows I'm here. The longer I'm here, the greater chance there is that he will see me. But I need to talk to Sascha first."

"Not now. Over dinner tonight," Owain said. "I have a meeting to attend and I won't have you talking to Sascha when I'm not here."

"I think I am old enough to decide who I do or don't talk to," Sascha said through gritted teeth.

Owain pulled himself to his full height, thrust out his chest and raised his chin. "I know you can do what you like when you're on Earth, Sascha, but I am the High King of Eratus. What I say is how it will be. Ken, leave now and take the dungeon entrance to my chambers. You can make it to the dining hall from there without anyone seeing you. I assume you remember where it is?"

Ken winced. "Yes, My King."

"And, Ken, one more thing," Owain said. "How did you awaken the creatures in the cave?"

Ken cleared his throat. "I hid in the bushes in the cave. I was worried about seeing Sascha, afraid of what she would say." He peeked over at Sascha before continuing. "I didn't see the little bird eating on the grass near the water's edge, and when I built up enough courage to leave the cave, I stepped on it, killing it. The cave erupted and I took off."

"You were fortunate to escape," Owain said. "Try not to kill anything when you leave. I'm not sure you would be so lucky a second time."

Ken bowed and then stepped into the cave mouth.

"Will he be able to pass through that barrier easily," Sascha asked "or should someone go with him?"

"The barrier is meant to stop people entering, not to stop them from leaving." Owain walked toward the ocean and watched as the waves washed up close to his sandals. Presently, he glanced at Sascha before walking toward the cave. "You both need rest," he called out as he entered the darkness of the cave. "Do not stay on the beach too long."

CONNELL AND SASCHA sat in silence. George and Soleil moved back to the pergola, but continued to watch them. They didn't move until the first sun started to set, casting a jade-colored shadow over the beach.

Connell grabbed his cane and levered himself upright. "As Father said, we should get some rest before dinner, Sascha."

"Yes." Sascha refused to look in his direction. She knew she was being childish, but, for once, she didn't care.

"Do you want me to show you back to your chambers?"

"No, I can make my own way," Sascha said. "Soleil will help me if I get lost."

Sascha heard Connell turn to walk away.

A deep, smoky voice echoed from the cave. "So this is where you have been hiding, little brother."

When Sascha twisted around to see who the voice belonged to, her mouth fell open. He was gorgeous. Tall with dark hair and the bluest eyes Sascha had ever seen. He wore a cobalt blue shirt that matched the color of his eyes. The top two buttons of the shirt were open, hinting at a tanned and well-maintained physique. His pants were white and loose-fitting and his sandals made of tan leather. Sascha stood.

"Sascha, you have grown into your beauty." The man's gaze lingered on her a little longer than she felt comfortable with.

George and Soleil raced toward her, George growling and Soleil hissing. Sascha stared at Soleil. She had never heard him hiss before.

"Drakon," Connell said.

Drakon nodded his head in acknowledgment. "Hello, Connell. You must have been busy to have persuaded Sascha to return to Eratus already." Drakon glanced at her. "And the girls, did you bring them?"

"How do you know about the girls?" Sascha asked.

He moved close to her with an elegant speed. His eyes held hers. "I know everything, Sascha." He tried to circle around her, sizing her up, but each time he moved, she matched his move.

"Damn it, girl, can you not stand still?"

"I can when I choose, but not when I am being assessed like a prized cow."

He laughed. "I would never describe you as a cow."

He was a powerful man and Sascha felt her heart start to beat faster and her skin begin to tingle in response to his presence. He stepped closer and lifted her chin in his hand. "You and I should become reacquainted, Sascha."

Connell hobbled up and slapped Drakon's hand away. "Leave her alone."

"Connell—" Sascha gritted her teeth.

"I know. You can fight your own battles. But the old Sascha would never have let Drakon treat her like that."

Drakon snapped around and faced Connell. "You didn't know everything about your sister. She had secrets. Don't make assumptions about what she would or would not let happen."

"Our sister," Connell corrected.

"No, your sister," Drakon answered. He faced Sascha and trailed his finger down the side of her face. "Sascha, I'm sure Connell - and others - will tell you how bad I am. It's up to you, but try to challenge what they say. I'm afraid they don't like me much."

He was so close that Sascha could feel his warm breath on her face and smell his aftershave of citrus and orange blossom.

"Don't trust them," he whispered. "They have many secrets to hide. I, on the other hand, am an open book."

Connell snorted. "An open book. Right. You won't get what you want this time, Drakon. Not this time."

Drakon smirked. "I had better go. I don't want to outstay my welcome."

Sascha watched as Drakon walked toward the cave. This man was dangerous, but Sascha felt the pull, the attraction. Her eyes followed him. By this time, Laela had arrived back on the beach. Drakon called out to her and she stopped mid-stride as she stared open-mouthed at him.

"It's nice to see you again, Laela. And no worse off for the disastrous experience during the healing ceremony. Mysterious." His laughter echoed in the cave as he continued back toward the castle.

When Laela arrived to join Sascha, she was furious.

"Where the hell did he come from?" she snapped. "I thought he was on Earth, or away, or something. He knows I'm alive. We must be careful. He is going to escalate his plans now."

CHAPTER 18

ERATUS

"I'm leaving," Connell said a few minutes after Drakon left. "Laela, will you walk Sascha back to her chambers? She doesn't want me around her at the moment."

"I will walk myself back," Sascha said. "Connell, what are the secrets that Drakon is talking about?"

"Drakon believes you will hate us when you get your memory back. He believes the only one you trusted when you left was him. He's wrong!" Connell slammed his cane onto the soft sands.

"If that's what he was talking about, then it's a strange way to say it," Sascha said. "Why would I hate you? There must be more to it."

"There is nothing more to it. Drakon is trying to stir up trouble."

"He may be. But he can't cause trouble unless there's something to cause trouble about."

Connell threw his hands up in the air. "Sascha, you can't believe him. He lies. He hated you, has always hated you."

Laela moved toward Connell. "I doubt Sascha wants to hear all of that now."

"She asked. But it's true, you know it's true," Connell said. "We used to joke about Drakon's hate for you, not your hate for us. You used to say he was jealous of your power, but that his hate could never beat us while we stayed as closely bonded as we were. Now look at us. You look at me through the eyes of a stranger. I have no sister anymore."

"Connell, don't let Drakon win," Laela said softly.

Sascha stayed silent, struggling to breathe, a band tightening around her chest. She was at the mercy of these people with no idea of the truth. "How do I know I can trust any of you?" Sascha said. "You all terrify me. Connell is right. I do look at you all as strangers. I don't know you. Everything I've found out since I arrived has shown who I can't trust, not who I can."

Sascha walked to the edge of the cave and looked in with unseeing eyes. "But I will learn the rules of whatever game it is you are playing. And when I do..." Sascha let the threat hang in the air.

"I'll come with you," Soleil said.

"No," Sascha answered, "stay with George. I need time to myself."

Soleil fell quiet, stung by her sharp words.

"I'm sorry, Soleil. No-one is who they seem. Even someone I thought of as my rock, someone I thought I could trust, wasn't who I thought he was. And trying to deal with who I was and the damage I seem to have caused..." Sascha took a breath.

"I will follow you to keep you safe, but I won't talk to you," Soleil said.

Her eyes pricked with tears. "OK, but you must give me space."

"Sascha, you shouldn't walk off alone," Connell said.

"I'm not alone," Sascha replied. "I have Soleil."

~

CONNELL STARED at Laela as she stepped ahead of Sascha and disappeared into the cave. Drakon's comment about Laela had left him feeling unsettled. It was a mystery that Laela disguised her injuries with magic. He wouldn't have realized she had been hurt either until she showed him. Why did she disguise them? He would have to ask her.

Connell followed Sascha out of the cave and into the castle gardens. He walked a distance behind, giving her the space she needed, but still keeping an eye on her. He smacked his walking cane onto the ground. It was stupid of him to think he could protect her. He wouldn't be able to do much if she was attacked, but he did still have some magic.

"In the shadows let it be, a ball of power for all to see."

A small ball of electricity floated in his open hand. He flicked it up in the air and let it follow him.

He kept going over his last conversation with Sascha. The secrets - he should have said something, but where would he start? What should he tell her about Marco and about Kira? Owain had said it was better to wait until she got her memory back. But was it? Maybe they should tell her everything. He sighed and shook his head. "I don't know. I honestly don't know the right way to do this," he muttered.

He looked up and saw Soleil circling in the air, watching Sascha as she wandered ahead, lost in the millions of thoughts that must be torturing her. It must be terrifying. Few things in their life were simple. And nothing in hers was, that's for sure.

He heard the whistles of the other pyrans as they called to Soleil and heard him whistle back in answer. George galumphed ahead of Connell, chasing the furry little hurlies that played in the bushes.

Connell's gaze drifted back to Sascha. She had been a brunette the last time she walked in these gardens and now she was blond. It certainly suited her, but he wished she had stayed a brunette. It would have made her seem more like the old Sascha, but did he want the old Sascha back?

They needed to know, to understand what had happened on that last day. They had to convince her to try to get her memory back. He knew it was selfish and that he might regret not leaving her be. But nothing could be worse than what he imagined, could it?

The creatures in the garden had gone quiet. Connell glanced around. Even the hurlies George had been playing with had disappeared.

It was then the magic ball above him spat, sizzled and shot off toward the trees. George roared and raced off after it.

Sascha sensed Soleil above her, and although she didn't want to talk, she did feel more comfortable knowing someone was watching over her.

"Careful, Sascha," he said, "you're being followed."

"I thought you weren't going to talk to me, Soleil. Anyway, I heard Connell walking behind me. He's hardly quiet and neither is George."

"It's not them I mean." A few seconds later, Soleil screamed. "Look out!"

A heavy hit to her shoulder knocked her down to the ground.

"What the—" Sascha sat up and searched for whatever it was that had hit her, but she couldn't see anything. A hit from the opposite direction slammed her back onto the ground. Sascha heard Soleil scream and George roar.

Whatever it was landed on her, pinning her to the ground. Sascha could feel its weight on top of her, but she couldn't see it. Its hot putrid breath covered her face. Something wet dripped onto her neck and shoulders. Sascha closed her eyes tightly and put her arms up to protect her face. Razor-sharp teeth bit hard and deep into her arms. They held on and shook hard. Sascha forced herself to ignore the pain as she tried to work out what to do. The thing was heavy and her arms weren't strong enough to hold it away for much longer. Something thumped into her side, and the teeth were ripped from her arms. George roared and darted in toward a shimmer that lay on the ground next to her. She bit at it, shook her head and then dived away. The pitch of the creature's screams vibrated through Sascha. Soleil flew in with his claws outstretched. The shimmer tried to avoid them, but Soleil and George were too fast.

"Sascha, move!" Connell pulled at her arms, dragging her away from the battle.

A few seconds later, Connell fell and dragged Sascha on top of him. Connell moaned.

"Connell, are you hurt?" Sascha called out.

"Don't worry about—"

A loud agonized scream echoed around the gardens.

"Soleil!" Sascha screamed. She scrambled up. She had to save Soleil.

"Sascha, Soleil's not hurt." Connell caught her leg with his cane as he tried to slow her down. "The sound you heard...Soleil and George have killed the creature. They're searching for its mate now."

"Its mate? What was it?"

Sascha leaned down and grabbed Connell by the elbow to

help him stand. It was the first time either of them noticed the blood pouring down both of her arms.

"You've been bitten." Sascha saw the color drain out of Connell's face.

"I'm fine. It's not bad," she said. The gouges on her arm were edged with green. "What is that green stuff?" Sascha started to feel giddy.

Connell stood for a moment, staring at her arms, and then hobbled over to the dead creature. Sascha followed. "A pit hound." A putrid gas filled the air as the creature sizzled and the flesh fell off its bones, leaving behind a dark glistening carcass.

"It was quick," Sascha said to Connell. "I didn't see it."

"You wouldn't have been able to see it. It's protected by an invisibility cloak, but its protection disappears once it's dead."

Owain and Laela arrived together, panting. "We heard screams," Owain said. "Is anyone hurt?"

"Sascha was attacked by a pit hound," Connell said. "It bit her on her arms."

"It what?" Laela said. "Can I have a look at your arms, Sascha?"

The ground started to move beneath Sascha. She leaned on Laela as she closed her eyes to get her balance back.

"Sascha?" Laela said.

"I'm fine. A little dizzy, that's all." Sascha opened her eyes and looked at Laela. "The attack was a shock."

"Of course it was," Laela said. "She needs treatment, Owain, and quickly, before the poison settles in her system."

"I will take her to the healer's room," Owain said. "You can treat her there. Laela, get your medicine."

"We will need more than medicine," Laela said.

"Get whatever you need," he commanded. "Now!"

Owain leaned over to pick Sascha up.

"What? I'm not being carried," Sascha said as she backed away from Owain. "I can walk. I'm not incapacitated."

"I am carrying you. That creature was poisonous. Walking will circulate the poison." A second later, Sascha was in Owain's arms as he strode toward the castle, Connell in tow.

"Soleil," Sascha said in panic, "where's Soleil? And George?"

As if in answer to her question, they both raced out of the bushes toward them.

"We didn't find anything," Soleil said.

"That's good then," Sascha asked. "Isn't it?" She twisted toward Connell. "Soleil said they couldn't find another pit hound. That's a good thing, isn't it?"

"Unfortunately, no," Connell said. "They usually travel in pairs. Its mate must be around here somewhere." He glanced at the trees around them.

"We will have to take extra precautions until we find it," Owain said.

"Why is Owain carrying you, Sascha?" Soleil asked.

"He's being ridiculous. I can walk, Owain. Please put me down. This is most embarrassing."

Owain continued to walk in silence.

"Humor Owain," Connell said. "It's important you don't spread the poison."

"Why? What sort of poison is it?" Sascha asked.

Silence.

"Connell? What sort of poison is it?"

"We are treating you, so everything will be fine."

"But?" Sascha said.

"If we did not treat you, you would be, um, changed."

"Changed?"

"Into a creature that destroys everything it's commanded to destroy."

An icy chill raced through her, but Sascha laughed. "I'm not that gullible. Commanded to destroy? What do you mean?"

"Whatever created the creature commands the spawn it produces. It's a dark magic, an evil we haven't seen for nearly five years. We thought it had gone."

Her stomach lurched.

Could it be connected to...

"Sascha, did you tell them about the gibleree?" Soleil said, as if he had read her thoughts.

"No, I—"

"You must tell them."

Sascha coughed. "When we were on the beach, I saw a creature scramble up the cliff to the top and then it stood and looked down at me."

Owain stopped. "What sort of creature?"

"Soleil told me it was a gibleree. He said I should tell you."

"Are you sure?" Owain snapped. "Why didn't you tell us this before?"

"How was I supposed to know it was important?" Sascha snapped. "And anyway, I didn't get a chance. It was before Ken arrived and I...I wasn't going to mention it."

"At least the damn bird has some sense," Owain said.

"What do you mean?" Sascha said as she squirmed in his arms. A thought occurred to her. "Connell, exactly how many years has it been since you saw this sort of dark magic?"

Connell stopped walking. "It's been..." He stared at Sascha as she continued to bounce in Owain's arms. He shook his head.

"What, Connell? What is it?"

"It was a coincidence," he said.

"Connell, please. I need to know."

"Not since you left," he replied.

Her stomach dropped. Why would a pit hound attack her, but that creature, the gibleree, not? If they were both made from dark magic, what was the difference between the two? And how was she connected to dark magic?

"Sweet souls and angels. What are either of those creatures doing in the castle?" Owain said.

"The gibleree couldn't have been watching us for long because George and Soleil would have sensed it." Connell tried to keep up with Owain's large strides.

"But, Connell, both sensed the pit hound the moment it appeared, but not the gibleree," Owain said. "Sascha, did Soleil sense it? I know George didn't."

"No, he didn't," Sascha answered. "That's strange, isn't it?"

"Maybe a pit hound requires a more powerful dark magic to create it," Connell said. "I wonder if it was created to kill Sascha?"

"Kill me? Why? Won't I be doing something good when I help to heal the Shield?"

"You are," Connell said, "but there is a religious group, fanatics, who think the Shield was created to lock them here, keep them away from Earth. The place they want to call home."

"But they can use the transporter, can't they?"

"It's not that easy to use. What Ken said about the portal nearly killing Pat isn't unusual," Connell said. "And it can only take a couple of people at a time...if they survive the guardians."

"The guardians?"

"Grotesque creatures that guard the portals." Connell stopped walking. "We're here."

"I've made up a bed for her to lie on while I treat her." Laela was standing in the healer's room. "If you could leave us, give Sascha some privacy."

"Once you have been treated, Sascha" Owain said, "have

some rest. We will all meet in my chambers before dinner and before Ken joins us. Ciara will let you know when it is time for you to meet us."

"Father," Connell said, "Laela and I need to talk to you about some information we have found. It might help to explain where these dark creatures came from."

"They came from dark magic. But who in the castle would have access to that amount of dark power? That is my concern." Owain turned and walked away.

CHAPTER 19

ERATUS

onnell climbed the stone staircase to his father's chambers with George racing ahead of him.

"No-one likes a show off, George," Connell said as he hobbled up one stair at a time. This morning had taken its toll and everything hurt. When Sascha had fallen on him, it had opened the burns, causing them to bleed. The healer had torn strips off him for being careless.

He finally arrived at the top of the stairs. The stone floor was covered by several large circular mats embroidered with the kingdom's crest a winged manticore sitting underneath a canopy of gray fangs. On the far wall were four glass doors that opened onto an ornate balcony. Tall decanters of prumble ale and silkar, and plates of meat appetizers, were laid out on a glass ebony-colored outdoor table.

"C'mon, George, let's sit out on the balcony."

Connell poured himself a glass of prumble, took a sip and felt his tension begin to ease.

No-one else had arrived yet. He stood at the edge of the balcony and looked down at the castle grounds. The air was filled with the sounds of shields smashing against other shields as soldiers practiced their skills in the training camps, and the screeching of children whose mothers were gathering them for dinner before night fell. Laughter echoed from the tavern where people were enjoying a couple of silkars before going home. He never had acquired the taste for silkar and the taverns couldn't afford prumble ale.

The second sun had nearly set and the two moons were rising. The early evening, when the light from the moon mixed with the light from the setting suns, was a beautiful time of the day. During the two-moon season, the sky was filled with the colors of fire and green ice, but during the season of the third moon the colors were darker purples, dark greens and tan.

Connell shivered in the breeze, but he preferred the freshness to sitting inside near the fire. He sat on the balcony chair nearest the wall. George snuggled into him. "I love you," Connell said as he patted her. George lay down at Connell's feet with a huge sigh.

The second sun had set and still no-one had arrived. "Maybe I misheard, George. But I'm sure we agreed to meet in Father's chambers."

Then he heard soft footsteps as someone sprinted up the stairs. "Finally."

Laela landed on the final step and smiled. She had changed into a soft green and gold dress, and her hair bobbed around her shoulders. No-one would believe she had been in a fire.

"I thought I would be late," Laela said.

"No, you're not. You're the first person here. How is Sascha?"

"She's been quiet," Laela said. "Even when I applied the potion she never called out, never said anything."

"They say the treatment is like burning acid."

"I know." Laela grimaced. "But there was no reaction."

"She must be in shock," Connell said.

Laela walked to the corner of the room, where she put her hands close to the fire in the wood-burning dragon-stone fireplace. "Well, can you imagine what it would be like to be dragged here, not knowing anyone, and then have to face everything she has faced so far?"

"True," Connell answered. "Did Sascha tell you about the gibleree?"

"Yes, she did," Laela said. "I told her it must be connected to the pit hound and then she went quiet."

"Like us, she must be trying to work it all out." Connell reached over and picked up a piece of spicy meat.

Laela glanced at the pair of plush tan chairs positioned next to the fireplace. They were covered in large white furs. She walked over, picked one of the furs up and carried it with her to the balcony. Once she had poured herself a glass of Silkar, she wrapped herself tightly in the fur and sat in the chair next to Connell's.

"I didn't think it was that cold, Laela," Connell said.

"You never feel the cold, Connell." She took a sip of the silkar. "What do you think Owain will say when we tell him about the darkness?"

"Not sure," Connell replied. "Father did say he was more interested in who possessed the dark power required to create those creatures."

"Only one person we are aware of," Laela said. "Drakon."

"Unless, of course, we throw Reya in the mix."

"She is powerful," Laela admitted. "And if Sascha hadn't been sent away—"

"I know. We would have to consider her too."

Connell heard slow labored steps as someone else climbed the stairs. "Sascha," he acknowledged when she reached the top of the stairs. "Those stairs are tough to manage when you are recovering from an injury, aren't they?"

"I'll be fine in a day or two," Sascha answered. She had changed into darker colors the same sort of shades she wore when on Earth.

"How are you feeling?" Connell asked.

"I'm fine," she answered. "Let's get this over with. I need to get back home to my girls."

Connell's shoulders sagged. It was hard to see her acting as if she was alone. But perhaps she was.

Sascha walked up to George, squatted down in front of her and gave her a big hug. "Thank you, George. You and Soleil saved my life." George nuzzled into her shoulder and then licked her on the cheek with a long, wet, rough tongue. When Sascha smiled at George, Connell felt the tug on his heart.

She used to smile at me with that warmth. How ridiculous to be jealous of the affection a creature receives. But we used to get on so well. It's sad to see us now.

Sascha walked over to the wall next to the staircase, where there were two large arched windows that led onto a balcony overlooking the mountains. She fingered the pictures engraved onto the glass scenes from within the cave that led to Ocean's Mouth.

Sascha walked over to join him and Laela.

"Would you like a glass of silkar or prumble ale?" Laela offered.

"The same drink I had on the beach, whatever that was. Thank you, Laela."

"That was prumble ale," Connell said to Laela.

As Laela handed Sascha her drink, Soleil landed on the balcony railing and then trotted along to perch close to Sascha. Sascha smiled at him. Connell tried hard to ignore the sadness that sliced at him. This had once been a familiar scene. Sascha and Soleil sitting with him while they waited for Owain to arrive. They would often joke with each other, but now they sat in silence.

Heavy footsteps announced the arrival of Owain. His official white, gold and silver armor glittered when he stood near the light of the fire. He walked onto the balcony and poured himself a silkar. He sat down at the end of the table where he could make direct eye contact with each of them. "Sascha, how are you feeling?"

"Fine, thank you."

Owain took a sip of the wine and turned to Laela. "Was the treatment successful?"

"I believe so, but only time will tell. Sascha will be taking some additional medication for the next few days to make sure. It was lucky we were able to treat her straight away."

Owain looked at Connell and Laela. "What is it that you believe explains the appearance of this dark magic?"

"Father, Laela and I have been reading some of the Chronicles owned by the Four Sisters. They were locked away in their library. That additional power I discussed with you the power that helped us in the healing ceremony..."

"Yes?" Owain prompted.

"The power was introduced by an inexperienced mage," Connell continued. "It was unfortunate that her lack of experience caused the massive fire storm."

"Unfortunate?" Owain said. "Interesting word to use."

Connell fidgeted with his glass of prumble. "Anyway, it was her lack of experience that made her the perfect target for a dark power that wanted to enter the healing ceremony. It used the mage as a conduit into the healing process. The dark power became part of the healing process and is now in the Shield. It is killing the energy that forms the Shield and causing the unusual white marks in the sky."

"What sort of dark power?" Owain asked.

"The power of the ancients, the necromancers that used to rule over us centuries ago," Connell answered.

"What?" Owain stared at Connell. "Is that even possible? Their prisons are guarded by strong magic."

"We didn't think it was possible in the beginning," Connell said. "But the Chronicles of the Four Sisters recorded events before the ancients came to power last time. These events were signs of their growing power, signs which the rulers at the time ignored."

"Give me an example," Owain said.

Connell glanced at Laela. "It started with the appearance of giblerees and pit hounds. It was documented that the only ones who were powerful enough to create these creatures were the servants of the ancients."

Sascha gasped, and the noise made everyone jump.

"Are you feeling alright, Sascha?" Laela said, getting to her feet, ready to help Sascha if needed. "Are you in pain?"

"I am fine," she said, waving Laela away.

Laela sat back down, but kept her eyes on Sascha.

"The rulers ignored the signs. They believed they were only isolated incidents caused by a few powerful dark mages," Connell continued. "But it wasn't. It was the beginning."

"The beginning?" Owain asked.

"The more dark creatures that were created, the more people that were attacked. The ones that were attacked and weren't treated..."

"I understand," Owain answered.

"I asked my soldiers to scout out and report back on any other sightings of these creatures," Connell said. "Appearances are restricted to the regions surrounding the prison where the ancients and their weapons are locked away...and now here."

Owain finished his ale. "But the prisons are fathoms

beneath our surface. How could they escape? And how are they appearing in the castle grounds?"

"The only way they could appear here is if we have something that connects back to the ancients or their weapons." Connell ate one of the sweet rolls. "But there is one more thing, Father."

"Of course, always one more thing," Owain said.

"The magical prisons were linked into the energy in the Shield. Each time the Shield was renewed, so was the magic that sealed the prisons. The Chronicles state that it was this link that would keep Eratus safe. Nobody thought someone would be foolish enough to destroy the Shield, because it was the Shield that protected the life on the planet. The Chronicles said the only way to open the ancient chambers was to destroy the energy of the Shield."

"But?" Owain asked.

"They made one major miscalculation. The Shield doesn't need to be destroyed, it only needs to be changed. By changing the Shield, the prison walls become weaker and the ancients can escape."

"But the darkness was locked away before the ceremony when the Shield was still strong," Owain said. "How could it have been a part of the ceremony?"

"Drakon found the prison on Eratus last year," Connell replied. "And he tried to open it. We believe there is a connection."

"Again, Drakon," Owain growled. "Who doesn't hate Drakon? Why would he bother opening the prison?"

"It is possible he wants to get his hands on their weapons." Connell said, looking down into his drink.

"He is going to be ruler of Eratus," Owain said. "Why would he bother with these weapons?"

"We don't know, Father. But there is a lot we still need to find out. We may be wrong."

"You must be wrong, Connell. It doesn't make sense."

"We need your permission to access the libraries of the Four Sisters, as well as the libraries of the Fire of the Phoenix," Connell said. "There must be something that shows what we are dealing with. If we can find it, we will find a way to stop whatever is happening." Connell turned to Sascha. "Or to be more accurate, we will find a way for Sascha and the girls to stop whatever is happening."

The sound of the flickering fire echoed in the silence.

"I need to think." Owain slammed his cup down onto the table. "I need to work this through. Time for dinner." Owain stood and walked to top of the stairs. "Ken will be waiting. Connell, use the cone, and take Sascha with you." Everyone sat still as they listened to the sound of Owain's footsteps echo down the stairs.

"Everyone move. Now!" Owain yelled, his voice as loud and powerful as if he still stood in front of them

*C*onnell wasn't happy with her. He had hobbled away in a huff when Sascha had refused to use the cone and go with him to dinner. She needed to walk, to digest what had been said in Owain's chambers. Her stomach knotted. She was not a servant of the ancients.

But how could I have a connection to a gibleree if I'm not somehow linked to them? Was this one of the complications that Soleil spoke about? It couldn't be, or he would have said something on the beach.

Sascha growled at herself and shook her head. So many questions. She needed to talk to Soleil.

She arrived at the dining hall and pushed open the large carved doors. Tall gleaming statues of manticores and dragons edged the long narrow hall. Burning torches were mounted on the walls, casting a soft, glowing light on the table. Guards stood silently in the shadows. The scent of honey filled the room. She stepped in, and as the doors banged shut, everyone swiveled toward her. Owain sat in an ornate gold and silver chair at the head of the table, drumming his fingers. Connell and Laela sat on either side of him and Ken sat next to Connell.

"Sascha," Owain said, "when I give directions, I expect for them to be obeyed. Do you understand me?"

Sascha raised her chin and stood straighter. "When you are talking about the laws of your land, I will comply. When you are trying to boss me around for the sake of it, I won't."

"For the sake of it," Owain spluttered.

"Yes."

"You were injured," Owain grumbled. "You should have used the cone. Your attitude to authority hasn't changed, but it should."

Sascha slid into the chair next to Laela. After several minutes of awkward silence, servants entered the room and served an odd yellow-colored soup. The smell was tantalizing, but Sascha didn't recognize whatever was in it. She debated whether she was brave enough to eat it. Everyone else seemed to be enjoying the soup, so she picked up her spoon and took a mouthful. They were right it was delicious but Sascha still decided against asking what it was.

"Ken," Owain said. "You have one hour before Drakon joins us."

Ken coughed. "Sascha, I wanted to tell you everything the night you came over for dinner. I knew Drakon's visit meant everything was going to change. But then I saw the necklace. I knew then that I wanted to - needed to - protect you."

"From Drakon?" Sascha asked.

"Yes. And I know how to do that."

Owain's chair flew backwards as he stood from the table and his ale crashed to the floor as he reached toward Ken. "I will only say this one more time stop spitting out these lies about my son."

Ken gulped and turned to face Owain, "I know you believe he saved her, but he saved her for a reason. He has the map showing where the weapons are hidden and he needs Sascha's help to unlock the magic that protects them."

"I've had enough of this," Owain snapped. "I will summon Drakon here and we will sort this out right now."

"No!" Laela and Connell yelled at the same time.

"You can't do that, Father," Connell pleaded. "You may not believe Ken, but there is some truth to what he is saying. At least give us the opportunity to find out more before you say anything."

"Connell, this fixation must stop. One day I will step down from my role as High King and I cannot have you two tearing this land apart with your hatred for each other."

"Please, Father. Give us time. If we're wrong, I will do whatever you ask of me."

Owain grunted and dropped back into his chair as the servants skittered around the table, tidying up the mess from the spilt ale and refilling his cup. "You are wrong, Connell, so remember what you just promised."

"So how can you protect the girls and me?" Sascha asked.

"His army the Awakening are preparing to capture you and the girls when you transport back here through the portal."

"How can he plan for it?" Sascha said. "I have no idea when I will be returning, so I don't see how he can know."

"He will have someone following you," Ken said.

Sascha fidgeted with the drink in her hand as she studied each person at the table in turn. "Ken, why should I trust you?"

"I need you to trust me." Ken twisted toward Connell. "An additional power joined the healing ceremony, didn't it?"

"That's old news," Connell replied.

"Early this morning I found the young mage responsible for the power and she told me what happened. She tried to save you from the fires, Connell, instead of doing what she was ordered to do. She was...punished. Dra—" Ken glanced over at Owain. "Her attackers left her for dead. She was still alive, but her body was mutilated. She had been attacked by fire dragons. She begged me to put her out of her misery, to kill her."

"You obviously think Drakon did that too," Owain said. "Where is she? Where's the proof?"

"I was interrupted," Ken said. "I hid in an alcove at the corner of the training square. When I went back to get her, she was gone."

"Convenient," Owain said. "So this could all be lies."

"With respect, My King, I swear that I'm not lying. Can I continue?"

Owain flicked his hand at Ken. "Make it fast."

"When I spoke to her," Ken continued, "she was too terrified to tell me much. But there was one thing she did tell me. She had been instructed to use her magic during the ceremony to set up a link to a second portal a bigger one that links back to Earth. When she was being punished, she was asked if the connection to the second portal worked. She lied and told them it didn't. But it does. And she told me why they needed it."

"What was the second portal for?" Owain asked.

"Drakon needed a portal big enough to transport a small army to Earth, to the site where the ancient weapon is locked away."

"All they would need to do is go to the second portal and test it," Owain said. "Then they would know the mage lied."

"But they need to know how to operate it first. Each portal is different. If Sascha leaves tonight, gets the girls and returns through the second portal..."

"That's not much time," Sascha said.

"Drakon's army will be waiting at the first portal," Ken replied. "We have time, but I don't know how long."

The aroma of hot meats and savory stews floated around the servants as they placed large plates on the table and then left.

While the others helped themselves to the food, Sascha continued to sip her ale.

"Sascha," Connell said as he lifted a forkful of food to his mouth, "I know you were given the necklace and the artifact, but did you ever see a copy of this map that we're all talking about?"

"I was sent a map," Sascha answered. "But I lost it."

"The vision was true," Laela stammered. "But how could you lose it?"

"I don't know," Sascha said, "Why did you send it to me if it was so important?"

"We didn't," Connell answered. "Laela believes Kalurth sent it to you."

"Kalurth?"

A guard appeared beside Owain, saluted and leaned down to whisper something to him. He saluted again and then dissolved back into the darkness. "Enough!" Owain said. "Ken, Drakon has arrived. It is time for you to leave."

"Before you go, Ken," Sascha said, "would you tell us where this second portal is?"

"I have marked it on this map for you," he replied as he handed over a piece of paper. "Please be careful, Sascha."

"Soleil will come with me," Sascha replied. "He will help."

"Marco will want to help too," Connell answered.

"We will need to know more about this weapon and the map," Owain said. "You have my permission to enter the libraries and to do the research. And, Connell, I give you until Sascha and the girls return to provide me with some evidence as to why I shouldn't talk to Drakon about this."

"Yes, Father," Connell replied.

Ken stood from the table and bowed to Owain. "I must go, My King."

"Yes, go," Owain replied. "And if this is all an elaborate lie..."

"It isn't, My King. I promise." Ken turned to Sascha. "Would you mind walking me out?"

She pushed her chair back and stood.

Connell coughed. "You should ask your King's permission before you leave, Sascha."

"What?" Sascha said.

"Don't worry about it, Connell," Owain replied. "She never asked before and she's obviously not going to start now."

Sascha shrugged her shoulders. "I didn't know. Am I excused?"

Owain waved his hand in dismissal and Sascha followed Ken to the door.

"I didn't want to say this in front of Laela," Ken whispered. "There's something about her that I don't trust. I left something with our favorite distraction. If anything happens to me, please open the locket I gave her."

"Our favorite distraction? What are you talking about? Oh, you mean R—"

Ken put his hand on Sascha's arm to stop her talking. "I'm sure these walls have ears," Ken whispered. "Please, Sascha, promise me."

"Yes, I promise." Sascha sighed. "This is all so sad. I wish none of this had ever happened and that we were still friends."

"Sadly, that isn't possible," Ken said as he melted into the darkness.

∼

DRAKON'S MUSCLES ached and his feet were sore. It had been a long time since he had taken part in formal military training, but it was good to see Chiane's army in action. They were operating as a well-trained military group, and Chiane was proving to be an effective leader.

They will be ready when it's time for them to travel to Earth...once we get that second portal working.

But now it was time to join Father and his sycophants for some food and wine. At least Sascha would be there.

As Drakon approached the dining hall, he heard a soft click and turned to see Ken skulking away. Ken was here! How did he get here? Another thing his people hadn't warned him about. And the last report from Novo said Ken and Pat were still in Sydney.

"Sokentash."

What was the point in having an army if they didn't know what was happening around them? And Ken was proving to be a liability. One that he couldn't afford. It was time to get someone to remove him and Drakon knew the perfect person to do that.

CHAPTER 21

ERATUS

*S*ascha stood on the castle roof and zipped up her black leather jacket. Everything was quiet as everyone was still asleep. She stared at Soleil, deciding how this was going to work. The sun hadn't started to rise yet. Flickering torches provided the only light, their echoes reflecting on the dark clouds that hid the stars and the moons.

"Connell, how do I ride Soleil?"

"Ask me," Soleil said, turning his head toward her.

"Sorry, Soleil. How do I ride you?"

Soleil brought his head and neck down low and Sascha walked closer to him. The warmth that emanated from his body was comforting.

"I'll give you a leg up," Connell said.

"Don't be stupid. You're not well enough."

Laela stepped forward. "I'll do it."

Sascha shoved her hands in her pockets to hide the tremors. "Why are all the transports up high somewhere? What's wrong with having them on the ground?" Sascha could sense Soleil shaking. "And stop laughing at me, you damn bird."

"You will be fine," Connell said. "You've done this before and survived. You need to trust him. He will keep you safe. He wouldn't risk your life."

"Is there no other way?" she pleaded.

"No, I'm sorry, there's not. You have to do this for the girls."

Sascha took a deep breath and squashed the nerves that threatened to incapacitate her. "I guess if I'm going to die—" Soleil's soft chuckle stopped her mid-sentence. "Are you laughing at me, you...you..."

"Damn bird?" Soleil said helpfully. "You're not going to die unless, of course, you wake the guardians. It is nearly time for their feeding. We had better go now or else we will be their breakfast."

Sascha squealed as Laela grabbed her left foot and helped her climb onto Soleil's back.

"Sascha, sit still for a moment," Laela said, "and let me set the straps on Soleil's back. Press this section when you get to the other end and the straps will release. And here is the paperwork I promised you."

"Thank you."

"When you get back," Connell said, "ask Marco to take you to the library of the Fire of the Phoenix. See what you can find to help us work out what is going on here."

"Where's the Fire of the Phoenix library?" Sascha asked.

Connell glanced surreptitiously at Laela. "Marco will know. He'll tell you all about the place when he takes you there. Get the girls and make your way back here as soon as you can. We will keep an eye on the second portal and be ready to protect you if we need to. Here are the transporter keystones so you can all go through the transporter together."

Sascha swallowed her scream as Soleil's strong wing muscles moved beneath her. They flew off the edge of the wall, and the ground beneath them disappeared. She clenched her eyes shut. Her stomach and heart both seemed to be resting in her mouth. Sascha felt the straps loosen as Soleil climbed into the air. She struggled to breathe and grabbed hold of the straps as she tried to scream, but nothing came out.

Soleil spoke to her in a gentle voice. "It will go quickly. Relax and enjoy the flight."

"Enjoy," Sascha snapped back. "I hate heights, and..." She looked down without thinking. This was not good. She felt queasy, convinced she was going to fall. Then the straps tightened around her, locking her back into position.

"What happened?" she asked Soleil.

"The straps automatically go back into position. You can't fall out," Soleil answered. "The shape was defined when Laela tied the straps around you. They will keep that shape until we separate them at the other end of the journey."

"I don't feel well," Sascha complained. "Maybe we should walk."

"We don't have time," Soleil answered. "But when we get close, please don't make any noise. The sound will wake the guardians and then we'll be in trouble."

It seemed an age before Sascha heard Soleil's whisper. "Here we are. The creatures are starting to waken."

"The guardians?" Sascha held tightly onto the straps and opened her eyes slightly. She was curious to see these grotesque creatures.

They were hulky hairy creatures with fluttering manes. Their long claws and horns were yellow and their teeth bloody, as if they had recently enjoyed a feast of meat. Sascha shuddered. One of them stretched and burped.

"They are revolting," she whispered.

"I'm going to have to circle high and fly hard and fast into the portal so that we can get through before they realize we're here. You're going to have to be quiet and not make a sound, otherwise we'll be breakfast."

"I promise to be quiet," Sascha said, shutting her eyes again.

~

DRAKON ARRIVED at the portal on Fenix's back. They circled the portal first to make sure the creatures were still asleep, but they were waking. He had to move. He caught a glimpse of movement ahead of them. Soleil! Why was that creature flying to Earth? Whatever Soleil was planning to do would only interfere with Drakon's own plans for Sascha. He had to stop him.

"Fenix, force Soleil into the guardians."

The muscles in Fenix's shoulders tensed as she pulled back and started to turn away. Heat flushed through Drakon's body. She was going to disobey him again.

Drakon leaned closer to her so she could hear him. "If you disobey me, you know what I will do to your young ones, don't you, Fenix?"

His threat was rewarded when Fenix changed direction and headed for Soleil. Drakon was glad he was locked into the saddle, as he wasn't prepared for the sudden stop when Fenix pulled up short of Soleil. He was lifting his whip to punish Fenix when he heard Soleil's screams as he was thrown into the claws of the guardians. Drakon smiled when he saw the claws tearing at Soleil's underbelly. But that voice. Sascha! That was Sascha's voice. The green lyrium had changed her. She was terrified of heights. She would never have flown him.

"Pull back," he said, tugging on Fenix's neck. "Pull back, Fenix."

Drakon watched Soleil lift himself above the guardians and then fly through the portal. He saw the gashes on Soleil's chest and wings. He was badly wounded, and while Drakon hoped he wouldn't survive the damage the claws had done, he had to make sure Sascha was safe.

Drakon followed them through the portal and saw them land on the platform. It was a rough landing, but at least Sascha was safe. He flew over the scene and saw the blood on Soleil's wings. Sascha was trying to undo the straps and didn't see him. He needed to get closer. Soleil was talking to her, the wind carrying his words to Drakon.

A cave? What cave? I will have to find it.

But he had another, more important job to do first.

THE WIND BLEW BY FAST, then faster. Sascha felt the powerful beats of Soleil's wings. Suddenly, she heard a cry of terror and felt a hard thwack as something warm gushed over her.

"Soleil!" Sascha screamed as she opened her eyes. "Are you hurt?"

The creatures were close to them. Sascha could feel their hot, rancid breath on her face.

Soleil grunted as they weaved in between the guardians. He pulled back up into the air, out of the reach of their claws. Again and again, the creatures swiped at them, trying to pull them down. Soleil sailed through the portal and crashed onto the rooftop of a city building.

"I'm sorry, Soleil, so sorry." Sascha scrabbled at the straps as she tried to undo them.

Soleil was silent.

She finally got the straps undone and jumped off to look

at him. His eyes were closing. Blood covered his wings and face.

"Soleil," Sascha cried. "We need to get you some help."

"Get Marco. He knows what to do. Tell him I will see him in the cave."

"In the cave? What cave? I need to help you here. Now!"

"Until you get your magic back, Sascha, there's nothing you can do."

"I will take you wherever you need to go," Sascha pleaded. "You can't fly."

"And how do you plan to do that?" Soleil asked.

"I don't know. I..." Sascha said as she realized the impossibility of the situation. He was too big to carry. "You're not going to die. Please don't die."

"I will make it. Tell Marco. He will help."

Sascha watched as Soleil attempted to stand. When he finally got to his feet, she was able to see the full effect of the damage. Several large gashes had been torn across his chest and under his wings. "Those creatures aren't poisonous, are they?"

"Get Marco. We will talk at the cave. And it would be good if you could hurry." He flew off the top of the building and sank several meters before finding enough strength to fly off in what Sascha assumed to be the direction of the cave.

Owain carried me to stop the poison spreading. If those creatures are poisonous, every flap of Soleil's wings is spreading the poison and I can't do a thing.

CHAPTER 22

* EARTH

*D*rakon parked the Ferrari behind some trees in the bushland opposite Pat and Ken's place. With one hand draped over the steering wheel, he relaxed into the soft leather seat as he studied their house. The sun had started to rise and the street lights were flicking off. His phone buzzed.

"Ken hasn't returned home yet, Prince Drakon" the voice said.

"Good," he answered. "Once you see me go in, give me five minutes and then join me."

He hung up the phone, placed it in his jacket pocket and stepped out of the car. Drakon walked to Pat's door and knocked. The door whipped open.

"Ken, where the hell—I'm sorry, My Prince," she said as she lowered her eyes and bowed low before him. She had a towel clasped in one of her hands, as if she had just been drying them.

"Stand," Drakon said.

"Thank you, My Prince," she said. She stood and then stepped back to allow Drakon to enter the house. "It didn't occur to me that it would be you. I thought it would be Ken."

"Ken's not home then?" Drakon said.

"No, and I have no idea where he is."

"You and I need to talk, Pat."

She gulped and Drakon saw a pink flush creep up her neck and cheeks. She was small, easy to intimidate. Drakon smiled at her. "I'm assuming I can trust you?"

"Yes, My Prince."

"How much?" Drakon asked.

"What do you...what do you mean?" Pat started to fidget with the towel in her hand.

"Can I trust you?"

"Totally, My Prince. I promise."

Drakon stopped for a second and stared at her. He could see the sheen of sweat on her forehead. "Enough to get rid of Ken?"

"What do you mean, *get rid of?*" she stammered.

"Pat, Pat, Pat. You know what I mean."

"I can't *kill* Ken."

"I thought you and I had something special. I thought you were one of my soldiers, someone I could rely on." Drakon shook his head slowly. "This is sad. I was obviously wrong."

"No, you're not wrong, My Prince. I was confused. I didn't realize he had done anything wrong."

"He has betrayed me. But I was hoping you were different, that you wouldn't have let him betray me if you had known about it."

"I would never have allowed that, My Prince. But killing him..."

"He is a traitor. I can't have traitors in my army. What sort of example does that set to the rest of my men? It is hard being a leader, and I thought that you would understand, that you would want to help me."

"I do, My Prince. I truly do."

"Then I can rely on you?" Drakon asked.

"Yes, My Prince. You can."

"I realize it has been a while since you were active, so I have organized for a couple of my men to help you. But it must be done. Tonight."

"Tonight?" she said weakly.

"I will be following up tomorrow, and if I find—"

A knock sounded at the door.

"Answer it," Drakon said. "It should be the two men I have asked to help you."

Pat kept wiping her hands on the towel as she walked toward the door and opened it.

"Enter," he called out.

Two men walked in and bowed. "My Prince."

"I have explained to Pat what is expected of her, and she has said she will do whatever is necessary to help me. Isn't that right, Pat?"

"Yes, My Prince," she stammered.

"Good. You will be well-rewarded for your work. You know that, don't you? I always reward those soldiers who do me proud."

"Yes."

"Did you bring the weapon?"

"Yes," one of them said. He stepped forward and handed Drakon a dagger.

Drakon rested the handle in his hand. The poisoned dagger needed to be treated with respect. "Be careful when you touch the blade, Pat. It's poisoned. Hold it by the handle, and keep your hand away from the blade at all costs. Here." He handed it to her.

Color drained from Pat's face, but she took the knife from him. She stared at it with wide eyes, fingering the design on the handle.

Drakon turned his back on her, waiting to see if she would try to use the dagger on him instead of Ken. He studied the faces of his men, who were, in turn, watching Pat.

After a minute, Drakon turned to face Pat. He expected to see uncertainty in her face, but instead he saw glee. He was right. She wanted to do this. He could count on her. "It's time for our plan to be put into action."

"Men, I will leave you to help Pat," Drakon said, walking toward the door. "And use this house as our base while we are here. We will take any items with us when we leave in a couple of days. And make sure you protect the house with magic. I don't want anyone stumbling in here by accident. You know the price for failure. You know what I expect. I'll be back tomorrow."

SASCHA STOOD DAZED as she watched Soleil disappear on the horizon. He was gone. She had to help him. The sun was rising, giving a bit of warmth, but the cool winds forced her to pull her collar up and push her hands deep into her jacket pockets. She moved closer to the middle of the rooftop, away from the edge. Marco, she needed to see Marco. He lived in this building. She had been here before. But what floor was it?

"Soleil," she whispered, "hang on. I'll be there as soon as I can."

She heard someone call her name and turned. "Marco." She wanted to race toward him, be wrapped in his arms and have him tell her everything was going to be alright. But she couldn't. Everything she thought they had was a lie. No matter how much she wanted it to be different.

Marco scanned the skies. "Where's Soleil?"

Her words spilled out, tripping over each other. "Soleil's hurt. Those revolting creatures ripped at him." Sascha shook her head, "There was blood, so much blood. And now he's flying, spreading the poison. They wouldn't let me walk. But Soleil's flying. We need to help him."

Marco moved toward her, his arms outstretched to hug her. Sascha stepped back and Marco let his arms drop.

"Sascha, tell me what happened. Slowly."

Tears threatened to burst, but she pushed them back.

"We need to—" Her breath hitched.

I must slow down.

Sascha closed her eyes for a few seconds, slowed her thoughts, then opened her eyes and faced Marco. "Soleil was clawed by the guardians of the portal. He's badly hurt."

"Where is he?" Marco asked.

"He said he'll meet us at the cave. We need to go there. Soleil said you would know where it is."

"I do. Let's go." Marco opened the heavy metal door to the stairwell and held it open for her. Sascha walked in and stood at the top of the brick stairs for a moment to allow her eyes to adjust to the dim lighting. Marco passed by her and led the way down the stairs.

Sascha hurried after Marco, their footsteps echoing loudly in the empty stairwell. "You know where he is?"

"I am assuming he means the cave at the Fire of the Phoenix headquarters. Everything we will need is there."

"Is that far?" she asked.

"Roughly a forty-minute drive toward the Sunshine Coast."

"Forty minutes such a long way for Soleil to fly."

"Flying is quicker than driving, Sascha. He'll be fine."

Sascha stopped, balled her fists and glared at his back. "How do you know, Marco?" Marco didn't reply and he didn't turn around, which was probably lucky. The last thing they needed to do was fight. Sascha started walking again. At the bottom of the stairs was a corridor that led to a set of polished silver lifts. Marco waved his card in front of the card scanner and they caught the lift down to the carpark.

In a few minutes, they were driving out of the carpark and toward the cave.

Marco pointed to her bandaged arms. "Did you hurt yourself?"

"I'm fine. I will talk to you about it later."

Sascha sat huddled in the seat and stared out of the car window.

What pain must the poor creature be in? What happens if we arrive at the cave and he's not there? Where will we start to look?

Her eyes stung.

They sat in silence for what seemed like an age, even the radio was off. Sascha didn't want to talk, didn't want to have to carry on a civilized conversation with Marco.

As if he knew what she was thinking, Marco glanced over at her and said. "You haven't said a word the whole trip."

"It was my scream that woke the monsters. I should have been quiet. That's all I had to do. Soleil was doing all the work. I promised him I would be quiet." Sascha buried her head in her hands.

"Soleil is a tough creature," Marco said. "He won't be that easy to kill."

"What if he can't make it to the cave? I shouldn't have let him go. We could have carried him, taken him in the car...something!"

"How? How could we have carried him?" Marco reached for her hand but Sascha pulled back further into the seat. He sighed. "Soleil knew the only way we could help him is if he flew to the cave. We can help him there, and he knows it."

"How much longer, Marco?"

"Ten minutes."

Sascha looked out of the window. She had no idea where they were. They were driving along a gravel track and all

Sascha could see was the bush. Sascha glanced at the arm she was resting against the car door. Soleil's gashes had changed color the same way her bites had. Sascha turned to Marco. "When you said Soleil won't be easy to kill, was that because an attack by those monsters is fatal?"

Marco didn't say anything for a few moments. "Normally, yes. But I have the antidote at the headquarters. The guardians have attacked our soldiers from time to time and the treatment has always worked well on them. It should work in the same way on Soleil."

"Should work?"

"We haven't used it on creatures before, so I can't be entirely sure. But Soleil has a will to live. I'm hoping it will work." Marco glanced at her. "There is something else I should tell you, Sascha."

"What?"

"You need to prepare yourself for the treatment process. It can seem rather brutal, but it works. Soleil will need you to be strong for him, and you will need to let me do what I need to do. If you ever trusted me, you need to trust me now."

"What do you mean by brutal?" Sascha stammered. "How brutal is it?"

"I will be as quick as I can. Don't look at what I do, just focus on being there for Soleil. I will be using strong pain killers to help him, but sometimes the shock of the treatment can cause the patient to pass out. Passing out can be a blessing, however."

Sascha's mouth went dry, and she rubbed her stomach to calm the sudden wave of nausea. "Pass out? How severe is this treatment?"

"We're here," Marco said.

They arrived at a large gated property surrounded by mountains and forests. A guard in red, gold and silver armor walked up to Marco's window.

The guard brought his gloved fist to his chest in salute. "Colonel."

"Sergeant," Marco answered.

The sergeant held out a machine, which Marco placed his hand on. The machine buzzed and a green light scanned his hand. The guard stepped back and the gate opened. "It's good to have you back, sir."

They drove past a water fountain. Sascha watched the shimmering water glide over a white stone carving of a bird that looked like Soleil. They turned into a parking lot in front of a large ivory-colored double-story mansion. Sascha stepped out of the car and followed Marco along a polished slate walkway to a large set of glass doors. The side panels on the three doors were engraved with scenes from the cave to Ocean's Mouth. It felt surreal to Sascha to see pictures of Eratus here on Earth. Marco put his hand on a scanner and the doors opened. They rushed along a marble floor toward a room with frosted glass walls and a pair of glass doors. A floral symbol was carved into one of the door panels. A caduceus - two snakes winding around a winged staff - was carved below the floral symbol.

"What's the floral symbol mean?" Sascha asked Marco.

"It's the plant that symbolizes medicine on Eratus. The symbol must be recognized by anyone from Eratus as well as Earth, which is why they also have the caduceus."

"Do you have soldiers here from Eratus and Earth?"

"Yes." Marco scanned his hand over the symbols and then typed in a code into a keypad on the wall beside the doorway. The doors whooshed open and they entered a large cool room with a tiled floor. Glass cupboards, metal tables and several fridges were dotted around the room. It smelled of anesthetic and something else - a familiar smell that Sascha couldn't place. Marco picked up a white box from one of the silver tables and walked over to the fridge that sat in the corner of the room. He took out a jar of green liquid and a glass vial of red powder and placed them in the white box. He then opened the glass cupboard next to the fridge and picked up a bundle of bandages, a handful of long matches and a sealed plastic tray on which were set several-brutal looking tools. He put these items in the box as well.

"Do we need to use those...weapons... on Soleil?"

"Yes, we do," Marco answered. "Before we treat the poison, we need to remove the damaged skin on the surface.

"But we're giving Soleil something to help with the pain?"

Marco picked up the jar of green liquid. "That's what this is for. It's selecine. It's used on Eratus for healing, but it also has numbing properties."

They rushed back to the car and drove out of the carpark and around to the back of the building, where they found themselves on a clay track covered in fine golden pebbles. A few minutes later, Marco stopped the car in front of a cave. The cave was hidden from the track by a lattice fence covered in grapevines. Marco picked up the white box and Sascha followed him into the cave.

The cave was large and cool, and the walls were gold, like the pebbles that covered the track. The sound of bubbling water echoed around the cave. As they walked in further, Sascha smelled the now familiar scent of cinnamon and pine. And then she heard the heavy breathing of an animal in distress. Soleil was lying on the sandy edge of a narrow creek at the back of the cave.

"Soleil, we're here," Sascha called out. A soft whimper sounded every time he breathed. Sascha sat down on the ground next to Soleil, picked up his head and rested it in her lap. Sascha caressed his feathers as he turned toward her, his eyes glazed over in pain. To see him suffering so much tore at her heart. Marco's words came back to her. She had to be strong for Soleil. "Marco, we need to save him. What do you need me to do?"

Marco bent down and inspected Soleil. "I need to move his wings so I can access the wounds. This will hurt him."

Marco braced himself and lifted the wings apart, forcing Soleil onto his back. Soleil gave a muted cry and pushed his head deeper into Sascha's lap. She caressed his face. "I'm here, Soleil."

The smell emanating from the wounds was putrid. Marco opened the jar of selecine and started to slather it all over Soleil's chest and wings. "Your pain will ease soon, Soleil. Hang on."

Soleil's eyes closed and the luster of his feathers dulled.

When Marco had finished applying the treatment, he squatted next to Sascha. "I covered his wounds with selecine, but they are too deep. I can't cut away the dead skin or burn the poison. He wouldn't survive and would suffer an agonizing death. We can't do that to him. I think we must make him as comfortable as we can. It is only a matter of time now."

"No." Sascha's eyes blurred with tears. She wanted to be strong, but the tears kept flowing. "No, that's an easy cop-out. You said he had a will to live, so let's give him a chance."

"Sascha, the only way of saving Soleil is with a specific type of healing magic, a magic that can only be found on Eratus."

Soleil opened his eyes. They looked empty and black. "Sascha, the necklace..."

"What about the necklace, Soleil?" His eyes had closed again, and his breathing was slowing. "Soleil? Talk to me," Sascha pleaded.

"Of course." Marco slapped his forehead with the palm of his hand. "You can save him."

"Me?" Sascha stammered. "How? You said only healing magic on—"

"I thought Soleil wanted us to come here because I could save him with the treatment, but it's not me he wants to save him, it's you."

Her stomach churned. "What are you talking about Marco?"

"Your magic must be alive if you can wear your necklace and if you can talk to Soleil. And this cave's walls are ingrained with an old magic. If we can combine whatever power you have with the magic in the cave and the jewel in your necklace..."

"This is lunacy. You want me to heal a badly wounded creature? I don't remember my magic. I could kill him."

"Or you could save him. You have a better chance of saving him with your magic and the necklace than I do with the treatment." Marco stood. "Well? Are you ready to try?"

Sascha looked down at Soleil. "And if I make it worse?"

"You can't make it worse. He's dying. You may be able to save him. Do you want to try?"

"What do I need to do?"

"Have you noticed any sort of magical abilities while you've been here on Earth? Anything at all?"

"I know I can move objects." Sascha squirmed beneath Marco's stare.

"Could you crush a stone, like the jewel in your necklace?"

"I don't know. I'll try. How would that help?"

"I will show you, but first let's see what you can do."

Sascha took off her jacket and bundled it under Soleil's head. "Why don't we use a hammer? That would smash it."

"A hammer wouldn't smash it as finely as it needs to be. We need it powdered. Magic is the best and easiest way to do that...if you can remember how."

"OK. Tell me what to do."

"The jewel in the necklace is magical. If we crush the jewel and mix it in with your blood and the fire starter - this red powder - we may be able to save him."

"What does the fire starter do? And why my blood?"

"The fire starter is what we use to burn away the poison. Your blood is the magic that will bring it all together and protect him from the shock of the fire starter."

Marco walked over to the creek, leaned down and picked up a small smooth stone. "Let's move away from Soleil."

They walked over to the cave's entrance. "Take this stone. Hold it in your hand. Then visualize it with a crack."

Her throat was dry, and her hands clammy. Sascha took the stone from Marco, held it in her open palm and closed her eyes. A warm flush crept up her neck and face. Sascha opened her eyes. "Marco, stop looking at me. Turn around. I feel stupid enough as it is without you staring at me."

"It's not like you're getting dressed or anything." He shrugged his shoulders and turned around. "But if it helps."

Sascha closed her eyes again and tried to visualize the stone. She knew she had to imagine it cracking, but nothing was happening. "Marco, I can't do this."

"You're panicking, Sascha. You need to calm down and focus properly."

"Easy for you to say. How do I even do that?"

Marco turned around to face her.

"Turn around, Marco. I told you I can't do it with you staring at me."

"But I thought—"

Sascha glared at him.

Marco gave an exaggerated sigh. "Very well, I will turn around. Again!"

Soleil moaned.

Soleil.

She had to do this. Sascha decided to change tactics. She sat down, crossed her legs and closed her eyes. She visualized the turquoise blue water of the creek bubbling over the golden stone bed. Sascha breathed in the scent of cinnamon and pine and breathed out the building tension in her shoulders and neck. She heard soft music drifting through the air - haunting, gentle sounds. Where was the music coming from? Is this music the magic Marco was talking about?

The stone moved in her hand. Sascha sensed it floating in the air in front of her and rotating slowly. She could see the composition, see its makeup. She pictured it breaking, each of the molecules separating. There was a loud crack and a whoosh of dusty air. The stone exploded, shattering into dust.

"I did it! I did it!" Sascha jumped up as Marco turned to look.

"Soleil was right," Marco said. "That's good. But we can't afford for the jewel dust to go everywhere like it did then. We won't have enough of it to work with. Wait a second. I know what we can do."

He raced over to the bundle of goods he had taken from the hospital, then hurried to the creek, leaned down and grabbed another stone. He came back to join her. "Explode this stone in the same way you did before, but see if you can control the blast." Marco put the stone into a white plastic container and gave it to her. "See if you can keep the dust within this container."

Sascha sat back down and closed her eyes. She sensed the container resting in her open palm. It was easier to concentrate on the sound of the bubbling water this time. The soft music returned.

Sascha pushed the thoughts aside and brought the image of the stone back into her mind. She could see it, see the amount of space she had to shatter it in. She visualized the stone becoming dust.

She heard a soft thud as the stone exploded, blowing the lid off the container and knocking the container out of her hand and onto the ground in front of her.

"Sascha, you need to focus more."

"You do it if you think it's so easy, Marco," Sascha snapped.

A strange gurgling sound made her turn toward Soleil. Blood was oozing from his beak. He panted and shut his eyes tightly.

"Soleil is not going to last much longer," Marco said.

Sascha wanted to snap again, do something to cover up the growing fear that gnawed at her.

Maybe I can't do it. Maybe I can't save Soleil. But I must. I must do this!

She took her necklace off and handed it to Marco. "Take the jewel out. Put it in the container you are preparing the treatment in."

"Maybe we should practice once more," Marco said. "The container I have to use for the treatment is glass. The fire starter would melt plastic."

"What if I explode the jewel in the plastic and then we transfer it to the glass?"

"We would lose too much of the crushed jewel. We need every bit of it."

"We don't have time for another practice, Marco. I have to do it now."

Once the jewel was in the glass jar, he handed the jar to her. Sascha stared at the jewel. Her heart pounded in her chest. Her head ached.

"You can do this, Sascha. You can save Soleil if you do this right."

"Thanks, Marco. I'm not under enough pressure already."

"Sorry. Are you ready for this?"

"Of course I'm not bloody ready." Sascha sat down again, crossed her legs and closed her eyes. She could hear Soleil's labored breathing. It echoed in her mind and took control of her thoughts.

The pain he must be in! What if I mess this up?

Her heart pounded even faster. She needed to calm down. She remembered the old magic Marco had talked about. If there was ever a time she needed help from old magic, it was now. But how could she ask the magic to help her?

"Hello, Sascha. It has been a long time." The singsong voice echoed in her mind.

"Who are you?"

"You don't remember me but my name is Athena. I give you your powers."

"Athena? The god of Eratus?"

"Sascha, we need to help Soleil now," Athena continued, "but a time will come when we can talk freely. For now, push aside the sounds of Soleil's breathing and concentrate on the task ahead of you."

Sascha knew this voice, but even if she hadn't, she would have accepted its owner's help to save Soleil. "Are you the old magic Marco talked about?"

"In a way," she replied.

A man coughed. "Excuse me, Athena, but this is my cave and my old magic."

"Not now, Zeus," Athena said. "Sascha needs my help. Leave."

"I am your father, Athena. And this is my cave. You don't speak to me like that."

"Zeus, now is not the time," Athena snapped.

"Very well," he said. "I will go. This time."

"Take a moment and breathe, Sascha" Athena continued. "You can do this."

Sascha pushed aside the confusion caused by the argument between Athena and Zeus and slowed her breathing. A sense of calm, of peace, flooded over her. She visualized the glass container resting in her palm and felt its weight. Sascha examined the amount of space in which she had to explode the jewel.

"Don't use the full space," Athena said. "Visualize a smaller space so you don't damage the glass."

"Good idea," Sascha answered. She examined the jewel.

Damn, it's softer than the rock.

There was some dust on one edge of the jewel.

"Start from the inside of the gem and work outward," Athena said. "Imagine each layer becoming like the dust you have found."

"Yes, that would work." Sascha flexed her neck and shoulders, took a deep breath and re-examined the jewel. She started at its core and visualized each layer becoming dust. It was working! Each layer of the jewel started to disintegrate. Then she heard a soft pop. She opened her eyes. The jewel was nothing but dust. Best of all, the jar was still intact. Sascha put the jar on the ground, raced outside and threw up.

A minute later Marco joined her and gave her a fistful of tissues. "You did it, Sascha. Well done. But we can't stop now. I need some of your blood so I can complete the final steps of the treatment."

Sascha followed him back into the cave.

"Give me your right palm."

Sascha offered up her hand without a second thought. She ignored the sharp slice along her palm as she looked over at Soleil. His breathing had worsened. His face was etched in pain. The thought of losing him...

"Pump your hand so your blood drips into the jar."

Once Marco had enough blood, he put the jar down and

took her hand to patch it up. Sascha had forgotten how gentle his touch could be. She pulled her hand away. "I'll do this. You fix up the treatment."

He stirred the blood, the crushed jewel and the fire starter together with the selecine. It smelt of sulfur and pine. He walked toward Soleil. "This is going to hurt him."

Sascha moved over to Soleil, removed her jacket from beneath his head and sat down. She put his head on her lap. His feathers, normally soft and silky, were stiff and cool.

Marco squatted and started lathering the treatment over him.

Soleil tried to pull away from Marco, but he didn't have enough strength.

"I'm so sorry, Soleil." Sascha closed her eyes. "Athena, help us."

"You can help him," Athena said. "You can diffuse his pain in the same way you turned the rocks and the jewel into dust. Visualize each area of pain and dissolve it."

The soft music filled the air and Sascha knew she wasn't alone. This time, instead of visualizing the jewel, she pictured Soleil's head resting on her lap. She could hear their two heartbeats. Sascha put her hand on Soleil's chest and felt the slow thud of his heart as it struggled to beat.

"Soleil, I'm here."

He groaned. Sascha pictured Soleil's pain and started to feel the burn. Red and black marks glowed on Soleil's wings and chest. She visualized her hand moving over the wounds. Pain slammed into her, she could feel his pain as if it was hers. She pushed past the crippling intensity of it and imagined the pain dissolving and healthy cells regenerating.

As Sascha melted each mark away, another layer covered with the same red and black glowing patches appeared. She focused on each layer at a time, dissolving the pain and visualizing the cells regenerating as the treatment burned away the poison.

"It's working," Athena whispered. "The pain is easing and Soleil will live."

Soleil's heartbeat began to even out. His breathing started to return to normal.

Gently, Sascha pulled her magic back, moving away from Soleil and back into the cave. "It's up to you now, my friend," Sascha said as she stroked his head. "You need to sleep so you can heal. Thank you, Athena."

Sascha jumped when Marco's hand rested on her shoulder.

"Here, drink this." Marco handed her a tall glass of iced water. "Soleil is resting. I think you should do the same."

Sascha stroked Soleil. He was sound asleep. She put her jacket back under his head and tried to stand. Her legs had lost their strength and they wobbled for a moment until she was able to find her balance.

"I have covered Soleil's wounds with fresh selecine," Marco said. "Soleil will survive this, thanks to whatever you did. I have never seen wounds heal that much in such a short time. If you ever need to go that deep into your magic again, let me know. You are vulnerable when you are so fully wrapped up in your magic. If anyone or anything wanted to attack you, that would be the perfect time to do so. I need to be ready to defend you."

"I never realized I could do that," Sascha answered. "What an incredible gift." She walked over to the wall of the cave and rested her hand on it. It warmed to her touch and then cooled. "Athena helped me."

"Athena what?"

"I heard Athena's voice, and she helped me. I know that sounds strange, but it's true."

"The stories say that this is Zeus's cave and that Athena visits here as well."

"Zeus said he was Athena's father," Sascha said. "Is that true?"

"Zeus said?" Marco asked.

"Yes, I heard him fighting with Athena."

"Then you were honored, Sascha," Marco said. "You never mentioned this sort of contact with the gods before. But as leader of the Four Sisters, I guess I assumed that you would have talked to Athena. But Zeus too? That is distinguished company."

"So is he her father?" Sascha asked.

"There are a lot of stories. Why don't you ask Athena next time? See what she says?"

"It was an amazing experience," Sascha said. "The most beautiful music I have ever heard surrounded me. You must have heard it."

"No, I heard nothing. I knew something was happening though. I was burning away the poisoned flesh and when I looked at you and Soleil, you were both at rest. He had moved his head closer to you, and your hands were resting on his face. He should have been in agony, but he wasn't. Even the color in his feathers had started to return."

"Athena gave me the idea of moving the pain, dissolving it in the same way I did the stone, but she helped me control it so I didn't harm Soleil."

"You were a powerful mage on Eratus."

"What magic did I have, Marco?"

"Sister Laela used to say you were the most powerful mage she had ever seen in healing and fire magic. You come from the land of Brun, which is also where I come from. Our people believed that anyone with healing magic was flawed. No matter how much we tried to stop the practice, each year our people gave sacrifices to the fire gods. If there were any flawed, they became the sacrifices."

"How barbaric."

"Yes. Owain tried to help us stop it, but nothing worked. He adopted you before your people realized how powerful you were and that you could heal. That is the only reason you're still alive."

The ground started to move beneath Sascha, and her vision started to fade. She felt Marco put his arm around her shoulders to steady her. His touch burned.

"You need to rest." Marco led her to a bundle of blankets and pillows bundled up on the sand next to Soleil. "Here, sit down."

Sascha dropped onto the blankets and then rested her head against her bended knees. The giddiness started to pass. "Sorry, Marco."

Marco squatted next to her. "There's nothing to be sorry about. What you did would have been exhausting even if you were used to using that amount of magic."

"Do you have anything stronger than water? I could use a drink."

"Yes, wait a moment." He walked to the opposite side of the cave, where he opened a door by pressing part of the wall. He walked through the open doorway and a few minutes later, came out with a glass of wine.

"I would give you a brandy, but since I know you don't like the stuff, I poured you a wine instead."

Sascha had a couple of mouthfuls of the wine and felt her strength begin to return. So many questions flooded through her mind, but she was too tired to deal with any of them. "I might rest now. Thanks, Marco."

Sascha lay down. Sleep came almost instantly.

CHAPTER 23

* EARTH

*K*en drove down his street. They needed more street lights it was too dark at night. He could see lights at his house. Pat was awake. That was good. It was time to talk to her, time to work out a way forward. He had to persuade Pat to stop trusting Drakon and start trusting him instead. But he wasn't sure if she would agree to his proposal. He must be careful not to tell her too much. He didn't want her to stop the plans he had put in place.

Once they had talked, they would pick up Rusty from Sascha's and go for a drive to the beach. A late-night stroll along the beach and an ice cream. That would be fun. But what would he do if she didn't agree?

He pulled into their driveway. Two men stood at their front door. Pat sat on the swinging chair on the front patio. Ken watched as she stood and walked toward the men. Something was wrong. Pat stood beside the two men as Ken stepped out of the car and walked toward her.

"Hello, honey," Pat said. "I've heard about what happened on Eratus."

"What? What are you talking about, Pat?" Ken stopped a few feet from her and glanced at the men. "What's going on?"

"Drakon visited me. He told me you had betrayed him. What did he mean?"

"Pat, you have it all wrong."

"Do I? You have gotten too attached to Sascha. You have forgotten where our loyalties lie. I told you she would be your undoing one day. I warned you!"

Ken backed away from her. "Pat, what are you doing? What have you been told?"

"We need to obey Drakon, not do our own thing. You know that."

"Pat—"

"I'm sorry for this," Pat said.

Ken heard footsteps. One of the men was now standing directly behind him. The stranger gripped Ken's shoulders, stopping him from moving. Pat moved toward Ken. When she was standing in front of him, she looked directly into his eyes. "I warned you that there would be a price for betraying Drakon."

"But, Pat—"

Pat thrust a blade into his stomach. "I am sorry, my love, but you can't stop this and neither can I."

Ken's legs gave way beneath him. He reached for her as if she might change her mind, and—

The pain!

He grabbed at his waist. He could feel the warmth of the blood as it oozed from the wound.

Pat's voice echoed as she talked to the two men. "It's done," she said.

He heard her footsteps as she turned away from him and walked up their patio steps. The pain burned through him like acid. One of the men lifted Ken's body up onto his shoulder and carried him inside and down the stairs to their cellar. The man threw Ken onto the floor and walked out. Ken felt his heart slowing, his body shutting down. He was grateful that he had put his plans in place before arriving home. Pat was right. No-one could stop what was about to unfold. He could hear Rusty crying next door. He would miss her.

"Bye, old mate," he whispered. "Look after Sascha and the girls." The crying stopped and Ken welcomed the relief of the darkness.

SOLEIL WAS STILL ASLEEP when Sascha left. He had slept well during the night, and when she had examined him an hour earlier, she could see he was recovering well. She had wanted to be there when he woke, but she needed to collect the girls. She still needed to update Marco and the girls on what had happened on Eratus. Marco promised to text her as soon as Soleil was awake.

Sascha drove up her driveway and the roller doors opened. As she unlocked the side door, Rusty leaped out and jumped up at her.

"Hello, Rusty. Are you staying with us again? Where are the girls?" Rusty whimpered and raced for the back door.

"Do you need to go outside?" Sascha dropped her bag and keys on the kitchen bench and walked over to let her out. Rusty pushed her way through the partly opened door and raced over to the fence. She paced up and down the fence line, then turned and raced inside to the front window.

"What's wrong, Rusty?"

She pawed frantically at the front door, then turned to Sascha and gave a bone-chilling howl. Sascha's skin prickled.

"I'll get your lead. Let's go and see what's happened." Sascha clipped on the lead and opened the front door. Rusty raced out, dragging Sascha behind her. Sascha walked to Pat and Ken's door and knocked. No answer. She tried to open it. Locked.

"Sascha, you're home." Sascha turned to see Pat standing at the gate. A man Sascha had never seen before stood beside her. Rusty turned, her back bristling and a deep growl vibrating in her chest.

"Pat. I wasn't sure if you and Ken were away."

"We were, but I had to come back for something. I'm heading off again shortly."

Pat made no mention of Ken's visit to Eratus, so Sascha decided not to say anything either.

A loud click sounded behind Sascha. She turned to see another stranger standing in the doorway of Ken and Pat's house. Her mark tingled. Rusty's snarl deepened and her lip curled as she showed her teeth. Rusty tried to push past the man and force her way into the house, but the man moved, blocking entrance to the house.

"Rusty seems desperate to get inside, Pat," Sascha said. "Where's Ken?"

Pat opened the gate and walked toward them. The man beside her followed. "It's alright, Rusty," Pat cooed. Rusty's growl deepened. "He's away on business. You know what that job of his is like. He'll be joining me in Sydney later on." She pointed to the man in the doorway. "I'm afraid Rusty doesn't like Jake. Jake is Ken's brother."

"Or me." The man standing beside Pat smiled at Sascha.

"Ken and I may be away for longer than we originally thought," Pat said. "Jake and Tim have offered to look after the house while we're away. Considering Rusty's reaction to them, would you mind keeping Rusty for a little longer?"

Sascha patted Rusty as she tried to work out what was happening. "You know we don't mind looking after Rusty. But I have never seen her react like this before. And she does seem more interested in what is in the house, not Jake."

"She's like this every time they visit," Pat said. "It gets very embarrassing."

Sascha glanced at the men. "Are you sure you're okay, Pat? There's nothing I can do to help?"

"I know Rusty's reaction is disturbing, but there is nothing to worry about. Take her back to your place and she'll calm down. You'll see."

"If you're sure," Sascha replied.

"If it's still OK, Ken and I will come and see you for that dinner you promised when we return."

"Of course," Sascha replied.

Rusty didn't want to leave, but Sascha bent down and rubbed her ears. "C'mon, gorgeous. Let's go home."

"See you soon, Rusty," Pat called out. "You be a good girl for Sascha."

Sascha led a still growling Rusty away.

As THEY ARRIVED BACK at her place, Sascha squatted down in front of Rusty. "I'm so sorry, gorgeous." Sascha stared at her mark, which still tingled. "I know you're trying to tell me something, but I don't know what it is."

Rusty leaned over and licked her.

"Let's go inside." Sascha nearly missed the note stuck to her door. She reached over, peeled it from the door and opened it.

Hi Sascha,

I was wondering if you wanted to drop by the club tomorrow (Saturday) at 4pm? Ken has been in touch with me. I have some information you might find useful.

Signed, your sketch artist.

Sascha glanced over at Pat and Ken's place. The yard was empty. She shook her hand to ease the tingling sensation from her mark. She decided it was time to call Ken. When he didn't answer, Sascha left him a voice message, asking him to ring her back. And then she sent a text to the girls to tell them she was home. A few minutes later, they texted back to say they were on their way. They had been shopping for groceries.

Sascha put the kettle on and was putting some miniature cakes onto a plate when the roller door went up. The girls were home.

"It's so good to see you," Kira said, racing in and giving Sascha a hug. "We want all the juicy details."

Without thinking, Sascha took her jacket off, revealing her bandaged arms.

"Sascha," Kira cried out. "What did you do to your arms?"

"It's a long story."

"But you're okay?"

"Yes, I'm fine."

"I'll finish making the coffee," Kira said. "And then you can tell us all about it. Do you need any pain killers?"

"No, it's all good. Thanks, Kira."

Twenty minutes later, the girls had finished their coffee and were discussing Eratus, excited at the idea of the adventure ahead of them and finally meeting their parents. Sascha's cell phone buzzed. "Soleil is awake," Sascha said. "Time for us to leave."

"Let's take Rusty with us," Kira said. "She was so sad last night. I think she needs company."

"She was strange when I arrived home today," Sascha said. "I can't help but feel something isn't quite right next door. Pat said Rusty was reacting to Ken's brother, but I'm sure there's something else."

"They've lied to us all these years," Kira said. "I'm not sure they're going to start telling us the truth now."

Sascha snapped her fingers. "I know what I'll do. I'll call the police. I have his station's phone number. I'll tell them something is wrong."

"And what if there isn't?" Kira asked. "What if it is exactly what Pat says?"

"But what if Pat is a hostage or something? I can't let it go. It's odd that Ken hasn't returned my call yet."

"This could backfire," Lee said. "If nothing is wrong, Pat could get cranky."

"I'd rather deal with that than thinking I should have done something."

Lee yawned and stretched. "While you're doing that, we'll pack some food to take to the cave for dinner."

Sascha stood and began to clear the table. "Don't forget food and treats for Rusty. Which reminds me; I need to get Marco to organize food for Soleil."

Kira bounced around the kitchen. "I'm so excited. We're finally going to Eratus."

"We'll need to be careful," Sascha said. "I'm not sure we can use the second portal now. It might be too dangerous. We will discuss tactics when we get to the cave. And we also need to do some research in the library before we leave here."

"This Drakon sounds cute," Kira said. "I can think of worse things than being kidnapped by a good-looking prince." The girls laughed.

Sascha shook her head as she smiled. "You won't be able to find your parents if he captures us."

"Point taken," Kira said. She opened the fridge and then stopped. "Sascha, you're fine with us talking about our parents, aren't you?"

"Of course I am," Sascha lied.

"We were talking about it when you were away. We don't

want you to feel you aren't important to us. We love you and we are so grateful you were the one they chose. But we need to know who our parents are and understand why they sent us away."

"I get it. But Marco said they sent you here to keep you safe. Don't be hard on them." Sascha clapped her hands. "Time for us to move it. I want to check on Soleil. You lot pack dinner. I'll call Ken's office and then we'll be on our way."

CHAPTER 24

*M*arco stormed out of the cave. Not being able to understand Soleil was causing him great difficulty, and Soleil was proving to be a terrible patient. "C'mon, Sascha. Where are you? Come back and control this creature of yours."

Marco watched as Soleil stumbled around, trying to find his balance.

"Your wings, you stupid bird," he yelled. "You need to rest and let them heal, otherwise you'll be useless to Sascha."

Soleil turned around to glare at him.

"You understood that? Good! I wouldn't want to be in your shoes when Sascha finds out what you've been doing."

Soleil let out a high-pitched scream, forcing Marco to cover his ears to block out the sound.

"Bird, I'm going to bloody well kill you if you don't stop doing that." When Marco glanced at Soleil, he could have sworn that Soleil was grinning at him, taking delight in being the cause of his fury. Marco stalked over to the bird, intent on doing something to shut it up, when Rusty came galumphing in toward Soleil. She was followed by a frantic Sascha and the three girls.

"Rusty, no, he's wounded," they screamed. Rusty ignored them. When she was close to Soleil, she stopped and stood looking at him, her body vibrating with the vigor of her wagging tail. Soleil warbled and leaned down as Rusty moved closer and gently snuggled her head into the bird's neck.

"Well, would you look at that!" Marco said.

"Good girl, Rusty." Sascha said, stopping to look at them. She let out a deep breath. "That's a relief. I thought Rusty was going to jump all over Soleil." She shuddered. "Even the thought terrifies me."

"Hello, Soleil," Kira said, walking over to stroke his head.

"Brave soul," Marco said. "That thing can bite."

Sascha laughed. "Ignore Marco. Soleil won't bite you. He might bite Marco, but that just shows he's an intelligent creature."

"Very funny," Marco answered.

"You certainly seem to be recovering well," Sascha said to Soleil as she walked around him to assess the scaring.

"He's weak," Marco said. "And won't look after his wings properly, but whatever you did...he is nearly healed."

Soleil glanced over at Marco and moved his head close to Sascha. Then again came that smile. Sascha laughed.

"He said something about me, didn't he?" Marco asked. "That bird is a hell of a bad patient, so don't listen to him."

Sascha laughed again.

"What? What did he say?"

Sascha grinned. "I'll tell you later, when we don't have an audience. It might be too embarrassing otherwise."

"That bird. Honestly, Soleil, one day..." Marco stabbed his finger in Soleil's direction, "Anyway, now you're here, I might find some fresh clothes and have a shower. When I come back, we can talk about what happened on Eratus."

WHEN MARCO LEFT THE CAVE, Sascha turned to Soleil. "It is so good to see you recovering, Soleil, but Marco is right. You do need to rest your wings and your chest, and give them time to heal. The selecine may be making you feel better than you are."

"You saved me, Sascha."

"Marco and I saved you. And Athena."

"Athena?"

"Yes. Marco understood what you meant by the necklace. He showed me what I had to do. Athena showed me how to heal you."

"I know you are still angry with Marco, Sascha, but he is a good man."

"Says the bird that has been giving Marco a hard time all morning."

"Yes, but that's fun. I think of him as my toy."

"Your toy?" Sascha laughed. "I am sure he would be happy to hear that. But let's not discuss Marco. I would rather you rest and recover."

"Sascha," Kira said, "are you talking to Soleil? How come you can understand him? You aren't wearing your necklace."

Her hand automatically flew to her neck. "You're right, Kira."

"You combined our bloods when you mixed your blood with the potion. What you did was similar to a bonding ceremony. Now that our bloods are joined, we are bonded again."

A warm glow flooded through her. "What a lovely thought."

"What did Soleil say?" Kira asked.

"When I healed him, we...bonded."

"You will need a necklace for Marco," Soleil said.

"For Marco? How could Marco wear it?"

"Oh, I mean Kira."

"You never did tell me why Kira could use the necklace but not the other girls."

Marco walked back into the cave. "I'm back."

"That was quick," Sascha said. Have you been to your place and back?"

"No, there are showers in the main complex. And I always keep fresh clothes there." Marco rubbed his belly and frowned. "We need to get some food. I'm starving."

"The girls packed food," Sascha said.

"I'll get it," Kira said as she raced out to the car. "It's in the car fridge."

Sascha turned to Marco, "We have food for Rusty. Have you got something for Soleil?"

Marco pulled some gloves out of his pocket. "Follow me."

Sascha trailed after him as he walked around to the back of the cave. He walked over to a tall fridge and opened it. The stench of fresh blood and bone almost made her vomit. "What is that smell?"

"Soleil's food." Marco grinned. "Put my gloves on and put some of the meat into this tray." Marco leaned down and picked up a huge tray. "I will carry it."

"This is so gross." The meat was slimy to the touch, and Sascha dropped a few pieces before managing to fill the tray.

They walked back into the cave, Marco leading the way.

"I am so hungry I could eat a wyvern whole," Soleil said.

"I have no idea what a wyvern is or what this food is," Sascha said, "and I don't want to know." She placed the tray in front of Soleil. "Eat it slowly. Your body has been through a shock." Rusty moved closer to sniff at Soleil's food. "No, Rusty. We have other food for you. Kira, can you give Rusty something to eat so she doesn't scavenge from Soleil's tray?"

"C'mon, Rusty," Kira said. "Look what I have for you."

Sascha turned to Marco. "Where can I wash my hands?"

He pointed to the door she had seen him open earlier. "In there, we call it the squad bay."

Sascha could still smell the stench after she washed her hands, so she lathered heaps of lotion on and joined the others back in the cave. "That's a good setup in there," she said to Marco. "Kitchen, bathroom, sleeping area."

"We use this cave as a base whenever we plan any major events. Sometimes people stay here several weeks."

A few minutes later, they all sat down on the sandy edge near the creek and helped themselves to the pizza and salad the girls had packed. Everyone except Kira had a couple of glasses of wine.

"Now that we've had something to eat and drink," Marco said, "you can tell us all about what happened on Eratus, Sascha."

Sascha updated Marco on the significant points. The girls sat and listened, asking a few more questions along the way.

"There is still something I don't understand," Kira said.

"And what's that?" Marco asked.

"Why did our parents feel they needed to protect us?"

Marco studied the girls. "Each of you were powerful mages. Many Eratians are superstitious. They believe that when powerful mages are born, a time of strife follows. So they figure that the disasters can be prevented by killing the powerful mages."

Sascha shook her head. "But that's stupid. It just means that they are killing the ones that could help them."

"I know, but it's hard to defeat superstitions with logic. When news of four young girls with powerful magic started to spread, the people were uneasy. There were several attempts on your lives, so your parents met with Connell and asked him to help protect you. You three were sent here."

"What happened to the fourth girl?" Kira asked.

"The sisters kept her for a while, but sent her here when she was older. She started to work for you, Sascha."

"Work for me?"

"Yes, the fourth girl was Jenny."

"Jenny? My bookkeeper?" Sascha asked.

"Yes," Marco replied.

Sascha picked up a second piece of pizza. "Wow. Does she remember her past?"

"Yes. They didn't take her memory away. She was older when she came here, and there were complications."

"Complications?" Kira asked.

"Yes, but I think that is a conversation for another time."

Kira pulled the paper off one of the mini cakes. "We always knew we were different, but it's hard to think of us as mages, let alone powerful ones. It does kind of make sense though."

"What do you mean?" Sascha asked.

Kira shrugged. "Things we can do."

Sascha stood and stretched her legs. "Marco, we have been asked to do some research in the Fire of the Phoenix library. Can you take us there? I was thinking of giving each of us a section to research. We can all come back here afterwards and compare notes."

"Good idea. Did you ask Laela where the Four Sisters headquarters were? Alex can have a look in their library too."

"To be honest, it didn't even occur to me," Sascha said.

"It doesn't matter," Marco replied. "Jenny must know where it is. Well, at least I hope so. Alex can ask her about it when he finds her."

Lee jumped to her feet and wiped the sand from her

jeans. "Who does what then? I would like to research the history of their Shield. It sounds fascinating."

"And I'd like to know more about the ancients and those weapons," Ella said.

Kira joined in. "I'll look into what they have on the dark creatures."

"This is easier than I thought it would be. Thanks, everyone. Marco, will you research the prisons? You might need to link in with Ella and Lee. I will research dark magic on Eratus. I might need to link in with you, Kira."

Kira gathered the dirty plates and cups into one neat pile. "All organized. Shall we go?"

Sascha looked over at Rusty and Soleil, who were curled up together. Both of them were fast asleep. "I'm worried about leaving Soleil and Rusty here by themselves."

"Um, I do have some magic," Ella said, studying her hands. "I can make objects or people disappear from view. They're still there, but I can make them blend into their surroundings so that they vanish. Sort of like a chameleon, but better."

"Show us what you mean," Marco said.

"Sure, but sometimes I need a couple of goes. I need to practice more." Ella sat cross-legged on the ground. "Keep your eyes on Soleil and Rusty." She closed her eyes. One second they were looking at Soleil and Rusty, and the next they were looking at the bubbling creek. They had disappeared.

"That's amazing!" Marco stammered.

"They are still there, aren't they?" Sascha asked.

"You should be able to sense Soleil," Marco said.

Sascha looked to where she knew Soleil was sleeping. She felt his soft warmth, sensed his heart beating stronger and stronger as his strength returned. "Oh, yes, I can. I hadn't realized."

"I'll show you, Sascha. You might feel more comfortable then." Ella closed her eyes again. Seconds later Soleil and Rusty were back. They were still sleeping soundly.

"I'll have to tell them what we're doing so they don't think we've left them." Sascha walked over and stroked Soleil's head. Soleil's eyes fluttered open. "We won't be long. We're going to the library to do some research. I want both of you to stay here. Soleil, please rest. Rusty?" Rusty lifted her head. "You make sure Soleil rests. And, Rusty, you must keep quiet. No barking. We don't want either of you attracting unnecessary attention. Ella will use some magic to hide you, but please be careful. Call me if you need me, Soleil."

"Stop worrying about us," Soleil said. "Go and do whatever you need to do. We'll protect each other here, and we promise to be good."

Sascha turned to Ella. "Are you ready?"

As they walked out of the cave, Sascha turned back to check that the magic had worked. The cave was empty.

DRAKON SMILED to himself as he drove away from Pat's place. The visit had been rewarding. Ken was no longer an issue. Pat had mentioned that there had been some sort of complication with Sascha and Rusty, but Drakon knew how to fix that. Once his plans were in place, Pat would be free to carry out his next assignment. But now it was time to check the supplies he had hidden in the basement of the Fire of the Phoenix headquarters for a time such as this.

Drakon had timed his arrival at the smuggler's entrance to the headquarters for when the sun was setting, thinking he could sneak in easily without anyone seeing him. But the place had changed. Guards were everywhere and lights lit up every corner of the grounds. Marco had increased security, probably following the disaster on Eratus. A few of the guards Drakon recognized as ones he could probably persuade to let him in, but he didn't want to attract attention. Drakon went into shadow and took advantage of the brief gap in security during the changing of the guards. It wasn't long before he found himself walking through the grounds toward the base of the main building.

Drakon placed his hand on the reader on the main door to the basement. The scanner beeped and the door opened. It had been Reya's idea to create human palm prints which they could use when they needed to access secure places like this. When she was younger, she had been quite brilliant. But times had changed and she had lost a lot of her edge.

Drakon pushed himself further into shadow and crept along the polished walkways, making sure to stay away from the cameras. He eventually found the place he was looking for.

"There's a secret here I know, element of air, the secret show."

The invisibility runes Drakon used to hide the entrance to his supply room lit up. He pressed the hieroglyphs in order and the doors slid open. Drakon ducked in, waved his hand in an arc over the runes and the doors closed. Roof lights, activated by his movement, lit up the room, revealing a number of glass display units. He walked to one at the back of the room. On one shelf was a charm bracelet more powerful than the one Reya had given him a few days ago. Drakon picked it up and pocketed it. He would need it for the meeting with Sascha at the club on Saturday.

Drakon then walked over to a shelf on which stood little vials of green lyrium. He pocketed a couple of the vials in case he needed some additional help with Sascha.

Drakon was about to leave when he glanced at the writing desk in the corner of the room. The envelope was still sitting on the desk. Drakon had written the letter five years ago when Reya had told him Marco and Sascha were back together. He would not let Marco take Sascha away from him again, not after everything he had done for her. In the end, Sascha and Marco had split up before Drakon had needed to use it. But now Marco was back in her life.

Drakon sat down at the desk and reworked the letter. Things had changed since he had written it. When he was done, he put the letter in his pocket. He would use it this time, just as soon as he found an opportunity.

Drakon left the room and raced to the back entrance of the headquarters. It was as he was preparing to leave that he heard her voice.

Sascha!

Drakon waited for them to walk past. Marco was leading the way, with the girls chatting happily behind him. Sascha tagged along at the end. They were coming in through the back entrance that led to the—

Of course, the cave. There's a cave in the paddocks out the back of here. That's where Soleil is.

He needed to kill off the creature before Sascha became too attached to it. And he knew just how to do that.

But first, Drakon needed to see where Marco was taking them. Soleil could live a little while longer.

THOUGH SHE KNEW Ella's magic was protecting Soleil, Sascha found it hard to relax after leaving him. But they needed to do this research. Sascha followed Marco and the girls in through the main building's back entrance.

A buzz of electricity shot down her arm and then it was gone. Sascha stopped, her stomach churning. She glanced around. They were being watched, she was sure of it. But who would be watching them?

"Marco," Sascha called. "How much further is the library? I don't want to be too far from Soleil."

Everyone stopped and turned toward her. "It isn't much further." He pointed. "Through that door and along the walkway."

Marco retraced his steps and joined Sascha. "I know you're worried about Soleil, but we don't need to be here for long. An hour at most. We can find the texts we need and take them back to the cave."

I'm being overprotective. I left him for hours with Marco and nothing happened then. An hour isn't a long time.

"OK. An hour," Sascha said. "And then we head back."

"Agreed," Marco said. "And once I have shown you to where you can do your research, I will organize for a couple of soldiers to guard the cave's entrance. They can make sure no-one goes in there until we return."

Sascha let out a deep breath. "That would be good. Thanks, Marco."

They walked out of the building and onto a marble walkway which connected the main building to the library. Everything was immaculate.

"Looking after this place must take a lot of work," Sascha said.

"Manuscripts containing centuries of wisdom are stored here," Marco replied. "It is worth caring for."

Several large archways circled the library's main room. In the center of the main room was a large sitting section with white cushioned lounge chairs set around a solid oak coffee table.

Sascha pointed at the lounge chairs. "Shall we use that as our base? Is everyone happy to meet back there in an hour?" Everyone nodded.

Marco strode off toward the first archway. "Follow me."

As she passed through it, Sascha noticed that there was a symbol etched into the side of the archway. She looked around. A different symbol was etched into the side of each of the archways. "What are those symbols, Marco?"

"They indicate which specific element is covered in that section of the library," Marco replied.

They followed Marco into a massive room lined with carved stone shelves. Each shelf was numbered and titled.

"Are all the rooms the same?" Sascha asked.

"Yes," Marco said.

Where are the guards?" Ella asked. "There's no-one here."

"We're all being watched," Marco answered, "and if anyone tried to do anything, they would be stopped."

"Watched?" Sascha asked.

"Yes, by hidden cameras."

"That seems sensible," Sascha said.

Perhaps that is what I sensed. It wasn't a person watching us but cameras.

"I don't know if I like that idea much," Kira said.

"There shouldn't be any need for privacy in the library. The information these rooms hold is priceless. We could never replace it, so security is critical."

"How come they let us take the texts to the cave then?" Sascha asked.

"I will check each of the texts out using my ID. You would normally have to use them here," Marco said. "Ella, this is where you'll find information about the ancients. I'll show the rest of you to where you'll find the information you're looking for and then I'll go and organize the guards for the cave. Try not to get lost while I'm gone."

CHAPTER 25

* EARTH

*D*rakon touched the charm bracelet in his pocket as he followed the group. Marco was joking around with the girls. He seemed to be getting on well with them. And he was always walking back to talk to Sascha. Drakon was pleased he had picked up the note. He had to stop this friendship before it started up again.

Marco took each of them to different sections of the library. Drakon stayed in shadow near Sascha. He would have loved to have known what she was searching for. She was in the section that dealt with dark magic. And there was one text there he wanted her to read. Drakon took it off the shelf and left it on the floor. She wouldn't miss it.

And now it was time to use the letter. Drakon wandered out to find Kira. She had left the section of the library that dealt with dark creatures and was drifting toward the entrance to Zinnath's cave.

She won't be able to open that door. It's always locked.

She turned the handle and it opened.

The door opened. That's not right. The magic traps could kill her.

Kira opened her cell phone, turned on the torchlight and wandered into the darkness. She stepped onto the plate before Drakon had a chance to call out. A ball of fire flew through the air. He dived at her, pulling her below the path of the fireball with only seconds to spare.

She was breathing heavily. Drakon jumped up and then held out his hand to her. She took his hand and stood, then gathered her bag and a few of the things that had fallen out.

"Who was stupid enough to put that here?" Kira said.

"Young lady, you can't blame Zinnath and Kalurth for protecting their home."

"Who are they?"

"They are powerful dragons. A lot of magical traps have been placed along this passageway to stop the unwary from stumbling into their cave. Until you know where those traps are, I would suggest you leave here."

"Is there something I can study to find out where the traps are?" Kira asked.

"I'm not certain. But you might find some reference to the traps in the texts on the other side of this room. The truth is they don't know if the dragons still live here. No-one has made it past the traps to tell us."

"It sounds like an adventure," Kira said. "Something I would be interested in."

Drakon leaned toward the ground and pretended to pick up an envelope. "Did you drop this?"

"No, I..." She looked at it and saw her name. She rubbed her forehead. "Oh. I didn't think it was mine, but..."

"Come with me," Drakon said, "and I'll show you where you can look for information on the traps."

Kira stuffed the letter in her bag and followed him.

"Here we are," Drakon said. "I'll leave you now." Drakon pointed to a door not far from where they stood. "When you leave, use that door. I would hate for you to walk into another trap."

"Thank you. I didn't catch your name."

"Consider me your guardian angel."

She had a lovely smile, much like Sascha's.

Drakon walked a short distance away and slipped back into shadow. He wanted to see what she would do. Eventually, she opened her bag and retrieved the envelope. She dropped onto the floor, crossed her legs and then opened it. Drakon could see her mouthing the words as she read the letter. The further she read, the paler her face became.

Good. Let's see Marco explain this one away.

SASCHA LOVED SEARCHING the texts on dark magic. She could spend a month in here and not even read a quarter of it. She glanced at her watch for what seemed like the hundredth time. She knew it was stupid but she was worried about Soleil. Once she had gathered some texts to study, she started to make her way back to the lounge chairs.

She cried out as she tripped on something. She looked down to see what she had tripped on. There was an old book on the floor. Someone must have dropped it. Considering how spotless the place was, it seemed strange that it hadn't been put back. She picked the book up and looked inside. It was a study text and showed how to learn a pictograph type language. It seemed familiar, but she couldn't quite place it. She wasn't sure why, but she decided to take the book with her. She wouldn't mention it to the others, not yet anyway.

Everyone but Kira was already there, lounging in the chairs with their texts bundled on the coffee table.

"Where is Kira?" Sascha asked.

"She won't be long," Ella said. "She was finished before us, so she said she would use that extra time to explore."

"Where did you see her?" Sascha asked.

Ella nodded. "She wandered over to that narrow doorway with what looks like an angry lizard above it."

"Angry lizard?" Marco asked. "You mean the dragon wings. But she shouldn't have been able to get in there. That door is always locked."

"It's open now," Sascha said. "I can see it. What's in there? Is something wrong, Marco?"

"That leads to Zinnath and Kalurth's cave."

"The dragons?" Sascha asked.

"Yes. She doesn't know about the traps in there." Marco raced toward the door. He called Kira's name out. There was no response. He turned back to Sascha. "I'll meet you back at the cave."

Sascha jumped out of her chair to chase after him. "I'm coming too."

Marco stopped and turned back to her. "Please," he pleaded. "You need to trust me. I'll find her and bring her here."

"Sascha!" The voice screamed in her head.

"Soleil." Sascha turned to Lee and Ella. "Soleil's in trouble. Lee, stay here and wait for Marco and Kira. Guard our books. Ella, come with me."

Sascha raced to the cave and saw the guards standing outside the entrance.

"Did you see anyone go into the cave?" Sascha snapped.

"No, ma'am," the taller of the two guards answered.

"Sascha!" Soleil cried out. "Stop Rusty."

"We're coming," she answered. She turned to the guards. "Someone snuck past you! Stay here and watch our backs. But this time, keep your eyes open." She pushed past them and raced into the cave.

She froze when she saw the two pit hounds lurking around the cave. Their claws clicked on the ground, and the air in the cave vibrated with the sound of their sniffing and snorting. They turned as one and headed for where Sascha knew Rusty and Soleil were hidden and then disappeared.

"Rusty!" Sascha heard Soleil scream out as Rusty appeared out of nowhere. She was ready to attack and confused to find the enemies were no longer there. Rusty turned in circles as she looked for the creatures.

"They're near Rusty," Soleil screamed out.

"I can help," Ella said. She raised her hands and a flash of light raced toward Rusty and covered her in a protective white ball.

Electricity sizzled as one of the creatures leaped at Rusty and was stopped by the shield Ella had created.

"The shield won't last long," Ella said. "Sorry, Sascha, but I'm not that good at magic."

Rusty launched herself at the shield as she tried to escape.

"Rusty, stop it," Sascha screamed. "Stay!"

Sascha darted to one side of the cave, looking for the tell-tale shimmer she had seen on Eratus. They were still near Rusty, but then she saw the shimmer change direction. They had stopped chasing after Rusty and were heading for her.

"This is my home, and you're not welcome," Sascha said to the creatures. She raised her hands and pictured fire. Fire came to life and flowed between the palms of her hands. She manipulated the fire and formed a ball. Using all her strength, she threw the fireball at the pit hounds and smashed them against the cave wall.

They staggered back to their feet, still alive, but no longer protected by their invisibility cloaks. Dark liquid oozed from their wounds.

Now they were visible, Rusty growled and tried even more desperately to escape the shield Ella had locked her in.

"Rusty, stay!" Sascha commanded.

Ella created another ball of white light, renewing the shield around Rusty.

"We have more time now," Ella said. "Finish them."

Sascha raised her hands, her fingers working quickly to manipulate another, larger ball of fire. She threw it. It picked the creatures up and smashed them against the wall again. This time they lay still. A putrid gas filled the air as the creatures sizzled and the flesh fell from their dark, glistening bones. Sascha raised her hands and stared at them.

"We were incredible. That was amazing." Ella said as she raced toward Sascha and gave her a powerful hug. "I feel so—"

"Alive?" Sascha asked. "But I can't believe I knew what to do. I didn't have time to think, it was instinct."

"It was the same for me," Ella said. "I knew I had magic, but that was amazing. We have to do that again." She jumped up and down, "Let's kill another monster."

Sascha laughed. "I don't think so, Ella. Let's check on Rusty. We have to make sure she wasn't bitten."

When Ella waved her hands in the direction of Soleil, the magic lifted and Sascha could see him again. Then Ella released Rusty from the ball. Rusty galumphed over to them. Sascha managed to avoid her huge wet tongue long enough to check her over and heaved a great sigh when it became clear that Rusty was fine.

"Soleil, how are you?"

"I'm good, thanks to you. But that dog is stubborn. She doesn't listen."

Sascha looked down at Rusty. "She's like someone else I know."

Soleil snapped his beak. "I'm not as bad as *her*!"

Ella had wandered over to the wall of the cave and was

staring at the bones. "Everything has melted away. The only thing that remains are the bones, and they stink."

"I know. One of those creatures attacked me on Eratus."

"That's the creature that attacked you? That must have been terrifying."

"It was scary. At least I knew what we were fighting this time. Ella, would you mind going to the library and collecting the others? I'll stay here with Soleil and Rusty."

"Wait until I tell them what happened here," Ella said as she raced out of the cave.

Sascha opened the door to the squad bay and walked in to freshen up. The adrenaline was wearing off and she was exhausted. After she had washed her face, she leaned on the basin and stared into the mirror. If pit hounds were here, someone in the Fire of the Phoenix headquarters must have powerful dark magic. But who could it be?

"We're back," Ella called out.

Sascha left the room and joined them in the cave. Ella was still bouncing around the cave, still full of energy. Marco and Lee carried bundles of books.

"Where's Kira?"

"She stayed in the library," Marco answered. "She's in a foul mood. She snapped at me when I asked her to bring some books back here."

"Something must have happened in the library," Sascha said. "I'll talk to her when she gets back."

"Are you OK?" Marco asked.

"I'm fine. Ella told you then?"

"You bet I told them," Ella said. "Lee, Marco, come and have a look." Marco and Lee followed Ella over to look at the skeletons.

"Parents used to scare their children with stories about pit hounds," Marco said. "Most adults think they're just creatures from their kids' story books."

"There's nothing made-up about those bones, is there?" Sascha said.

"Sascha, can I talk to you." Kira stood at the entrance to the cave. She looked over at Marco. "In private."

"Looks like it was me that upset her," Marco whispered.

Kira stormed outside to a little wooden seat near the lattice fence.

"There's something different about the little redhead," Soleil said.

"I haven't seen her this angry for years," Sascha said.

Sascha followed her. "Kira, what's happened? Marco said you are angry at him."

Kira snorted. "For once he's right. How much do you know about Marco?"

"I used to know him a long time ago. Why?"

"You shouldn't trust him."

"Why do you say that?"

"Someone gave me a letter." She handed Sascha an envelope. "Here, you read it."

"It's addressed to you," Sascha said.

"I know, but read it."

Sascha opened the envelope.

Dear Kira,

I know you want to know about your past, but you need to start looking closer to home before you go anywhere. Marco has a lot of secrets, secrets he should have shared with you when you first arrived. Marco's father raped your mother and you were the result. Marco knew, but he never did anything about it. When your mother's health suffered as a result of the rape, she asked her best friend a close friend of Marco's to care for you, but Marco stopped her. You have been badly treated.

Marco was given the chance to make everything right, to give you the family you should have had, but he threw it away. You never needed to be sent to a strange land. You could have stayed on Eratus all this time and grown up surrounded by people who love you. Don't trust Marco. Your safety depends on it.

You need to convince the others not to trust him too. He has too many secrets.

Signed, a friend of your mother.

SASCHA STARED BLINDLY at the note, then read it again. "This can't be right. Surely he would have said something to you. I'm so sorry, Kira." She read the note a third time. "I wonder who your mother is."

"I don't care," Kira said. "They can all go jump. I don't want them in my life. And I'm going to tell Marco that right now."

Sascha grabbed Kira's arm. "Why don't we go home first and talk? Everyone else can stay here. This letter might be a lie."

Kira choked. Her voice wavered. "Don't tell the girls yet. We all dreamed our parents were these incredible heroes, and now I find out I'm the result of a rape. No wonder she never fought to keep me. And Marco knew all along, but never told me. It would kill me if the girls found out. I'll meet you at your car."

Sascha's mind was numb. She sagged back against the seat. Marco had lied about everything from the beginning. And so had Ken. And so had Connell. Who could they trust? But perhaps she was right. Perhaps the letter was a lie, and someone was using it to split them up. Either way, Sascha had a lot to think about.

CHAPTER 26

ERATUS

Fireworks exploded outside. The colors of emerald, honey and powder flashed on the inside walls of the castle, lighting Connell's path as he made his way to his chambers. The smell of sulfur and saltpeter filled the air, overtaking the aroma of roasted meats and warm sweet rolls. The Elemental Magic Fair had begun. "No-one will be sleeping much tonight, will they, George?"

George darted in front of him and sat, forcing Connell to step around her.

"I'm not taking those beads off you, George. It would break the little girl's heart. They're magical. They're supposed to protect you."

Connell smiled. He knew it was cruel, but he couldn't help himself. He stopped, turned toward George and patted her head. "Who's a pretty puppy then?" he cooed.

George bristled and gave a deep-chested roar.

"If it's that important to you, you can tell her you're not a puppy. But you're on your own. I'm not saying anything." He laughed.

Connell opened the door to his chambers. Reya, dressed in her black leather training gear, sat in the chair beside his desk. His laughter died in his throat. George sidled up to him, her eyes focused on Reya. Pretending to straighten the bottom of his pants leg, Connell leaned down, removed the beads from around George's neck and stuffed them into his pocket.

He glanced at Reya as he walked past her and dropped his cane on his desk. The healer, pleased with his progress, had released him from having to use it.

Connell turned to face Reya.

This should be interesting.

"Reya! I'm honored you deigned to visit me. Or has Drakon got you running errands?"

"Connell, I need your help."

He smirked. "You need *my* help. Really? What about my big brother? Why don't you go to him?"

"It's him I need protection from," Reya replied.

"Why? Have you two had another squabble?"

Reya looked down at her hands, which were fidgeting with a band on her wrist. "Your brother...he's changed. I've always been wary of him, but lately he scares me. I'm terrified he's planning to feed me to his fire dragons, like...."

"Like the mage that helped in the ceremony?"

She stared at the floor. "How did—"

"Reya, I'm busy. All I can say is that it looks like you're getting what you deserve. You have always had Drakon's protection. If you have lost that, then I'm sorry for you." Connell turned his back on her and moved toward the door. "Please leave."

"If you help me, I will tell you everything I know about Drakon's plans."

"I know what he is up to," Connell said.

Reya jumped to her feet. "No, you don't. You don't know

why he needs the weapons, what he's planning to do with them."

Connell frowned. "I doubt the information will be free."

Reya paced the floor behind Connell's desk. "You're right. I will tell you everything, but only if you protect me."

"You're a powerful mage. You could sort this out yourself, Reya."

Reya stopped pacing the floor and stood in front of Connell. "Have you heard of black lyrium?"

"Black crystals, yes, but not black lyrium."

"I hadn't heard about it before either. But adding it to the food or drink of a mage neutralizes their powers, makes them vulnerable to attack." She shuddered.

"How do you know that?"

"Drakon used it on the mage he punished—"

"I know all about the mage and what he did to her."

"You know how powerful that mage was. Didn't you wonder why she didn't fight back? Why she allowed him to do the things he did to her?" Reya stopped for a moment. "It was worse than you can imagine, Connell. And he made me watch."

Connell shook his head. "And you did nothing to help that young girl? You're as bad as he is."

"Yes." Reya hung her head. Tears rolled down her face. "I know. I saw her try to use her magic, saw her fail. Heard her screams as those creatures played with her before they started feasting on her. The damage..." She shook her head. "Ken showed her mercy. He put her out of her pain."

"Ken wasn't lying about that," Connell muttered.

"What?"

"Nothing. Why are you telling me all this, Reya?"

"I'm convinced that's what Drakon has planned for me. Please, Connell, you need to help me."

"I need some time to think. Go now and I will—"

Heavy boots sounded in the hallways. "I...I can't leave here now." Reya's face turned ashen. "That could be Drakon. He'll be suspicious if he sees me coming out of your chambers. He will want to know what we talked about."

"You're good at lying. I can't see that being of concern to you." Connell crossed his arms and stared at her. "What is it you're not telling me?"

"Drakon brought me breakfast in bed today. He never brings me breakfast. Then I realized that he must have poisoned the food, so I didn't eat it. I only had the vimberry he brought with it. That was my mistake. Black lyrium was in the vimberry."

"He gave you the lyrium? How do you know?"

"I drank half of it before falling asleep. When I woke, I tried to warm what was left. I couldn't even summon a warming spell. Please, Connell, help me."

Connell turned away from Reya. "Why should I believe you?"

"I told you, Drakon's changed. He keeps talking about how clever Chiane is. And when he's not talking about Chiane, he talks about Sascha. I've realized that if he wants to appoint a new general and acquire a new mistress, he needs to get rid of me, clear the way."

"Sascha's his sister. He wouldn't take her as his mistress."

"She's his adopted sister."

Connell turned to face Reya. "That's the same thing. And he hates Sascha."

"It's not the same thing. If he will sleep with me, he'll sleep with Sascha."

"What do you mean?"

"She's my sister. I'm your half-sister."

"Now I know you're lying."

"Look at me! Can't you see the similarities between Sascha and me?"

Connell tilted his head to the side as he studied Reya.

"I swear on Athena's life," Reya said. "It's the truth. I never realized either, but I never did see much of Sascha when she lived on Eratus. But when she turned up here a couple of days ago and Drakon found out, he demanded that I follow her, keep an eye on everything she was doing. I was near her when that *thing* attacked."

"You mean the pit hound?" Connell asked.

"Yes. Ugly looking beast." Reya went to the water jug on Connell's desk, poured herself a glass of water and took a few sips before continuing. "It was the first time I had been that close to her in years. I was shocked to see how alike we are. Her hair color was different, but her face! We look the same. I had to know who she was, so I went to the Four Sisters headquarters and checked through the register of mages."

"The register is locked away in their vaults. You couldn't have opened the vault without Laela's help."

"I know. Laela did help me."

"She never mentioned it to me."

"Well, she did. When I checked the register, I found out my mother had two girls to my father and a son to an unlisted father. When Mother died, Father took me. Owain took my sister and half-brother. We're kin."

Son to an unlisted father!

"What do you mean, *a son to an unlisted father?*"

"I don't know who your father is Connell, but he wasn't our father. Father used to say he was glad Mother was dead, because she was a whore. I used to think it was his way of coping with her death, but now it all makes sense."

Connell walked to his chair and sat down.

"I know it's a lot to take in, Connell," Reya said. "I'll get you a drink of water." She poured a glass of water and passed it to Connell. "Here, drink this."

"It doesn't make sense. If this is true, why am I only finding out now?"

"Laela told me she has known for years. She has her reasons for saying nothing. Have a drink, Connell. You're looking pale."

Connell gulped the water down and put the glass on the floor next to him. George walked over to it, sniffed at it and started to snarl. She turned to Reya and Reya started to back away from her. "That animal doesn't like me," Reya said.

"Do you blame her?"

George's snarl deepened. She took a step toward Reya.

"Connell, would you mind putting her in your sleeping quarters while we talk?"

"This is her home, not yours."

"I know, but please."

George stalked toward Reya, her body poised to strike.

Connell pointed to the floor next to him. "Calm, George. Lie down."

George ignored him and crouched down, ready to attack.

She's going to attack her.

"No!" Connell jumped out of his chair and grabbed her collar. "Sorry, girl. This time I need to send you to the other room."

George pulled at her collar, but her gaze remained fixed on Reya.

"Come. Now!" Connell snapped. "What is with you, girl?"

Connell dragged George to the room and closed the door. He turned back to talk to Reya. "I—"

Where did she go?

The balcony curtains blew in the gentle breeze.

She must have gone outside.

He walked toward the curtains and heard the click of a lock behind him. He turned. Reya stood at the door to his sleeping chambers. She had locked George in. George's roar echoed around the room, the pitch rattling the windows. Connell's stomach churned. He had made a mistake. This was a trick and he had fallen for it. But why? What was she after? Connell heard the sound of George's nails scratching at wood as she began to dig furiously at the base of the door.

Reya laughed. "By the time you scratch your way out of there, George, it will be too late." She looked at Connell. "I had to lock her in. I don't want a long and complicated battle. It would draw too much attention." She walked over to his desk. "Did you enjoy your water?"

"My..."

George sniffed the water glass. That's when she went crazy.

Connell could hear George throwing herself at the door, trying to break through to help him.

"George, I'm okay. Have some water, rest and recover."

George quietened down.

"Reya, someone will have heard the racket George was making."

"Over the noise of the fair?" Reya grinned as she walked over to the balcony doors and pushed them fully open. As the familiar sounds of the fair echoed around Connell's room, he realized no-one would have noticed the noise. His only hope was that George remembered her training.

George, please don't fail me.

"I assume everything you told me was a lie," Connell said. "We aren't really kin."

"Oh, but we are. It's surprising, isn't it?" Reya walked away from the balcony and toward Connell. "Do you want to see if you can do one of your cute electrical ball spells?"

Connell looked over at the glass on the floor. "The water was clear."

Connell looked up at Reya. She was smirking at him. "That's the thing about the lyrium," she said. "It's called black lyrium because of the magic used to create it. Unlike all the other lyriums, it's not named for its color. It is clear and tasteless. Go on, humor me. Try one of your electrical spells."

Connell walked over to his desk and picked up his cane his only weapon. She wasn't going to win. She couldn't. "You'd better hope it worked, Reya, because there's no way I'm going to humor you."

"Never mind. I already know how helpless you are. I just wanted to see you try."

"What are you going to do now? Use your magic to kill me?"

"No, no. I've worked out a way to get rid of you without me being blamed. Laela would sense my magic if I used it and she would be angry at me. Sorry, I should have said that she would sense my magic if I used it *now*. But if I had prepared something earlier..."

Connell watched Reya as she walked to the picture on his wall and shifted it to the left, opening the secret passageway to his room. "Drakon told me about this secret tunnel. He wanted me to investigate how to get in and out. I have to admit that it's very handy."

Connell heard snorting and sniffing, and saw a shimmer move out of the dark entrance. He swallowed. "A pit hound? Really, Reya. It was you?"

"Without George and Soleil," Reya said, "oh, and your magic, my baby here will be able to kill you. And then you will become my creature and do my bidding." She cackled. "I will have the true son of King Owain under my power."

"The true son?" Connell asked. "What are you talking about, Reya?"

"I guess if you're going to die, it is only fair if I tell you why. I did learn who your father was. You are Owain's son. It was Drakon's father who was unlisted. Well, he wasn't actually unlisted. Laela deliberately had his name excluded.

Unlisted father seemed so much better. And his mother died giving birth to him, so she won't care."

"Laela knows?" Connell stammered.

"Of course she knows. She has known for years. Never underestimate Laela. She has big plans, bigger than you or Drakon ever realized. But the plans involve Drakon, not you. To save any complications, I think it is better we get rid of you. I don't like loose ends. She doesn't agree, but she can't have everything her way, can she?"

"I should have known," Connell said. "You're as evil as Drakon."

Reya stepped into the secret passageway. "Time for me to go." She turned toward the shimmer, "He's all yours, my pet."

Reya pressed a button and the wall closed. "Have fun, you two," she called through the wall, her laughter echoing in Connell's ears.

*T*he screeches of the lorikeets and the monotonous caws of the crows flying overhead woke him. The sun's heat warmed the air and its glow lit up the cave. Marco stretched out on the blanket and stared at the roof of the cave. Kira hadn't come back after she and Sascha had talked. Sascha said she needed more time with Kira to determine what was wrong.

She wouldn't look me in the eye. Whatever I did must have been bad. What did Kira say to her?

He had searched his mind, tried to remember if he had said something, done something that might have upset Kira. She had been fine when he left her in the library, and Lee and Ella hadn't known anything when he had asked them.

Marco sat up and turned toward Soleil and Rusty. He could smell bacon and coffee. One of the girls must be up and cooking breakfast in the squad bay. His stomach rumbled. He was hungry, but he couldn't face food, not yet, not until he found out what had happened with Kira.

His phone rang and he grabbed it. His heart sank. It was Alex, not Sascha.

"Hi, Alex. How's it going? Have you had any luck in finding the safe house?"

"We think we've found it. Eham has been very helpful. We're about to drive out to see it. It's in a remote part of Scotland, near Achmelvich. Someone fitting the description of Jenny lives there. Mind you, we have had a few false leads, but we're hoping it's legit this time. One second, Marco." Alex's voice was muffled, but Marco could still hear him. "Yes, that's fine, Eham. I'll come over in about ten minutes."

There was a heavy thud as a door closed. A pause.

"Marco, something's not right with Eham. Have you noticed?"

"What do you mean?" Marco asked.

"It's strange. It only happened once. I dropped Eham off at your house, but had to go back in when I realized I'd left my keys behind. I saw this black creature twisting around Eham's feet. It had beady eyes and sharp white teeth. Eham clicked his fingers and the creature disappeared."

"I saw it too," Marco said, "but I thought I was imagining it."

"It couldn't have been a dread wisp, could it? Only dark mages use dread wisps. Eham's not a dark mage, is he?"

"I honestly don't know," Marco answered. "We've been researching dark powers and dark creatures. I don't know if they have anything on dread wisps, but I'll have a look."

"I have this uneasy feeling," Alex said. "But I know he's Jenny's grandfather. He wouldn't do anything to hurt her."

"I hope not," Marco said. "I'm the one that sent him to you."

"He has been useful in the search for Jenny," Alex said. "I guess I shouldn't complain."

"Let me know how you go at the house. Ring me after you've been there. And be careful."

"Yep, I'll call you. You be careful too, Marco. Speak to you tomorrow."

Marco heard the dial tone. Alex was right. There was something wrong with Eham, but Marco was sure he wouldn't hurt Jenny. He loved her. Marco hung up the phone.

MARCO WALKED OVER TO SOLEIL. "Soleil, would you move your wings so that I can have a look?"

The wounds were healing better than he could have hoped, and the scars now looked like fine golden lines. It wouldn't be long before Soleil would be completely healed. Sascha's magic was clearly more powerful than he had first thought.

"You're quiet, Soleil. You're angry with me too, I suppose."

Soleil stood and gently stretched his wings. He glanced over his shoulder at Marco and walked out into the morning sunlight. Marco and Rusty followed.

"Don't you do anything stupid, Soleil. Your wounds may be healing, but you need to give yourself moretime before you fly."

Soleil walked around to the back of the cave and tapped his beak on the fridge.

"You're hungry," Marco said. "I'll get some food for you." He picked up a tray and opened the fridge.

Soleil snapped his beak.

"OK, OK! I'm hurrying. Do you always have to be so difficult? You're not the only one with problems." Marco sighed. Not for the first time, he wished he had the necklace. Sascha was lucky she could hear Soleil without it. How would he explain to Sascha that he could wear it? That would open a whole bucketload of issues.

Soleil leaned over and tapped the fridge again. Marco turned around, intent on letting all his frustrations out on the bird. Soleil moved his head until he and Marco were eye to eye, then moved deliberately around him and touched his beak to the same spot.

Marco glanced at him, then squatted and peered into the fridge. "Are you trying to tell me something, Soleil?" Then he saw it a little door on the inside of the fridge. He placed the tray on the ground and ran his hand over the fridge wall, searching for a button, something to open the door. His fingers found a small raised spot, which he pressed. The door slid open. Inside was a necklace, money and a phone.

Marco picked up the necklace and put it on.

"Finally," Soleil said.

"Is this an emergency kit for Sascha?" Marco asked. "How did you know it was here?"

"She organized this stash before she was deported from Eratus," Soleil replied. "About six years ago."

"A year before she was deported? So she visited Earth when she was leader of the Four Sisters. But why? And why didn't she tell me?"

"Perhaps she was being cautious."

Marco examined the phone. It was dead. Then he flicked through the money. "There's several thousand dollars here."

Soleil ducked behind Marco, picked up a chunk of the meat from the fridge and swallowed it in one gulp.

"So you are hungry," Marco said. "I'll put some meat on a tray for you."

Rusty leaped around the fridge. "Ar-ruf."

"No, Rusty this is Soleil's food. I'll find you something else in a minute." Marco picked the tray up again, filled it with portions of meat and placed the tray on the ground in front of Soleil, who inhaled the meal in a matter of moments. "You greedy guts," Marco said.

He picked up the money and stared at it. "What made her think she needed to organize this?"

"She told me there might come a day when she would need it."

"Why would she hide everything in this fridge?" Marco said. "It was a bit risky. It could have fallen into anyone's hands."

"Good luck to them. She protected the fridge with powerful magic."

"What sort of—"

The sounds of twigs cracking and gravel crunching underfoot came from the clump of trees nearest to them. Rusty gave a low growl and stalked toward the sound, the hair on her back bristling. Marco was about to call Rusty back when he remembered the necklace. He reached up and took it off, but held it in his hand so he could still talk to Soleil. "I hope that's not Sascha returning," Marco whispered. "I'll have to be careful. How would I explain to her that I can wear this?"

A guard walked out of the bush, glanced at a still growling Rusty and strode toward Marco. The guard saluted. "Colonel, we have added Sascha's name to the security system, so she will have no issues when she wants to return."

"Very good, sergeant," Marco said, returning the salute. "Update the guards at the gate."

"Yes, colonel," he said before turning on his heel and marching away.

"You wanting to hide the necklace is exactly what I wanted to talk to you about, Marco. You must talk to Sascha, really talk to her. Tell her everything! I don't know what happened yesterday afternoon, but I have a bad feeling."

"I know what you mean," Marco said as he rubbed his stomach.

"Drakon is out to take advantage of the secrets you,

Connell and Owain have. You need to tell her before she finds out some other way."

"How do I do that?" Marco asked. "Can you imagine what Sascha will do?"

Soleil clicked his beak at Marco. "Can you imagine how Sascha will react if she is given bits of the truth? She won't know who to trust. This could all explode."

Marco glanced at Rusty, who was sitting several feet away from Soleil. She was watching them with her head tilted to one side. He walked over and patted her.

"Drakon is back here on Earth," Soleil said.

"How do you know?"

"He came through the portal at the same time Sascha and I did. He tried to send his pyran to destroy me, push me into the claws of the guardians. Then he realized Sascha was riding me and he backed off."

"Sascha thought it was her fault that you fell into the guardians," Marco said.

"Her fault? But she was there."

"It looks like I'm not the only one that needs to talk to Sascha."

"I'm surprised she thinks it's her fault. Anyway, Drakon's intention is to capture her," Soleil continued. "He could use your secrets to destroy your relationship with her. I'm concerned she'll decide to put her trust in the wrong person." Soleil looked up into the sky. "I need to heal. Flying will help me to regain my strength."

"Flying isn't a good idea, Soleil. It's only been a couple of days. Give yourself more time."

"I can't afford to let the joints seize. Are you going to talk to Sascha?"

"Sascha is angry with me."

"So sort it out. This isn't about you or Sascha. It's about

doing whatever we need to so we can heal the Shield and save the people on Eratus."

"You're right."

Tyres on gravel sounded from the front of the cave. Marco's stomach knotted. Sascha was here. He shoved the necklace into his pocket. Rusty left them and bounced around to the front of the cave to welcome Sascha back. Marco walked far enough to see the parked car. Sascha stepped out of the car alone.

"This is your chance, Marco," Soleil said. "Before Lee and Ella realize she is here and come out to talk to her."

Sascha greeted Rusty in a low voice. Her despondence was obvious, even at a distance. "Uh oh, things didn't go well last night with Kira."

Soleil glanced at Marco and then turned toward Sascha. He half-flew, half-walked over to greet her.

Marco studied Sascha as she checked Soleil's wounds. She looked up and saw him staring at her. She said something to Soleil and stroked his neck. As she walked toward Marco, he pressed his hands deep into his jeans pockets. He knew that look. He was right. He was in trouble.

She stopped about five feet away from him. "When were you going to tell me your father raped Kira's mother? Why didn't you give me a chance to tell her?"

Marco felt the ground disappear beneath him. "What? How did you find out?"

"Kira found a note that had been left for her by a friend of her mother."

"A friend of her mother? Who would—ah, Drakon."

"I see what Owain was talking about. Drakon is the perfect patsy for everything that goes wrong, isn't he? Everyone who I'm supposed to trust has lied to me. The only one who has been honest with me is Drakon." Sascha took a breath. "You haven't answered my question, Marco. When were you going to tell me?"

Marco's mind whirred with possible answers, but he still couldn't decide what to say.

The truth. I need to tell her the truth.

"I couldn't," he said.

"What do you mean, *you couldn't*?"

"Your instructions were clear. I was never to tell anyone."

"My instructions? What are you talking about? I never said any such thing."

"You did. Before you left Eratus."

"How convenient. Too convenient. Marco, I don't believe you." The muscles in Sascha's jaw flickered as she clenched her teeth. She shook her head. "I might have forgiven you for lying, but to let Kira find out what happened to her mother in a note. A note!" Sascha squared her shoulders and took a step closer to him. "You could have told us everything years ago, but you lied and flew off to Scotland to live with some floozy you married."

"Sascha, you and I need to talk about this when you're a bit calmer." Marco glanced over at Soleil and saw the bird wince.

"When I'm a bit calmer? Really?" Sascha crossed her arms and stood in front of Marco, sneering and tapping her foot on the ground. "That's all you can say? This news has destroyed Kira. We could have helped her, made the truth a bit easier to digest. But it's me who needs to be calmer?"

"What I meant was—"

"I'm not interested in what you meant," Sascha said. "She was only one little girl. Why should you worry about her? I'm sure you had far more important things to do!"

An intense fury burned inside Marco, a flash of hate for this person he thought he loved.

Tell her the truth. You're an idiot for taking this. Destroy her!

Marco looked away from Sascha. Soleil and Rusty were watching them. Soleil moved toward Marco, but he raised his hand. "No, you stay out of this. This is my battle."

Sascha turned and stared at Soleil. "He asked me to me gentle with you. He said you were a good man. I never thought Soleil was gullible, until now. I want you to leave, Marco. I don't want you here, Kira doesn't want you here. The girls and I have a job to do. You're a distraction we could do without."

Marco didn't understand why Sascha calling him a distraction was inflammatory, but it was. "How dare you, Sascha. You have no idea—"

"Please go," Sascha said. She turned her back on him. "I can't deal with you."

Hatred ate at Marco like acid. He grabbed her by the arms. "Don't you dare turn your back on me. You may think you know everything and think you have a right to take the higher moral ground, but you don't. You are more to blame than me or Connell or Owain."

She pulled her arms free from Marco's grip. "What are you talking about?"

Marco stormed to his car. Sascha followed. He opened the door and threw himself in. "And another thing. The note couldn't have been from a friend of her mother. You're her mother and you have no friends."

Marco turned the ignition on, revved the car and pressed his foot to the accelerator. He sped off, leaving dust in his wake. Marco glanced in the rearview mirror and was pleased to see all the color had drained from Sascha's face.

DRAKON HOPED Sascha had read the note he had left on her door. She should be here soon. He glanced at the mirrored wall at the entrance to the club. Yes, his disguise was in place.

Drakon walked to the bar and ordered wine and some wedges with sour cream. He carried the ice bucket to the same table they had sat at last time. He assumed it was somewhere she liked to sit. Drakon turned the bottle of Angel Cove, the same wine Sascha had been drinking on the day they met, in the ice. He took the two glasses out of the ice bucket and put them on the table as a waitress delivered the wedges.

Drakon fingered the charm bracelet in his pocket. He might have had a problem if she had stayed on Eratus for too long. Laela would have helped her to fully activate her magic and then the bracelet would have been deadly. In that case, he would have had to settle for using the green lyrium. But it would be a last resort. The last thing he wanted to do was hurt Sascha. She was his, and he loved her. She just needed a bit of time to realize how much she loved him too. It felt exhilarating to admit what he had hidden for all these years.

I love her! Marco was a fool to let her go. I would have fought for her.

Soleil should be dead by now. The pit hounds should have made short work of him. And if Kira showed Sascha the note, her friendship with Marco would be damaged permanently, and the path would be clear. Drakon chuckled and rubbed his hands together. This was his chance.

Together they would convince the girls to join them and then they would be unstoppable. They would heal the Shield and then work to release the weapons that would give them the power to rule not only Eratus but Earth as well. Drakon was so absorbed in his thoughts that he didn't see Sascha until she was standing next to him.

"Hi," she said. "Deep in thought?"

"Yes, I was. Sorry, I didn't see you arrive. I organized wine and wedges. Seemed perfect for a Saturday afternoon." Drakon pointed to a seat opposite him. "Please, sit." He poured a glass of wine and gave it to her. She sat, took a mouthful and relaxed back into her chair. Drakon could feel her eyes on him as he leaned over to pick up the wedges. "Can I tempt you with a wedge?"

"Thanks," she said.

"Some days really take it out of you, don't they?" he said. "You look weary."

She looked down into her glass of wine. "I am weary. A lot has happened."

"I've been told I'm a good listener."

"I'd prefer not to talk about it," she said. "But thanks for the offer." She took another mouthful of wine.

"Let's change the subject," Drakon said. "How did you and Ken meet?"

"Ken?" She smiled. "I've always thought of him as my dad. He seems to want to look after me, but I guess I'm not that easy to look after."

"I find that hard to believe," he said. "That reminds me. I have a favor to ask. Do you mind?"

"It depends on what the favor is."

"I bought a bracelet for my girlfriend and I want a second opinion before I give it to her. Would you mind having a look at it and giving me your opinion?"

"That's a nice thing to do, but women can have quite different tastes."

"This is it," Drakon said as he put it on the table. "What do you think?"

The braided golden bracelet reflected the light. It glittered.

"It's absolutely stunning," she said. "What is it made of?" She picked it up and looked closely at it.

"Three types of gold and that glitter is diamond dust. Put it on. Show me what it looks like."

She did so, twisting her wrist back and forth. The light caught the bracelet as it moved, making it sparkle like the stars in the night sky. "It is truly beautiful."

Drakon could see her face relaxing, the stress lines around her eyes softening. The bracelet was doing its job. "You think she would like it?"

"She should love it and..." Sascha sat back in the chair and closed her eyes. "I'm tired. I'm so sorry, I'm being rude."

She shouldn't be responding so quickly to its power.

"You probably need some fresh air. Why don't we go outside? Maybe we could go for a walk on the beach? It's not far from here, and the fresh sea air should help you wake up."

"No, I need to—" She stopped. "Yes, okay."

"I'll drive. You shouldn't drive if you're tired."

She didn't appear to have heard him and continued to sit in the chair with her eyes closed. As Drakon watched her, the color drained from her face.

I need to move fast to get that bracelet off her.

"Sascha, I think it's time we left." Drakon jumped up and helped her out of her seat. She was compliant. Too compliant.

She couldn't have activated her magic, could she?

Drakon shook his head.

It's not possible. She wasn't on Eratus long enough.

Drakon put his arm around her waist and guided her out of the building, moving as fast as he could without attracting attention.

It was dusk. It surprised him to see how high and bright the sun still was. He shielded his eyes and frowned. The sun was moving closer, getting brighter.

How is that possible?

Drakon realized too late that it was Soleil.

As Sascha raised her arms to protect her eyes from the glare, Soleil dived toward her, ripped the bracelet from her wrist and shot back up into the sky. Sascha screeched in fright. Soleil swooped down at Drakon, forcing him to move away from Sascha.

The blasted bird was dead. It should be dead. How did Soleil survive the pit hounds? He was badly wounded. He should have been an easy target.

Drakon looked over at Sascha, who stood a short distance from her car, massaging her wrist and shaking her head as the magic from the bracelet started to weaken.

Drakon moved forward quickly, grabbed at her and tried to hold her. She stomped down hard on the instep of his foot with her high heel. Pain shot up his leg and he released his grip. She raced toward her car. The club's sliding doors swished open and a group of people, which included a couple of security guards, came out to see what the ruckus was.

The security guards were watching them both, but one of them seemed to be focusing more on him. More people came out. Drakon could only watch as Sascha jumped into her car, started it and sped off. As he stood in the center of the carpark, he watched her glance in the rearview mirror. It was then he realized that, in his rush to protect himself from Soleil, he had focused his magic on creating a protective shield and not on maintaining his appearance.

Drakon picked up his phone. He would need to use his backup plan. He didn't have long. They would be planning to leave Earth soon. Drakon needed to get to Sascha before she left for the portal.

~

SASCHA SHOOK HER HEAD. It felt like it was full of cotton wool, but she couldn't think why. She was turning out of the carpark and into the street outside the club.

How did I get here? I feel...drunk. I shouldn't be driving. Perhaps I should go back into the club, have a drink of water and call a cab.

"No," a voice screamed at her. "Keep going."

"Soleil?"

"Yes, it's me. You're in danger. Keep going."

Sascha looked in the rearview mirror to search for Soleil. Among a crowd of people watching her drive away was Drakon. "What the hell is Drakon doing here?"

Sascha drove back to the cave. She jumped out of the car and looked for Soleil. He was sitting next to Rusty and the girls at the cave's entrance.

"Soleil, what happened? And what were you thinking of when you flew all that way to the club?"

"That's ripe," Soleil said. "I saved you from Drakon, but the first thing you do is tell *me* off."

Guilt slashed at Sascha. "I wasn't telling you off."

Lee and Ella came running to her and threw their arms around her. "Thank the heavens you're okay."

"Why shouldn't I be okay? What happened?"

"I'm sorry," Lee said. "Ella and I were guessing who this sketch artist was, the one you were meeting." Lee glanced around at Soleil. "He heard us talking about him and took off. We tried to stop him, but he ignored us."

Soleil clicked his beak at them and turned to Sascha. "Everyone wants to tell me off. I knew something was wrong. I had to check. I'm worried that you didn't sense the bracelet. Didn't you realize what Drakon was up to?"

"What are you talking about, Soleil?"

Soleil gave an exaggerated sigh. "Think back. What were you doing?"

"What did Soleil say?" Lee asked.

"He asked me to try to remember what I was doing today, but everything is blank." Sascha rubbed her eyes as she tried to remember. She ran her hands through her hair. "I honestly can't remember a thing."

Lee put her arm around Sascha. "Let's go inside, let you sit down."

Sascha let Lee guide her to the kitchen in the squad bay. She sat down at the table, and Ella brought her a glass of wine. Soleil and Rusty stood in the doorway.

"What's the time?" Sascha asked.

"Five-thirty," Lee answered.

"The last thing I remember was Marco speeding off from the cave this morning."

"You came back in here," Lee said. "You helped us gather the research together."

"Did I?"

"You were quiet, not yourself, but that wasn't surprising considering you had fought with Marco. We reminded you of your appointment with your sketch artist and you left."

"The sketch artist! Now it's coming back to me. I hope I didn't embarrass him. Or myself. He was showing me a bracelet and then everything went blank. He—"

"The sketch artist was Drakon," Soleil said.

"Drakon? But that's not possible, Soleil. They look completely different."

"It's magic," Soleil said.

"Magic?" Sascha repeated. "But why would he..."

"It's so hard getting only parts of your conversations with Soleil," Lee said.

"Sorry," Sascha replied.

"It's OK. It's just that sometimes it's hard to work out what you two are talking about when we only hear your side of the conversation. If Drakon tried to use magic to kidnap you, he must be determined to capture us, like Ken told you."

Sascha sighed. "It seems that's what Soleil thinks."

"Lee is right," Soleil said. "Drakon is desperate to capture you. And that time he nearly succeeded. We need to gather everyone together and leave for Eratus."

"Will we be any safer on Eratus?" Sascha's stomach churned at the idea of seeing Connell and Owain again.

"We have to be," Lee said. "None of us can remember our pasts. It's like we are all fighting our own private pit hounds, creatures we can't see, creatures that are capable of tearing us apart."

"That's a great analogy, Lee," Ella said. "That's exactly what it's like."

"But you and Marco need to talk before you leave, Sascha," Soleil said.

Sascha's phone buzzed. "It's Kira." Sascha read the message, typed her response and turned back to Lee and Ella. "She asked if she can stay with her school friend, Tanya, for tonight. I said yes, as long as Tanya's mum is fine with the idea. I'm worried about her. She's only fifteen, and she has to face so much."

"So she's still upset?" Lee asked.

Sascha slipped her phone into her pocket "Yes, she is."

"What happened?" Lee asked.

"Do you mind if we don't talk about it yet? When Kira is back, we can all sit down and chat about it together. After all, it's Kira's secret to tell, not mine."

She couldn't be my daughter. I was only nine when she was born. What Marco said makes no sense. But I wish I was Kira's mother. Any mother would be proud of that girl.

Sascha stood, walked over to the fridge and poured herself a glass of chilled water. She wanted time to work it all out, but they needed to start preparing for the return to Eratus. Sascha turned to the girls. "How did you go with the research?"

"We found some real gems." Lee grinned, her eyes sparkling. "Did you know that three gods fought over who should rule Eratus?"

"Three gods?" Sascha asked.

"Yes. Athena, Ares and Hades. Ares and Hades were the ones who helped the ancients create those weapons that Drakon is after. And once they were made, they wanted to test them out on the people of Eratus. There was a massive war when Athena found out what Ares and Hades were planning. Athena won and has protected Eratus ever since. She locked the weapons away using the magic of the Shield. Every time the Shield is renewed, so is the magic that locks away the weapons."

"So the gods helped to create the weapons?" Sascha said. "Wow! I bet none of the others know that."

"We gave the texts back to the library after copying what we needed," Lee said. "Perhaps we can all go home now and look at everything there?"

"We still need to talk about how we're going to return to Eratus but we need everyone together to do that." Sascha glanced around the cave. "It would be good to get away from here. I'm sorry we left you two to do a lot of the work."

"You've all had other things going on," Lee said. "And we enjoyed ourselves. Marco did a lot of work last night before he fell asleep. He said he would stand guard, but we know he spent most of the night researching."

Sascha flinched as she remembered what she had said to Marco, particularly what she had said about his wife. She had been cruel, but then so had he.

"How are your wings after the long flight, Soleil?"

"They're good. They're a bit tender."

"Flying to the club wouldn't have helped. Do you think you can fly to my place, or would you like to rest first?"

Soleil shuddered and fluffed up his feathers so he

appeared to be twice his size. "I would prefer not to spend another night here."

"I agree. Girls, I'll pack some of Soleil's food. You pack our gear and the research papers in the car. Rusty, you help the girls."

Lee laughed. "Thanks, Sascha. That's all we need."

"Ar-ruf." Rusty bounced around Lee, her tail wagging.

"No games, Rusty," Lee said as she walked toward the squad bay.

"Once we're done, we can leave," Sascha said. "We have a lot to do." She remembered the ancient text she had hidden away in the cupboard in the squad bay. She retrieved it and placed it at the back of the boot, away from prying eyes

SASCHA HEAVED a sigh of relief as they arrived home. A tall narrow bag and a bunch of roses sat on the front step.

"It looks like someone has an admirer," Lee said as she jumped out of the car and raced to pick up the gifts, beating Rusty by only seconds.

"The envelope says they're for you, Sascha," she said as she retraced her steps. Lee breathed in the sweet aroma of the roses. "Open the envelope."

Sascha put her case down and glanced at Lee as she took the card. There was nothing on the envelope to identify the florist, and the writing didn't look familiar. She opened it.

Sascha,

I'm sorry about what happened at the club today. I didn't want to upset you. In fact, that's the last thing I wanted to do.

I didn't get a chance to tell you who I was, but I guess you know now. Please accept this bottle of wine as my apology.

Maybe one day we can catch up on Eratus and I will tell you why I wanted to meet you today. You can blame Ken.

Drakon.

"Well, don't keep us in suspense." Lee put her hands on her hips "Tell us who sent it."

Sascha smiled at Lee. "You're so impatient!" Sascha read the note out to them.

"Don't trust him," Soleil said. "I don't believe it was Ken's fault."

Lee handed Sascha the bag. "He sent you wine, so he can't be all bad. I'll take the flowers."

"Females!" Soleil scoffed. "Why are they so easily impressed by such trivial things?"

Sascha ignored Soleil's barb. She unlocked the front door and stepped inside. Lee followed her in, cradling the bunch of flowers like a baby.

Sascha's mind kept going over the note. Why would he blame Ken? She pushed her thoughts aside, walked to the kitchen and put the wine in the fridge. Then she went out to the patio to check Soleil's wounds. She was pleased to see there was no visible damage after the day's adventures. "Rusty, make sure you keep an eye on Soleil, and, Soleil, please take it easy. No wild flights to rescue anyone."

She walked back inside. Lee had placed the flowers in the vase in the middle of the kitchen table, and was sitting at the kitchen bench talking to Ella as she made coffee. The rich scent of ground coffee filled the house.

"We've ordered Chinese for dinner," Lee said. "It'll be here in an hour."

"Perfect." Sascha sat down at the table as Ella arrived with the coffee.

"I thought I would organize lunch for tomorrow," Lee said. "We should gather everyone together so we can go through our notes from the library."

"Good idea," Sascha said.

"What time will Kira be coming home?" Lee asked.

"I don't know. You'll need to text her."

"What about Marco?" Lee asked. "Do you mind if we invite him too?"

Sascha felt her throat closing up. "I need time before I face him again."

"But we need to know what he found out last night," Lee insisted.

"I know." Sascha wrapped her hands around her coffee cup. She could feel Lee's eyes boring into her.

"The timing is interesting," Lee said, "don't you think?"

"What do you mean?" Sascha asked.

"We know Kira found something at the library, and we know that's what you three are fighting about. Ella and I saw you and Kira talking outside the cave. We saw how upset Kira was. We have been searching for our pasts for so long and couldn't find anything. Then, when we finally start to get somewhere, this thing appears out of the blue, causing you and Kira to start hating Marco."

"There's more to it than that, Lee," Sascha said.

"Can you tell us about the note?" Lee asked. "What it said?"

To give herself time to think, Sascha got up from the table, walked to the fridge and took out a packet of chocolate biscuits. "I would prefer to let Kira tell you. But it was cruel."

"Was it true?" Lee asked.

"Yes...I think..." Sascha stopped on her way back to the table as she thought about what Marco said.

Did I give him time to tell me the truth?

"Actually, I assumed it was true because of Marco's reaction."

"How did he react?"

Sascha opened the packet of biscuits and offered it to the girls before taking a biscuit for herself. She sat down. "He asked me how I found out. He wouldn't have asked me that if it wasn't true. And then he told me I needed to be calm."

Lee coughed as she glanced at Ella. "That wouldn't have gone down well," Lee said.

"No, it didn't. Everyone has lied—"

"But that's the thing," Lee said. "It's like everyone who wants to be our friend is being set up as our enemy. Even the note you got from Drakon blamed Ken for what happened at the club."

"Lee has a point," Ella said.

Lee leaned over and put her hand on Sascha's arm. "There is so much we don't understand, Sascha. Perhaps you do need to get your memory back. Perhaps we all do. That way we'll know who our enemies truly are. Not knowing is proving to be dangerous. Don't you think so?"

Sascha's heart pounded and her palms were damp with sweat. "There may not be a way to do that."

"There might be a way." Lee glanced at Ella. "But we are missing a jewel."

"A jewel?"

"Yes," Lee said. "There's a ceremony that uses that artifact you were sent, but it also requires a gem or jewel."

Sascha took a sip of her coffee. "Did you find that out at the library?"

"Yes," Lee said. "But the texts kept referring back to the chronicles of the Four Sisters. You can only access it at their headquarters. We need Alex to investigate it for us once he finds the place."

"So we still need Marco," Sascha muttered.

"Yes, we do." Lee picked up a teaspoon and traced imaginary designs on the tablecloth. "I also found some texts that referred to a combination of magic skills which can be used to defeat the darkness that is attacking the Shield protecting Eratus. I couldn't find any detail on what type of magic the texts were referring to, so I asked Marco to see what he could find. That's what he was doing last night."

"We need to find out what he discovered," Ella said.

Sascha sat at the table in silence and stared out the window at Soleil and Rusty. She knew Lee and Ella were right.

They finished their coffee in silence, each of them watching Soleil and Rusty. Rusty had snuggled in close to Soleil, and Soleil had draped his wing across Rusty in a protective gesture.

"We need to tell work we won't be coming in," Lee said. "We'll need to agree on a story and keep it consistent. I'm assuming we will come back?"

"I don't know," Sascha said. "I guess we're going to have to wait and find out what happens."

Lee pushed herself up from the table and walked to the window. "What about Rusty? Perhaps we should take her with us?"

"I can take Rusty," Soleil said. "My magic will be sufficient to protect her."

Sascha nodded. "Soleil will take her." She glanced at the fence that bordered Ken's place. "I haven't heard from Ken or his office yet. I must call them again."

Lee walked to the fridge and plucked a menu off the side of it. "Maybe we should organize something tasty for lunch tomorrow. And wine, of course. Good food and wine can fix a lot of things."

"It's Kira we need to look after," Sascha said. "She might refuse to see Marco again." Sascha flinched. "And I was pretty blunt when I told him to stay out of our lives, so I'm not sure how keen he will be either. I need to call him."

"I'll organize Kira and lunch," Lee said. "We'll buy Kira's favorite Indian. Even if I didn't text her, I wouldn't be surprised to see her roll up when the food does."

Sascha pushed herself up from the table. "I'll get this over and done with. I'll call Marco now." Sascha plodded through to her bedroom. "He'd better answer my call. He only gets one chance at this."

"We need him," Lee called out after her.

"I know, I know. But if he so much as—"

"Sascha, please be nice," Lee said as Sascha closed the door to her bedroom.

CHAPTER 28

*M*arco dropped onto the gym bench, exhausted. He used to think of his apartment as his and Sascha's refuge. But after they split up, the memories of their time together haunted him, followed him every moment. He often thought about selling the place, but every time he received an offer, he changed his mind.

After a quick shower, he made his way downstairs to his lounge room. He stopped in front of the delicately carved owl that sat in the doorway. Sascha had given it to him for a birthday present. He never could find the courage to dispose of it, even though it was a constant reminder of what he had lost. Even after all this time and everything that had happened, he still loved her.

He couldn't imagine how hard it would be to have forgotten your past. But what she said was cruel and her words cut deep. It was her fault he hadn't spent time with Kira. They could have had a happy life on Eratus. But he knew that wasn't fair either. He found his anger building again. The intense hatred he felt for her at the cave surprised him. He thought he had recovered enough for it not to eat away at him the way it used to, but he had been wrong. Seeing Sascha at Caloundra made him realize he had never and probably never would get over her.

He needed to escape. He would go to his coffee shop and pick up some wine to help his mind switch off. He had no idea how they were going to recover from everything that happened today. They said too much. And Kira. How could he explain everything to her when the only person who could support his story couldn't remember her past?

He was picking up his keys when his phone rang. He ignored it and walked out of the house, locking the door behind him. His phone vibrated in his pocket.

Can't people leave me alone?

He drew in a quick breath and released it slowly before looking at the phone.

Alex.

He needed to answer it. "Hi, Alex. How's it all going?"

"Marco, I wanted to let you know that Jenny is safe. I'm with her and Eham. We're all going out for brunch to debrief on the past week's events."

Marco held the phone between his ear and shoulder as he pushed his keys into his jeans pocket. His hands now empty, he took the phone in his right hand and started walking toward his coffee shop. "She's in the safe house in Achmelvich?"

"Yes, she is, but..."

"But what?" Marco asked.

"Oh, nothing. It's just my overactive imagination. You know what I'm like. You okay, Marco? You sound...flat."

Marco ran his free hand through his hair and sighed. "It's been one of those days. Feeling tired and guilty, that's all. I had a huge fight with Sascha and both of us said more than we should have. Her inability to remember her past makes life difficult, to say the least. And Kira thinks Father raped her mother."

Alex gasped. "Raped her? He didn't rape her."

"It seems he will never be free of the taint, no matter how innocent he is." Marco stopped at the traffic lights at the intersection at the end of his road and pressed the button several times, as if doing so would make the walk signal turn green more quickly.

"But who would have known about it?" Alex asked. "I thought that whole debacle was dead and buried."

"I don't know, but I'm sure Drakon is involved somehow."

"Geez, how are you going to explain this one to Sascha?"

The walk signal turned green and Marco walked across the road. "I don't know. And to make things worse, I ended up telling Sascha she's Kira's mother. To be honest, though, I'm more worried about Kira than Sascha and myself."

"Man, that's a fine mess you've got."

"Tell me about it. I really need Sascha to get her memory back, but I've no idea how to help her do that."

"The Four Sisters headquarters is not far from the safe house," Alex said. "They have a huge library. I'll start looking into it as soon as I get back from the debrief."

"I've done some research myself and so have Lee and Ella. I'll email you a summary of what we found when I get home."

"Sounds good," Alex said.

"Any help you can give us would be appreciated."

"I'll see what I can do. Speak to you tomorrow."

"Speak to you then." Marco hung up. His phone vibrated again.

Sascha.

He had arrived at the coffee shop. He stood and stared in the front window with unseeing eyes. "Marco speaking," he answered.

"Hi, Marco, it's Sascha."

"Yes?"

"I'm here with the girls. We were wondering if you'd join us for lunch tomorrow. We're having Indian."

His heart pounded. His stomach knotted.

"Marco, are you still there?"

"I'm here."

"Did you want to come for lunch? After lunch, we'll discuss what everyone found at the library."

"I'd prefer you and I talk alone first. We need to come to some agreement about how we deal with what was said. Would you come over to my place tonight?" Marco heard her gulp.

"Come over there? Um, okay. But I can't stay for long. I need to keep an eye on Soleil."

"That's fine," Marco answered. "I'll organize some food. How is Kira?"

"She's okay, considering everything. She's staying with a friend tonight."

"That's probably the best thing for her."

"Yes, probably. I'll let the girls know you'll come for lunch tomorrow."

Marco hung up. His heart went out to Kira.

She must be finding it so hard to come to grips with everything. Sascha and I must find a way to help her through this.

Marco walked into the coffee shop. The solid timber counter was gleaming. The bubbling water fountain in the middle of the shop and the soft music playing over the speakers helped to create a relaxing atmosphere. It was clearly doing a good trade there were people everywhere. He loved hearing his patrons laughing and chatting with the staff. Mike was at the front of the shop, showing people to their seats, blasting them with his abundant charm. He had given the boy a share in the coffee shop and it had proven to be a worthy investment. He had paid the investment back tenfold.

Marco waved at him, walked out to the kitchen, and grabbed some pasta and a couple of bottles of wine.

He returned home and put on a navy shirt and black pants. He sprayed on some cologne and went downstairs to wait for Sascha.

Marco's phone beeped. He read the text. It was from Sascha, telling him she was on her way. His stomach lurched. He was dreading tonight. He opened the wine and swilled down a glass. His stomach muscles started to unwind.

A few minutes later, there was a knock on the door and he opened it to see Sascha standing there, dressed in a simple black dress, her blond hair loose and floating around her shoulders.

She's beautiful.

"Come in." Marco stepped aside and Sascha walked past him.

"We do need to—"

Marco turned. She was staring at the owl.

"You kept it?" she asked.

"Yes."

"I thought..."

Marco closed the door. "You thought I would have disposed of it?"

"Yes, well, after everything..."

"Sascha, I never—"

"Sorry, I shouldn't have said anything." Sascha walked into the lounge room. "Let's get this over with. What did you want to say?"

"It's not all about what I have to say," Marco said. "It's about both of us. Let's slow down at least long enough to have a drink."

"I can't. I'm driving."

"Since when has that stopped you?"

"If you're going to spend the night insulting me, I'll go."

"I was joking, Sascha, trying to lighten the mood."

"Marco, please, what did you want to say?"

"One glass? It will help."

She gave a deep sigh. "OK, OK. But a small one. And one of *my* small glasses, not one of yours."

Marco smiled as he walked to the kitchen. "You never complained before."

"Before was a long time ago," Sascha answered.

Soleil told him he had to tell her everything. Help her understand. So that's what he would do.

"Alex phoned," Marco called out from the kitchen. "He found Jenny."

"He found her? That's good. Where?"

"At a house not far from the Four Sisters headquarters near Achmelvich in the north of Scotland."

"Eham must be pleased," Sascha said.

Marco walked back into the lounge room. Sascha was sitting in the armchair next to the sofa, still holding her purse and keys. "Yes, he is pleased." Marco leaned down and handed her a glass of wine, his hand brushing her arm as he did so. "Here you go. You can put your purse and keys on the table if you like."

"No, it's fine. Thanks." She took a sip. "You remembered my wine."

"I picked up some of your favorite pasta for dinner if you can stay." Marco sat down on the sofa. "Soleil asked me to talk to you. He said he was worried you would learn only parts of the story and not know who to trust."

"Soleil asked you to talk to me?" She frowned. "How could he have done that?"

"Before we talk about Soleil, let's talk about Kira."

Sascha repositioned herself in the armchair and crossed her legs. "Yes, OK. Why did you say I was her mother? And what you said about me having no friends..."

Marco winced. He shouldn't have said that, but she was so incredibly frustrating. "I'm sorry. It was a cruel thing to say."

Sascha sighed, put her phone and purse down by the side of her chair and sat back. "I said cruel things too. So what's Kira's story?"

"It's a long story, but the short version is that we were both good friends with Kira's biological mother, Tamarina."

"The one your father raped."

"He didn't rape her." Marco glanced over at Sascha. She moved again and sat on the edge of the chair with her chin raised and her legs crossed. She was studying him in much the same way a lioness studies its prey moments before she consumes it. He forced himself to relax. Another fight wasn't going to get them anywhere.

"My father is the Duke of Kilmarnock. Kilmarnock is a city in the kingdom of Brun on Eratus. Mother died when Alex and I were young. Father was out riding one day when he noticed a woman fending off a group of thugs. Father flew in on his pyran and rescued Tamarina. They soon fell in love. A countess in Father's court became jealous of Tamarina and thought that she could split them up by spreading the rumor that my father had raped Tamarina and then blaming Tamarina for starting the rumor. And she was right it did split them up."

"So the note was a lie?"

Marco finished his glass of wine. "Yes. And it seems that somehow that lie is still alive."

"Where is Tamarina now?"

Marco got up, walked into the kitchen and brought back

the open bottle of wine. He topped up Sascha's glass, refilled his own and then placed the empty bottle on the coffee table. "She was pregnant, so she returned to live with her mother."

"Why didn't your father marry her?"

"He wanted to but Tamarina refused. Not long after Kira's birth, she was offered a position in the Academy of Magic, a day's travel from Owain's castle. She accepted it. You see, Tamarina was flawed, so she couldn't stay in Brun."

Sascha gasped. "She had healing magic?"

"Yes. She tried to hide it, but there were religious fanatics everywhere. It wouldn't have taken long for her secret to be discovered if she stayed in Brun. You and I became friendly with Tamarina while she was at the academy, but a few years later, she came to us and told us that she needed to go back to Brun because her mother was very ill. She had decided to leave Kira with the Four Sisters because she too showed signs of having healing magic."

"Surely they wouldn't sacrifice children?" Sascha asked.

"Anyone with healing magic was fair game."

Sascha sat open-mouthed. "What brutal people."

There was a knock on the door and Marco got up to answer it. It was someone collecting for a local charity. He pulled out a ten dollar note, waved off the need for a receipt and returned to the lounge room. "I'll be back in a second." Marco picked up the empty bottle and returned to the kitchen. He took a fresh bottle of chilled wine out of the fridge, a packet of spiced nuts from the cupboard and rejoined Sascha. He opened the packet of nuts and placed them between him and Sascha. He topped up their wine glasses and then sat down. "Sorry about that. Just a local charity collecting money."

"That's OK," Sascha said. "What happened next?"

Marco folded his hands together and hung his head.

"Tamarina was branded a traitor to Eratus and sacrificed a few months later."

"She what?"

"We were both gutted and Kira really struggled. But you visited Kira often and I think that helped her make it through what was a very difficult time. When Kira turned seven, she asked you for help. She wanted to become an enchantress for the Four Sisters, but couldn't because her mother was a traitor. The laws of Eratus don't allow the children of traitors to accede to positions of power. It was your idea to adopt her so that she could take on a new name. As a princess, you were in a position to do so. You persuaded Connell to help and together you convinced Owain to allow the adoption papers to go through. Once she was your daughter, she was allowed to apply to become an Enchantress."

Sascha wiped away some droplets on the side of her wine glass. "So I adopted her?"

"Yes. And when you and I married, she would become *our* daughter. I had never been happier. I had what I had wanted for years, you and a family. And then you...left."

"But why would I leave when I had so much?"

"I don't really know. I hated you - truly hated you - when you left. Losing you nearly destroyed me."

Marco looked up to see tears rolling silently down Sascha's cheeks. "I'm sorry, Marco. I seem to have hurt so many people. You were right I am worse than you or Connell or Owain."

"No, you aren't. We all had a part to play in this. It wasn't all you. I loved you, Sascha. In fact, I still love you. When I found you in the cabin, I thought we had been given another chance. But then Zinnath contacted me."

"The dragon?"

Marco picked up the packet of spiced nuts and offered

them to Sascha, before taking some himself. "Yes. You and Soleil had built a strong friendship with Zinnath and Kalurth. A few months before you left, you found out a group was plotting to destroy the dragons. And everyone who could helped to protect them had died. Zinnath believed that's why your mother was killed and that Tamarina was set up for the same reasons."

"So there's more to my mother's death?"

"Yes, and Tamarina's. Zinnath was surprised when you attacked Owain. It was never planned for you to be deported, and your memories taken away. But as it was, Zinnath was pleased it happened that way because those actions protected you. You were no longer a threat to the group."

"But Zinnath and Kalurth were still in danger?"

"Yes, but you were safe. And the dragons believed that with you gone, the group might be more likely to show themselves."

"But attacking Owain wasn't part of the plan?" Sascha asked.

"No."

"Then why would I have attacked him?"

"There's only one way you can know for sure, Sascha."

"And that's by trying to get my memory back." She nodded. "But I'm so scared of becoming who I was."

"Sascha, you were a very powerful mage who could use both dark and light magic, but that power didn't destroy the good in you. You saved Kira, gave her back her dream. And there were plenty of people who loved you, not to mention Soleil. Your only real weakness was your addiction to green lyrium, but that shouldn't be a problem since you haven't taken it for years. The one thing we do have to consider, however, is that getting your memory back is likely to put you in danger."

"From the people who want to kill Zinnath and Kalurth?"

"Yes."

Sascha sat back in her chair and had a mouthful of wine. "I don't understand how it impacted what we...had."

"Zinnath explained to me that staying with you might make the group think the transportation was a ruse. They would have gone after you again, and you didn't have your magic to protect yourself. Or they could have demanded that you be sent back to Eratus and given the death penalty, as the law required. Until the time was right, we had to make sure everyone believed that you remembered nothing about Eratus."

Sascha went quiet. "So us being together here would have made people think that I still remembered Eratus. Wait, so you were my fiancée?"

Marco met Sascha's eyes. "Yes."

"The one everyone has been telling me was killed?"

"Yes."

Sascha closed and then opened her eyes. She stood, but collapsed when her legs crumpled beneath her. Marco rushed toward her, but she held her hand out, stopping him from coming any closer.

"Please, I need a moment. Of course they would think it was all a ruse. They wouldn't believe that we just happened to fall in love a second time."

Marco shook his head.

Sascha sat back down, poured herself another glass of wine. She drank it down in one gulp and poured herself another. "Does your wife know about any of this?"

Marco fiddled with the stem of his wine glass. "I never got married. I only said that to you because it was the only thing I could think of that would make you hate me and not come looking for me."

"You never..." Sascha reached down to pick up her purse, but she kept dropping it. "I'd better go."

She's had too much to drink.

Marco stood. "Maybe I should warm up that pasta. You need something to eat."

"No, I'm fine."

Sascha stopped trying to pick up her purse and sat silently, resting her head in her hands. Marco could see her shoulders shaking. He crouched in front of her. "I'm sorry, Sascha." He put his hands over hers. "The truth is I still love you, have always loved you."

She pulled her hands out from under his and wiped away her tears with the back of her hand. "I need to go. I need to—"

She looked up at him. The memories of the taste of her flooded through him. His eyes followed the trail of his hands as they caressed the soft skin of her neck and shoulders and rested at the curve of her breast. She closed her eyes and sighed. She smelled of vanilla and jasmine. With one hand, he cupped the back of her neck and pulled her to him. Their mouths touched. He brushed his lips against hers, tasting the wine and spiced nuts. Her breaths were coming in shallow bursts and he felt his body respond. She groaned and moved into him as she deepened the kiss. Desire flooded through him. The world disappeared. He was lost in her. Then he felt her hand on his chest, gently pushing him away.

"I can't, Marco. Not now."

His head spun. "I'm sorry. I didn't mean to...not now, not like this."

"I'm sorry too, Marco. I need time. Time to take everything in."

Marco rested his forehead on hers. "I need you back in my life, Sascha. I am only half a person without you."

"Please call me a cab," Sascha said.

"Have something to eat before you leave. The pasta won't take long to warm."

She hesitated for a moment. "No, I think I'd better go."

Minutes later, as he stood looking at the door Sascha had closed behind her, Marco heard the sounds of a car door slamming shut and tires crunching on loose gravel. She was gone.

CHAPTER 29

ERATUS

*D*arkness surrounded Drakon. Even the lights in the midnight sky didn't dare cast their beam in this valley. Drakon stepped off the transporter and looked over at the darkness of Earth's moon. It looked so close, so large, that he almost thought he could reach out and touch it.

The last time he had been here, he was thirteen. He hadn't known what he had been in for, hadn't known the dangers. He never did understand how he survived, but perhaps the gods were helping him even then.

Now, with the battles ahead of him, it was time to take on his father's powers, and there was only one way he could do that. But first, Drakon had to understand why Ares was so interested in his father.

He glanced over at the edge of the valley. He could see the massive golden pillars at the entrance to Ares' castle, even in the darkness. What was it about the Master that had Ares worried enough he wanted him dead? He shook his head to stop himself from fixating on what Ares was up to. The next part of the journey needed his full concentration.

It's time to get a move on, get this thing done.

"There's a secret here I know, element of air, the secret show."

The winding trail that led into Peaceful Valley glowed with an iridescent white light. The trail was devoid of any vegetation, but littered with the many skeletons of the intrepid explorers that had been fooled by the valley's name.

This valley was anything but peaceful. Many deadly creatures lived here, the worst of which were the massive black desert serpents that lived beneath the sands on either side of the trail. They were always waiting for those who unwittingly left the trail to take a shortcut across the open plains. The ghostly screams of those explorers echoed around him. They would never find peace.

Drakon heard the wails of the huens as they circled above him, watching him as he made his way toward the tower, waiting for him to stumble, waiting for a chance to feast.

Drakon smiled as a warmth spread across his chest and through his body. Soon, he would be firing the first shot in the battle he had spent his whole life preparing for, the battle for the leadership of Eratus. The potion was in the top pocket of his jacket. The knowledge comforted him.

An hour after starting his journey, Drakon stepped up to a solid stone door in the side of the tower, leaned against it and used all his strength to push it open. He stood on the edge of the doorway as he surreptitiously took the potion out of his pocket and concealed it in his left hand. He stepped into the room. The room smelt like stale ash, but it was cool and lit only by a few weak lights. He could hear claws skittering across the floor as the creatures they belonged to sought the best positions from which to view the meeting.

His father was waiting for him, his scrawny form resting on his throne. Drakon looked around the room and saw only the eyes of his father's creatures staring down at him.

Everyone knew why Drakon was here. Everyone was ready for the show.

His father looked up, his glowing eyes taking in all who were there. "Drakon. The time has come?"

"Yes, Father. I am about to embark on a journey, and I need to take on your powers."

"I am the Master, not your father."

Drakon rested his right hand on his dagger and ambled several steps closer to the throne. "My mother told me who my real father was before she died. To ensure her position in the court, she needed to provide the High King with a son. A powerful son. Something you could guarantee. It was the winter solstice, and you were real for long enough for Mother to convince you to take her and give her your child."

The Master's body jiggled. "No. I wouldn't—"

"Tut, tut, Father. You don't remember the beautiful blond, standing naked in the middle of the stones, her skin the color of pure milk? Singing to you?"

"She was your...your mother? No, that's not possible. I cannot father normal children." He waved his hand around the room. "These are my children."

"Which is why I thought she was lying. But I know now she didn't lie. You are my father." Drakon laughed. "And you never knew. I'm surprised you didn't wonder about the powers I came into when I turned thirteen."

The Master scanned the balconies before he rested his gaze on Drakon. "Are you sure you want my powers, Drakon?"

"That is the law. The father must always pass his powers onto his son, once his son is of age and has proven himself. I am of age, and I think we can agree I have proven myself. So, dear Father, what do you think?"

Drakon heard the snickers as the Master's creatures whispered to each other. The Master raised his hand and the noise stopped. As he brought his hand down, the door Drakon had entered through slammed shut with a deafening thud.

Something fluttered in Drakon's stomach. "You'd better have it right, Chiane," he muttered. "This must work."

Drakon had the potion ready. He would have to get his timing right if he were to have a chance of beating the Master. "Father, there is one thing I would like to ask."

"Speak."

"You seem to worry Ares. He asked me to kill you. Why do you think that is?"

"So you here for more than just my powers? You are Ares' pawn? I expected more of you."

Drakon smirked. "He also said you had been talking to Athena and you had...changed."

"Athena," the Master said wistfully as he touched the golden arm band he was wearing. "Now that is an intelligent god, one who knows strategy." He stroked his bony chin with his long narrow claws. "It would be a mistake to back Ares over Athena. History shows he has lost every time he has taken her on." He cackled. "I would be careful if I was you, Drakon. There is so much you don't know about the games of gods. Ares has another agenda, one that will only benefit him."

The Master stood; his long skinny frame three times the height of Drakon. He looked scrawny, but only the foolish underestimated his power. "Drakon, or should I say, son," he drawled. "I hope you know the price for taking on my powers?"

"I am willing to pay any price."

The Master spat, "You don't know what I'm talking about, do you? But you soon will."

"I don't need to know. This is just the stepping stone to my fate."

"You are right, Drakon. But the fate you could have had when you entered this room was an entirely different one to the fate you will have when you leave it." The Master started to walk toward Drakon, his limbs jiggling with every movement.

A little closer. Move a little closer.

He stopped two steps from where Drakon needed him to be and stared at him. "You think I'm a fool, Drakon?"

"My mother had no trouble outwitting you."

"The potion. What is the purpose of the potion you are holding?"

There was no point in lying. Drakon lifted the bottle to show him. "It's to kill you."

The creatures on the balconies roared into life. High-pitched primal screams echoed around the room, and loud thuds surrounded Drakon as the creatures bashed against the balcony walls.

Again, the Master raised his hand, and again, the balconies went quiet.

"In that case, you need to see what it is you're killing." In the blink of an eye, his appearance became that of a man, the man his mother had seduced, his father. They did look very much alike. Any doubts Drakon might have had were gone. His mother had become pregnant in the way she had told him. Screams of pain echoed around the chamber as the creatures fell to the floor. One by one, they stood, the sound of their screams growing duller until there was silence. When Drakon looked again, the balconies were filled with women and children.

Mother's description of what she saw that night was true.

"You think you can save yourself by copying my form, Master? You told me earlier you couldn't have human children, yet now you are saying you can. If you are going to lie, you need to be consistent."

"Your obstinacy is unfortunate," the Master said. "If you kill me, you set in place a sequence of events you will not be able to control, even with the powers you believe you will gain from my death. When you say you are willing to pay the price, I hope you truly know what it is you are saying. This can never be undone, and this time, this place and your role will be marked in history."

Drakon took two steps forward, threw down the potion and waited for it to take effect. A white ball of light shot up from the floor, flew toward the roof and leaped onto the balconies. Bloodcurdling screams echoed around the room as the Master's creatures were engulfed in the white fire that roared its way across them.

An explosive crack fractured the air, shaking the building violently and flinging Drakon and the Master to the ground.

"What the hell was that?" Drakon stammered.

The Master cackled, "It is done."

"What is done?"

The Master sniggered. "That sound was the Shield dying. You can blame your friends, Ares and Hades, for that. Death is only days away now. Enjoy your last days on Eratus, and remember this is what you wanted."

"But you are on the side of the ancients. You have been helping to destroy the Shield."

"You have so much to learn, Drakon," he said as he touched the arm band again. "Athena gave me the power to make a stand against the ancients. I was the one keeping the darkness under control, slowing it down. Nothing is ever as simple as it seems, is it?"

Drakon's heartbeat thrashed in his ears as he realized the Master was telling the truth.

I must stop this.

But he knew it was too late. He watched helplessly as the light circled the Master and then consumed him. The guttural screams seemed to last forever, but when they finally stopped, the Master was dead.

The light moved toward Drakon, becoming brighter the closer it came. Soon he couldn't see a thing. Then he felt it, the pain. His skin was being torn from his body. This time, the screams Drakon heard echoing in his ears were his own.

CHAPTER 30

* EARTH

Sascha stood in the shower and let the warm water wash over her. The smells of bacon and coffee wafted through to the bathroom. Her stomach rumbled. Aside from the few nuts she'd had at Marco's, she hadn't eaten since lunch yesterday. Lee and Ella's laughter echoed through the house. Sascha hadn't been ready to face them last night and was grateful they had gone to bed early. But she knew they would be full of questions this morning and had decided to tell them about the conversation...most of it, anyway.

The phone rang as Sascha walked into the kitchen. Lee picked it up. "Hi, Marco. Do you want to speak to Sascha?" She turned to Sascha and smiled.

Sascha shook her head, pointed to her room and mouthed, "I'm asleep."

"Yes, she's right here. I'll get her for you."

Sascha stomped her foot, gave Lee a dirty look and snatched the phone from her. "You wait," Sascha mouthed. Sascha took a deep breath and steadied herself. "Hi, Marco."

"How are you feeling today, Sascha?"

"A bit shell-shocked, but I'll work it out. How are you?"

"I didn't sleep last night. Someone left me feeling very frustrated. Even an icy shower didn't help."

Sascha felt butterflies in her stomach as she thought about what had nearly happened. Her reluctance was hard to understand, but something just didn't feel right.

"But that's not why I called. Alex phoned from Dubai airport."

"Alex?"

"Yes, he's coming over to visit. He couldn't sleep either and spent hours in the library at the Four Sisters. He said he found something we need to know before we go back to Eratus. And he said he found out what you need to do to get your memory back. He's asked us not to do anything until he meets with us. It sounds important."

"It sounds promising." Sascha replied. "We were going to ask him to do some research, but it sounds like he's ahead of us."

"His flight isn't due in until 12.50 a.m. tomorrow. After we've finished going over our research, I'll leave from your place to pick him up. If that's OK with you, of course."

"That sounds fine."

"We can have pasta for dinner. I have plenty and I don't want to throw it out."

Sascha's stomach clenched at the thought of Marco being in her house for so long. She rubbed her stomach to ease the cramps.

"When is Kira getting back from her friend's place?" he asked.

"She will be here in time for lunch. Lee's organized it."

"When she arrives," Marco said, "do you mind if I take her somewhere quiet to talk? I need to tell her what I told you last night."

"Yes, she needs to know. I was going to tell her, but it might be better coming from you."

"So is it OK if I get there about noon." Marco asked.

"Yes, that would be good."

"Oh, and I'll get one of my staff to pick up your keys and drive your car back to your place."

"You don't need to do that, but I appreciate it. Thanks, Marco." Sascha hung up.

"What did Marco say about Alex?" Lee asked.

"Alex called him late last night to say he's on his way to Brisbane. He's found some information he wants to tell us before we return to Eratus, and he knows how I can get my memory back."

"Fantastic," Lee said. "I wonder if he discovered the same thing we did?"

"If it is, I hope he has some idea where we can find the jewel. I wish he had talked to us before he left Scotland. I guess we'll just have to wait until he arrives to hear what he has to say."

"You wouldn't think he would fly all the way over here if what he found wasn't important," Lee said.

"That's true. Marco will be here at noon. Lee, did you text Kira?"

"Yes, I did," Lee answered. "She hasn't replied yet, but I'm sure she'll have seen it. If she's not here by eleven-thirty, I'll call her. When is Alex due in?"

"Marco said early tomorrow morning. Let's have breakfast."

"Will you tell us what happened last night?" Lee asked. "You can say no..."

"But if you tell us, I'll make you some waffles to go with the bacon," Ella said.

"You can't talk about this to Kira until I say you can. Is that clear?"

"Of course," they both replied.

An hour later, they knew all about Zinnath, Kalurth and Kira. They spent the next half an hour drinking coffee and talking about Eratus and the dragons. Lee glanced at her phone. "Kira still hasn't replied yet. I'll give her another half-hour."

"I'll clean up, girls," Sascha said. "Thanks for a yummy breakfast."

Ella pushed back from the table and grabbed her bag. "I'm slipping out. Do either of you need anything?"

"I'm fine. Thanks, Ella," Sascha said.

There was a knock on the door as Ella pulled away, her car radio blasting. "I'll get it," Lee said.

"Hello, Lee," Marco said as he leaned down and gave her a kiss on the cheek.

Sascha took a slow, deep breath as she tried to stop the fluttery sensation that had taken flight in her stomach at the sound of Marco's voice.

The back door slid open and Sascha turned as Rusty bounded toward Marco and then launched herself at him. Laughing, Marco managed to put his bags down and brace himself so that he wouldn't be knocked to the floor.

"Rusty," Sascha called out. "Leave the poor man alone."

"It's okay, Sasch. Isn't it, beautiful?" Marco gave Rusty a big hug. "We've become good friends over the last couple of days."

Once satisfied she had given sufficient greeting, Rusty raced back outside to join Soleil.

Sascha picked up the dirty dishes from the table and took them into the kitchen. Marco followed her. "Can I put the pasta in the fridge?"

"Yes, wherever you can find a spot." Sascha turned on the hot water tap, poured in some detergent and then frothed the water up.

"I brought some extra sauce and cheese to add to the pasta when we heat it up. I also bought some blueberry cheesecake. The girls tell me that's their favorite."

Sascha started to wash the breakfast dishes, putting them in the rack on the sink when they were clean. "That was thoughtful of you, Marco. The girls will love you."

"I'm not averse to using bribery." He picked up a tea towel to dry the dishes she had washed.

"You're a guest, Marco. You don't need to do that."

"If this is what I have to do to be next to you..."

"Marco..."

Marco stood, tea towel still in hand, and looked at her. "I know. You need time. But I can wait."

The door slammed and Ella raced into the house.

"Marco, that plane your brother was on. What flight was it?"

"Why?"

"Turn the TV on," Ella said. "It's been on the radio. There's been a crash. It's a flight from Glasgow to Brisbane via Dubai. Due into Brisbane at ten to one tomorrow morning."

Sascha looked over at Marco. He was frozen to the spot.

"What?" he finally gasped.

Lee turned the television on.

"...and we will let you know as soon as we find out more," the broadcaster said.

Lee flicked to another channel.

"The flight from Glasgow to Brisbane has disappeared. It was due to arrive at 12.50 a.m. tomorrow. No details are available at this time, but we will advise you as soon as we know more." The male broadcaster's face was devoid of expression.

Marco had gone pale. Sascha watched as he moved to the

dining table and dropped into one of the chairs. "That's not possible."

Sascha walked over to him. "He might not have been on that flight, Marco. He might be on another one."

The room was silent. Lee had muted the adverts on the television and everyone was staring at the screen.

Sascha put her hand on Marco's shoulder. He shook it off, leaped out of his chair and spun around toward her. "Tell me, Sascha, why is it that every time you come into my life all I find is heartache?" He put his head in his hands. "Last time I lost my life, my daughter. This time, my brother..."

Marco's words sliced at Sascha. She stared at him, rooted to the spot. She couldn't think, couldn't speak.

Marco let his hands drop and faced Sascha. "I'm sorry, Sascha. That's not true. I need to go, I need to phone around, learn what I can."

"We'll help you, Marco," Sascha said.

"No, I want to do this alone." Sascha stared as he walked to the door. He was right. She had brought him nothing but bad luck.

A knock sounded on the door as Marco was about to open it. He opened it to see two police officers standing on the doorstep. "No," he said. "Please, no."

"Is Sascha Morgan home? Hey, are you okay, buddy?"

Sascha and the girls raced to Marco.

"Marco, are you okay?" Sascha asked. She put her hand on his shoulder. This time he didn't shake it off. He leaned against the doorframe. "They're here for you, Sascha."

"I know." Sascha turned to them. "Yes?"

"Are you Sascha Morgan?"

"Yes."

"I am Constable Miller," the shorter one said, "and this is Constable Archer. We found this wallet. Do you recognize it?"

Sascha looked at it and her heart dropped. "Yes, it's...it's Kira's." Everything seemed to be moving in slow motion. "Why?"

Sascha could see them speaking, but the sound of their voices took a long time to reach her ears.

"Is she here?"

"No, she's out," Lee answered for Sascha.

"When did you see her last?"

Again, it was Lee who answered. "A day ago. She's due back home at lunchtime. She spent last night with her best friend."

Constable Miller opened his notebook and took out his pen. "What is her friend's name?"

Sascha's voice returned. "Tanya Schofield. I'll call her now. I have the number."

Everyone stood in silence as Sascha dialed Tanya's number. "Tanya? Yes, hi. It's Sascha. Can I speak to Kira? When did she leave? Last night? But I thought she was staying the night with you? No, it's okay. Thanks, Tanya."

Sascha could feel her blood draining away. She felt cold and weak. "She's not there," she stammered. "She didn't stay there last night after all. And I didn't follow up. I should have followed up."

"I'm sorry to say that we found this wallet on a body late last night," Constable Miller said. "We need you to come down to the station. We think it may be Kira."

"No," Sascha whispered.

"I'll come with you," Marco said.

"No, you have enough to deal with."

"Sascha, Kira is important to me too. I need to be there with you."

"You need to determine if that flight was the one Alex was on."

"Which flight?" Constable Archer said.

"The flight that crashed—" Marco closed his eyes and then opened them again. "We think my brother was on that flight that crashed."

The officers looked at each other. "You poor bugger. We'll look into it, see what we can do."

"Thank you," Marco replied, wiping his face with the back of his hand.

SASCHA AND MARCO sat in silence in the back of the police car as they were being taken to the morgue. Sascha felt hot, then cold and clammy. The trip seemed to take forever, though Sascha knew it took only minutes. She wanted to scream, to lash out, to hurt someone, but all she could do was sit in the back of the car, stunned. She couldn't even cry.

When they arrived, the officers took them to a room in the basement and stood with them in front of a curtained window.

"Are you ready?" Constable Miller asked.

Sascha nodded, unable to speak.

Everything moved so slowly. The curtains were pulled back. Sascha couldn't look. Instead, she stared at the deep graze on the lower edge of the window. She had come too far for Kira to end up lying dead on a cold metal table. It couldn't be her. Sascha wrapped her arms around her waist, took a step toward the window, lifted her eyes and stared at the face on the other side of the glass pane. Sascha could only see half of it, the rest having been covered with a white sheet. Constable Miller was saying something about the fire, the damage to her body. Sascha let out a cry. The room went dark as Sascha dropped into Marco's arms.

CHAPTER 31

* EARTH

The hum of distant voices echoed in the hallway. Sascha leaned against Marco's arms as she pushed herself up from the floor. The aroma of citrus, spices and sweet wood drifted around her. Marco was too close. She needed to move away from him, get some distance. But her legs had lost their strength and they refused to move on their own.

"Sorry. I don't know what happened," she slurred. She sounded drunk.

"It's the shock," Constable Miller answered. "It's understandable, given the situation. Come with me and I'll get you some water. I'd like to ask you a couple of questions."

"That's fine," Sascha said.

The constable escorted them down a narrow passageway and past an open work area to a room with a large window facing out into the work area. He opened the door to the room. "Have a seat. I'll be back in a minute." He reached over and closed the blinds. Then he left.

Marco guided Sascha toward a tan couch in the corner of the room and lowered her into it. The room was sterile no pictures, just a couch, a couple of chairs and a coffee table. A musty smell filled the room. The couch's soft cushions moved beneath her as Marco sat next to her.

"It's not her," Marco whispered. "It's not our Kira."

Sascha took a minute before speaking. When she did speak, she focused on each word so that she didn't slur them together. "Yes, thank God. But my heart aches for the girl's poor parents, for what they are going to suffer when they see how she died."

"A horrible way to go," Marco said.

"But where is Kira? And how did her wallet end up with that girl?"

"Maybe they were friends."

Someone knocked on the door and Constable Miller entered the room. He placed a jug of iced water and a couple of glasses on the coffee table. "How are you feeling, ma'am?"

"I'm Sascha, not ma'am. But I'm better, thank you. Who is that girl, and why did she have Kira's wallet?"

"We were hoping you could help us with that," he said. He opened a manila folder and showed them a picture of a pretty young girl with fiery strawberry-blond hair and bright blue eyes. She was laughing at the camera. She looked happy, as if she had not a care in the world. "Have you seen this girl before?"

"Is that the girl?" Sascha asked.

He nodded.

"What a tragic waste." Sascha shook her head. "No, I've never seen her before. Was she murdered?"

"Yes, so any help would be appreciated. Sir, have you seen her?"

"No," Marco replied.

The constable dug his fingers into his jacket pocket and pulled out a business card. "When Kira contacts either of you, would you ask her to come and see us? She may be able to help."

Marco nodded.

"Yes, of course," Sascha said.

"Let me know when you're ready to leave and we'll take you home." The constable walked out of the room, closing the door behind him.

Marco stood and held out his hand. "Do you want some help to stand?"

"Yes, thank you." Sascha took his hand, grateful for the help. His touch stirred up memories she seemed incapable of forgetting. It would be so easy to lean into him, let him hold her, but the moment was gone when he stepped back and turned away.

Her bag came alive with the muffled sound of crickets. "My phone. It could be Kira. Oh! I forgot to text Ella and Lee."

"I've already texted the girls," Marco said. "They know it wasn't Kira."

"Thanks." Sascha opened her bag and retrieved her phone.

"Hi, Sascha. Sorry you had a terrible scare. I called home and Lee told me what happened. I'm sorry about the girl. I heard she had my wallet. I hadn't realized I had lost it. I'm fine and I'll be home by 7pm. It's later than we had planned, but I'll tell you everything when I get home. I'm really sorry to have worried you all. Please forgive me. Love, Kira."

Sascha breathed a sigh of relief. "It's from Kira. She's safe." Her fingers moved on the keyboard as she typed a response.

"What does she say?" Marco asked.

Sascha handed the phone to him. "You can read it if you like."

Marco read the message and handed the phone back. "Maybe it's time to get out of here. Are you ready to leave?"

Sascha nodded. "Were the police able to give you any more information about Alex?"

Marco shook his head. "No, they can't find any sign of the plane. I've left several messages for Alex in case he didn't catch that flight, but he hasn't rung me back. Anyway, I've booked a flight to Glasgow. I have to see what I can find out."

"But didn't you say he called you from Dubai?"

"I'd be going in blind if I went to Dubai. I don't have contacts there. But I've called Alex's office in Scotland and they're investigating his last movements, including whatever he was doing in Dubai. They may find a lead, something we can follow up on. I'll catch up with them in Glasgow and work out what to do from there. Now I understand why Eham needed to be involved in the search for Jenny. I'm not good at waiting around either."

"When are you flying out?"

"Tomorrow evening. I'll let the officers know we're ready to leave."

It wasn't long before they were heading for Sascha's home in the back of a police car. Constable Miller and Constable Archer chatted as they waited for the traffic lights at the end of Sascha's street to turn green. Constable Miller turned around to Sascha. "Is this area always so dark?"

She glanced down the street. The silvery light of the crescent moon provided some light, but most of the area was in darkness. "No. Normally the few street lights we do have are on. I hope we haven't lost power." A reflection caught her eye. Sascha nudged Marco and pointed. "That's the black car."

Marco leaned over her to see what she was pointing at. "What black car?"

"The one Ken reported." Sascha picked up her phone and checked for messages. "He still hasn't answered any of my texts."

Sascha leaned toward the front of the car. "Constable Miller, would you be able to check in on my neighbor? Some strange things have been happening there lately and I'm worried."

"What sort of strange things?" the constable asked.

The lights turned green and they started to turn. "See that black car up ahead? Ken reported that car days ago and now it's back."

"Who's Ken?" he asked.

"He's a police officer," Sascha replied. "A superintendent."

"Where is he based?"

"In the city. He hasn't answered any of the voice messages I've left for him, which is highly unusual. I asked his office to follow it up, but nothing seems to have happened."

"I'm sure they would have taken it seriously, but I'll call it in anyway."

Constable Archer slowed the vehicle as they drove past the car, and Constable Miller shone a torch into the vehicle. "There's no-one in there. Are you sure it's the same car?"

"It looks the same," Sascha answered.

"Maybe it belongs to one of your neighbors or their visitors. Which house is Ken's?"

"That one." Sascha pointed. As she did so, the lights in the lounge room flicked off, leaving the house in darkness.

"We can check on it tomorrow," the constable answered. "It looks like no-one is home."

"Someone is there. Didn't you see the lights switch off?" A blue light shone through the narrow window in Ken's cellar. "Look!" Sascha called out. "There are lights. Someone is in the house."

Soleil's call sounded in her head. "Sascha!"

"Soleil, what's wrong?"

"It's Rusty. She's going crazy and won't calm down."

The car pulled into Sascha's driveway. The moment

Sascha opened the car door, she could hear Rusty barking. Lee was talking to Rusty, trying to calm her down.

Sascha turned back to the two constables. "Please, I know there is something wrong."

Constable Miller nodded to his partner, pulled out his radio and wandered toward Ken's place. "Leave it with us."

Sascha and Marco stood in Sascha's front yard and watched. Lee joined them on the lawn, while Ella stood at the lounge room window. Ella was holding Rusty's collar in an attempt to stop her from launching herself out of the window.

"Rusty is desperate to get home," Lee said.

Sascha glanced at Rusty. "Soleil told me she was going crazy. Where is he?"

"Out the back," Lee answered.

"I'm on the roof," Soleil answered. "I can't see anyone in Ken's yard, but Rusty certainly senses something."

The two constables spoke to each other, then Constable Miller went to the front door, while Constable Archer walked down the side of the house.

Miller knocked on the door. One of the curtains on the second floor twitched, but no-one answered the door. Miller called out. When there was no response, he wrote something in his book and stepped back to look at the front of the house. He went to the car and spoke into his radio. A couple of minutes later, Constable Archer joined him at the car. The two of them chatted for a few minutes and walked over to join Sascha on the front lawn.

"Sascha, we checked and the city station did follow up on your call. Everything is fine. Pat called them yesterday to tell them Ken will be away for a week or so. They're stuck in Sydney. Ken has caught the flu and they can't fly until he's better. You don't have to worry," Constable Miller said.

Sascha clenched her teeth.

Everything is not fine.

"How do you explain the lights?" Sascha asked.

"Pat mentioned she has had some sort of security system installed," the constable said. "It's set up to make it look like someone is home."

"How convenient that Pat happened to mention it. Don't you think it's strange? Did she mention Ken's brother or his friend?"

"Pat was being diligent. She didn't want anyone wasting their time on investigating strange lights in the house. She didn't mention visitors, so they must have left. She did mention, however, that you were looking after Rusty. I would suggest you all go inside and get a good night's—"

"I saw the upstairs curtains move when you knocked. If no-one is home, how did that happen?"

The constable glanced back at the house. "That could be anything."

"And what about the car?"

"We've run the plates. Ken phoned through a different registration number to this one. And this car isn't stolen. The owner must be visiting one of your neighbors."

"But—"

Miller held up his hand. "I've taken down the details in case something else comes up." His radio came to life and the constable mumbled something in response. "We have to go now, but you have our card. Call us if anything else happens."

They got back into their car and drove off.

"This is totally ridiculous," Sascha said. "I'm going to find out for myself."

"Sascha," Marco said, "do you think that's wise?"

"I am going to find out exactly what's happening. You can help me or you can stay here. It's your choice."

"I'll get the keys for you," Lee said.

"Thanks."

As Lee opened Sascha's front door, Rusty pushed past her, leaped over the fence and raced to Ken's house. She stood on the lawn and barked, then glanced back at Sascha. When she was certain that she had Sascha's attention, she sat down and stared at the house. When Lee returned with the keys and Ella, the four of them joined Rusty.

"I'll go in first," Sascha said. "If the police come back, would you stall them for me?"

"I'll come with you, Sascha," Marco said. "You're not going in there alone."

Sascha nodded. "Lee and Ella, you stand guard."

Sascha put the key into the lock. It was the loud sharp crackle that told her she was in trouble. A split second later, a bright flash of white burning light sparked through the air, and Sascha was thrown off the porch and into the flowerbed near the stairs.

"Sascha," Marco said as he raced toward her.

Sascha lay on the ground, winded. "What the hell was that?"

Marco squatted next to her. "They must have electrified the door somehow. Are you hurt?"

The mark on Sascha's hand burned. She sat up and stared at it. The last time it burned like this was when Laela touched her. She shook her hand to ease the pain. "If it was electrified, how come the police could knock on the door and not be sent flying like I was?" Sascha asked.

"I don't know," Marco said. "Is your hand alright?"

"Yes, it's fine."

"You used to say that the mark on your hand protected you," Marco said. "Maybe it's protecting you from something now."

"But why now? Nothing like that has ever happened before." Sascha clambered to her feet. "What if it's magic? What if this place is protected by magic?"

"We might need some help if it is," Marco said.

"Damn it," Sascha said, "we need to get in there now. Whatever is in there could be gone by tomorrow. I refuse to give up."

"If only there was another way in," Ella said.

"Don't they have an outside door to the cellar?" Lee asked.

"They do," Sascha said. "Good on you, Lee. I wouldn't be surprised if they had put a spell on that too, but it's worth a shot."

As they walked around the back to the cellar door, Sascha stopped, causing the girls and Rusty to crash into her. "The cellar door is open. For once it seems luck is on our side."

"Someone must still be here," Marco said.

Sascha glanced at Marco and turned to Lee. "Would you keep hold of Rusty's collar?" she whispered. "The last thing I need is Rusty chasing after me. She's not exactly quiet."

"You can't go in there, Sascha," Marco said. "We'll call the police back. Someone is in there. You could get hurt."

"Try and stop me," Sascha said as she grabbed hold of the banister that edged the stairs leading down to the cellar. As she stepped on to the first step, her feet lost purchase and she slid down the staircase, banging against every step on the way down. A putrid icy breeze assaulted her as she crashed into the floor at the bottom of the stairs.

"Ouch, that hurt," she mumbled as she rubbed her back.

"Of all the—you could have killed yourself, Sascha," Marco said. "I'm coming down."

"Keep your voice down, Marco," Sascha whispered. "And stay where you are. There's no point in both of us being down here. I'm going to turn on the light. Phew, what is that smell? It smells like blood and bone mixed with rotten eggs and dirty dog."

She groped blindly along the wall until she reached the

light switch. She flicked it. Nothing happened. She flicked it back and forth several times. Still, nothing happened.

"Of course the light switch doesn't work," she moaned. She groped her way back to the stairs. "I need a torch," she whispered. "The light switch doesn't work."

Running feet sounded above her, racing toward the front door. "Marco," she hissed. "There's someone in the house. They're running toward the front door."

"I'm coming down. When the front door doesn't open, they'll make for the cellar door. Ella, call the police."

A loud crack reverberated through the house, followed by the crash of a door being slammed open.

"No, don't come down here. They've opened the door. How the hell did they do that? Hurry, Marco! They're getting away, damn it."

"Stop. Police. Stay where you are."

Constable Miller. What's he doing back here? He couldn't have responded to Ella's call that quickly.

The sound of skittering claws came from near the cellar door.

"No, Rusty. Stay," Lee called out. "Sorry, Sascha but Rusty is coming your way. She got out of her collar."

Rusty yelped as she lost her footing and dropped onto Sascha, sending them both crashing to the floor.

"Damn it, Rusty, I told you to stay with Lee." Rusty leaped to her feet and rushed to the other side of the room. A high-pitched, mournful cry reverberated around the room.

"Rusty," Sascha called out as she raced over to Rusty, hitting her shin on the corner of something sharp in the process.

"Ouch, that—"

Wow, the stench is so much worse here.

She crouched down next to Rusty. "Are you hurt?" Rusty's

cry softened and changed to a low, mournful howl. Goose-bumps raced across Sascha's skin.

The lights flicked on. The sudden brightness forced Sascha to cover her eyes. Cautiously, she removed her hand and looked at Rusty. Her head was resting on a large bump underneath a green tarpaulin. Sascha lifted the corner of the tarpaulin. "Ken! My God, it's Ken."

She dropped the cover back in place and covered her mouth as her stomach lurched. Ken was dead.

Footsteps clumped down the stairs. A man in a suit led the way. He was followed by Constables Miller and Archer. "What is this dog doing here? Madam, please step back. This is a crime scene. Constable, take this woman up to the kitchen and keep her there until I can talk to her."

"Yes, sir," Constable Miller said.

And get forensics to check this mutt for evidence before it's released." He shook his head. "You'd think people would have seen enough television to know they shouldn't mess with a crime scene, wouldn't you?"

Sascha snapped to her feet. "How dare you be so rude. Ken was my friend, and this *mutt* was someone he loved. You could have learnt a lot from Ken. He had manners."

"Constable, show this woman out."

"I don't need anyone to show me to the kitchen. I know where it is. I'll make my own way there. Come with me, Rusty." Sascha reached for Rusty, but Rusty pulled away. Sascha squatted next to her. She tried not to breathe in, to ignore the smell. Rusty raised her head and stared at her with glazed eyes. "Sorry, gorgeous, we have to move." Sascha stroked Rusty's head. "Let's go upstairs." Rusty let out a cry, its pitch causing Sascha to shudder. "I'm so sorry, girl." Rusty staggered up and moved toward the stairs with Sascha.

"Constable, go with her. Make sure you get the dog checked for evidence, and organize a change of clothes for the woman. I'll have some questions for her when I've finished here, so don't let her leave until then."

Sascha stomped up the stairs to the kitchen, Rusty following close behind. The kitchen lights were on and Marco was waiting for her. He had made tea.

"Here, Sascha, this will help."

"Thanks, Marco."

Constable Miller arrived and put a plastic sheet down on the kitchen floor for Rusty to lie on until the vet arrived. "Did you catch him, Constable? Do you know who it was?" Sascha said.

"She got away, unfortunately. Someone was waiting for her."

"Don't tell me they drove away in a black car?"

The constable looked a bit sheepish. "You were right about the car too." He turned around and went back down the stairs.

Sascha turned to Marco. "A woman? I didn't expect it to have been a woman. Unless...unless it was Pat."

Marco shrugged. "She did lie to the police when they asked her where Ken was."

"Ken said that Pat would betray anyone for Drakon. But betraying someone is different to killing them. Ken was only worried about what Drakon would do to him."

"Anything is possible."

"By the way, Kira is home now, Sascha. When you get a chance, perhaps you can talk to her. Tell her what we've talked about?"

"Yes, I'll talk to her tonight," Sascha said.

Sascha sat at the kitchen bench and took a sip of tea as she glanced around the kitchen. There were so many happy memories here, but now everything had been turned upside down. She put her cup down and walked over to the fridge to look at the photos stuck onto it. There were the familiar photos of her and the girls with Pat and Ken on holiday or at parties together. One picture was separated from the rest, so she moved closer to have a look. It was a picture of Ken and Pat sitting at a table with a slim brunette. They all held glasses full of what she supposed was champagne and were making a toast. The woman looked strangely familiar.

Sascha took the photo and held it under the light. "Look at this, Marco. That's Laela with Pat and Ken. What would she be doing with them? I didn't realize they knew each other."

"Laela looks younger," Marco said.

Sascha studied it. "There's a strong family resemblance between her and Pat, don't you think?"

"I guess so," Marco said.

"Look at their eyes and the way they both smile they're so similar. When was Laela here?" Sascha reached over to the put the photo back, knocking a couple of the magnets and some papers onto the floor in the process.

Marco leaned down to pick the things up. "Hello." Marco stared at the piece of paper he was holding.

"What is it?"

"It's a fragment of a map." He turned and showed it to her. "And look at where it was torn. There's part of a circle and the coastline around Achmelvich. That's where the Four Sisters safe house is. Why would Pat and Ken have a map of that specific area?"

"Do you think Jenny or Eham are in danger?" Sascha asked.

"We can warn them, but Eham will be able to protect Jenny if Pat tries anything."

"But what would Pat and Ken want to find Jenny and Eham for?" Sascha asked.

"I have no idea," Marco said.

Constable Miller and a female officer stepped into the kitchen. "Excuse me, Sascha," Miller said.

"You want me to come with you?" Sascha asked.

"Yes, please."

"I have to give the police my statement," Marco said. "I'll do that while you're getting changed and then I think I'll slip home. I have a lot to organize before I leave tomorrow, and you and Kira have a lot to talk about. I'll let the girls know you won't be long."

"Will you come by later?"

"It's late. I'll catch up with you tomorrow."

Sascha gave Marco a half-smile before following Constable Miller down the hall.

WHEN SASCHA HAD LEFT with the officer, Marco grabbed the photo of Pat, Ken and Laela off the fridge and pocketed it as well as the map. It worried him that Laela was friends with Ken and Pat. He needed to do some investigation, find out what Laela was up to.

After giving his statement to the police, Marco walked to his car, which was parked out the front of Sascha's place. Lee and Ella were sitting on the swinging chair on the front patio, while Kira and Sascha were sitting arm-in-arm on the step with Rusty beside them.

He knew he probably should stay with Sascha. He sighed. Everything was a mess. He dug into his jeans pocket and pulled out his car keys. He looked back at Sascha's place before diving into his car. Movement on the roof of Sascha's house caught his attention. Soleil was watching him.

He sighed again and drove away. The radio was on, and the plane crash was the topic of choice. He changed the station, but only found more news stories about the plane crash. He turned the radio off. His stomach knotted. He couldn't lose Alex. It was too unfair that something like this happened every time he was around Sascha.

There's no point thinking about it.

He pressed the phone icon on the touch screen in his car and called Alex's number again, leaving yet another message for him. Then he called Jenny's cell phone and got her voice-mail. He left a message for her to call him as soon as she could.

Assuming she even looks at the phone.

When Marco got home, he went upstairs for a shower. As he walked back down the stairs, a male voice talking to the answering machine penetrated his thoughts. He caught the tail end of the message. "...we haven't heard anything yet, but we'll be in touch as soon as we can confirm if Alex was on the flight." He walked over to the answering machine and listened to the full message. There was nothing new.

He's not dead. I would know if he was dead.

He needed to switch off. He walked down to his coffee shop, picked up a few bottles of wine and then phoned the pizza shop. He planned to get drunk and stuff his face with food.

THE STENCH of stale wine and pizza hung heavy in the air. Marco groaned. He sat on the edge of the sofa and rested his pounding head in his hands. A wave of nausea surged through him.

Never again. I will never do this again.

He took a couple of slow, deep breaths and waited for the nausea to ease. When he was sure it was safe to move, he pushed himself gingerly up from the sofa and made his way to the kitchen.

He washed down a couple of painkillers with a Bloody Mary and put a few homemade sausage rolls in the oven before climbing the stairs to the bathroom. Feeling a bit more human after his shower, he returned to the kitchen to check his cell phone. There were no messages.

"Alex," he said, "where the hell are you?"

He had a breakfast of sausage rolls, ketchup and several mugs of fresh black coffee.

He forced himself to tidy his unit, then picked up his car keys. A soft roar echoed from outside his front door.

That sounded like George. But that's impossible.

Marco walked to the door and opened it. Sitting on the front step was a winged manticore. George stood up and raced toward Marco, swishing her tail in the air with excitement.

"George! How did you get here?"

Marco held the door open. "Inside. Quickly, before anyone sees you. And be careful with that tail." Marco scanned the area outside his unit. Connell wasn't there. Marco's stomach dropped. Connell never would have sent George here by herself unless something was wrong.

He walked back inside and closed the door behind him. George was lying on the thick woolen mat in the middle of the lounge room, her wings folded neatly by her sides.

If George had come by herself, then she must be carrying a message. Marco put his keys on the table and strode over to the mat. He squatted next to George. "Do you have something for me?"

George pushed her wings further back and Marco could see she was wearing a harness.

"You do have something." As he leaned forward and undid the straps, a small parcel fell onto the mat. Marco picked it up and took it to the table. He unwrapped it. Inside was a sealed packet attached to a yellow envelope. He opened the packet first. There were eight keystones.

"Eight keystones?" Marco said. "Why are there so many?" He picked up the yellow envelope. It was Connell's writing on the front, and it was addressed to Marco. His stomach tensed. This couldn't be good news. On the back of the envelope was the royal seal of the Grayfang realm a winged manticore sitting underneath a canopy of gray fangs. He broke the seal and took out the letter.

Marco,

I don't have long to write this, but I hope to get a chance to explain more when you and the girls return to Eratus. I'm sure it's a surprise to see George. Unfortunately, I'm not well enough to travel. I have enclosed keystones for the first portal. I'm not sure how safe the second portal is, so I wanted you to be able to choose the safest way to get back here. You all need to return as soon as you can. The Shield has suddenly worsened and I am sure we have only days until it collapses. You and Sascha need to work out how to heal it, and soon. Time is not on your side. When you return, it might be worth bringing Alex, Eham and Jenny with you. Their safety is at risk.

Marco stopped reading. Connell wouldn't know about the crash. He rubbed his stomach to ease the growing tension and continued to read the letter.

I don't know if Sascha told you, but she was attacked by a pit hound when she was here on Eratus. We weren't able to find the second hound at the time, but I later learned that Reya was behind the attack when she sent the second pit hound after me. George saved me with the help of a magical necklace given to her by a little girl. Who would have thought the necklace was magical? But I am rambling. There is so much to say, but George is waiting to deliver this to you before the others return. Since Reya's attack, I have discovered some disturbing news, which I am documenting in my journal in case the healer's treatment doesn't work. I will have the journal hidden in the secret place we used to use as kids.

I don't want anyone to know about this letter. I am not sure who I can trust.

If the treatment doesn't work, I have given instructions for my body to be destroyed so that I don't come under Reya's control. Please make sure my instructions are followed. I know what I'm asking, but I cannot become a creature of the dark. As my friend, please see that this is done.

Connell

P.S. Please look after my George. I know she is exhausted after what she did to save me. And bring everyone home soon. I miss you all.

Marco dropped into his lounge chair. Connell was in trouble again and he wasn't there to help him.

A slow, deep growl echoed from George's chest as she stared at the front door, the hair along her back bristling. She held her tail aloft as she got up and stalked toward the door, her claws clicking against the floorboards.

"What is it, George?"

Marco followed her, placed his hand on the door handle and whisked the door open. He looked. Nothing was there. George gave a quiet rumble, turned and walked back to the lounge room, where she threw herself onto the mat with a loud thud. Marco took one last look outside, closed the door and turned back to George.

"What was that all about?"

George let out a huge sigh, curled up and closed her eyes. Goosebumps covered Marco's arms. He glanced around the room, unable to settle. George appeared to be happy now, so everything should be safe.

I'd better check through the unit. I can relax then.

The place was clear. He took a deep breath to calm

himself. It was time to call Sascha. He picked his phone up from the dining table and dialed Sascha's number.

"Hello, Marco."

"Hi, Sascha. I'm sorry I took off last night."

"That's fine. I understood. Have you heard anything about Alex?"

"No, but I refuse to believe…" He swallowed the lump in his throat. "I've just had a visitor. You'll never guess who it is. It's George."

"George? What's she doing there?"

"Connell sent George with keystones for the first portal. He said he wasn't sure how safe the second portal was, and he wanted to give us the option of using whichever was the safest."

"It's strange he didn't come with her," Sascha said.

"Um, there is a reason. I will tell you when I get there."

Marco's phone beeped. He glanced at it. It was Jenny. "Sascha, do you mind if I ring you back? I've got a call from Jenny."

"No, of course not. That's fine."

"I'll call you," he said. Marco hung up and tapped the screen to accept the call from Jenny.

"Jenny, hello. It's Marco."

"Hi. I'm ringing with good news. Alex is safe."

Marco's legs turned to jelly. He pulled out one of the dining chairs and dropped into it.

"Marco?" Jenny said.

For a moment, Marco was speechless. He shook his head, as if waking from a dream. "Did you say Alex is safe?"

"Yes, he is," Jenny replied. "I can't imagine how hard it has been for you, not knowing whether Alex was alive or dead. He is in Sydney. He and Eham are about to board the flight to Brisbane."

"Thank Athena," Marco said. "You've made my day, Jenny. Thank you so much for letting me know."

"I would have called earlier if I'd heard about the plane crash, but there's no television or radio in the safe house. The Sisters believe in isolating themselves from the outside world."

Marco could hear a female voice on a PA system announcing the boarding details for the next flight to Sydney, Australia. "I've got to go," Jenny said. "I'm on my way to join you too. By the way, Alex asked if you and the girls would meet him at the Fire of the Phoenix headquarters. He thinks that's the safest place to meet."

"Safest?"

The female voice on the PA system sounded again. "Yes. He will tell you more about it when he catches up with you. That's my last boarding call. I'd better go."

"OK," Marco said. "I'll speak to you when you get here."

Marco hung up the phone and closed his eyes. Alex was safe. He was actually safe. Marco walked to the kitchen and made himself a strong coffee. He took the coffee to the sofa and then dialed Sascha's number. He left a message when the call went through to voicemail. "Jenny's call was good news. Alex is safe." Marco swallowed hard as he tried to push down the emotions that were whirling through him. "They're due in Brisbane in a couple of hours, and they have asked us to meet them at the Fire of the Phoenix headquarters. I will call you later to make sure you get this message."

CHAPTER 32

ERATUS

*D*rakon coughed. His throat was dry and his eyes stung. When he tried to take a deep breath, he gagged on the fine salty dust that filled his mouth and coughed again. Presently, he gathered enough strength to push himself to his feet. As he stood, a gray powder drifted off him. He looked around. The Master's skeleton lay next to him. The fire had destroyed every living creature, and ash and bone and a faint, slightly metallic odor was all that remained. But he was alive. Somehow he had survived the white fire. He attempted to brush himself off, but there was a sticky residue covering him that made the dust impossible to remove. He needed new clothes and a long hot bath.

"It's time for you to fulfil your destiny," a voice echoed around the room.

"What? Who's there?"

Laughter reverberated around the chambers, the sound of it sending chills through Drakon.

"You will find out soon enough. For now, all you need to know is you have work to do. You need to release us. And when it is time, we will help you destroy the Four Sisters."

"Us? Who is us?"

Again, the voice laughed. Then it continued. "Together we will release the weapons."

"Those weapons are mine and I have no intention of—" A screeching, sharp pain sliced through Drakon's head, bringing him to his knees.

"You will do what you are told. It is you who chose this path."

"I won't…" The pain increased and Drakon gripped his head in his hands.

"The longer you take to agree, the worse the pain will get," the voice said.

Drakon screamed as the pain continued to build. "Stop," he called out.

"Do you agree to do as we tell you?"

"Yes," Drakon said, "I agree."

"Good," the voice replied.

The pain eased and Drakon clambered to his feet. There had to be a way to free himself from this creature's control. The realization hit him with a sickening thud.

The voice belongs to one of the ancients. I'm being controlled by one of the ancients.

He shook his head.

No. I will not allow this to happen. I haven't worked this hard to have them take control now.

Torches set in wall sconces burst into flame. "Time to get out of here, Drakon," the voice said. "You must return to the castle. Finally, after all these centuries, we will be free to rule again."

Drakon glanced around him, desperate for some way to regain control. He glanced at the Master's body. And then he saw it the armband the Master had been wearing. An olive tree and an owl the symbols of Athena were engraved on it.

Of all the gods you could have chosen to help you, Master, you chose Athena? But if this is what gave you power over the ancients, it should work for me too.

He leaned down to pick up the band.

"No," the voice screamed out.

Drakon gasped as the screeching pain returned with an intense ferocity. His vision blurred, making it hard to see in front of him. He needed to move fast.

"Do not put that band on," the voice bellowed.

Drakon half-fell, half-dived onto the arm that wore the band. The Master's bones were brittle and broke easily. He grabbed at the band and slipped it on. A second later, the voice quietened to a soft whisper. Relief flooded through him as the pain disappeared. He smiled. The band would serve until he could another one made that possessed the same sort of magical properties, and then he could dispose of it. He wasn't going to rely on any of the gods for help, even Athena. All the gods offered was betrayal.

Fire erupted around the edge of the chamber. He gathered all his remaining strength and raced to the door. He waved his hand and the door slammed open, shattering against the wall. Drakon stared at the remains of the solid stone door. How could he possibly have smashed that? The fire was coming closer. He had to move. Drakon raced outside just as the chamber imploded. The morning suns were bright, forcing him to cover his eyes until they acclimatized to the bright light. It was time to go home.

Drakon surveyed what was left of the site where his life had changed forever. He had no idea how he survived the white fire storm that had engulfed the room and swallowed the Master. But he had. The voice was right he had work to do.

Drakon began his journey back to the castle. When he arrived on Eratus, he looked up at the sky. The white cracks were everywhere. The Master was right the Shield had worsened and there wasn't much time. He was going to have to change his plans. His priority must be to protect Sascha, to help her heal the Shield. There was no point in rushing to capture her now. There would be plenty of time once this disaster was behind them. He wanted his kingdom and it seemed that Sascha was the key to that.

DRAKON SNUCK into the castle through the dungeon entrance. Once he reached his chambers, he bathed and changed before summoning his guard.

The guard started to raise his arm in a salute, but then took a step back, a look of surprise on his face.

"Is something wrong?" Drakon asked.

"No." He saluted. "You asked for me, My Prince?"

"Send Novo to me. Tell him to meet me in my war room."

"Yes, immediately. And, My Prince, the High King has requested your presence in his chambers."

Drakon nodded. "Advise the High King I will be there."

Drakon strode into his war room minutes later.

"Hello, my pets," he said as he stood for a moment, half expecting Ares and Hades to make an appearance. They would be keen to know what happened, unless, of course, they already knew. He wasn't sure what he was going to say to them. The one thing he did know, however, was that he wanted revenge for the way they had set him up. Drakon clenched his fists. He needed to be patient, wait until the time was right. Drakon glanced over at his creatures. They had stopped eating and were staring at him.

"You're not talking today?" Drakon said as he walked toward them. The young ones backed away from him, but the leader stayed where he was, studying Drakon. He stretched to his full height as Drakon walked closer.

"It's me, my pets. What's wrong?" The fire dragons started to sing in a pitch Drakon had never heard before. They circled him and moved closer. Drakon watched them, his senses on high alert. They knew he was different. The leader of the pack gave a loud, sharp call and they lay down at Drakon's feet as one. Drakon leaned down cautiously and caressed the head of the leader. "I am different, my pets. But I still love you." A soft crooning sound filled the room. The leader suddenly pulled back and gave a sharp click of his beak as he stared at the doorway.

Drakon turned to see Novo standing there, staring at the fire dragons as he fidgeted with the hilt of his sword. "You needed me, My Prince?"

"Yes," Drakon said, taking a handful of berries from the fruit bowl on the table as he moved toward the window that overlooked the training grounds. The berries tasted so sweet and luxurious. He suddenly realized he hadn't eaten since before leaving for the Peaceful Valley.

"What has been happening in the castle, Novo?"

Novo kept glancing at Drakon and then looking away. "I expect you know the High King has been looking for you."

"Yes, I know."

"He wants to talk to you about the healing of the Shield and what happened to Connell," Novo said.

"Connell? What are you talking about?"

Novo cleared his throat. "Connell is very ill. He was attacked. The healers aren't sure he will survive."

"What attacked him?"

"Rumors say it was a pit hound," Novo said.

Drakon stepped toward Novo. "A pit hound? Are you sure?"

"Yes, they say it was Reya."

"Why would Reya attack Connell? Guard, bring me Reya."

"Reya's disappeared, My Prince," Novo said. "But we are searching for her."

Drakon stood silent for a moment as he digested what Novo had said. "Bring her to me as soon as you find her. Is that clear, Novo?"

"Yes, My Prince."

"And what about the other things I asked you to do?"

"We have taken over a small village outside of Cirrone. There is a compound there where we can keep Sascha and the girls. It is only accessible from one area and cannot be found unless you are looking for it. We bought it from one of the wealthier families in Dalhurst. They could not have been more helpful after we mentioned how much we knew of their family secrets."

"Good," Drakon said. "But we will put any plans for capturing Sascha on hold until the Shield is repaired. You've seen the sky. We need her to focus on the healing."

"Yes, My Prince. I have some other news that I am sure will please you. Reya was acting strangely, so I decided to follow her. She snuck into the Four Sisters headquarters to hide a piece of paper. I retrieved it when she left."

"Show it to me."

Novo gulped. He stepped into the war room, unable to tear his gaze from the fire dragons. He handed a folded piece of paper to Drakon and then skittered back to the doorway.

Drakon opened it. For a moment, he stared open-mouthed. It was the original map. Attached to the map with a dragon clip was a card with a code written on it. Reya had been holding onto the map all this time and never told him.

Four symbols were embossed in the corner of the card fire, ice, earth and water. He read the words below the symbols.

Your faith will reveal the next steps you must take. Do you destroy the dark, or allow the light to awake? The circles will slow and the protection will rise. The future will then be yours to decide.

He was sure the meaning would become clear when they arrived at the site. Maybe they could use the code to retrieve the weapons sooner rather than later.

"Novo, you have done well."

"Thank you, My Prince. There is one other matter. Chiane has asked for a meeting with you. Reya asked for his help before we knew what she had done. He's concerned about the assistance he gave her. Do you want me to send him to you?"

"Yes, but tell him to meet me here later this afternoon. I must meet with Owain and Laela first. And I may have another task for you."

"Yes, My Prince." Novo saluted, turned on his heel and strode away.

"Guard," Drakon called out. "Bring my aide-de-camp to me."

"Yes, My Prince."

Curious about everyone's reactions to his appearance, he walked over to a small mirror on the wall beside the doorway. His eyes were now a deep charcoal color and his olive skin was two shades darker than normal, as if he had been sunbaking in the deserts of Brun for a month. His hair was different too, with streaks of silver showing through at the sides. The changes made him look distinguished, something which pleased him. He couldn't help but wonder what Owain would say.

The aide-de-camp gave a small cough to announce his arrival. "Yes, My Prince."

"Find Laela. Let me know where she is," Drakon said.

"But she—"

"I don't care how you do it, just find her." Drakon rubbed his hands. "It is time for us to have a little chat."

"Yes, My Prince." The aide scurried from the room.

Drakon chortled to himself. Laela would panic when she saw him, but her part in the disaster at the healing ceremony couldn't be ignored. Faking her death had been a good idea, but she hadn't even been able to do that properly. Fortunately, he was generous. He would promise forgiveness, but only if she helped him.

DRAKON LEFT HIS WAR ROOM. He was ready to face Owain now. He glanced around the castle grounds. Amazed to see how well the people were handling the changes in the Shield, he stopped a noble as he strode past him.

"Is no-one afraid to see the worsening condition of the Shield?" he asked.

The noble frowned. "They are, but the High King's speech gave them hope."

"His speech?"

"Yes, My Prince. He promised that he was only a day or two away from healing the Shield. He told us we have nothing to fear."

Drakon nodded, dismissed the man with a flick of his hand and then raced up the steps to Owain's chambers. "The fools," he muttered.

Owain's chambers were empty, so Drakon sent the guard to let him know he had arrived. He walked out to the fully laden table on the balcony, poured himself some ale and took a couple of sweet meats. He looked out over the balcony rim and studied the crowds gathering at the taverns. Some of the people clearly weren't as gullible as the noble he had spoken to. The people in these crowds carried banners warning the end was near and demanding that the portals be opened so everyone could flee to Earth. Maybe things weren't as peaceful as he first thought.

"Where have you been?" a voice behind him boomed.

Drakon hadn't heard the High King arrive. He turned toward Owain, who was dressed in tan-colored pants and a white shirt. "Father, what's with the casual gear? This is so unlike you."

"Don't change the subject," Owain said. "No-one could find you."

"I had duties to perform. Don't forget I have businesses to manage. As, of course, do you," he said, bowing and giving a flourishing sweep with one hand.

"Don't mock me, Drakon." Owain studied him. "What have you done to yourself? You're different."

"Father, I'm sure you didn't summon me here to discuss my appearance."

Owain sat in one of the tan leather chairs in front of the fireplace. "You're right, of course. We need to work out how to fix the Shield in the few days we have left."

Drakon leaned against the balcony rim and stared at a small group of nobles who were chatting and pointing animatedly at the crowds in front of the tavern. "One of your people told me the Shield would be healed in a couple of days."

"Don't be a fool. I had to say something to stop the people from panicking."

Drakon nodded in the direction of the tavern. "Not everyone believes you."

"There are always fanatics," Owain said. "You should know that."

"Are you going to open the portals?"

"There are no portals big enough to send all of the people to Earth. Besides, if Eratus is destroyed, Earth will be as well.

It won't survive the destruction of a system that is so close to it."

"It might be worth telling that to the people so we don't have to deal with another rebellion." Drakon turned his back to the balcony and faced Owain. "What do you want from me, Father?"

"Make sure Sascha returns to Eratus, and soon. We need her to activate her powers and perform the healing. She's our only real hope."

"I will do that, but she can't restore the Shield on her own. We need to work out how to help her."

"I know. We already have a plan to send all the powerful mages to Zinnath's Peak to support Sascha throughout the healing. With Sascha taking the lead, we may be able to do the impossible. Assuming she still has her powers."

"Novo tells me Connell was attacked by a pit hound."

Owain was silent for a moment as he stared at the floor. "Yes. It was Reya. I trust you had nothing to do with it, Drakon?"

Drakon walked to the fireplace and stared into the dancing flames. He flexed his shoulders. "Would you believe me if I say I didn't?"

"Of course I would."

"Well, I didn't," Drakon replied. "I would find a more creative way of getting rid of Connell."

"That gives me little comfort, Drakon."

"Why would Reya want to kill Connell?" Drakon said as he watched the flames leap from log to log, shuddering as he remembered what had happened at the Peaceful Valley. "How would she benefit from his death?"

"Connell said he had no idea, but I know he is hiding something. He is very ill, so I can't push him too much. Did she say anything to you? Did she hate Connell that much?"

Drakon shook his head. "She never talked about Connell

specifically. She wasn't overly impressed with any of the court, but I wouldn't have said she hated him."

"There must be a reason," Owain said "We need to work out what it was. Perhaps you can oversee the search for Reya?"

Drakon debated about whether to tell his father that he had already taken control of the investigation, but decided against it. "Yes, Father."

"Good. I will organize for the mages to be sent to Zinnath's peak. Temporary accommodation can be set up not far from the ceremonial area so that we can commence the healing as soon as Sascha is able."

"Father, I'm not sure the mages will be enough. And the area must still be recovering from the last disaster."

"People are already preparing and cleansing the site," Owain said. "And we will have to hope the mages are enough, because they are all we have." Owain sighed. "One thing, Drakon. Sascha has been told a lot of bad things about you. She will be wary."

"She's heard bad things about me? Surely not, Father," Drakon said as he headed for the stairs. "I must leave. It appears I have work to do."

"Let's hope that whatever we do is enough to save Eratus," Owain said.

~

Drakon's aide was waiting for him at the entrance to his chambers.

"My Prince, this is where Laela has been staying since the disaster," he said, handing over a slip of paper.

"Good. Now, I want you to travel to Zinnath's peak. You will assess what is happening there and report back to me."

"Yes, My Prince."

"Go," Drakon snapped.

Drakon stepped into his chambers, closing the door behind him. He paced the room, eventually stopping in front of his desk. He leaned over, picked up the photo frame that held a photo of Reya and studied it. He had a feeling that Reya had more reason for visiting the Four Sisters headquarters than simply hiding the map. Why would she choose to hide the map there of all places? She was an apostate. She hated everything the Sisters represented. "Why would you go there, Reya?" He started to pace again, the frame still clasped in his hand. He stopped mid-stride. "The Register of Mages," he muttered. What could she have hoped to find in the register? His stomach twisted. Surely it couldn't have been something to do with him or Connell. The only person who knew anything about the secret was Laela and she wouldn't tell Reya. Would she?

Drakon threw the frame to the floor, smashing it into pieces. "Sokentash!" None of it made sense.

He had to fix this. He would do it properly this time. Now that he had the Master's powers, he could fix it so that he never had to worry about it again.

Fifteen minutes later, Drakon arrived at the underground entrance to the Sisters' headquarters and sent himself into shadow. "So, Father, let's see how much power you really had," he whispered.

Though there was no-one around, he stayed in shadow as he crossed the tiled floor of the reception area and headed for the stairs at the back of the building. He climbed the stairs and opened the panel that allowed him into the room where the register was hidden. He walked past the many library shelves to the far back corner of the room. The register was sitting on a podium.

Drakon pushed aside the fear he felt and moved closer.

This time will be different. It must work.

Last time he had visited here, the ancient magic that protected the register nearly killed him. This time, however, he had his father's magic.

If it didn't work—

Drakon pushed the thought away. There was no room for failure. He rested his hands on the book's cover and closed his eyes.

"Breath of darkness, let it be, a change to the records of our history. Let it be, that I'm the High King's son, and the records for Connell Grayfang be undone."

A blue flame licked around the edges of the book, the heat forcing Drakon to pull his hands away. Drakon could hear the chant repeating itself, getting faster and faster. The flame twisted around the book and then the podium, the flame's colors changing from blue to yellow to orange and, finally, to red. There was the sound of a muffled explosion and then the smell of sulfur before everything fell quiet. Drakon glanced around him, thinking that somebody must have heard what happened, but no-one came. He stared at the register. He had to check, see if the changes had happened. He opened it to the records of births for Connell and himself. He took a deep breath, relaxed his shoulders and looked down at the words.

The sound of voices came from the staircase. He had to go. He closed the book and slipped back into shadow. As the door opened, he slid out and hurried back down the stairs and outside. Everything was exactly as he wanted it to be. Excitement welled up inside him. He had done it. After all these years, he was finally free. He was now Owain's son, and it was Connell who was the outsider. He rubbed his hands together. It was time to visit Laela.

∿

LAELA'S HOME was well hidden. His aide had done well to

find it. Drakon slid from Fenix's neck and walked over to the vines hiding the gated entrance. He waved his hands and the vines flicked aside, revealing a track leading down a steep hill to a little cabin. The cabin was quaint, made of terracotta stone with cream edging. Laela sat cross-legged in the garden, her eyes closed and ignoring everything around her. The lush garden was full of dragonberries, moonflowers and fruit trees, all of which attracted an abundance of bird life. Little ground runners played happily around her. She turned her head toward the door to her cabin. Drakon watched as Owain stepped outside to join her in the garden.

What was he doing here?

Owain walked over to Laela, pulled her to her feet and embraced her.

Laela and Owain? No.

Owain released her and then wandered up the track toward where Drakon was standing. Drakon pushed himself into shadow and waited for him to pass. When Owain was out of sight, he stepped back onto the track and glanced at Laela's house. She had moved inside.

He walked down to the house and strolled in through the open front door. The room smelled of the sweet peppermint scent of healing medicines. Dry bundles of herbs hung from the roof beams, and various colored liquids bubbled away in glass tubes suspended over burners placed on the kitchen benches. Laela was grinding some herbs in a mortar at a table. Her hair was pulled back, revealing her markings.

"Hello, Laela. It's been a long time."

She jumped, dropping the pestle into the mortar with a thud. The color drained from her face. "What are you doing here? How did you find me?"

"I think it's time we talked, don't you?" Drakon leaned over her shoulder to look into the mortar, enjoying the power his height gave him. As he walked around the room, he took down one of the hanging bundles of herbs and sniffed it. He raised his eyebrows. "Cedarwood? Isn't it good for increasing a man's virility. Nothing to do with my father, I hope?"

Laela stormed toward Drakon and snatched the herbs out of his hand.

Drakon laughed. "I am here because I need your help. I figure you owe me after the part you played in the healing ceremony."

"I don't need to be afraid of you anymore, Drakon."

Drakon studied her. "You don't? It doesn't worry you that I might tell Owain it was you who introduced the darkness into the Shield, killing your sisters and wounding his precious Connell?"

A bright pink flush creeped up Laela's neck and into her cheeks "What do you want, Drakon?"

"A small favor, that's all. And then we're even. You'll be free of me."

"What small favor?"

"We need to ensure Sascha arrives here safely. I know she trusts you. I want you to visit her on Earth and offer to help her. Tell her that Owain sent you to protect them."

The muscles in Laela's neck and shoulders relaxed as she let out a huge breath. "And then my debts are cleared?"

"Not quite. There is one more small thing you need to do for me."

"Of course," she sighed.

"One of my people delivered a bottle of wine to Sascha. It was a gift to her from me. I have only recently become aware that it has green lyrium in it."

She raised her eyebrows. "Green lyrium?"

"Yes. I need you to destroy that bottle. I think it is in all our interests to stop her from drinking the lyrium. Don't you agree?"

"You knew nothing about the green lyrium being in the wine, Drakon?" Laela asked.

"Don't get lippy with me, Laela."

Laela picked up a piece of cloth and the pestle. "There will be no more requests?"

"No more, I promise," Drakon said, touching his hand to his heart and smirking.

"I mean it, Drakon." The muscles in her jaw twitched. "This has to be the end of it. If it isn't, I might have to start revealing a few of your secrets. I am sure Owain would be interested to know who his true son is."

Drakon laughed. "That would be me."

She cleaned the pestle and placed it next to the mortar. "The register records—"

"The register? Never threaten a man more powerful than you unless you already have the ace up your sleeve."

Laela pressed her lips together as she stepped back and crossed her arms. "I do have this ace. The register is protected. You cannot touch it."

Drakon laughed again. "You really don't know what I can do, do you? You might find the magic protecting it has...changed."

Laela's eyes widened.

"You have work to do, Laela," Drakon said as he walked toward the door. "Don't disappoint me." He stopped. He was sure there was no connection between Laela and Reya, but he had to check. "I'm sure Reya has told you what I do to those who disappoint me." He glanced back. Laela stood staring at him, her mouth open, her face a ghostly white.

No denial? So they really do know each other. That could be a problem.

"Do as I have asked, Laela, and soon. We don't have much time before the Shield collapses."

"Timing isn't a problem. Once I find them, we can travel

back here as a group now that—" Laela put a hand to her mouth and lowered her eyes. "I will try my best to convince Sascha and the girls to return to Eratus. I know what's at stake."

Drakon turned and strolled out of the cabin. He thought about that last part of their conversation as he walked along the path. What had she started to say? How could they travel as a group? The first portal wasn't big enough. The only way she could make that promise was if the second portal is working. He smirked. He needed to talk to Chiane.

"Fenix," he said as he set himself into the straps on her shoulders, "take me home and then follow Laela. Make sure she protects Sascha. I don't trust her."

CHAPTER 33

* EARTH

Sascha changed into jeans and a black shirt. Hearing Marco's voice this morning had renewed the overwhelming guilt she felt over Alex's disappearance. She dropped onto the edge of the bed. She was finding it hard to breathe, to think. What she wanted to do was dive back into bed, pull the covers over her head and forget about everything and everyone. But she couldn't. She clenched her fists to try to stop her hands from shaking.

The confrontation with Pat kept circling in her mind. Perhaps she should have forced the situation when Rusty was so desperate to get inside the house. Ken may have still been alive. Maybe she could have saved him. She rested her head in her hands. It was Pat and Ken's house, and Pat had been there. What could she have done? Pushed past the strange man and barged into Pat's house? She massaged the sharp pain in her temple.

"I can't do this, Ken," she whispered. "I need you." Tears trickled down her cheeks.

You can do this. Take one step at a time.

She wiped the tears away and pushed herself up off the bed.

I must do this.

Sascha opened the sliding door that led to the patio and walked outside. She stopped for a moment to breathe in the sight of her two favorite creatures – Rusty and Soleil – huddled together. The tension in Sascha's shoulders began to ease and she let out a deep sigh. She couldn't give up while they were in danger.

She walked over, squatted next to Rusty and stroked her head. "How are you going, gorgeous?" Rusty lifted her head, shuffled over and nuzzled into Sascha's shoulder. They stayed like that until the kitchen door slid open several minutes later. Sascha looked up to see Kira watching them. The aroma of freshly baked croissants and brewed coffee drifted outside.

Sascha stood up as Kira walked over to her. "How are you feeling after our chat last night, Kira? I know there was a lot to take in. I struggled to accept what Marco said. It would be so much harder for you."

Kira leaned over and hugged her, tears in her eyes. "There is so much I still need to understand. To think you knew my mother and that she is dead. I need to know what happened to her."

"So do I, Kira. And we will find out."

"But you looked after me, even on Eratus. Finding that out made me love you more."

Sascha's eyes stung as a tingling warmth flowed through her. "Thanks, Kira. I love you too. And I hope you know that I will always be here for you."

Kira stepped back, a silly grin on her face. "I've made breakfast. I want to tell you why I disappeared and I thought it would be better over croissants and coffee."

"Sounds good to me," Sascha said as she walked inside with Kira.

Lee and Ella were sitting at the table.

"Do you want some orange juice?" Kira asked.

"No, thanks. Black coffee is fine," Sascha said.

"Are you OK?" Ella asked.

"I will be." Sascha glanced out of the window at Rusty and Soleil. "Last night was…well, we all need time to get over it. But we have a lot to do. So, Kira, do you want to tell us what happened?"

Kira cleared her throat. "Firstly, I am so sorry to have given everyone such a scare. I have no idea who that girl is or how she got my wallet."

"I will need to take you to the police so that you can tell them that," Sascha said.

"We can take Kira," Ella said. "We doubt you want to go back there."

"Thanks, Ella. Kira, my biggest issue is not that you took off – I totally understood that – but that you lied to us and didn't tell us where you were. If something had happened to you, we wouldn't have known where to start looking. I know the note was a shock and that everything is changing so quickly. We must know that we can trust each other completely."

Kira stretched out her arm and rested her hand on Sascha's. "I know. I'm so sorry. I won't do it again. I promise."

"OK." Sascha wiped her face. She was becoming way too emotional. "So where were you?"

"I went back to the cave, the one with the dragon wings."

"How did you get there?" Lee asked.

"A friend drove me."

Lee frowned. "A friend? A male friend?"

"Lee, do you want me to tell the story or not?"

"Continue," she said, sitting back and studying Kira.

"I wanted to see if I could find the man who found the letter on the floor. I wanted to know if he was the friend mentioned in the letter."

"And did you see him?" Sascha asked?

"No, he didn't turn up. I waited for as long as I could. And then I got this idea. Dragons are supposed to know everything, and I knew there was a dragon cave somewhere below the library. I thought it might help us if I could find more information on the two dragons that stranger mentioned." She held up three books. "I found these texts."

"You stole those from the library, Kira?" Sascha said, staring at the texts.

"I borrowed them. Marco can return them once we've finished with them."

"That place is monitored like Fort Knox. How did you get them out of there?" Lee asked.

Kira shrugged. "I watched how Marco checked out the other books, waited until it was dark and then did the same."

"But you didn't have Marco's card," Lee said.

"Yes, I did," she said, holding the card up proudly. "I took it from him when he was giving me a hard time for not helping with carrying the texts back to the cave. I was angry with him and it seemed like a good way to get back at him."

Lee chuckled. "You've got to give it to the girl."

Sascha shook her head. "*You* can tell Marco what you did, Kira."

"I will." Kira sat up straight in her chair and put the books on the table. "But you will thank me for this. I found a series of stories about Zinnath and Kalurth. One of them tells of a plot devised by one of the Four Sisters to attack the dragons."

"That ties into what Marco was telling us," Lee said.

"But this attack was a long time ago. See, I did well, didn't I?" Kira said. She grinned.

Sascha tried to smother her smile, but she knew Kira had seen it. "Don't push your luck, Kira."

"Did it say who was behind the attack?" Lee asked

"The text said that it was the Enchantress the leader of the Four Sisters that organized the attack. She was sentenced to die in the sulfur pits. The texts said the punishment was so severe to stop anyone else from doing the same."

"It clearly didn't work," Lee said. "Sascha, do you think it's the leader of the Four Sisters that's behind this group planning the attack on the dragons?"

Sascha shrugged. "I don't know. Laela makes me uneasy, but I'm not sure why. I could be wrong, but she doesn't seem the type to be planning that sort of attack. She's friendly with Connell. And Owain as well, I think."

"I couldn't find any more information on the Enchantress the dragons punished," Kira said, "but the dragons might know."

Sascha sat back in her chair and glanced at each of the girls in turn. If the dragons were the ones who had all the information, then visiting them had to be the next step. "So that's what we're going to do."

"What are we doing?" Lee asked.

"If the cave below the library at the Fire of the Phoenix belongs to the dragons, then we're going to the cave and we're getting answers."

"We're what?" Lee and Ella said in unison.

"Now you're talking," Kira said, rubbing her hands together and bouncing in her chair.

"But we'll have to find out how to get into the cave first," Sascha said.

Kira opened one of the books and pulled out a sheet of paper. "I did find this. But I couldn't understand it. It's a map, but it's in some sort of code."

Sascha looked at the paper. "It does look like a map.

Those strange-looking pictographs could be a language. But I have no idea what language it is." Sascha spread the map on the table. "Girls, do you have any ideas?"

Everyone leaned forward in their chairs to study the map.

"The pictures..." Sascha said. She snapped her fingers. "I'll be back in a minute. I have an idea." She bolted out to her car, retrieved the text she had hidden in the boot and then raced back into the dining room.

"I have a translator," Sascha said as she held up the text.

"A what?" Kira said.

"A translator! It's a text on the language of the ancients. The pictographs in it look very similar to the symbols on the map."

Kira folded her arms. "That book isn't from the same place I retrieved these ones on the table, is it?"

"It could be," Sascha said. She smirked. "C'mon, girls. Let's do this."

"I'll make some fresh coffee," Lee said.

An hour later, they had translated most of the words on the page. "Read it out, Lee," Sascha said. "What does it say?"

" 'Let fire be your guide, with ice by your side. On earth you will stand, while the air shapes your land.' " Lee looked at Sascha with wide eyes.

"It's very cryptic," Kira said. "Perhaps we need to be in the cave for it to make sense."

"It's worth a shot," Sascha said. "We have nothing to lose. It's time to visit the library. I think we should all prepare as if we weren't coming back. We might have no choice once we meet with the dragons."

"Ella and I will take some emergency leave," Lee said. "And we'll take Kira to the police to give her statement."

"Do we have to go to the police?" Kira whined. "What difference does it make? We're leaving."

"You might know something that will help them," Sascha

said. "I saw that young girl. We have to help in any way we can." Sascha pushed herself up from the table. "While you girls are doing that, I'll organize lunch and visit my surgery. Marcie can look after things for me while I'm away. And I might pick up those two fans I was sent."

"The sharp ones?" Kira asked.

"Yes," Sascha said. "Maybe they were sent to me for a reason. Everything else I've received so far seems to be important."

"Shall we meet at the library?" Lee said.

"Let's meet in the squad bay instead," Sascha replied. "We can have some lunch there and plan exactly how we're going to do this. Do you remember how to get there?"

"I do," Lee said.

"Good. Let's all meet there at noon."

"Now the fun begins," Kira said, her eyes sparkling.

Sascha picked up her phone. "I should call Marco and tell him what we're up to." She glanced at the screen. There was a missed call and a message from Marco. "Wait a minute, girls. Marco called." She dialed her voicemail and listened to the message. Then she replayed it. She hung up and stood for a few seconds, staring at the phone.

"Is Marco OK?" Lee asked.

"Yes, he couldn't be better. That message was to tell me Alex is alive."

The girls squealed and hooted as they hugged Sascha first, then each other.

"What fabulous news," Ella said.

"This is all going to work out," Kira said. "Alex being alive is a good omen."

"And it appears he and Eham want to meet us in the library," Sascha said.

"Eham?" Lee asked. "He's back? He gave me the creeps."

"Me too," Kira said.

"Girls, we have to be nice."

"Did he say Jenny was coming back too?" Lee asked.

"No. Alex and Eham should be at the library soon," Sascha said, "so let's make sure we're on time."

THE ROLLER DOOR slammed shut as Sascha climbed out of her car. It always felt good to get home, even if it was only for an hour or so. The clinic seemed to be doing a roaring trade without her. Sascha wasn't sure if she liked that or not. It would have been nice to have felt needed. But Marcie and the team were doing well, and it was good to know that she didn't need to worry. Marcie had also agreed to look after the house while they were away – another weight off Sascha's mind.

She went inside to pack for the trip. Half an hour later, Sascha looked at her watch, her packing done. She had finished earlier than she had expected to.

Rusty barked as a knock sounded at the door.

"Visitors." She rolled her eyes. "Perfect." Sascha opened the door. Her mouth dropped open. Standing on the doorstep was Laela. She was dressed in a slim-fitting jade-colored shirt and white jeans, and was carrying a bag containing a bottle of wine.

"Laela? Of all the people—what are you doing here?"

"Surprise," Laela said, giving a quick, high-pitched laugh. "Ah…can I come in?"

"Oh, I'm sorry." Sascha stepped back to allow Laela to walk into the house. "You surprised me. You're the last person I expected to see."

"I knew it would be a shock, but I thought you might appreciate some extra support after what happened to Connell."

"What happened to Connell?"

"Haven't you heard? I assumed Connell would have let you or Marco know. He was attacked by the mate of the pit hound that attacked you."

Sascha gasped, her hand flying to her mouth. "Attacked? Did it bite him?"

"Yes, but George killed it, and Connell is being treated for the bite."

"Was it bad?"

"I won't lie to you. It was a bad attack. But he's tough, like you. He'll recover."

"So that's why—"

"Careful what you tell her, Sascha," Soleil said. "Something isn't right."

Sascha glanced out of the window. Rusty was watching Laela, but Soleil had disappeared.

Laela tilted her head to the side as she studied Sascha. "What were you going to say?"

"It explains why Connell was so worried about the second pit hound not being found," Sascha said, scratching a sudden itch on her ear.

"Yes," Laela said. "They always travel in pairs. But there's something else. Owain asked me to get you back to Eratus as soon as possible. The Shield is breaking down a lot faster than first thought."

"How much time do we have?"

"We think we only have a day or two before the Shield collapses."

"That soon?" Sascha's stomach lurched. "But that's not enough."

"It has to be enough. That's all we have."

Sascha felt the blood draining from her face. "So little time. What has caused this sudden change? It didn't look that bad when I was there."

"We don't know. But we are looking at ways to help you during the ceremony. Some powerful mages live on Eratus. Though they are not as powerful as you used to be, they may be able to assist you."

Sascha dropped into one of the dining chairs. Laela joined her at the table. "Sascha, I know you're scared, but we will be there to help you."

Sascha swallowed the fear.

There's no point in worrying. I will do what I must do and if it isn't enough...

She stood. "There is something the girls and I want to do before we leave here."

"I could come with you," Laela said.

"You don't have to do that, Laela. How about we meet you at the second portal?"

"You don't want me to join you?" Laela dropped her gaze. "Don't you trust me?"

"Aside from the girls, I don't know who to trust. I don't mean to offend, but I have to be careful until I get my memory back."

"I don't blame you, Sascha. But Owain has asked me to stay with you. I must follow his orders. I'm happy to stay in the background until you learn to trust me."

Sascha sighed as she stared at Laela. "You can come with us to the Fire of the Phoenix headquarters. But the girls and I need to do something together. Alone. You can wait for us in the squad bay."

"That's fine. Does it help that I bought some wine?" she said, her voice wavering. "I thought it might give us all the courage we need to face what's ahead of us."

"We can have the wine with our lunch. Do you want to come with Rusty and me in my car, or do you have your own?"

"Thanks, but I have a vehicle. I'll follow you."

"Give me a minute to lock up the house," Sascha said, "and then we can leave."

"Sascha, be careful," Soleil said. "I'm not sure what's wrong, but please be careful."

"I will, Soleil. I don't trust her either."

SASCHA SET up lunch in the squad bay with Laela's help. They decided to sit outside in the warmth of the sun to wait for the girls. The sound of bubbling water echoed around them.

"I'll get us some wine while we're waiting," Laela said, standing up and striding toward the squad bay.

Rusty sat fifty feet from where Sascha was sitting and was watching Laela's every move. Soleil was flying overhead, having refused to join them.

"Soleil, you will need to come down here sooner or later," Sascha said.

"Not until I'm sure what Laela is doing here."

"And here we go," Laela said as she returned with a bottle in an ice bucket and a couple of glasses. "This will help with the nerves." She filled the glasses with wine.

"Thanks, Laela," Sascha said, taking one of the glasses. She studied the wine. It looked a slightly different color to the wine she was used to.

"What wine is this?" Sascha asked.

"I brought it with me from Eratus. You'll love it. Try it."

Rusty screamed in pain, dropped to the ground and started twitching.

"Rusty!" Sascha yelled as she put the glass down and raced over to her. "Rusty, what's wrong?"

Rusty's eyes rolled back in her head. Sascha squatted next to her. "Soleil, we need to get help…" The twitching stopped just as suddenly as it had begun and Rusty lay there, her eyes closed.

There was a loud whoosh of wind as Soleil flew in low toward them, low enough to force Laela to duck. Then came a splintering crash. Sascha and Laela turned to see the bottle of wine and the glasses smashed on the ground, wine spilling everywhere.

Soleil landed twenty feet inside the cave entrance and sat hunched, his eyes watching Laela's every move. Rusty leaped to her feet and raced over to join Soleil.

"I'm so sorry about this, Laela," Sascha said as she stood up and studied Soleil and Rusty. She moved toward the broken glass and started to pick up the shattered pieces.

"Rusty seems to have recovered quickly," Laela said. She leaned down and brushed Sascha's hands aside. "I'll clean this up. Accidents happen. Luckily, I brought a second bottle." She picked up the glass pieces, put them in the ice bucket and stood. "I'll be back in a minute." She glowered at Soleil and Rusty as she strode back to the squad bay.

"Rusty is fine, isn't she, Soleil?" Sascha said.

"Yes."

"What's going on?"

"The wine has green lyrium in it," Soleil said. "And Laela knows about your addiction. I don't think it's a coincidence."

"But why would she do that? I wouldn't be able to heal the Shield if I was high on drugs. How do you know there was green lyrium in it?"

"I could smell it."

Sascha sniffed the air. "I can only smell cinnamon and pine."

"Sascha, if you get addicted again, there will be no going back. It will kill you."

Laela returned with the second bottle. She stopped when she saw Sascha and Soleil. "You know, don't you, Sascha?"

"Know what?" Sascha asked.

"You know about the wine." Laela pointed at Sascha's neck. "How can you talk to Soleil without your necklace?"

Sascha's hand went to her throat. "Of course. You wouldn't know that I don't need the necklace anymore." Sascha's glance flicked to Soleil. "You didn't think Soleil would be able to tell me what you were doing."

Laela stared at the bottle in her hand. "Drakon told me to do this."

"So much for trusting you, Laela," Sascha said.

Tears welled in Laela's eyes. "He is blackmailing me. I would never have agreed otherwise. I'm so sorry, Sascha."

"He's blackmailing you?"

"Yes," she stammered.

"I don't understand why Drakon would want to drug me. Surely that would weaken my powers."

"He wants to control you. You heard what Ken said on Eratus."

"She's lying," a voice screamed in Sascha's head.

A flash of ebony and scarlet feathers screeched and flew past the entrance to the cave and landed in the trees a hundred feet from where they stood.

"Fenix?" Soleil spluttered. "What are you doing here?"

"Drakon sent me to protect Sascha," Fenix said. "Laela's lying."

"What in the name of the ancients was that?" Laela glanced around her.

"You're lying, Laela," Sascha said.

Laela sighed as she faced Sascha. "You should have stayed on Earth, stayed out of things that no longer concerned you."

"What things?" Sascha asked, flexing her neck and shoulders as she prepared to use her magic.

"Watch out," Soleil cried out as circles of yellow light

shimmered around Sascha. Sascha tried to move, but every muscle in her body was frozen. She was paralyzed.

"Sascha, you have been a thorn in my side for long enough. It's time to get rid of you." Laela stood and stared at Sascha "What? No witty comeback? Oh, that's right. You can't speak." She cackled as she walked toward Sascha. "Silly me." She trailed her fingers down Sascha's throat. "You'll be able to talk now. What fun would it be if I couldn't hear your pleas for help? By the way, no-one out there will hear you. I have made sure of that. What's the point of magic if you can't use it when you need it?"

"Soleil, take Rusty and get away from here," Sascha bellowed.

"No! We won't leave you." Soleil leaped toward Laela, but froze mid-movement and then slowly floated to the ground. Sascha heard him grunt. "I can't move, Sascha," Soleil said.

Rusty let out a ferocious growl, but Laela flicked her hand to the side. There was a yelp and then silence.

"What is it with you and animals, Sascha?"

"Why are you doing this?" Sascha croaked.

"I will work and talk. I hope you don't mind. I'm not meaning to be rude, but my magic never lasts as long on Earth as it does on Eratus. I need to move quickly."

"What are you going to do?" Sascha asked.

"Give me one moment." Laela moved to the entrance of the cave, retrieved a wand from a pocket inside her shirt and extended it. She circled the wand in the air and mumbled a chant Sascha couldn't understand. A soft whirring sound echoed in the cave as a large circle of spinning air opened. "There," Laela said, stepping back and placing her hands on her hips to examine her work. "It won't be long before it's completely open."

She walked back toward Sascha. "I don't have enough time to explain everything to you. But what I can tell you is that once you are gone, everyone will turn to me to help them heal the Shield. Owain is already organizing mages to help me with the healing. But I will heal it in my way, without destroying the ancients. The ancients will rule, and I will be there to help them. Together we will destroy the dragons. And then I will finally be in charge of all magic on Eratus. Can you imagine how much power that will give me?"

"Laela, you're crazy. Linking up with the ancients? They were brutal. What's to stop them from destroying you once you have released them?"

Laela tutted. "So many questions. But I may be a little crazy. That much is true."

Laela moved her hands together and lifted the portal, moving it closer to Soleil. "Soleil, would you like to know where this portal goes? It will take you to where you should have gone years ago the fifth dimension."

"No," Sascha screamed. "Laela, let's talk about this."

"The time for talk has gone, Sascha. But before I destroy you, I want you to see me destroy your precious Soleil. This creature messes everything up. Even Drakon can't get rid of him."

Sascha tried to move, but it felt like she was buried in sand. She remembered the last time she had been in the cave and forced her mind to imagine a fireball forming. But her mind was so sluggish. She listened for the bubbling water echoing in the cave and forced herself to relax. She imagined a ball of fire forming and used all her energy to send it flying toward Laela. But all she could do was send a spurt of fire in Laela's direction. Laela dodged it and laughed.

"Well done, Sascha. With a little more practice, you might have passed the magical tests our graduates have to go through. But I guess that doesn't worry you now, does it?"

"Help!" Sascha yelled.

A high-pitched screech echoed around the cave, followed by a loud scream. Fenix landed next to Sascha. She stared at Laela, who was doubled over, blood all over her back. The portal started to flicker.

"I will help," Fenix said.

"Fenix, take Soleil out of here," Sascha said.

"You think you can save them, Fenix?" Laela said as she pushed herself up. "Good luck with that." Ignoring her bloodied back, she lifted her hands and moved them in large circles to the right. The portal steadied, and the winds inside increased speed. Soleil screeched as a flash of white light engulfed him and carried him toward the portal.

Sascha tried to move her hands, her legs, anything, but her body refused to obey. She had to do something.

"Soleil's too far away from me," Fenix called out. "I can't get to him in time."

"Stop Laela then," Sascha called out.

Fenix flew at Laela, but she was surrounded by a white shield that was protecting her. Fenix bounced off the shield and landed at Sascha's feet.

"Not this time, Fenix," Laela said.

Soleil was nearing the mouth of the portal. One small push and he would be gone forever.

Laela turned toward Sascha. "Say goodbye to Soleil," she cackled.

Fenix leaped into action, all claws and beak. The power she exuded pushed Sascha over. A second later, Sascha realized she could move and scrambled to her feet.

The cave echoed with frustrated shrieks as Fenix threw herself at the shield time and time again. Laela laughed and then sent a final burst of air toward Soleil.

"Sascha," Soleil screamed.

There was a loud, piercing howl as a brown and white

streak launched itself at Soleil. At the same time, Fenix crashed through Laela's shield.

Soleil and Rusty landed in a bundle against the cave wall. The portal wobbled, then flickered out as Fenix crashed on top of Laela.

"Soleil," Sascha screamed. She raced toward the bundle of wings and legs.

Laela lashed out with a blast of wind and sent Fenix sliding along the ground toward the back of the cave. She stood, blood pouring from the deep gashes that covered her.

Sascha armed herself with a fireball and stood in front of Soleil and Rusty. "Leave, Laela."

Laela assessed the damage to her arms. "Sascha, this isn't over. You may have won this time, but it was only a minor victory. Do you really think that you can heal the Shield? Your magic isn't even activated yet, and time is running out. When you fail, everyone will come to me for help. Then I will destroy you." Laela chuckled, shimmered and disappeared.

Sascha's arms dropped to her side as the fireball vanished. She turned around to check on Rusty and Soleil. Soleil had managed to stand, but his legs were shaking. He leaned over and nudged Rusty, who wobbled to her feet. Fenix stretched her wings as she assessed her injuries.

"Fenix," Sascha said, "you saved us. Thank you."

"I couldn't let anything happen to you," Fenix said.

"Why?" Soleil spat. "Because Drakon told you to save Sascha?"

"Soleil! She just saved us. Show a little more gratitude."

Fenix snuck a look at Soleil. "I don't blame him, Sascha. I do belong to Drakon."

"But Drakon wanted you to protect me?" Sascha asked.

"There'll be a reason," Fenix said. "There always is. Can I ask you something?"

"Anything," Sascha said.

"If you ever remember the secret to releasing us from our bonds, would you show me what to do?"

Soleil gasped. "You would go through with it? You would free yourself from Drakon?"

"Yes," Fenix said. "I would."

Sascha studied the two birds. Was it possible Soleil was in love with Fenix? "There's a lot I need to do and not much time to do it in. But if—when I get my memory back and find out what that secret was, you will be the first one I tell."

Soleil snapped his beak at her.

Sascha smiled. "Perhaps the second one."

"Thank you," Fenix said, nodding her head. "I will be indebted to you forever, Sascha."

Sascha smiled weakly and brushed her hair from her face. She had work to do. There would be no second chance. Laela had voiced Sascha's greatest fear when she had said that she would fail. Sascha took a deep breath and pushed the sting of the words away.

Laela is wrong. For the sake of everyone I love, she must be wrong.

CHAPTER 34

* EARTH

*S*ascha sat in the chair in front of the cave. The sun was setting, turning the sky orange and gold. Fenix had flown off only minutes before to warn Drakon about Laela. Rusty and Soleil were resting, both exhausted after the battle.

Sascha took a sip from a glass that held soda water and lemon. Wine had lost its appeal after the encounter with Laela.

She picked up the box that was sitting in her lap, opened it and took out the artifact. It looked nothing more than a particularly attractive wooden pen, but now she knew what it really was. She lifted the pen and pointed it toward the sky.

"Hocus pocus, let me get my focus." Sascha laughed.

"That's pathetic," Soleil said. "You'll need to be more creative than that."

She smiled. He was right. But there were a lot of things she needed to do. She took a deep breath, refusing to let the panic overwhelm her. She couldn't fall apart, not now.

Rusty wandered over to Sascha and sat down in front of her, her back leaning against Sascha's legs. As Sascha patted

Rusty's head, Ken's words came back to her. *"I left something with our favorite distraction. If anything happens to me, please open the locket I gave her."*

What would he have left with Rusty? Sascha put the pen back into the box and carefully placed the box on the ground near her chair. She leaned down to Rusty. "I need to borrow your collar for a minute." She reached down and took it off. Rusty stood, shook herself and stared at Sascha.

"Ar-ruf"

"I won't be long, Rusty, I promise."

Sascha prized open the locket. Nestled in a bed of yellow wool was an amber-colored jewel. She picked it up and held it in her hand as she leaned down to retrieve the pen. As she lifted it, the jewel began to warm in her hand.

Rusty had the jewel all along. But how did Ken get it?

Sascha heard the sound of car doors slamming shut. The girls were back.

"We're here," Kira called out. "You look like you've had a relaxing morning in the sun." She strolled over to join Sascha.

Sascha packed the pen and the jewel into the box. "I could think of other ways to describe our morning." Rusty began to bark and prance around in front of Sascha. "Sorry, Rusty You want your collar." She leaned down and put the collar back on.

"Hey, Sascha," Lee said. "Where's your knapsack? We'll put our bags with yours."

"I put it under the kitchen table."

"What happened this morning?" Kira asked.

Sascha stood. "Let's all have a quick bite of lunch while I fill you in. Then we had better head off to see if Eham and Alex have arrived. And you might like to know where I found the jewel."

THIRTY MINUTES LATER, Sascha and the girls were walking toward the library.

"Where did they say we were to meet them?" Kira asked.

"All Marco said was in the library."

"There's Eham," Ella pointed.

"So that tall dark stranger is Alex," Kira said. "He's a bit yummy, isn't he?"

"Kira, behave," Lee said.

"I always behave." Kira smiled.

Sascha watched as Alex strode toward them. He would have been nearly six feet tall. He had shoulder-length blond hair and sparkling blue eyes. Both he and Eham were wearing jeans and t-shirts. He leaned down and pecked Sascha on the cheek. "I don't suppose I should have done that. You wouldn't remember me."

"I wouldn't mind some tall good-looking stranger kissing me on the cheek," Kira said.

Alex glanced at Kira and then bowed before her. "You have grown into a beautiful woman, Kira."

Kira did a double take. "So you knew me too."

"Yes, I knew all of you," Alex replied. "Eratus is my home too."

Eham joined them a minute later. "There's no time for reunions," he said. "We have work to do."

"Eham," Alex said, "do you always have to be so abrupt?"

"You mean rude?" Kira muttered.

"Eham is right," Sascha said. "We do have work to do and not a lot of time to do it in. Have either of you heard that the Shield has worsened?"

Eham nodded. "Yes."

"So it's true," Sascha said. She rubbed her stomach to try to ease the tension she felt.

Alex looked around. "Where's Marco?"

"I don't know," Sascha said. "But I know he'll be on his way. He's the one that told us to meet you here. Now, the girls and I need to meet with Zinnath and Kalurth before we leave for Eratus. We know they have a home in the cave below this library. We need some answers."

Eham and Alex glanced at each other. "That's exactly why we suggested meeting here," Alex said. "You do need to meet with the dragons. The chronicles of the Four Sisters say that the dragons are the only ones who know how to activate your magic. You must activate it before you go back to Eratus."

"Why?"

"Jenny can see things. It's complicated, but the short version is that she had a vision. There are strong forces on Eratus that will work against you, stop you from regaining your powers. You must do it here. I should probably warn you that there are a couple of tests you must pass to prove you are worthy of your powers. I found a clue in the chronicles that may help. Only one person has ever been given their powers back. Luckily for us, she recorded the words she had been given to help her pass." Alex retrieved a card from his pocket and gave it to Sascha.

An icy chill swept through Sascha. "Only one person has ever been given their powers back?"

Alex studied the ground, then looked at Sascha. "To be more specific, only one person survived the trials. So, yes, only one person has completed the ritual and been given their magic back."

Sascha pushed down the panic. "What chance do I have of succeeding when so many others have failed?"

Kira put her hand on Sascha's arm. "Sascha, you've survived so much already. We know you can do it."

Sascha read the card. " 'Your faith will replace what your

mind cannot face. Do you destroy the dark, or allow the light to erase?' "

"Another cryptic message," Lee complained.

"Another?" Alex asked.

"Yes, we received this," Sascha said, plucking a piece of paper from her shirt pocket and handing it to Alex. "It tells us how to get through the traps set along the way to the dragons' cave. Well, that's what we hope."

"It seems dragons like to make things difficult," Alex said.

"Dragons and gods," Eham grunted. He walked back to where he and Alex had put their bags. "We need to hurry. Time is running out."

"I'll wait here for Marco," Alex said. "You go on ahead. We'll catch up." Alex went to hand the piece of paper back to Sascha.

"You keep it," Kira said. "I have a copy. You and Marco might need it."

Sascha turned to Alex. "Are you sure you're OK to wait for Marco?"

"I think it's important. After the crash and everything, he'll want to talk to me."

"He will. He was in a bad way," Sascha said. "See you in the cave. We'll try to leave the traps disarmed, but double-check everything in case things don't go as planned."

"Please be careful." Alex said. "Hopefully big brother isn't too far away."

Sascha, the girls and Eham entered the library and walked toward the cave's entrance. The door to the entrance was open, revealing a dark stony passage.

"Is there enough space for you in there, Soleil?"

"I won't be able to fly, but I can walk," he replied.

"We need a torch," Sascha said. "It's dark in there."

Eham groaned. "We have five mages here, yet we need a torch?"

"I don't think this is the right time to practice our magic," Lee snapped. "Do you, Eham?"

"I think it is the perfect time," Eham answered.

"I've got a torch," Kira said, taking a torch from her pocket and handing it to Sascha. Sascha turned the torch on and shone it into the passage. But for one burned patch just inside the cave's entrance, the walls were almost entirely covered in green moss.

Sascha touched the burned patch. "I wonder what happened there."

"I think that might be from when I was here before," Kira said. "I stepped on a trap, which triggered a fireball."

Sascha looked over at Kira. Now was not the right time to tell her off for taking risks. "Where were you standing when the fireball was triggered?"

Kira pointed "About fifty feet up that way."

"Fire can't hurt me like it can you and the others," Soleil said, turning to Sascha. "Let me go in there first and have a look around."

Sascha nodded. "Be careful, Soleil." Sascha turned to Ella. "Will you put Rusty on her lead and keep her with you? The last thing we need to worry about is Rusty killing herself by setting off one of the traps."

"Sure thing," Ella said.

"The plate is down," Soleil called out. "It looks like it's still disarmed. I'll test it." A moment later, Soleil called out again. "It's disarmed. And come and have a look at what I found."

"Soleil has found something," Sascha said. "Everyone, please tread carefully. I don't want anyone hurt."

They joined Soleil a couple of minutes later. "What is it, Soleil?" Sascha said.

Soleil tapped the wall behind him. Four holes had been carved into the wall, one below the other, and four colored candles sat in a bundle on a ledge beside them.

Lee leaned forward to pick up the candles. "It looks like the candles fit in these holes," she said as she reached down to put one in.

Soleil screeched.

"No, Lee," Sascha screamed out. "Everyone, drop to the ground!"

They all ripped their knapsacks off their backs and fell to the ground with a loud whompf. Ella threw her jacket over Rusty. They made it to the floor just before a large fireball screamed overhead, singeing the edges of a few of the bags as it smashed its way to the entrance. For a few minutes, nobody moved, the sounds of their heavy breathing reverberating down the dark passage.

"It's safe now," Soleil said.

They all clambered to their feet and wiped the dirt from their clothes.

"Sorry," Lee said.

"No-one was hurt." Sascha picked up her bag and slung it over her shoulder. "But we need to be careful if we want to make it to the cave. Let's make a deal. Before we do anything, we all have to agree that it's the right thing to do."

The girls nodded their heads in agreement.

Eham sighed with irritation as he flexed his neck. "Why are these passages always made for short people? My neck and back are going to be killing me by the time we get to the other end of this. Let's not take forever about it."

"The first clue," Sascha said, "was 'Let fire be your guide'. That must mean we do something with the candles. Perhaps if we need to light them in a particular order. But how do we know the right order?"

"How many candles are there?" Lee asked.

"Four," Sascha answered. "Red, light blue, brown and white."

"The same colors as the elements in the cryptic clue – fire, ice, earth and air," Ella said.

"So perhaps that's how we place them?" Sascha said. "Get ready, everyone. I'm about to try it out."

"Let's get on with it," Eham muttered.

Sascha held her breath each time she placed a candle. She placed the red candle – fire – first, the light blue – ice – second, the brown – earth – third and the white – air – last. But still, nothing happened. "Now what?" she said.

A rumble shook the ground beneath them. "Oh no," Sascha said. Her stomach dropped. "I've done it wrong." Everything went quiet. The only sound was that of Rusty panting. Suddenly, each of the candles popped as they burst into flame and little pockets of fire lit up along the ceiling.

"You did it, Sascha." Kira clapped her hands. "You did it." She studied the ceiling. "They look like little torches. I think they're showing us the way."

"So the next clue," Lee called out, "is 'with ice by your side'. Maybe there is something in the walls?"

Their heavy knapsacks meant progress was slow. They finally arrived at a junction where the passage split in four.

"Which way?" Kira asked.

"Look." Sascha pointed to the passage on their far right. "The lights in that one are lit up."

As they neared the entrance, they saw that they had a steep uphill climb ahead of them. The next part of their journey was going to be hard work.

"Wow, this is awesome," Lee said.

"Glad you're having fun," Eham grunted. "As if it's not tough enough for a normal person to navigate a short person's tunnel, we must now climb. I'm beginning to wish I'd never come here."

"Why did you come?" Sascha asked.

"I have my reasons," he snapped as he pushed past Sascha and started the climb.

Sascha waited for the others to pass her before beginning the climb.

A high-pitched scream echoed along the passageway. "Lee" Sascha yelled, racing up the passage to join Lee. "Are you OK?"

Lee was covering her mouth with her left hand and pointing with her right. "They're all dead."

Sascha turned to look where Lee was pointing. The next section of the passage was covered in thick ice. In the middle of the floor were frozen bodies, some with twisted, agonized expressions on their faces, others the open-mouthed look of shock.

"Back up, everyone," Sascha said. "Quickly! Get back to where the lights in the roof finish." They all slid or ran back along the passage. As they arrived underneath the warmth of the torches, an explosion of ice covered the area they had been standing in only seconds before.

"We would have been killed," Lee said.

Sascha stared at the icy graveyard ahead of them.

"Maybe we should move further back," Ella asked.

Sascha shook her head. "I don't think we need to." She looked up and pointed to the torches in the roof. "They're still alight. If they go out, we run."

"So what do you think the next clue means?" Lee asked.

"Perhaps there's a door or a secret panel to take us around this." Sascha said. "If fire is to be our guide and it has taken us safely this far, let's trust in it and see if we can find a panel in the wall along this area. There must be something."

"Perhaps this whole exercise is ridiculous," Eham said. "We should go back outside and search. We're obviously in a mountain, so we should just search the mountain."

"And how long do you think that would take us, Eham?" Sascha said. "We don't have time."

"It would have to be safer than this," Eham mumbled.

"Stop your bellyaching," Lee said, "and help us find the panel."

Kira screeched, causing Sascha to jump. "Found it," Kira said. A soft rumble echoed in the wall and a door slid open. Torches popped and lit up in the ceiling of the new passage. "This must be the right way," Kira said. "The fire is showing us."

They followed the path. There was a sharp right turn thirty feet from the entrance. "With ice by your side," Lee said. "Ice is by our side through that wall. Those poor people."

"We don't have time to think about it," Sascha said. "We must keep going."

"I still think my idea was better," Eham mumbled as he shifted the bag on his back and pushed past Sascha to get to the front.

"So the next clue," Ella said, "is 'On earth you will stand, while the air shapes your land.' What do you think that means?"

For a while, the journey was uneventful. But then they came to a section of the passage where the floor fell away into a wide, deep chasm. There was no bridge to the other side and no other passage.

"That's just great," Eham said. "We've made it all this way only to find out we can't make it to the cave."

"There has to be a way," Sascha said. She walked along the ridge of the chasm as she recited the verse. "On earth you will stand, while the air shapes your land."

"I can't fly you over, Sascha," Soleil said. "There's not enough space for me to open my wings."

Sascha could see a set of steps in the middle of the ridge

on the side on which they were all standing and a pathway on the other side of the chasm that was directly in line with the steps.

"Ella, the magic you used in the cave to hide Soleil and Rusty, can you use it to reveal things?"

"What sort of things?"

"See this little set of steps in the middle of the ridge? It lines up with that pathway on the other side of the chasm."

Lee gulped as she looked down. "You think there's an invisible bridge across the chasm? And we have to cross it?"

"We have to get across. And unless you can come up with another idea, that's the only option we've got."

"Let me see what I can do," Ella said.

Sascha's stomach turned as she watched Ella walk up the steps on the edge of the ridge and stand on the top step. "Ella, please be careful," Sascha whispered. Even a small breeze would blow her over the edge. Ella closed her eyes and her hands flowed together.

"Let my powers reveal what others conceal," Ella chanted.

Presently, her hands slowed and a soft white light spilled from her palms. The light moved across the chasm, shimmered and then disappeared.

Ella repeated the chant for several minutes, but the lights kept disappearing.

"It was worth a try," Sascha said. "Come down from there. In some ways, I'm glad. The idea of crossing that terrifies me."

"Perhaps that's it," Ella said. "Let me try something else." She let her hands flow together again and bowed her head. "Let my powers reveal what others conceal, so that our faith can replace what our minds cannot face."

Pale white lights sprung from her hands and moved together across the chasm. Within seconds, they had outlined the shape of a bridge across the chasm. And this time, the lights remained where they were.

"Ella, you used part of the cryptic message Alex gave us," Sascha said. "That was clever."

Ella shrugged her shoulders. "Not clever, exactly. I can't explain it. It seemed right, so I said it. And it worked."

"That looks like a bridge," Sascha whispered. "But the lights are only at the top of the bridge. There's nothing to show there's a base to it." Her stomach churned. She was covered in perspiration. "Even if we decide we're sure the bridge is there, you can see straight through it. It will be like walking on glass."

Kira stood next to Sascha, dug into her bag and pulled out a high-heeled shoe. She threw it. It landed with a soft thud in the middle of the lights. "Yep," Kira said. "There is a bridge."

"You have high heels in your knapsack?" Sascha stared at Kira.

"A girl never knows when she will need a pair of heels," Kira answered. She dug into her bag and pulled out the other shoe. "Take this with you," she said as she shoved it into Sascha's bag. "It could come in handy."

Sascha stood for a moment and looked at the lights. "We have to cross that?" Sascha turned and walked fifty feet down the passage through which they had entered, leaned against the wall and threw up. She stayed for a second, wiped her mouth with a tissue and then walked back to join the others.

"Oh, gross," Eham said. "Really? You choose to be sick when we're stuck in here and can smell it. Thanks, Sascha."

"Be grateful I've given you an incentive to cross the bridge then, Eham." Sascha concentrated on the nausea, forcing her stomach to settle. "I'll go first. You can all follow me. Don't stay too close behind me in case there's a problem. There's no point in us all dying." She walked to the top of the stone steps and closed her eyes.

"I'll stay with you," Soleil said. "If you fall, I'll catch you. That, or we'll die together."

Sascha snorted. "Is that supposed to make me feel better?" Sascha took a deep breath and stepped out. There was something solid beneath her foot. She took another step and another. She refused to listen to the noise around her. She refused to look down, concentrating instead on staying inside the lights. She had to keep going, and each step she took brought her closer to the other side of the chasm.

"You can stop walking," Lee called out. "It's safe to look down now. You've made it."

Sascha stopped, her legs like jelly. She looked at her feet. Lee was right. She was on solid ground. Then Sascha was being pulled into a big hug with the three girls, Rusty prancing and barking around their feet.

"We're so proud of you, Sascha," Kira said. "And look at what is there now."

Sascha glanced at the chasm. The lights had disappeared and in their place was a solid brick and stone structure that formed a bridge. "That's unfair. Now it becomes visible?"

They all laughed.

The climb ahead of them steepened, as did Eham's grumbles and complaints. It wasn't long, however, before they arrived in a huge cave. It was large enough to comfortably fit several dragons with their wings outstretched.

On the wall furthest from Sascha was an entrance. Though the entrance was partially covered by trees and scrub, she could see that the sun was low in the sky, its soft golden light shimmering on the leaves of the trees. Several large torches set into the walls of the cave were burning, making Sascha feel as if they had been expected. Despite the light from these torches, it was still hard to see clearly. The walls of the cave were a polished black stone, and long narrow holes lined the top of the cave wall.

"I wonder what those are," Sascha said.

"They're arrow loops," Eham replied. "In the olden times, they were used by archers in battles. A good high position gave them the best advantage to pick off their enemies, one by one."

"It would be a blood bath," Sascha said.

Kira raced to the edge of the cave. "This is magnificent."

"Kira, slow down...don't get too close, girls." Sascha shook her head.

What is the use? I can't blame them for being excited.

"Come and have a look, Sascha. It's beautiful," Kira said. "The sunset looks like fire."

"I'm fine where I am, thank you," Sascha said. "I have had enough adventure for today."

"Your adventures haven't even begun yet, Sascha." The smooth baritone voice echoed around the cave.

Sascha looked around to see where the voice had come from. "Who are you?" she called out.

"My name is Zinnath." A large majestic creature of gold and bronze flew into the cave on a breeze of pine and honey. He was closely followed by another creature, smaller than him and the color of emerald and diamonds.

"And I'm Kalurth," the smaller one said.

"Dragons," Sascha whispered. "They're beautiful."

CHAPTER 35

*D*rakon sipped at his prumble ale as he stood on the ramparts and watched as Novo and Chiane directed their men in training maneuvers. He was still in his training gear, having spent a couple of hours sparring with Chiane. Chiane was a tough and fit warrior, a worthy competitor.

Drakon had noticed that the incident at Peaceful Valley had changed more than his looks and his magic. His strength had increased ten-fold.

Down below, Chiane called to Novo. They both glanced up at Drakon and nodded. Drakon turned and walked into his war room and stood staring at the cryptic message Novo had found.

What does it mean?

The sound of heavy boots thumped along the battlements and a chained fist knocked on the open door.

"Enter," Drakon said.

"My Prince," Chiane flicked a glance at the fire dragons and then joined Drakon at the war table. Novo took up his usual position just inside the doorway.

Drakon smiled to himself. Chiane was the only man he knew who wasn't terrified of his pets.

"You wanted to talk to me, Chiane?"

"Yes, My Prince." Chiane cleared his throat. "I was told you were looking for Reya. She came to me, saying you wanted some of my best men to accompany her to Earth to hunt down a traitor. I learned later that she was after Sascha. I have also since been advised that you gave no such order."

Drakon clenched his fists.

Reya!

"You are correct. I gave no such instruction." Drakon pushed himself away from the table and walked over to the window overlooking the mountains.

"Novo, I believe the second portal is working. Test it and then take a small group of warriors to Earth with you. Find Sascha and Reya. Stop Reya by any means necessary. She has outlived her usefulness. Sascha must be protected until the healing ceremony is complete. Is that understood?"

"Yes, My Prince."

"And once the mages are no longer required for the healing ceremony, take a group of them to the ancient weapon site in Brun and see if they can translate the meaning of the code you found."

"Yes, My Prince."

"Chiane, if this second portal is working, you and I will be returning to Earth. I want you to prepare a small army to go with us. I need your most intelligent men, as well as some skilled warriors and a few select mages. We will take a copy of this code to the site of the ancient weapon on Earth and see if we can work out what it means. We have to finish our mission before the three-moon season begins."

"Yes, My Prince.'

"Novo, you are dismissed. Chiane, stay."

Drakon waited for the sound of Novo's steps to disappear. "Chiane, you did me a great service. Though it had some side effects, your potion worked. It saved my life."

"My duty is to serve you, My Prince."

"Now that we know the potion works, I have an idea. But we will need more of the potion."

"Yes, My Prince."

"And, Chiane, it looks like I have an opening for the position of general. You keep performing at this level and the position will be yours."

"I am honored, My Prince," Chiane said as he bowed before him.

"Dismissed."

"Yes, My Prince." He saluted, then turned on his heel and left.

Drakon summoned Fenix. The click of talons on the ramparts announced her arrival. The fire dragons swished their tails and chatted as they glared at her.

They sense something in Fenix. They don't want me to trust her. But why?

Drakon studied her. "My pets think you are...different, Fenix."

Fenix clicked her beak at them. "Fire dragons. They hate pyrans. But there is something you should know."

"And what is that?"

"Laela tried to kill Sascha."

"She what? Is everyone in this place going crazy? We need Sascha to heal the Shield, and yet they all insist on trying to kill the damn woman. You did well, Fenix. I will be returning to Earth in the next couple of days, but you won't be coming. I have another task for you, so I will need you to prepare one of the other pyrans to take me. And don't worry about Laela. I will sort her out."

Fenix clicked her beak and flew off toward the gardens in the castle grounds.

And the task will show me if the fire dragons are right. But I need to update Novo first. After he disposes of Reya, he will need to keep an eye on Sascha and be ready to protect her.

CHAPTER 36

*M*arco unlocked the door to his apartment. It had taken longer than he had expected to sort everything out, but he had no idea when, or even if, he would return. He walked into the lounge room. George was still asleep, but her food was gone and the bowl of water was nearly empty.

He squatted down next to her. "We have to leave, George. Everyone will be at the library by now. We'll be late."

George lifted her head, grumbled and dropped it again.

"You can sleep in the car after we find somewhere private for a pit stop. I don't want you making a mess in my car."

Marco raced up the stairs. He picked up Soleil's necklace and put it on. He walked over to the bed, picked up his bag and then walked down the stairs to collect George. "Come, George. Let's go."

Marco got the lift down to his car. He decided to take the four-wheel drive. He opened the boot and patted the floor. "Jump."

George half-flew, half-jumped into the back of the car. Marco glanced at the cameras dotted around the car park.

He would have some explaining to do if anyone saw George. He shrugged his shoulders. There wasn't much he could do about that now.

George started to grumble when she realized the space was a lot smaller than she would have liked.

"You're going to complain even more in a couple of minutes. I'm afraid I will have to put a cover over you. Nobody on Earth will have ever seen a manticore before, and I have no idea how I would explain what you're doing here."

An unhappy roar rumbled in George's chest when Marco put the cover over her. But she was good and didn't try to push it off. Marco started the car and turned on some relaxing music. George stopped the noise she was making the moment the music started.

"I don't suppose you've heard this sort of music before, have you?"

After a brief pit stop in the middle of a pine forest, they were on their way. It wasn't long before Marco heard soft snores. George was asleep.

As they turned onto the gravel road leading to the head-quarters, George leaped up with a roar and looked out the front of the car. She tried to leap into the front, but she was too big.

"Stay," Marco said. "What's wrong with you? We're nearly there."

George leaped again.

Marco's heart pounded and his skin prickled. George was warning him. But what was she warning him about? He slowed down. The rumble of the tires on the gravel did nothing to ease his tension.

Marco could see the gate ahead, or rather, what was left of it. The twisted metal hung on its hinges. Marco pulled over to the side of road and leaped out of his car. He crouched down and snuck toward the security hut, George not far behind him.

Marco glanced in the hut's window. The swarm of flies inside told him the men were dead. But he had to know what killed them.

He held his breath, stood up and stepped in through the hut's open door. The room was filled with the stench of feces and blood and bone. The men's bodies were crushed, as if they had been attacked by several people with enormous hammers. Their throats had been sliced open.

Habit made him reach for his sword. It was then that he realized he wasn't armed. He moved away from the hut to breathe in some cleaner air and to give himself time to think "Shit! What happened? Where is everyone?"

Marco squatted by the edge of the water fountain. The statue had been destroyed, and the water was pink with blood. He looked down the driveway toward the headquarters' front entrance. Patches of scorched earth formed a path to the doors. The dead bodies of his men littered the grounds. Like the guards, they had all been massacred. Interestingly, none of them had been attacked by fire. What had caused the scorch marks?

"It took you long enough," a voice behind him said.

Marco's heart leaped into his throat. He turned. "Alex! You're alive," he said. "Thank Athena. But what happened here? Where's Sascha and the others?"

"They're alive. Well, they should be anyway." Alex crouched down beside Marco and put his arm around him. He jumped when a low rumble sounded behind him.

"It's OK, Alex. It's George."

"George?" Alex pivoted around to see George's head inches away from his. "Don't take this the wrong way, George, but you need to do something about your breath."

George leaped onto Alex, pinning him down and licking him all over the face as Alex struggled to release himself.

"That's enough, you two," Marco said. "Save that for after the fight."

George released Alex and Alex sat up, smiling and wiping his face with the back of his hand. "I've missed you too, you dumb oaf," he said.

"What did you mean when you said they should be alive?"

"They left to visit the dragons over an hour before this all happened," Alex said.

"No. Of all the—there are traps protecting the cave."

"You don't have to worry. At least, I hope you don't have to. They had some clues to help them. And I got a chance to talk to them before they left. It's a long story, but the essence of it is that Sascha needs to meet the dragons here, on Earth, if she wants to activate her magic. So they're doing the right thing. And the dragons should be able to protect them. I hope."

Marco sighed as he shook his head. He glanced around the grounds. "How did this all happen? Did you see who the attackers were?

"It looked like a group of the royal elite, headed by a woman in a flowing black and red coat. There were also a group of soldiers dressed in the armor of the Awakening with them."

"The royal elite?" Marco said. "That's not possible. And you're sure the group was headed by a woman in a black and red coat?"

"Yes."

"There's no way."

"No way it's what, Marco?"

"The army that attacked me, destroyed our wedding, was dressed in the uniform of the elite. And they were headed by a warrior in a black and red cloak."

"No. I still feel guilty I wasn't there to help you fight, Marco."

"Your illness saved your life. I'm glad you weren't there. So it looks like they're back. And they must be after Sascha. Again. We must get to Sascha and the girls. Now."

George's deep rumble vibrated through them. Marco turned to her to see what was wrong. She was braced to launch into the air. Her focus was on the dark scorch marks on the ground near the entrance to the headquarters. "George, what is it? What's wrong?"

George let out a huge roar as she leaped into flight. She flew straight toward the shadowed areas. The scorch marks disappeared and suddenly George was attacking an invisible enemy with her claws and tail. The air around her shimmered.

"Pit hounds," Marco stammered. The scorch marks are pit hounds." He looked around the grounds. All of the scorch marks had disappeared.

THE DRAGONS PIROUETTED in the air and then landed in the cave with the grace of ballet dancers. They faced Sascha and the girls as they stretched their wings, then tucked them in by their sides. The clicking of their sharp talons echoed in the cave as they settled themselves down on the polished stone floor.

Zinnath turned to Eham, who bowed and then, with a flick of his wrist, lit the candles that were positioned in a semi-circle around the two dragons.

Sascha stared at Eham. She wasn't sure why it hadn't occurred to her that he had magic. After all, he was an advisor to the Four Sisters. And she had stupidly dismissed his comment about there being five mages as a mistake. But it wasn't a mistake. He was the fifth. He met her eyes, smiled and nodded. Eham stood as if he was a soldier standing at ease.

So what is Eham's relationship to Zinnath?

"Step forward into the light so I can get a better look at you," Zinnath said. "You do not need to be afraid."

The girls joined Sascha and together they moved toward Zinnath and Kalurth. As they moved closer, the aroma of pine and honey intensified, as did a lingering smell of sulfur.

Zinnath towered over them as he stared at each of them in turn. "The girls have grown into beauties, Sascha."

"Yes, they are quite stunning."

"And they all want to know who they are? Who their families are?"

"How did you know that?" Kira asked.

Zinnath made a deep-chested sound, his body shaking, his scales glinting in the setting sun. "I am a High Dragon. It's my job to know these things."

He turned back to Sascha, his eyes flashing in the glow of the candles. "You have changed, and by the look of you, for the better. I hope your time on Earth has helped you to heal and regain your strength."

"I thought I was already strong, a powerful mage," Sascha said.

"Your magic was powerful and your body was fit, but your mind struggled with the cruelties you had faced," Kalurth said. "You relied on green lyrium to help you, but it was killing you. We came to you because we needed your help. A group of traitors was working in the shadows to destroy our kind. We believed it was the same group who killed your mother. You pledged to free yourself from the addiction and to work with us to bring the traitors out into the open."

Kalurth glanced at Zinnath. "We were surprised when you decided to go to Earth."

Sascha's stomach lurched. "So I really did choose to be sent to Earth?"

"We don't know what happened between you and Owain," Zinnath said. "But what we do know is that being sent to Earth gave you a chance to heal, a chance you might never have had if you stayed on Eratus. It kept you safe. And it certainly flushed some of the group out into the open. Laela is very much involved. You also suspected Owain, but we haven't seen anything to prove that."

Kalurth lowered her neck and her head snaked in Sascha's direction. "The others can't hear me, Sascha, but I need to know before we go any further. Are you still taking green lyrium? I am sure I can sense a whisper of it on you. There shouldn't be anything after all these years."

Sascha felt her cheeks flush hot. It was stupid to feel guilty she hadn't done anything wrong. But why would Kalurth have smelled it on her?

"Laela tried to give her some this morning," Soleil answered. "But I destroyed it. She didn't take a drop."

"Soleil," Sascha said, "I can answer for myself."

"You were taking too long. I didn't want Kalurth to think you guilty."

"How did Laela do that?" Kalurth asked.

"It was hidden in a bottle of wine," Sascha answered.

"When you prepare for the ceremony, you will have to be sure to wash carefully. Green lyrium and magic are a deadly combination in this sort of ritual. It could kill you."

"Kalurth," Zinnath said, "are you listening to me?'

"Sorry," she answered. "I was distracted. What did you say?"

"My heart," he answered, "it's time to prepare for the ceremony."

"What ceremony?" Sascha asked.

"To activate your powers, of course," Zinnath said. "That is why you're here, isn't it?"

"Yes, but—"

"Let's not waste any more time," Zinnath said.

"I was told that only one person has ever completed the ritual and had their powers returned."

"That is true," Zinnath said. "But you must at least try. Time is running out. We need to heal the Shield."

"We?"

"Yes, we will help you. We created the Shield centuries ago with Athena's help. We can heal it together, but not until the darkness is destroyed. Only your magic can destroy the darkness. That's what we hope, anyway."

"Will my memory return along with my powers?"

"That is something you will need to ask the gods during the ceremony. Zeus is the only one who can give permission for that to happen."

"What about us?" Kira asked, glancing at Lee and Ella. "Can we get our powers and memories back too?"

"In time, with the grace of the gods," Zinnath said. "But first we must save the Shield. Then we can help you to get back what was stolen from you."

"Don't worry, little one," Kalurth said. "Everything will be revealed. You only need to be patient for a little while longer."

"Zinnath," Soleil screeched.

Zinnath and Kalurth's heads whipped up as they listened to voices Sascha couldn't hear.

"I will go with Soleil," Kalurth said. "You must hurry, Zinnath. I have a feeling we don't have long. Our guests have arrived."

"What guests?" Sascha asked.

"I think we're about to find out," Zinnath said. "But let us worry about that. You have work to do, Sascha."

"Soleil, I will join you in a few moments," Kalurth called out as she trotted over to an entrance that Sascha hadn't noticed earlier. "I want to organize a few surprises for our guests, see if we can slow them down a little."

With a whoosh of warm air, Soleil leaped into the mouth of the cave and flew off into the setting sun.

*G*eorge's roar shook the air around them.

"We're coming, George," Marco screamed as he smashed down the raw terror that threatened to incapacitate him.

Focus, Marco. Focus.

"Alex, grab the weapons off the dead soldiers. Hurry." Marco shoved the body closest to him onto his back, grabbed the man's sword and raced toward George. Alex hesitated before doing the same.

"What are we fighting?" Alex called out. "I can't see anything."

"There's a pack of pit hounds here," Marco said. "But who would have that amount of dark magic?"

"Pit hounds?" Alex said. "But they're nothing more than creatures from scary children's stories."

"I would say these ones are real enough, wouldn't you? Aim for the shimmering air. Don't let them bite you."

"Don't let them what? Why don't your soldiers have guns? Normal soldiers have guns." Alex screamed as he swung his sword at the shimmer George was attacking. "This is not cool, Marco. Not cool at all."

A loud screech echoed in Marco's ears as Alex's sword hit its mark and the creature's blood poured all over the ground. Its invisibility shield flickered and then disappeared, making it an easy target.

"Kill it," Marco said, swinging his sword at the creature's head. There was a blood-curdling scream as the creature's head rolled onto the ground in front of them. Seconds later, its body melted away, leaving nothing but a sizzling heap of bones behind.

"Phew, what a terrible smell," Alex complained. "They smell worse dead than they do alive."

A high-pitched screech reverberated through the mountains behind the library, followed by the booming roar of a dragon.

Soleil and the dragons have come to help.

"Soleil," Marco called out. "We're over here."

"We're coming," Soleil said.

George greeted Soleil with a lively yelp as he landed on the ground next to her.

"Are Kalurth and Zinnath with you, Soleil?" Marco asked. A flicker of movement caught his attention. "Duck, Alex," Marco called out. He took two strides toward Alex and swung his sword through the air just above Alex's head. He felt the satisfying thud and heard the scream as his sword connected with the pit hound. Blood spurted out of the creature at the same time as the sound of a horn pierced the air. The sound shuddered across the grounds, the pitch of it forcing Marco and Alex to cover their ears. The bleeding pit hound raced toward the front of the building.

George leaped to her feet to chase after the pit hound, but fell when he lost purchase on the ground, which was slippery with the hound's blood.

"Come, George," Marco ordered. "Stay with us."

George grumbled, looked toward the front of the building and then retraced her steps back to Marco and Alex. Soleil trotted over to join them. A deathly quiet descended on the grounds.

"This isn't good," Alex said. "Quiet is never good."

"Where did they go?" Marco asked. "There were plenty of them. How come they're not attacking?"

A gust of wind blew around them as Kalurth landed next to Soleil.

"They're protecting the building," Kalurth said. "They must have been instructed to stay and guard the building. We need a plan. One is wounded, but there are still three pairs that haven't a scratch on them."

"That's not so bad," Marco said. "We can fight them. It could be worse."

"It's nearly dark," Alex said. "Can you see the shimmer in the darkness?"

Marco shivered. "I don't know. I need to get into the building," Marco said. "There are weapons near the front entrance. If we could get to them…"

"What about guns?" Alex asked. "Do you have guns?"

"Guns won't kill pit hounds, Alex. They'll only slow them down. Pit hounds are created with a specific type of dark magic. If you can't kill them with magic, you must decapitate them." Marco glanced at George. "Or get help from magical creatures."

"So what are these weapons like?" Alex asked. "The ones that you think will help kill the monsters."

"They're magically crafted blades and daggers of fire called the Vengeance of Hephaestus. They were designed to kill creatures of darkness. They only need to touch a creature to destroy it. But we need to get to them first."

"Why not get Zinnath to fly overhead and blast them all with fire?" Alex asked. "He has magical fire."

"He's with Sascha," Kalurth answered. "An army is making its way through the mountain to destroy Sascha and the girls. Zinnath must stay to protect them. We'll have to work out another way. I'll help in whatever way I can, and you have George and Soleil."

"Are you sure these weapons are still there, Marco? The elite warriors could have taken them," Alex said.

"They look more like ornaments than weapons, so people dismiss them."

"But we still have to work out how to get to them," Alex said. "We have about half a dozen pit hounds in between us and them."

"We need to create a distraction," Marco said.

Marco heard something snorting and sniffing behind him.

"Oh no," Kalurth said.

"What?" Marco said as a chill of fear raced through him.

"They weren't guarding the house, or waiting for the dark. They were waiting for their back-up. There are almost twice as many pit hounds behind us. They have us circled."

FAINT SCREAMS BLEW into the cave on the early evening air.

"I have to go," Sascha said as she turned to face Zinnath. "I have to help Soleil."

"We will come with you," Lee said.

"No," Zinnath's voice boomed out, bouncing off the polished walls. "Kalurth will help Soleil. You must stay." He snaked his head closer to Sascha. "I understand how you feel, but you must activate your magic. We need to save Eratus. If you leave now, you will doom us all. But if you stay, we can prepare for what is ahead. Soleil understands what's at stake."

Kira's gaze bounced between Zinnath and Sascha. "What do you want to do, Sascha? I'm with you whatever you decide."

Lee and Ella nodded. "We are too."

Sascha rolled her shoulders as her gaze darted toward the mouth of the cave.

What if something happens to Soleil? Could I ever forgive myself?

She sighed. "I'm putting my trust in you, Zinnath. I will stay. I pray I don't live to regret this decision."

Zinnath's gaze fixed on her. "I pray that you have the powers we all need you to have. Let's get on with this then. Sascha, did Ken give you the jewel?"

Sascha's mouth dropped open. "How did you know he had the jewel?"

"That man cared for you. When he thought you were in trouble, he visited Kalurth to see how he could help you."

Sascha shook her head. A warm rush flooded through her. "You did care," she whispered as tears stung her eyes.

"Against my wishes," Zinnath continued, "Kalurth gave him the jewel and asked him to protect it until you were ready. I thought she had made a mistake, but it appears she was right. He could be trusted."

Sascha took her knapsack off her shoulder and pulled out the long narrow box. "I have the jewel and the pen."

"Pen?" Zinnath asked.

"The…artifact," Sascha replied.

"Eham," Zinnath called out. "Take the girls to the rooms at the back of the cave and keep them safe."

Eham nodded.

"I want to stay," Kira said.

"No, this journey is for Sascha and Sascha alone."

"But I read somewhere that someone can help her on the journey," Kira said. "I want to help her."

Zinnath chortled. "The only exception is when a mage has a soul mate. A soul mate can help to strengthen the magic."

Sascha leaned over and hugged Kira. "Thank you. Don't worry. I will survive this. Only the good die young."

Kira chuckled. "Very funny, Sascha."

Sascha hugged Lee and Ella and watched as Eham led the girls to the back of the cave and into a narrow corridor.

"Now we must begin," Zinnath said.

Sascha gulped and wiped the palms of her hands on her jeans. Her heart was pounding in her ears. "What happens now?"

"The process has three stages. First, you must choose your god. The god you choose will determine your powers. Then your magic is activated. You will get your memory back in the final stage, but only if the gods allow you to do so."

"But I would have chosen a god when I was on Eratus."

"You have changed, Sascha. You may make a different choice this time." Zinnath nodded at a hollow in the wall next to the maw of the cave. "In there you will find a mage. She will give you everything you need to prepare for the ceremony. Then she will take you to where your ritual will begin." He altered his position so that he could see out the maw of the cave. "Your first challenge will be to cross the bridge to the island."

Sascha stared at the gaping emptiness that lay between the cave and the island. "What bridge? Seriously?"

"You know how to do this. Have faith in yourself." Zinnath turned and strutted toward the back of the cave. "May the gods be kind to you, Sascha."

"What do these people have against doing things on solid

ground?" Sascha muttered. She rubbed her stomach to ease the building tension. "You will stay close, won't you, Zinnath?"

"I will guard the entrance to the cave, but I cannot help you during the ceremony. This is your path, your journey to take."

Still carrying her bag, Sasha walked toward the hollow. She felt ill. She found the entrance to the hollow and entered. The room was toasty warm and filled with the aroma of minty citrus and wintergreen. Little candles, shaped like stars, lit up the area. There was a large pond of clear blue water with a soft white mist floating on its surface.

A female mage, dressed in a long golden robe stood on the edge of the pond. "Everything you need is here, Sascha. You must bathe yourself in the water. There are cloths for you to use and a robe for when you have finished." The mage pointed to a chair in the far corner of the hollow. "I have placed your gown on the seat over there. When you are dressed, come to the entrance and I will take you to where your journey starts."

Sascha stepped into the pool of water. It was warm and comforting. And her muscles began to unwind. But she needed to make this quick. Her friends were at war, and she had a job to do.

"Sascha." Athena's voice echoed in the cave. Sascha leaped in fright, splashing water over the edge of the pool.

"You scared ten years' growth out of me," Sascha snapped, her heart pounding.

"I apologize," Athena said. "But you need to focus on this journey and what is ahead of you. Let the others take care of themselves."

"It would be easier to concentrate if I didn't have to worry about my friends. You could help them, Athena."

"Who says I'm not helping them?"

"But you are here with me."

"Am I not a god? I am looking after your people. You must prepare for the journey. Many lives depend on this, Sascha."

"And you will save Soleil?" There was no response. "Athena?" She was gone. Sascha punched the water. "Damn it. I wish I knew what was happening," she muttered. "Soleil, please look after yourself."

As she climbed out of the pool, a thought hit her. Alex and Marco where were they? If they were together, they should be OK. But if they weren't...Sascha shook her head. They had to be OK.

I wish this was all over and we were all back together.

"Athena, I'm trusting you to do what you promised."

Sascha dressed herself in the long white robe the mage had left. The robe was embroidered with silver stars, which glittered in the candle light. A silver pendant which held a crystal the color of fire had been left with the robe. She put it on. Finally, she brushed her hair and left it flowing loose around her shoulders.

"The fans. I need to take the fans."

She walked over to her knapsack and retrieved the two fans. She removed the oiled cloth she had wrapped them in and then put them in one of the robe's deep pockets. She wasn't sure if she was allowed to take them, but she wasn't going to ask. They had been sent to her for a reason.

Sascha picked up the box that held the pen and the jewel, and walked toward the mage. The mage handed her a satchel. "Take this with you," she said. "In it you will find a spell book. I have marked the page you will need. The satchel also contains some candles and a vial. It is important that you only drink the contents of the vial when instructed."

"Instructed?" Sascha asked.

"It will all make sense if you follow the spell book. You

can place the artifact and the jewel in here too. Oh, and the fans."

"You saw me." Sascha couldn't stop the flush that spread across her cheeks.

The mage smiled. "Follow me."

She walked with Sascha to the edge at the cave's entrance. Sascha looked down and saw three steps set into the stone. "Stand on the top step. It is from there that you will cross over to the island. I will leave you now."

"But how do I get over there?" Sascha asked.

"The answers you need are within you," she said as she turned away.

"Wait," Sascha cried out. "I don't even know what that means."

Sascha stood at the base of the steps. The idea of doing this again, crossing another invisible bridge, terrified her. The bright torches that shone along the maw of the cave lit up the chasm, but she wasn't sure if that was a good thing or a bad thing. Perhaps it would have been better not to see. She wrapped her arms around her waist as she leaned slightly closer to the edge to see how deep the chasm was. It seemed to go on for miles.

The island is so far away.

A wave of giddiness swept over her.

Who are you kidding, Sascha? You can't do this.

She swallowed. She had no choice. She had to do this. She closed her eyes for a second, took a slow deep breath and then lifted her foot onto the first step.

She wished she had Kira's high-heeled shoe so that she could throw it out in front of her, as Kira had done earlier.

"I do have it," she yelled. "I have the shoe."

Sascha stepped back down, raced to the hollow and dug the high heel out of her bag. She stopped for a moment and breathed in the sweet aroma that surrounded her as she forced herself to relax. With her sanity somewhat restored, she left the hollow and returned to the mouth of the cave.

I can do this.

Standing on the top step, Sascha positioned herself so that she faced the island and then threw the shoe. Her stomach churned as she watched it fly through the air. What would she do if it didn't stop, if it just kept falling?

There was a soft thump. The high heel landed fifteen feet from where she was standing.

Thank you, Kira.

Sascha's stomach rolled as she balanced on the top step, all her weight on her left foot. She raised her right foot carefully and used it to search for the bridge. Her foot found a solid surface almost immediately. She put her foot down and eased her weight onto her right foot.

Giddy with relief, she stopped for a moment, exhaled and then put all her weight onto her right foot. She brought her left foot from behind and used it to test for a surface in front of her. Again, she found it.

I'm doing it. I'm doing it!

The wind started to howl and whip at her body. She stopped, hunkered down and waited. The wind soon eased. Her legs felt hollow, but she stood and took another step.

It took what seemed like an eternity to reach the shoe. She squatted down to pick it up. As she did so, a sudden gust of wind blew across the bridge, causing her to wobble. She dropped her hand to the surface next to her foot and balanced herself again. Her heart pounded. She squeezed her eyes shut, refusing to look down. The wind ceased and Sascha opened her eyes. She reached for the high heel. Her finger caught one of the straps on the shoe and knocked it. It was only a slight movement, but it was enough. The shoe teetered on the edge before falling. "No," she whimpered. "No."

What do I do now?

Alex's voice came back to her. "Your faith will replace what your mind cannot face."

Was this really a test of faith? Her body trembled. She glanced over at the island, resisting the building desperation to look down. She was only a third of the way there. She glanced back to where she started. The journey had been a straight line so far. Perhaps she might find it easier if she focused on something on the island that was in line with the spot where she now stood. Several feet from the edge of the island was a rock with one single orange iridescent flower on it. That is what she would focus on.

She stood, her gaze fixed on the flower. "Your faith will replace what your mind cannot face," she muttered. "Athena, guide me safely." She balanced herself on her left leg, took a deep breath and put her right foot in front of her. She planted her right foot and took another step. Then another.

Progress was slow and she started to feel as if she had been walking for hours. But then she felt the ground beneath her feet change. She had done it. She was standing on solid ground. She was safe.

As she looked back, the bridge appeared for a few seconds before shimmering and disappearing. It was so narrow. How she made it over to the island without falling off was beyond her. By now, the moon had appeared, giving her a brief glimpse of the chasm. For a moment, she forgot to breathe. The walls were littered with the sun-bleached bones of those who had tried to cross the bridge and failed.

CHAPTER 38

*T*he sun had set, and any light from the moon and the stars was hidden behind thick clouds. The snuffling and snorting sounds of the pit hounds reverberated across the grounds. "Are we all agreed?" Marco whispered.

"Yes," everyone replied.

"All we need now is the luck of the gods," Marco said. He pointed to a red metal box sitting next to a short brick wall. "Alex, the red box over there is the electrical box. The top four switches will turn on the lights in the grounds. They're halogen lights, so they should be effective."

"If they work," Alex said.

Marco gulped. "Yes, if they work. Remember to stay behind the brick wall until Kalurth gives the signal."

"I know, I know," Alex said.

Marco turned to Soleil and Kalurth. "If the plan works, the lights should blind the creatures for long enough to give you two time to get behind the pack. It should also give us the time we need to grab the weapons. Wait as long as you can before you start the attack."

"Agreed," Kalurth said.

"You will need to hurry," Soleil said. "They will work out what's going on soon enough."

A flicker of movement caught Marco's attention. He glanced to his left to see a spindly ape-like creature with glowing red eyes and large red talons standing beside him.

"Marco, there's a gibleree standing next to you," Soleil screamed out.

Pit hounds aren't enough? Do the gods hate us that much?

Marco twisted on his left foot at the same time as he drew his sword.

"No," Kalurth cried out. "Don't attack him, Marco. The gibleree is here to help us, not hurt us. He's a friend."

"But they're creatures of the ancient," Soleil said, "creatures of the darkness."

"No, they're not," Kalurth replied.

Marco stood with his sword raised as he stared at the creature. It flinched, its arm raised in panic to defend itself.

"Bibacr is friend," the creature said. "Bibacr is friend."

"Every time the pit hounds appear, so do the giblerees," Soleil snapped. "They are made of the same dark magic. Marco, kill it."

"No," Kalurth growled. "They appear at the same time because they come to aid in the fight against the hounds. They destroy magic, not use it. They can dissolve the invisibility barriers that hide the pit hounds."

"Which means we can see them," Marco said, lowering his sword.

"Yes," Kalurth said. "And without their protective shields, the hounds are easier to kill."

Marco glanced at Kalurth. "If it is willing to help us destroy the hounds, it is considered a friend. For now."

Bibacr stood up straight and thrust his chest out. "Bibacr is not an it. Bibacr is a he."

"If *he* is willing to help us, he is considered a friend," Marco said. "For now."

"Bibacr," Kalurth said, "did you set those traps in the cave, as I asked you to?"

"Bibacr do good with traps. Army face many dangers." He chuckled to himself.

Kalurth nodded. "Good. Have you brought your clan with you?"

The creature nodded. "Bibacr's clan is in the shadows." He pointed a gangly limb in the direction of the security hut. "Bibacr's family help Marco now?"

Marco pointed at Alex. "Alex will be flicking a switch and these grounds will be flooded with light. Are you able to destroy the hounds' shields the moment the lights come on? It would be good to know exactly where they are and how many we have to fight."

The creature nodded. "Bibacr agree."

Marco turned to Kalurth. "With the giblerees' help, I think we have a chance of winning this."

"Those weapons would help…a lot," Kalurth said. "I hope they're as good as you believe they are, Marco."

"I hope so too," Marco said. "But I just had a horrible thought. Giblerees destroy magic, right? What about the magic in the weapons? Will they destroy that?"

"If you attack Bibacr's family with it, they might," Kalurth said. "But not if you only use the weapons against the hounds."

"Bibacr can't stay," Bibacr said to Kalurth. "Bibacr has to help Sascha. Bibacr's family help in the battle."

SASCHA WALKED around the small island. It was breathtaking.

Bottlebrushes and banksias covered in red, purple and yellow blossoms grew in all shapes and sizes. Emerald-leafed vines were wrapped around the bases of many of the trees. Lorikeets screeched at one another as they settled into the trees for the night. A sweet citrus and honey smell travelled on the breeze across the island. A grassed path led Sascha to the middle of the island, where she found a marble pedestal. Flat stone discs set into the grass formed a circle around the pedestal.

"We must begin, Sascha," a voice said, the sound of it echoing around her.

"Is that you, Athena?" Sascha said.

"Yes. It is time to choose the god you will follow. When you have made your choice, your magic will be given to you."

"How do I do that?"

"Open the spell book to the page marked and prepare the ritual area as shown. You can only share the circle you create with one other. You will be given three choices. Each choice will take the form of a different creature, and each creature will be acting as a representative for one of the gods. Trust in all of your senses. Whoever you choose will define not only your future but the future of Eratus as well. When you have made your choice, you will then need to activate your staff. You must complete the tasks before the protective barrier dissolves."

"What barrier? Why would it dissolve?" Sascha asked.

Athena was quiet.

"Athena, why would the barrier dissolve?"

Still, no answer.

"You're a very frustrating god, Athena." Sascha opened the spell book to the page marked and read the instructions. She placed the candles on the stone discs and pocketed the little vial of red liquid. She stood before the pedestal and visualized a protective ball, like the one Ella had used to protect Rusty against the pit hounds, surrounding the area. As she did so, she recited a chant, "Cleanse this area so I can see the future the gods have planned for me."

Sascha watched as a shield formed around the area she had lined with the candles. She stepped forward and placed the pen and the jewel on the pedestal.

Sascha closed her eyes and drank the vial as she cleared her mind of everything that was happening around her. She would worry about everything else when this task was complete. She flexed her shoulders and took a deep breath as the muscles in her shoulders and stomach began to unwind.

She opened her eyes. Standing in front of her was a guardian. That he was on the other side of the protective barrier made him no less intimidating. The hulky, hairy creature stared at her, his mane fluttering in the wind, his long claws and horns yellowed with age and grime. Slobber dribbled down his chin and was infrequently wiped away by a long purple tongue. He hunkered down and rested his claws on the ground. Sascha shuddered. She couldn't help but wonder which god the creature represented.

"Sascha, over here." She turned toward the sound of the voice. "Marco, what are you doing here?"

He smiled. "We won the battle and I am here to help you. We need to save Eratus. Time is running out."

Sascha walked toward Marco and stretched out her hand. This would be an easy test. Marco obviously represented Athena. She stopped, suddenly unsure. She looked over at the guardian. Maybe the obvious choice wasn't the correct one. She shook her head.

How am I supposed to know who I should choose?

A whoosh of wind sounded behind her. As she turned, a third creature appeared. A gibleree!

She moved toward it. "You? I've seen you before. On Eratus. Who are you?"

The guardian reacted instantly to the gibleree's presence. It stood, roared and flexed its claws.

"Sascha, stay away from that," Marco called out. "You know giblerees are creatures of the darkness. This is your chance to make your life different, to be the person you wished you were, to be someone other than the Sascha you came to hate. Stay away from that creature."

The guardian roared again and started to move toward the gibleree.

"Bibacr friends with Sascha," the gibleree said.

"No." Sascha shook her head. "Marco is right. You are a creature of the ancients."

Bibacr started to fidget, his glance shifting between the guardian and Sascha. "Bibacr left family with Marco." He pointed at Marco. "Bibacr know that not Marco."

"Sascha," Marco said, "I know I have failed you many times. Don't let it happen this time. How can I convince you to stay away from the gibleree? Don't waste the only opportunity you will ever have to start your life anew. Please don't let me fail you again."

"Bibacr," Sascha said, "you said you just left Marco. Where was he?"

"Bibacr met Marco out the front of this building. Marco was going to kill Bibacr, but Kalurth saved him. Bibacr's family helping Marco and his friends fight the pit hounds."

Pit hounds. Sascha's stomach sunk. That's why Soleil and Kalurth had taken off in a rush. If the creature was telling the truth, it at least meant that they were all alive.

"Sascha, do I look like I'm fighting pit hounds?" Marco asked.

Sascha glanced over at Marco and then at the guardian. The guardian was only a few steps away from Bibacr.

"Why are you here, Bibacr?" Sascha asked.

"Bibacr was told you were to be tested. Told he could help Sascha."

The guardian swiped at Bibacr, but he managed to dodge the claws.

"Get out of here," Sascha said. "I've seen what damage guardians do. Go, leave here."

"Bibacr can't leave. Bibacr promised to stay with you, and that is what he will do."

"Who did you promise?" Sascha asked. "What god told you to stay?"

"Bibacr can't say."

"Sascha, don't let the darkness into the circle," Marco said. "Choose a different life this time."

The guardian swiped at the gibleree, and again, Bibacr managed to duck away from the claws. Why was the guardian only attacking Bibacr and not Marco?

"This is ridiculous," Marco said, pulling out his sword and moving toward Bibacr. "Soon you will be out of time, Sascha. Your shield is shimmering. It won't be long before it will disappear and then all of this will be for nothing. You must choose, but I won't let you choose that evil creature."

Sascha glanced at the shield. He was right. Patches of the shield were disappearing.

Bibacr glanced from side to side. Marco and the guardian were both hunting him down now. The creature would be dead in minutes.

The guardian launched itself at Bibacr, claws out, fangs dripping. Sascha couldn't do it. She couldn't let the poor creature die. She put her hand through the barrier and pulled Bibacr into the circle. The guardian disappeared mid-launch, but Marco had time to turn to Sascha and scream before disappearing in front of her eyes.

Bibacr began to jump up and down. "You saved Bibacr. You trusted Bibacr. You saved him."

More patches of the shield were starting to shimmer. "What is happening? Can you tell me who sent you?"

"Bibacr sent by Athena. Guardian sent by Hades. Marco sent by Ares."

"Then I have chosen Athena?"

"Bibacr and Sascha can talk later." The creature dragged Sascha by the hand to the pedestal. "Sascha stand here, close her eyes and focus on Bibacr's words."

Sascha did as she was told.

"Athena, goddess of wisdom and protection, give me the powers I need to change direction. Let me be the shining star that allows your people to know who you truly are."

Lightning flashed and thunder rolled. A powerful shock-wave sent Sascha and Bibacr flying to the other side of the circle. Sascha found herself on the ground, her staff in her hand. It was glowing. The ceremony had worked. The pen was no longer a pen. It was a staff, a staff with a jewel set into the top. As she inspected the staff, the shield around her dissolved, snuffing out the candles.

"You did it," Sascha said. "You did it. The staff is healed."

"Now Sascha begin the final step. Bibacr have someone coming to help her. The true Marco."

CHAPTER 39

* EARTH

*M*arco and George snuck toward the main building's basement. Marco could hear the pit hounds. They were close, but George would warn him if they were in danger.

He placed his hand on the reader on the main door to the basement. The reader beeped and the door opened. Marco and George crept along the polished tile walkways, staying close to the walls.

They made their way to the door that led to where the weapons were stored at the front of the building. He hoped the army of the elite hadn't stolen them, though he was sure no-one would believe that such powerful weapons would have been left out in plain sight. Adrenaline rushed through him as he stood at the door and waited for Kalurth's signal. Every sound in the building was magnified. His heart was pounding, but his mind was clear. All he needed was for the lights to work. He hoped they hadn't been damaged in the attack.

Kalurth's shout thundered around the grounds and the lights burst on. Marco flung the door open and raced for the weapons. The giblerees had already done their work and Marco took a second to gauge the number of pit hounds. Twenty, give or take a few. One of the them stood outside the window, but right next to the weapons. This was it. He had to move.

Marco took a step forward as the hound turned and saw him. It gave a screeching call to the others as it leaped at the glass window and bounced off. It shook itself off and raced toward the doorway. Marco took a rolling dive for the weapons just as the hound burst through the door. His hand clutched a blade, which burst into life, flame streaming out of it. The pit hound realized the danger a moment too late. Marco sliced at it and there was a loud screech as the creature died. Its flesh melted and a pile of sizzling bones dropped to the floor.

Marco grabbed the second blade and the daggers, and raced out through the door the hound had crashed through moments earlier. George followed with a roar and then raced off to join Soleil and Kalurth.

Marco searched for Alex and found him fighting one of the pit hounds. He raced toward him and thrust the blade into his hands.

"I still think we need guns," Alex yelled as he took the blade and sliced at the hound. He stood momentarily stunned as the blade's magic sprung into being and consumed the creature in a blaze of fire. The hound died screaming.

"They work, Marco." Alex slapped Marco on the back. "Good call, bro. Maybe this time we can do without guns."

Marco gave Alex the second blade and armed himself with the daggers. Together they marched toward the pack. A soft blue shimmer covered the grounds as the giblerees repeatedly dissolved the creatures' shields. The air was filled with screams as one hound after another fell, devoured by the fire that sprung from the weapons. Finally, there was silence.

"We have won," Alex said. "We have won."

Marco's limbs felt heavy as the adrenaline started to wear off. He walked over to the steps leading into the building and allowed himself to collapse onto the top step. He surveyed the devastation. Who was powerful enough to have created so many of those creatures? Unless…unless some of the creatures they had fought were his men, the ones that had been turned. He shuddered. He couldn't think of a worse fate.

"We need to destroy all these bodies," Marco said as he got back to his feet. "Nothing is to be left of them."

An hour later, they stood in silent prayer around the pyre covering the bodies of his men. "It is believed in some countries that fire liberates the souls of the dead, allowing them to journey to heaven. I pray that is true for these men." Marco retrieved the daggers, leaned over and touched the blades to the wood. The pyre burst into flame.

They watched the flames for a couple of minutes and then returned to the steps at the front of the building.

One of the giblerees trotted up to Marco. "I am father of Bibacr," the creature said. "Bibacr told Father to bring you to him as soon as battle is finished." The creature looked around him. "The battle is finished. Father to follow Bibacr's wishes. Marco to come with him."

"Where are we going?" Marco asked. "And what about the others?"

"Bibacr say only George and Soleil come with Marco."

Alex waved Marco off. "You go, Marco. Kalurth will take me back to her cave to join the others, won't you, Kalurth?"

Marco raised his brows. "Can you ride dragons, Alex?"

"Ride dragons? Of course I can," Alex spluttered. "How hard can it be?"

Marco smirked.

The gibleree tugged at Marco's sleeve. "Bibacr need Marco. We go now."

~

"BIBACR HELP SASCHA ACTIVATE HER MAGIC," Bibacr said as he hopped from foot to foot. "Sascha lucky. Sascha have soul mate, someone to help her."

"Soul mate? What do you mean, Bibacr?"

"Bibacr's father bring Marco here. Soleil and George come to protect Sascha."

As if on cue, George landed on a patch of grass about twenty feet from where Sascha stood. She was followed by Marco and Soleil, Marco having ridden on Soleil's back. Last to arrive was a gibleree. They all looked too weary for words They were covered from head to toe in dark rust-colored stains and smelled of copper. But they were safe.

Bibacr walked over to the other gibleree and hugged him. "Bibacr thank Father."

"Is that your father, Bibacr?"

"Yes," he said, nodding his head vigorously. "Bibacr's father go now." Bibacr stepped back as his father leaped off the edge of the island and landed in the maw of the cave.

"Wow, your father can jump a long way."

"Bibacr's father fly, not jump."

Sascha walked over to George, leaned down and hugged her. "How did you get here?"

Marco climbed down from Soleil's shoulders. "Connell sent her here with the keystones for the first portal in case we couldn't use the second one."

Sascha walked over to Soleil and stroked his neck. "It's good to see you're safe, Soleil." She turned to face Marco. "And I'm glad to see you're safe too, Marco." There was an awkward silence as Sascha debated whether she should hug Marco, but since he didn't seem to care one way or the other, she decided against it. "Laela told me Connell was attacked by a pit hound. Is George here because Connell didn't make it?"

"Laela told you?" He glanced around the island. "Is she here?"

"It's a long story. But is Connell alive?"

"Yes, he is. He's being treated. You survived the treatment, so he should too. He is certainly as stubborn as you."

"I'm not stubborn," Sascha said. "But for the creature to attack Connell! It seems so cruel, especially after the healing ceremony. I wonder who created the pit hounds."

"Do you remember Reya?" Marco asked.

"The name isn't familiar."

"She is Drakon's lover. She attacked Connell."

"Why would she—"

Bibacr jumped up and down. "Bibacr worried. Sascha can't wait any longer. We must go."

"Where?" Sascha asked.

Bibacr walked over to the pedestal and pushed a button. A stone stairwell opened, leading down into darkness. He flicked his wrist and a torch just inside the stairwell burst into flame.

"I didn't know you had fire magic, Bibacr," Sascha said.

"Bibacr not use magic, Bibacr destroy it. Bibacr use matchling," he said, holding up a stick that looked nothing more than a large match.

"You use matches?" she said. "Really?"

"Everyone, move." Bibacr glanced over his shoulder. "Danger not far now."

"What danger, Bibacr?"

"Bibacr and Sascha talk later. Sascha ask Soleil and George to stay here and guard entrance. Sascha needs friends to protect her. Dark ones know what Sascha is going to do. Try to stop her."

"Soleil, do you mind?" Sascha asked.

"Mind being ordered around by the devil itself?" Soleil snapped. "Why should I mind?"

Sascha rolled her eyes. "Let's give Bibacr a chance. He helped me, Soleil."

"And his family helped us fight the pit hounds," Marco said.

Sascha glanced. "How do you know what he said?"

Marco's hand went to his throat.

Sascha gasped. "So that's how you knew what Soleil wanted you to do. You can use the necklace!"

Marco flinched. "When this is all over, I will tell you everything. But Bibacr is right. We'd better go."

"Come and get us if you need help," Sascha called out as she started moving down the stairs.

"That's it," Soleil snapped. "Insult us even more."

Sascha laughed. She turned to Marco. "I think it might take a while for Soleil to trust Bibacr."

"All his life he's been told that giblerees are evil, so I'm not really surprised," Marco replied.

"Bibacr not evil," the creature said. "Bibacr friend."

"I know," Sascha said.

"So what are we doing here?" Marco asked.

"Sascha and Marco are soul mates," Bibacr said. "Marco help Sascha activate her magic."

"Soul mates? That might have been true before I left Eratus," Sascha said. "But so much has changed."

"Marco still Sascha's soul mate," Bibacr said. "Magic says so. And Sascha need strong magic. Many dangers ahead. Sascha and Marco part of ceremony together, make magic strong."

They walked down the stone stairs, Bibacr leading the

way and lighting the torches as they went. It wasn't long before the stairwell was filled with the smell of beeswax and honey. Presently, they arrived at the entrance to a large cave with a star-shaped hole in the roof. The walls were covered with glowing lights shaped like stars. On one side of the cave was a swimming hole edged with flowers and grass. Sascha's skin tingled and the staff in her hand warmed. She glanced down at the staff and noticed the mark on her hand glowing. This room was full of magic. On the ground was a circle of star-shaped candles.

Sascha stood at the opening to the cave. "This is breathtaking."

"Marco follow Bibacr. Sascha stay here and wait for him to return," Bibacr said as he got behind Marco and started shoving him.

"Alright, alright," Marco said, raising his hands in surrender. They disappeared down a side corridor and Sascha stepped into the cave. She walked closer to the stars set into the walls. They flickered as if they were alive. She glanced up at the hole in the roof and saw only darkness. She shivered.

"Marco clean now," Bibacr called out. "The ceremony can begin."

Sascha turned to Marco as he re-entered the cave. He was dressed in a black robe embroidered with gold stars, gold braided cord wrapped around his waist.

"Black?" Sascha said. "For some reason I thought he would be dressed in white, like me."

"Opposites make good magic. Sascha and Marco stand in center of circle and drink this potion." Bibacr handed Sascha two vials. "Sascha read chant to Athena. They bring Sascha's memory back and fix her magic. Bibacr leave now."

Sascha stood and watched as Marco wandered around the room, studying the stars. He turned around and looked at her. For a moment, time seemed to stand still. She couldn't take her eyes off him. Memories of the passionate nights they had spent together flooded through her. Butterflies filled her stomach as she remembered the feel of his touch. She shook her head. This was about activating her magic, renewing her memories. This wasn't about them.

But Bibacr said he was my soul mate.

She coughed. "Do you mind doing this with me?"

"If I minded, I wouldn't be here," Marco said. "Anyway, I think it could be a bit late for me to change my mind now."

"It's the perfect time to stop if you don't want to be here."

Marco closed the distance between them with surprising speed. He put his arm around her waist and brought her to him. Sascha felt his warm breath on her face and breathed in the aroma of citrus, spices and sweet wood that still lingered despite the cleansing.

Stay with him, Sascha. Let this moment happen.

Her body screamed at her as she stepped back and freed herself from his arms. "If you're sure. Let us begin."

They moved to the center of the circle and stood facing each other.

Sascha, focus! Don't think about his eyes, his chest, his touch...

She handed one of the vials to Marco. He was still watching her, studying her. She looked down and concentrated on the vial in her hand. "Once we have taken the potion, I have to read the chant to Athena. I'm not sure what happens next, Marco, but I must admit I am afraid. Afraid of what will happen, of who or what I become."

"Sascha, I am with you all the way. You are not alone. I will never leave you again. Read the chant."

She closed her eyes and drank the potion. "Athena, goddess of wisdom and protection, give me the powers I need to change direction. Let me be the shining star that allows your people to know who you truly are."

Nothing happened. She glanced over at Marco.

"Relax, you can do this," he said. "I'll turn around so you don't feel as if you're being watched and then we can do it again."

Despite the tension storming through her body, she laughed.

"That's better," he said. "Do it again."

She raised the staff, closed her eyes and shut down the millions of thoughts that were racing through her mind. "Athena, goddess of wisdom and protection, give me the powers I need to change direction. Let me be the shining star that allows your people to know who you truly are."

The room roared to life. Wind howled around them, pushing them closer and closer to each other. She threw her head back and thrust her hands upwards into the gale as she increased the volume of the chant. A storm pounded on the roof of the cave. There was a boom of thunder as the wind whipped at the torches, dousing their flames, leaving the cave in darkness except for the light of the stars in the walls.

Sascha savored the sweet taste of the magic that surrounded her, breathed in the heat that streamed through her blood. She became aware of Marco's hands resting on her shoulders, giving her strength against the battering storm. His touch burned. She felt his arms slide around her waist. Passion flooded through her as he pulled her even closer to him. Their bodies fitted together perfectly.

The beat of a drum echoed in the cave, a soft sound keeping time with the beating of their hearts. Muted voices began to repeat the chant Sascha had been calling out moments before. The voices vibrated in her blood, calling to her, urging her to satisfy her desires. Marco's fingers trailed down the front of her gown, the heat of his touch burning through the material. She craved his touch, yearned to feel his skin against hers. He leaned down and kissed her, a total and consuming kiss.

The winds pounded louder, the drums beat faster and the chant increased in pace. Marco gave a flick of his hand and her gown dropped to the floor. She stood before him naked. He cupped her chin and kissed her again.

Her skin chilled without the heat of his touch as he took a step away from her and stepped out of his robes, allowing them to pool at his feet. His lean muscled body glinted in the lights of the stars. She stepped toward him, leaned up and pulled him down to her. She was lost in the sensations, his touch, the sounds.

He lifted her and carried her to the soft grass that surrounded the swimming hole. He lowered her gently onto the ground and lay on the grass beside her. Sascha studied his face. She could see the same desperation in him that was flooding through her.

He trailed his lips down her neck, across her shoulders and down to her waist. She groaned as his lips assaulted her body, leaving trails of fire and ice. She called out as her body responded to him, arching her back so she could move even closer. She was consumed with the mindless wonder of being so close to someone who belonged to her, who she knew loved her, truly loved her. The powers crashed around them as they moved together as one, filled with a desperate desire that consumed them both. She could hear Marco calling her name.

"I love you, Sascha. I will never lose you again. Never." They took each other to the brink and together crashed over the edge into the darkness.

∽

SHE NEVER EXPECTED THE PAIN. It sliced at her, burned deep into her skin. She could hear Marco calling her, a distant voice in the darkness. He was saying he was sorry. What was he sorry for? Then another flash of crippling pain.

"My head," she cried out, gripping her head in her hands.

The heat in her body started to build and kept on building. She was going to burn to death. "No," she cried out as she tried to move, find some way to ease the pain.

Then she was standing naked and alone. The world around her had vanished and had been replaced by mists and dark clouds. The pain disappeared.

"Sascha." It was Athena's voice. A figure stood in the mist for a moment before moving closer, taking shape. The woman who stepped into view had olive skin, flowing dark brown hair and sparkling gray eyes. She was dressed in white and gold. She smiled at Sascha.

"You have made it this far then," she said, handing over a golden cloak. "Well done. We are to meet with Zeus. He must approve the return of your memory."

"Athena." Sascha looked around her. "Where am I?"

"This is the last stage of the ceremony, the stage in which your memory is returned to you. But we cannot do that without Zeus's permission."

"And why should I give this fragile mortal back her memory?" a voice reverberated across the sky.

The mists parted and Sascha saw a series of shapes standing in a semi-circle behind a regal-looking giant with a beard and thick curly hair. He was dressed in a white toga with a golden sash around his waist.

"Father, we need her to help us heal the shield that protects Eratus. And for that, she needs her memory. Returning her powers is not enough. We need her to remember her training and the years she spent on Eratus."

"Save Eratus," Zeus spat. "It's their fault they're in the mess they're in. They deserve whatever happens to them." There was a roar of approval from the figures behind him.

"It isn't their fault," Sascha said. "It is the fault of a few traitors." The figures behind Zeus gasped as they stared down at Sascha.

"Who gave you permission to talk to the gods, mortal?" Zeus snarled.

Athena stepped forward. "I did, Father. And what she says is the truth. Which is another reason why we need her to regain her memory. I believe she knows who the traitors are. We need her help to bring them down, but only after the Shield is repaired."

"It still sounds to me like the issue is something they need to sort out on their own."

"They can't fight gods on their own," Athena said.

"Gods?" Zeus said. "Do you believe gods are behind the disaster?"

"As if gods would bother themselves with Eratus, Athena," one of the figures shouted out. "Zeus, she is mistaken." The other figures murmured their approval.

Athena turned to face the figure. "Yes, Ares, we believe gods are behind this. And I will stop them once and for all." She turned back to Zeus. "Please, Father."

"Daughter, I hope you're right. You do know you will be called in front of the council to provide evidence of this."

"Yes, Father. I know."

"In that case, I give you my permission."

He turned to the council. "I, Zeus, god of the sky, ruler of Olympus, allow this mortal to have her memories returned. Let no god stand in her way."

Athena turned to Sascha and smiled. "Travel safe, Sascha."

The mists dissolved as pain crashed back into Sascha with force. Memories flooded back, each memory hacking its way into her mind, burning and slicing. She doubled over in agony. Her legs collapsed beneath her and she crumpled to the ground.

Sascha pushed herself to her feet.

I must keep moving.

She glanced around her. There was a door. How come she hadn't seen that before? She stumbled toward the door, opened it and fell through. The pain disappeared. Then she was floating in the air as she watched Marco trying to pump life into a body that looked like her. Soleil was circling above Marco's head and shrieking. Zinnath and Kalurth were calling out to Soleil in an attempt to calm him.

Sascha heard the body cough and everything went blank.

She woke to the sounds of battle as the early morning sunlight cast a shadow over her. "George, stay there and protect Sascha." That was Marco's voice. Sascha used her remaining strength to push herself up. Bibacr was with them and they were fighting another pack of pit hounds. A soft blue shimmer covered the area. Soon the hounds were gone, fire having devoured them.

Sascha felt different, as if Athena was with her.

"I *am* with you, Sascha," Athena said. "I'm afraid you won't get time to rest and recover. But Bibacr will give you something to help you regain your strength and magic. How much of your memory has returned?"

"Enough to know we are heading for dangerous times," Sascha said. "After we heal the Shield, we need to talk."

"I agree. We do need to talk," Athena said. "Your memory may take a couple of weeks to fully return, so you will need to be patient. But you have another challenge to face before then. When you have succeeded, the dragons will bring you to me so we can finally heal the Shield."

"Thank you, Athena. For everything."

"You're welcome, Sascha."

"She's awake," Marco called out as he raced back to join Sascha. "I thought I had killed you."

Memories of Marco came flooding back. He squatted next to her, tears in his eyes. "I thought I had killed you."

Sascha pulled him down to her and kissed him, savoring the taste of Marco. "The first thing we are doing when this is all over," she whispered, "is get married."

He hugged her as he laughed. "Welcome back, my love."

"You're back," Soleil said. "Really back?"

Sascha smiled. "Hello, my beautiful creature. Yes, I'm back. Thank you for trusting me and not going to the fifth dimension."

"I could never leave you. I guess we all have work to do now you're back?"

"Yes, we do."

Bibacr trotted up to her. "Sascha remember Bibacr?"

Sascha laughed. "Yes, I do remember you. Thank you for helping my friends, Bibacr."

Bibacr blushed and shuffled his feet. "Bibacr happy Sascha is back. But Sascha must drink." He pulled out a vial of purple liquid. "It help Sascha heal."

Sascha took the vial and drank the fruity liquid down before handing the empty vial back to Bibacr. "Marco, will you help me to my feet? Let's deal with whatever is next so we can finally heal the Shield." She looked around her. "Where are Zinnath and Kalurth?"

"They've gone to their quarters below the cave. They said they're preparing for the army. It's nearly here."

"What army?"

"The army that created the pit hounds. They're coming here...for you."

"Let's return to the cave then," Sascha said. "Athena said I had another challenge to win before I could heal the Shield. I guess this is it."

a deep rumble sounded below them as they landed in the cave.

"No," Soleil called out. "A cave-in. Zinnath and Kalurth are in trouble. We must help them."

"This is not a coincidence," Sascha said. "Go, Soleil. Take George. See if you can free them. Bibacr, can your clan get here?"

"Bibacr will gather family, take them to Zinnath and Kalurth, and then come back to help Sascha."

"Good. Marco, can we send others to help?"

"We only have Eham, Alex and the girls. And I think we're going to need their help."

"If there is an army coming, we'll need the dragons," Sascha said. "Let's hope they are freed soon. Would you go and tell Alex and the others what is happening?"

"Yes," Marco said. "I won't be long."

Sascha took the satchel she'd carried with her from the island and placed it on the ground. She opened it. Crossing the bridge seemed so long ago. She retrieved the fans and examined them. What would it be like to use them? The sunlight glinted on a faint engraving on the sides of the fans. She lifted them up to get a closer look. Her mouth fell open. The mark on her hand was the same as the design on the blade a sun with a blade of jagged lightning across its face. How could she have not noticed this before? The ground seemed to tilt, everything seemed to blur. She moved her foot to get her balance as partial memories flashed in front of her. A woman's smile, a bloody fight, blades flying through the air.

These must be Mother's fans. But they had a name, a specific name.

The memories evaporated. How was it possible that the mark on her hand was the same as the marks on the fans?

They are blades, not fans.

"Sascha, prepare yourself." It was Zinnath's voice.

"Zinnath, are you OK?"

"It isn't me I'm worried about. I can hear Bibacr and Soleil arguing, so the wall locking us in can't be too thick."

A heavy black mist of creatures buzzed past her. "It looks like Bibacr's family is here," Sascha said. "With everyone helping, I pray you will be released soon. I have a feeling we will need you, Zinnath."

The sound of heavy boots on stone thundered into the room. Sascha slipped the blades into the pocket of her robe. She flexed her fingers, wiped her hands on her robe, then walked over to where she had placed her staff and picked it up. A small army of soldiers, all of them dressed in polished black plate armor, marched into the cave. They positioned themselves around the room with their backs to the wall.

"Eyes front," a voice called out. As one, the soldiers lifted their heads and locked their gazes. "Stand at ease." The soldiers moved into position chin up, chest out, shoulders back, armored gloves gripping large metal shields. The flickering torchlight glinted on the polished swords strapped to the sides of their bodies. They stood without moving a muscle, an eerie silence filling the cave.

A soft click of a weapon came from above her. Sascha glanced up to see metal glinting in each of the arrow loops.

Even if we somehow manage to kill these soldiers, we'll be cleaned out by the armed men above in the loops. These people are taking no chances. But why?

It was then she noticed the design on the chest plate of one of the soldiers. It was the emblem of the Awakening a red fist holding a raised sword. These men belonged to Drakon's army.

They mustn't be here to kill us. Drakon doesn't want me dead.

A glimmer of hope flickered through her. Sascha strode to the middle of the cave and stood with her staff in her hand. She held herself high, lifted her head and looked slowly around at the men. "And what is this about?" she called out, her voice sounding stronger than she felt. She glanced up at the arrow loops. There was no response.

"Again, I ask, what is this about?" she said. "If you wish to live, answer me now."

"Tut, tut, tut, Sascha. Threatening my men when they have done you no harm." Sascha turned to the sound of the voice. A woman dressed in a red and black cape stood at the entrance to the cave.

A red and black cape. Why is that so familiar?

"But I have heard about your violent tendencies," she continued. The cloaked figure ambled into the cave, her footsteps falling silently on the stony ground. She stood only inches from where Sascha was standing, turned to face her and flicked back her hood.

Sascha gasped as blond hair tumbled out of the hood and her own eyes stared back at her.

The woman laughed. "I see you're as surprised as me to

see how alike we are. I must be honest. I dyed my hair blond so that you got the full impact."

Sascha's mouth was dry. "Reya, I remember you. How come I never noticed the similarities before now?"

Reya flicked her fingers through her hair. "I felt the same, which is why I wanted to find out more. But you seem different from when I saw you last. Is it your magic? Has the ceremony worked? There were plenty of people who bet that it wouldn't. Laela certainly hoped it wouldn't work. She really seems to want you dead. But after what happened between you, I promised her I would seek revenge for her as well."

A cold sense of dread flooded through Sascha. "Why do you want revenge, Reya? What have I done to you?" Sascha looked over at the men. "And these men are Awakening. What has Drakon got to do with all of this?"

"Oh, honey, this has nothing to do with Drakon. It has to do with me seeking revenge on my sister."

Sascha's heart skipped a beat. "Your what?"

"I was surprised to find out we were sisters too, but there had to be an explanation for us looking so much alike."

"That's not possible. You think that we must be sisters because we look so much alike. But if that were true, Owain would have adopted you when he adopted Connell and me. Or is that why you want revenge? Because he took us in and you think he should have taken you too?"

She cackled. "I don't want revenge for something as petty as that. You killed our father. That's what I want revenge for."

"Killed our father? What are you talking about, Reya? You've been a part of the court for long enough to know I've been trying to track down those who killed Mother for years. I didn't realize they also killed our father."

"I'm not talking about those who killed our weak,

pathetic mother. You killed our father...and his friends Gregorio and Lurthel."

Sascha felt the blood drain from her face. "Gregorio and Lurthel?"

"I saw the devastation, what you did to them. You were more brutal than I have ever been. You mutilated them."

Sascha shook her head. "Reya, they kidnapped me, tortured me. I don't remember killing them, and when I realized what I had done...I didn't know Father was there too."

"And what is your excuse this time? Still under the influence of green lyrium? You always made excuses, always blamed the green lyrium for everything you did wrong. And everyone just accepted what you said. But not anymore. I am here to make you pay for what you did to Father."

"What's going on here?" Marco said, pushing his way through the circle of men and storming toward Sascha.

Reya laughed. "Wonderful! Your timing, as always, is impeccable, Marco. Men!".

Warriors dressed in fine black leather raced out from behind the soldiers and lunged toward Marco. Marco twisted and dived away from them. He drew his sword, ready to attack.

Sascha was so worried about Marco that she didn't see the men who came up behind her until it was too late. One of them levelled a kick at the back of Sascha's knees, sending her flying to the ground. Her staff fell out of her hand. The man dragged Sascha to her feet and pressed a knife to her throat, pushing hard enough to break the skin and cause a trickle of blood to flow down her neck.

"Marco, I wouldn't if I were you," Reya said. "We will kill Sascha if you don't give yourself up, and I can assure you that her death won't be pleasant."

Marco stopped fighting, turned to Sascha and dropped his weapons.

"Good boy, Marco. Now, where was I? Oh, that's right. Sascha, before you die I want you to see your loved ones suffer in the way our father did. Who do you think we should start with?" Reya strolled closer to Marco. "This handsome man? Or perhaps one of these lovely people?" She swung around and pointed to a group of captives who were being ushered into the cave. "You pick, Sascha."

"Sascha," Kira yelled, "destroy them." She grunted as one of the warriors bashed her on the head. She fell to the floor, unconscious.

"Kira," Sascha screamed.

Reya glanced over at Kira. "Of course. You went to a lot of effort to adopt that precocious child, didn't you? Let's start with her."

Reya flicked her fingers and one of the soldiers picked up Kira's unconscious body, swung her onto his shoulder and marched over to Reya. He threw Kira down at her feet. Reya kneeled and brushed the hair from Kira's face. "She is such a pretty girl too. What a shame."

"I will not let you hurt my family, Reya," Sascha said. "Please, if you have a problem with me, fight me. Make me pay for what you think I did." Sascha glanced at her staff. Her mind made up, she dived toward the staff, grabbed it and pulled it close to her as Reya shot a bolt of electricity at Sascha, sizzling the earth beside her. Sascha twisted away and pushed herself up into a crouching position.

"Reya, stop. I'm sorry I killed our father, but if he was there, it was because he was part of the group who was torturing me. He may have been a father to you, but he wasn't to me."

"You're too late, Sascha," Reya said, sending a bolt of magic from her hands that wrapped around Sascha and dragged her toward Reya. "You will stay right here and watch everything I do to Kira. And every move you make will bring you excruciating pain."

"No," Marco screamed. "Leave them alone."

Reya gave a flick of her wrist and Marco fell to the ground, scrabbling at his neck as he tried to breathe.

"And not only will you feel the pain of Kira's death but the band I have put around Marco's throat will tighten every time you struggle against your bonds. He will slowly and painfully suffocate." She rubbed her hands together. "Oh, the power. How I love the power."

CHAPTER 41

* EARTH

"Well, well, well. What have we got here?"

Everyone turned to the soldier standing at the entrance to the cave. He was a head taller than Sascha and built like a mountain. He was dressed in the same polished black plate armor as the men who stood around the cave.

"Who are you?" Sascha stammered.

"It's the drunkard Novo," Reya said. "I have this under control, Novo. Go while you still have your head."

Novo chortled as he strolled into the cave, followed by a dozen highly armed warriors. "Yes, you certainly look like you have this under control, Reya. But you have been a naughty girl. Torturing Sascha, commanding the men to kill when Drakon gave no such orders. In fact, I believe he wants Sascha protected until she heals the Shield."

Novo stepped up to Sascha and bowed before her. "My Lady, Drakon sends his regards. He commanded me to save you from this witch."

He turned to the men. "I assume you heard me, but in case

you didn't, Drakon wants us to stop Reya. Those of you who think they are doing what their commander-in-chief asked them to do should think again. You will not get a second chance. Join me, or Zinnath and Kalurth will deal with you." He glanced around the cave. "I know they must be around here somewhere. And if you happen to survive them, you will be declared a traitor. Either way, it will not end well for you."

"How do we know you're not the traitor?" a voice called out from the back of the cave.

Novo raised his brows. "Show yourself. Who said that?"

The group parted as a lean figure stalked toward Novo. "I did," the man said.

Novo glanced to his left and nodded. Arrows whizzed through the air and into the man's arms and legs. The man's screams echoed around the cave.

"That was a good question," Novo said as he turned back to Reya. "The truth is that you don't know. In Athena's name, put the poor man out of his misery," he said to the nearest man. "His screams are putting me on edge.

Anyone else have any questions?"

The men stood in silence.

"That is good to see. Release the hostages."

"I will do no such thing." Reya tightened the band around Marco's throat and then sent a fireball at Sascha.

Novo flicked his fingers at the soldier nearest to Reya. The soldier slammed his shield into Reya and sent her flying to the ground. The magic holding Marco and Sascha dissipated. The fireball sputtered and disappeared, leaving behind a whiff of sulphur. Marco collapsed, gasping for breath. Sascha raced over to him and helped him to his feet.

Novo walked toward Reya, who lay stunned at the soldier's feet. "Tie her hands behind her back."

The soldier pulled some rope out of a pocket in the cloak

he wore over his armor and tied Reya's arms. He dragged her to her feet.

"Now, Reya. What will we do with you?" Novo smiled.

"These are my men, Novo," Reya said. "You will not get away with this."

He laughed as he glanced at the man who was holding onto Reya. "Well, it appears I will. But let's be clear about who these men serve. They are not your men, Reya. They are Chiane's men. And Chiane is loyal to Drakon." He paced in front of her, rubbing his chin. "I don't understand why you would be so foolish as to go against Drakon. Unless you never planned to go back to him." He licked his lips as he stared at her. "Are the rumors about you and Laela true?"

Reya shuddered, but Novo ignored her. He leered at her as he walked around her, his hand resting on the pummel of his sword. "Laela is your lover," he sneered.

"Novo, I could be a very powerful ally. If you let me go, I will do whatever you want of me. All I ask is that you let me do what I came here to do."

"And what did you come here to do, Reya?"

"I'm here for revenge." Reya nodded at Sascha. "She killed my father in a way that sickened even me. You would know the pain of losing your family, the desperate need for revenge. Weren't your family slaughtered and didn't you seek revenge on the ones who killed them?"

He stopped mid-step. "You dig into everyone's past, don't you? Anyway, it doesn't matter how you found out, because you won't be alive to do anything with it." He pulled a dagger out from the scabbard at the side of his leg.

"No," Sascha cried out. "There's no need to kill her."

"Sascha, you are far more generous than Reya. Have you forgotten what she had planned for you?" Novo said.

"Don't be a fool, Novo," Reya said. "Together we can have more power than you could ever imagine."

Novo stood in front of Reya and studied her. "So you really believe you are seeking revenge for your father's death? I would love to see you get your revenge. Do you know who really killed him?"

Reya frowned. "I have evidence. It was Sascha."

"It wasn't Sascha. It was Drakon, you fool."

"Drakon?" She shook her head. "No way, he couldn't have—"

"And what is more," Novo said, glancing over at Sascha as he stepped quickly toward Reya, "I found out who set Sascha up, who organized for her own sister to be captured and tortured. And when I tell Drakon…"

"No," Sascha shook her head. "Reya, tell him you didn't do that. You couldn't have hated me that much."

"It was Sascha who killed father," Reya said, staring at Novo. "It had to be Sascha."

Novo put one hand on Reya's shoulder and smiled as her eyebrows rose in confusion. With the other hand, he thrust his dagger into the soft spot below Reya's rib cage.

"No!" a female voice screeched.

"Laela," Sascha stammered. "That scream was Laela." She spun around, searching for Laela. There was a click from the arrow loops and suddenly she knew where Laela was.

Novo hadn't heard the sound, didn't recognize the danger as he thrust the knife upwards into Reya's chest. "You foolish, foolish woman. You disobeyed Drakon." Reya fell in a crumpled heap at his feet, blood pooling around her.

"Everyone, head for cover," Sascha screamed as arrows began to rain down upon them. The soldiers surrounded Novo, raising their shields above their heads to create a barrier against the arrows, protecting Novo and themselves. As one, they shuffled toward the rear of the cave.

"Girls," Sascha screamed, racing toward them.

"Everyone is OK, Sascha," Ella called out. "None of us are hurt."

"Thank Athena," Sascha said. "Reya! Marco, I have to get Reya."

Marco grabbed her by the arm. "No-one can help her now, Sascha. It's too late."

"She might still be alive." Sascha turned and readied herself to run to Reya. "I have to try to help her."

She stumbled as the ground shook beneath her. Zinnath flew out of a passageway, his roar echoing around the cave and forcing everyone to cover their ears. He dropped onto the ground in front of Sascha and the girls and gave a blood-chilling screech.

Screams echoed from the arrow loops as white flashes of lightning crackled along the walkway behind the sloops.

"Stop this now, or you will all die," Zinnath called out.

The cave was silent except for the whimpers of those who hadn't managed to make it to cover before the arrows had fallen.

Kalurth flew into the cave and landed next to Zinnath. "The arrow loops are clear," she said.

The soldiers silently lowered their shields and formed a line behind Novo, blocking Sascha's view of Reya.

"Now, that was exciting, wasn't it?" Novo eyed what was left of his army and then strode toward Sascha. "Now that you are safe, Sascha, I will take my leave. Drakon has asked you to please prepare to renew the Shield at your earliest convenience. It seems that we are in a crisis. But as I believe you are already aware of the situation, I will say no more. Zinnath and Kalurth," he said, bowing low before the drag-ons. "It is an honor to finally meet you. Thank you for saving us."

Zinnath gave a slight nod.

"I will take Reya's body with me." Novo waved his men

aside so he could have one final look at Reya. "I am sure Drakon will be pleased when—" Novo stopped and pivoted around to Sascha. "Where is her body? Where is Reya's body?"

"What are you talking about, Novo?" Sascha walked over to join him in the center of the cave. "She's over—"

Reya had disappeared. The pool of blood remained, but her body was gone. Sascha glanced around the cave.

"Did anyone take her body?" Novo's voice boomed around the cave. No-one answered.

He turned back to Sascha. "We will find it. If you have taken her, Sascha, you will be sorry. Reya belongs to Drakon." He looked at his men. "Let's get out of this place. Commander, collect our wounded. Leave the dead."

Novo stalked toward the entrance to the cave, but turned back to Sascha at the last moment. "Oh, and the second portal has been cleared for your use."

Everyone watched in silence as the army marched out of the cave.

"This could be a trap, Sascha," Soleil said.

"We will take precautions," Sascha replied. "Did anyone see who took Reya's body?"

Zinnath and Kalurth were the only ones who didn't shake their heads. who glanced at each other but said nothing.

"Is she still alive then?" Sascha asked.

"I certainly hope not," Marco answered. "For all our sakes." He turned to the dragons. "You didn't say much to Novo."

"There was nothing to say," Zinnath replied. "He is a dead man walking. He just doesn't know it yet."

CHAPTER 42

ERATUS

"They're safe, Sascha," Zinnath said. He was circling high in the air above the second portal with Sascha strapped to his back.

Sascha smoothed the silk mesh overlay on her white fur gown as she glanced at the sky. It looked like finely shattered glass in the moments before it explodes into tiny fragments. "Only if we can heal the Shield," Sascha said.

"We don't have long. Come, my heart," Zinnath snapped, glaring down at Kalurth, who was deep in conversation with George and Alex. The girls, Marco, Soleil and Rusty stood beside them.

Sascha smiled. "It looks like she has last minute instructions."

"Humph," Zinnath snorted. "That female can talk, that's for sure."

"How come there are no guardians there yet?" Sascha asked.

"They'll come…in time, once they realize the portal is open."

"Where do the guardians come from?"

"Some say the gods send them, but I believe it's simpler than that. I believe they are attracted to the hum the portals make."

"I didn't notice any noise when we flew through," Sascha said.

"It's in the ground. A gentle murmur emitted by the energy that circles the portal."

Sascha heard the powerful beat of Kalurth's wings as she flew up to join Zinnath. She was followed closely by Soleil.

"Finally," Zinnath said.

"Soleil, what are you doing here?" Sascha asked.

Soleil nodded at Kalurth. "I'm here with Marco."

Strapped to Kalurth's shoulders was Marco. "What are you both doing here? Who will protect the group if you're with us?"

"George and Alex will protect the girls," Kalurth said.

Marco fidgeted with the straps, then relaxed. "We're hardly going to let you do this without us. Besides, you will need protection too. Soleil and I are your...guardians. We will protect you."

Kalurth laughed. "It's like the old gang is back together."

"Have we heard from Eham yet?" Sascha asked.

"He is going to wait for Jenny," Marco replied. "And then they will both join us at the castle."

"Sascha," Soleil said. "Your memories must be returning, and without the green lyrium, you're no longer afraid."

"Afraid?"

"Of flying," Soleil said. "You're no longer afraid of flying."

Sascha's hand flew to her chest. "You're right."

A soft rumble echoed around them, followed by a loud snap.

"Let's move it," Zinnath ordered. "Time is running out."

When they arrived at Zinnath's Peak, it was crowded with

mages and soldiers. Tents had been set up as temporary accommodation.

"What in Athena's name are they all doing here?" Zinnath exploded.

"I remember Laela saying something about Owain organizing mages to help with the healing ceremony," Sascha said.

"What?" Zinnath yelled. "Have they learned nothing after the first disaster? Another inexperienced mage could be the last straw. They could destroy this planet."

Sascha peered over Zinnath's neck at the crowds below them. "They want to help us, Zinnath."

"Help? I have a mind to blast them all off the mountain top. We can't perform the healing ceremony while they're all hanging around. We need to get rid of them."

Sascha slapped Zinnath's neck. "Zinnath, remember there are traitors who want you dead. How we handle this will have lasting consequences."

"Blasted mortals," Zinnath said. "Do they always have to make things so difficult?"

"Is there somewhere else we can go?" Sascha asked.

"What about Tasuna, where we created the Shield?" Kalurth said.

"I thought you did that here," Sascha said. "Isn't that why the peak was named after you, Zinnath?"

"No, we didn't. The Sisters found this site. They named it after me in memory of what I did." He nodded toward the second highest peak in the mountain range. "They named that peak after Kalurth for the same reason."

Sascha shrugged. "Let's go to Tasuna then. But we must say something to these people. Give them something to do. We can't ignore them."

"What if we tell them the site has to be changed because the power of the land is needed for the healing and this land still needs time to heal," Kalurth suggested. "We could ask them to prepare for a magical celebration after the healing is done. Tell them we're trying to bring the people back together, show them the planet is safe again."

"That could work," Sascha said. "It's worth a try."

"Marco and I will tell them," Kalurth said. "We will join you after we're done. You three can go and prepare for the ceremony."

"Don't be long, Kalurth," Zinnath said. "We need your healing powers for the ceremony."

"I'll be as quick as I can. But I think this is an important thing to do. Sascha is right. How we deal with this will have a lasting impact on what people think of our kind. We will meet you in Tasuna."

Zinnath flew up high into the air and headed north-west.

"Where in Tasuna are we going?" Sascha asked.

"To the peaks near the ocean. We will be too far from the mages for them to interfere."

Fifteen minutes later, they flew down to an ice-capped mountain range. An icy breeze whipped around them, forcing Sascha to rub her arms in an effort to warm herself. "It's freezing here," she said.

Zinnath flew lower as they approached the peak of one of the tallest mountains in the range. "The magic will warm you."

Ornate golden torches circled a flat area at the peak. Inside the circle, four stone pillars, engraved with the symbols of fire, water, air and earth, stood on the edge of a carved stone platform.

They landed a couple of minutes later. Sascha released herself from the harness, unhooked her satchel and clambered down from Zinnath's shoulders. She shuddered as she glanced around her. They were being watched. Soleil landed beside her. She turned to him and met his eyes.

"Sascha, the darkness is near," Soleil said. "I can sense it."

"I can sense it too, Soleil."

"The darkness knows what we're here to do," Zinnath said. "We'll be safe once we're inside the circle, but we'll have to be careful out here. It has been centuries since we battled the darkness. But it is you who must battle them this time our souls are too...tired. I'm not sure what tests the darkness has in store for you, but you must be prepared. And you must stay inside the circle."

"I'm terrified, Zinnath. How do I do this? How do I destroy the darkness?"

"The magic will show you, Sascha. You must have faith in yourself...and in us. We will do this."

Sascha walked around the cliff top to burn off some of the stress that was storming through her. "This is a beautiful place," she said.

"It is ancient. My ancestors used to come here regularly for local ceremonies. But now it lies dormant."

She walked over to a heavy metal door that was set into the side of the mountain and tried to open it. It wouldn't budge. "What was this door used for?"

"I don't even know if it opens any more. The mages of old used to go in there to prepare for the ceremonies. But we have everything we need with us, so we don't need to use it."

"Talking about preparations," Sascha said, walking back to her satchel and retrieving the fans. "Have you seen these before, Zinnath?"

Zinnath spluttered as he stared at them. "Where did you get those?"

"They were sent to me when I was on Earth. The note said they were a gift, but didn't say who they were from."

"Your mother told me those weapons existed, but I never believed her."

Sascha gasped. "In your cave, I saw a vision, a face which I knew was my mother's, and she was using these blades?"

"She wanted to use them to help us. They're called the Blades of Light. They're supposed to be powerful weapons, weapons used many centuries ago when Eratus was whole."

"Used by who?"

"Mages. I always thought the weapons had been destroyed."

Sascha stared at them. "Were they good mages?"

Zinnath sighed. "They were powerful mages, sworn to protect the dragons. They were...friends."

"These weapons must be powerful then?" Sascha asked.

"Yes. But who would have sent them to you?"

"I have no idea," Sascha said, placing them and a vial of dragon's blood in the pocket of her gown. "A symbol is etched into the surface of both weapons. It is the same as the mark on my hand."

"That sounds like a very good omen, Sascha," Zinnath said.

Thunder boomed, its echo reverberating across the sky. The stars started to disappear and bright arcs of green fire and ice collided with the growing darkness. Zinnath snarled. "We must prepare for the ceremony and start the healing soon. Sascha, it is time to light the torches."

Sascha walked around the circle and lit the torches with a flick of fire. Despite the icy winds, the flames burned strong and true, and soon the aroma of beeswax, minty citrus and wintergreen drifted around them.

A roar of powerful winds announced Kalurth's arrival.

Marco climbed down, walked toward Sascha and pulled her into his arms. "You must promise to be careful, Sascha. We have come too far for anything to happen to you now." He cupped the back of her neck and pulled her to him. He leaned down and touched his lips to hers. Then he deepened the kiss and Sascha felt her body respond. She put her hand on his chest, gave herself a moment to recover and gently pushed him away.

"I will do my best," she croaked. "We will continue this… conversation when this is all over. How did it go on Zinnath's Peak?"

"To be honest, I think they're grateful they don't need to be a part of the healing. The memories of what happened last time are too fresh."

"Sascha, it is time," Kalurth said.

"Marco and Soleil, would you guard the door over there?" Zinnath said. "I don't believe it still works, but it would be good to know you have it covered."

Sascha retrieved her staff from her satchel and took her place in the center of the circle. Kalurth and Zinnath stood on either side of her.

"May Athena guide and protect you," Zinnath said. "Let's begin."

Zinnath and Kalurth lifted their heads back and stretched out their wings. They started to sing, a sweet harmonious tune. Sascha breathed in the sound and forced herself to relax. She looked up at a sky filled with slashes of light the colors of fire, ice and evergreen leaves.

She raised her staff. "May Athena cleanse this staff, give it the power to heal and me the wisdom to guide its healing."

She sensed a golden magic wind itself around her. The dragon-eye stone at the top of her staff began to warm. She retrieved the small vial of dragon's blood from the pocket in her silk mesh overlay and drank down the sweet liquid.

A thunderous boom exploded around them and the ground vibrated from the force of the blast. The sound of the dragons' singing was replaced with loud, piercing cries of agony.

"Marco…Soleil," Sascha called out.

Dark clouds filled the skies and then parted as a figure glided toward her. The figure had long ebony hair, olive skin and sparkling blue eyes. "I'm sorry, Sascha, but it's too late for them. They've gone. I destroyed them."

"No," Sascha cried, clutching her arms to her chest and turning in circles as she looked for Marco and Soleil. The smoke and fire that billowed all around her made it impossible to see.

They can't be dead. They can't be.

"You remember what happened at the last ceremony," the man said. "Will you people never learn? But you can save yourself."

Sascha heard the thud of a metal door. She turned toward the sound. The air started to clear as the fire pulled back. The door in the mountain was open.

"This is a magical place of the ancients," the man said. "If you go in there, the ancients will protect you."

"No," Sascha said.

"Go now," the man said. "Protect yourself from the fire."

"No," Sascha snapped. "I am here to destroy you."

"Oh, how precious. You think you can make a stand against *me*." He chuckled. "You mortals have always been amusing."

"I know who you are. You will not win. You will not take over Eratus."

A loud series of cracks shook the skies.

He sighed. "Oh well, I tried. If that is your choice..." A staff appeared in his hand and he used it to draw a cross in the air. A mist of red magic drifted away from the staff and toward Sascha. When the magic reached her, each droplet of it burned into her skin and kept on burning. She screamed. She tried to wipe it off, but instead spread it further. It was melting her skin.

He laughed. "And you were going to destroy me?"

This isn't real, Sascha. You are in the circle. This isn't real.

"Sascha, I will not lie to you. This pain will kill you. Slowly. But if you go through the door, you will be saved. But only if you go through the door. Of course, there will be a price, but it would surely be better than what you are going through now."

"You are evil," Sascha cried. "I will not let you win."

The man roared with laughter. "You do realize that you're the one who is bent over in pain, the one who is alone because all of your friends are dead. And me, well, I'm getting stronger and stronger and have a whole army to help me. Yet *you* are going to stop *me*."

Sascha forced down the pain. She had to think.

"The dragons should never have trusted you, Sascha. You can't do this. You don't even know what to do."

There must be a way, but how?

Something Alex had said flashed into her mind. "Do you destroy the dark or allow the light to erase," Sascha mumbled. "And what did Zinnath call the fans? Blades of Light?"

"Sascha, you are dying," the man said.

The light to erase. Alex was wrong. The second part of that sentence wasn't about the activation ceremony. It is about the healing.

The mark on Sascha's hand started to tingle, then burn. She looked down to see the blades in her pocket glowing. She knew what to do. She remembered how to use the blades.

"Athena, I hope you're still there and none of this is real," she prayed. "If you are there, and if I am right, then you need to prepare for what is to come next."

Sascha put her hands in her pockets and retrieved the blades. She glanced up at the man standing before her. He was smirking.

"You're running out of time, Sascha. Soon this will all be

over." He moved his head to the side as he studied the weapons in her hands. "And what do you plan on doing with those?"

She grasped the tips, her thumb on one side of the blade and her fingers on the other. She bent her wrist back toward her forearm, swung her arm forward and released the blades.

The blades spun in circles, becoming brighter and brighter the faster they spun.

"They're pretty," the man said. He moved his hand to touch them and gave a bloodcurdling scream. Sascha watched as the man's hand disappeared, then his arm. Slowly, his whole body disappeared. Then the fans raced toward the sky and Sascha heard screams as the fans erased the darkness.

She had done it. She fell to the ground, exhausted. The cool air returned and she saw Zinnath and Kalurth standing on either side of her. Athena stood before her. They merged their magic, weaving it together into a white line of glowing light. The light moved upwards, high into the sky and the healing began. The light regenerated the weave almost instantly and then raced along the sky, searching for and repairing all the damaged threads. In a matter of minutes, the Shield was healed and had merged with the night sky.

A SOFT TRILLING noise echoed around the bed chamber. Sascha opened her eyes and glanced around the room. Soleil was sound asleep in his nest, his head buried beneath his wings. Next to him, fast asleep in a smaller and more heavily padded nest, was Rusty.

Not wanting to wake Marco, Sascha sat up slowly and padded over to the window. She looked up at the sky. It was clear. The healing had worked. She sat on the window ledge and breathed in the cool, peppermint-scented breeze as she studied three of the most precious things in her life. For the first time in many years she was happy, truly happy.

She knew there would be work to do when her memory fully returned, but for now she would savor every moment she was given. She padded back to bed and snuggled into Marco. His arm slid around her waist and pulled her closer.

She let out a huge sigh. She was home.

THE END OF BOOK 1

INDEX ON TERMS AND CHARACTERS
IN THE STORY

An aid to assist with the pronunciation of the names/titles in this novel.

BIBACR – (Pronounced Bib-a-car) A gibleree.

BREYTH – (Pronounced Brair-th) One of the Kingdoms in Eratus.

CIARA – (Pronounced See-r-a) A healer and maid for Sascha.

CONNELL – (Pronounced Kon-il) Adopted son of the High King of Eratus.

CRUDOURAKS – (Pronounced Kroo-door-aks) Creatures that protect the entrance to the High King's meeting place – Ocean's Mouth.

CRYSTAL – (Pronounced Kris-tal) The Mirror.

DRAKON – (Pronounced Dray-kon) Son of the High King of Eratus.

EHAM – (Pronounced Ee-ham) Mage advisor to the Four Sisters.

ELLA – (Pronounced El-a) Powerful enchantress, yet to find her parents and discover her true magical powers.

GIBLEREE – (Pronounced Gib-al-ree) A creature, believed to be made from dark magic.

GEORGE – Bonded pet of Connell.

JENNY – Sascha's book keeper and granddaughter of Eham.

KIRA – (Pronounced Kee-ra) Powerful Enchantress, yet to find out what happened to her parents and discover her true magical powers.

LAELA – (Pronounced Lay-la) A powerful enchantress and current leader of the Four Sisters.

LEE – (Pronounced Lee) Powerful enchantress, yet to find her parents and discover her true magical powers.

MANTICORE – (Pronounced Man-tee-core) Mythical creature with the body of a lion, wings of a dragon and tail of a scorpion.

MARCIE – (Pronounced Mar-see) Vet in Sascha's business.

MARCO – (Pronounced Mar-ko) Leader of the Fire of the Phoenix, connected to Sascha.

OWAIN – (Pronounced O-wayne) High King of Eratus.

PIT HOUND – A mythical beast that is said to be created from dark magic.

PYRAN – (Pronounced Pie-ran) A bird, a larger version of the mythical creature called Phoenix.

REYA – (Pronounced Ray-a) Drakon's lover who has many secrets to hide.

ROGER – Sascha's accountant.

RUSTY – (Pronounced Rus-tee) Ken and Sascha's favorite distraction.

SASCHA – (Pronounced Sash-a) Adopted daughter of the High King of Eratus.

SELECINE – (Pronounced Sel-e-ceen) It's used on Eratus for healing, but it also has numbing properties.

SOLEIL – (Pronounced Sew-lay) Bonded pet of Sascha.

SOKENTASH – (Pronounced Sok-en-tash) An Eratian swearword.

TASUNA – (Pronounced Tas-oo-na) A Kingdom in Eratus.

DID YOU ENJOY THIS BOOK?

Please consider leaving a review once you have read this book. Every review makes a difference and helps other readers discover our stories.

Once you have left a review, if you would like to join an exclusive team of readers who are sent an advance copy of my books, please email me at: anaya17.writer@gmail.com.

Should you wish to find out more about the author you can also go to the following social media sites:

Website: https://www.anayamacleod.com
Amazon Page:
https://www.amazon.com/author/anayamacleod

Facebook: https://www.facebook.com/anayabooks.

Twitter: https://twitter.com/macleodanaya
Instagram: https://Instagram.com/anaya_macleod_author

A Dark Mage. An Enchantress.

An Ancient Secret That Could Destroy Them Both.

***

Drakon, son of the High King and a Dark Mage, finally possesses the map that will lead him to the hidden ancient weapons, giving him the power to destroy his enemies and rule over Eratus. But the deadly storm season is quickly approaching, and the weapons hold a secret so dark, the gods will use any means necessary to keep it out of Drakon's hands. His only hope for survival—and victory—is an Enchantress, Sascha.

But Sascha has battles of her own to fight as the nightmares that plagued her on Earth have returned, this time with a disturbing prophesy of death. Now Drakon and Sascha must work together if they are to save their home and those they love, but the cost of winning may be higher than either of them bargained for.

The adventure continues in the second book in the Four Sisters series, where magic and mystery come in together in a fast-paced read that transports readers into an imaginative fantasy world.

If you like adventure, engaging stories, magic and mystery then you'll love this book.

CLICK ON THE LINK SHOWN BELOW TO CONTINUE YOUR EPIC FANTASY ADVENTURE:

https://anayamacleod.com/books/**in-magics-shadow**/

FOR MORE INFORMATION ON THE AUTHOR

Website: https://www.anayamacleod.com

Amazon Page: https://www.amazon.com/author/anayamacleod

Facebook: https://www.facebook.com/anayabooks

EXCLUSIVE OFFER TO NEW READERS

Don't want to miss out on opportunities to grab any free novels or novellas?

- Don't want to miss out on chances to enter competitions which include giveaways?
- Don't want to miss out on receiving an advance copy of the next book in the series?

Click on the picture of Soleil (below) and he will fly you to my website.

Or *Visit, https://www.anayamacleod.com*

Have a look around and then *go to* my *Contact Page.*

Prepare for your next epic fantasy adventure.

SOLEIL

I am very conscious of your privacy and I promise not to spam you. I will only send you emails when special offers or exciting updates are available. For information about my privacy policy feel free to visit my website:

https://www.anayamacleod.com

ACKNOWLEDGMENTS

I would like to thank all those who have supported me in my endeavor to finally publish my first fiction novel. While this is very much the beginning of my journey, and I still have a lot to learn, I have been incredibly blessed to have been given so much support to get this far.

Thanks to my parents and my family, and a very special group of friends. They have kept me going and never allowed me to give up. I am grateful to have them in my life.

I would specifically like to mention those who were brave enough to read my unpolished manuscript, and who have given me invaluable feedback: Michele George, Michelle Bleakley, Cydoni Ikin, Sarah Millin, Christine Winkler and Paquita Fadden

Not to mention a very special group of fellow writers – the Infamous SLQs.

I would also like to thank my brilliant and very patient editor: Tegan Holmberg (Sprout Editing Services), my talented cover designer, Angie Ayala, And my wonderfully creative map designer, Ren at Renflowergrapx.

SOLEIL'S WORDS ABOUT THE AUTHOR

Hi.

My name is Soleil.

I told Anaya she was supposed to write a bio about herself as an author on this page, but she doesn't like being the center of attention. She said she had a better idea. When she asked me to write about myself and introduce readers to my world, a planet which is fighting for its life, how could I say no?

For those who don't know me, I am a pyran, and I live on Eratus. Pyrans look similar to the birds of fire called the Phoenix, although we have a larger build. We come in all the colors of the rainbow. I have ochre-colored eyes and my feathers are a mixture of reds, greens and burnished gold.

Eratus is a planet that resides in a star system next to Earth's solar system. Our world is protected by a magical shield that works in much the same way as the atmosphere protects Earth. But our shield has an additional protection. It cloaks Eratus so that we remain invisible to all our enemies and even Earth's powerful telescopes can't locate us.

But in this isolation our corrupt have grown even more vile, our Gods have developed an insatiable dark lust which can only be sated by the spilled blood of our people. And once they have consumed Eratus they will be searching for another home to destroy. And their next target is Earth.

This is why my friends and I visited Anaya MacLeod late one winter's night. We are hoping that by sharing our stories with you, one day you may read them and see them for what they are. A warning.

My prayer to Athena is that you don't discover these stories before it is too late to save yourselves.

Soleil